T0340069

Imaginings

Imaginings

An Anthology of Long Short Fiction

edited by Keith R.A. DeCandido

an Albé-Shiloh effort

POCKET BOOKS

New York   London   Toronto   Sydney   Singapore

POCKET BOOKS, a division of Simon & Schuster, Inc.
1230 Avenue of the Americas, New York, NY 10020

ISBN: 0-7434-6665-9

First Pocket Books trade paperback edition August 2003

10 9 8 7 6 5 4 3 2 1

POCKET and colophon are registered trademarks of Simon & Schuster, Inc.

Manufactured in the United States of America

For information regarding special discounts for bulk purchases, please contact Simon & Schuster Special Sales at 1-800-456-6798 or business@simonandschuster.com

To my father, Robert L. DeCandido,
who encouraged me to follow my imaginings. . . .

ACKNOWLEDGMENTS

Scads of thanks go to Faith L. Justice, Gordon Linzner, Natalia Lincoln, Roy L. Post, and Robert E. Murphy for their magnificent editorial assistance. I couldn't have done it without you guys.

Thanks also to the folks at Pocket Books: Scott Shannon, who said yes; Jessica McGivney, who herded the book through production with grace, wit, and aplomb; and Elisa Kassin, who kept the paperwork mill grinding as smoothly as possible.

I have to thank the 400+ people who submitted their work, yet who got turned down. The sheer volume of material I got meant I had to reject over 98% of what I received, and many of the stories made that task exceedingly difficult, for which I'm grateful. At a time when doomsayers are predicting the collapse of the genre (of course, there's no time when they *aren't*), to see such an outpouring of quality material from all across the spectrum is truly heartening.

Other noble folks to whom I am excessively grateful: the Forebearance, for years of encouragement; the Malibu Lunch gang and the Geek Patrol; the good folks at the post office that houses Albé-Shiloh Inc.'s PO box, who professionally and kindly dealt with the massive influx of submissions in the last weeks before the deadline; the equally good folks at Greyware, who host the Albé-Shiloh Web site at www.albeshiloh.com; John Betancourt, Nancy A. Collins, Dinah Dunn, Laura Anne Gilman, Steven A. Roman, Josepha Sherman, Robert Silverberg, and Leonard Wolf, with whom I worked on assorted past anthologies; and my wonderful agent, Lucienne Diver.

Most thanks of all go to the love of my life, Terri Osborne—who put up with a lot of crazed commentary and pulling out of hair and gnashing of teeth as I plowed my way through the submission pile—and our cats, Marcus and Mittens, who were always there to distract me by looking cute and begging to be scritched. I couldn't have done it without you guys, either.

CONTENTS

Introduction:

Novelette, Over Easy

Keith R.A. DeCandido

Novelette is a really silly word.

Ask the average person on the street what a novelette is, and they're most likely to say that it's a kind of egg dish—or they'll think it's a malapropism for *novelty*. Most people are familiar with the terms *novel* and *short story*, but once you get into the more esoteric subcategories like *novella* and *novelette*, you are met with looks of abject confusion.

However, a novelette is the ideal length for a speculative-fiction story.

My personal definition of SF—which, for the purposes of this discussion, applies to fantasy, science fiction, and certain types of horror—is that it's the world we live in with at least one major change. Sometimes that change is as simple as moving forward or backward in time. Sometimes it's that vampires exist. Sometimes it's that someone from our world falls down a rabbit hole or goes into a wardrobe or travels through a wormhole. Sometimes it's that the Axis won World War II. Sometimes it's that the sun is eaten by a giant space goat. Often, it's more complex, of course, but what's important is that the author has to create a new world—sometimes several—or, at least, a new way of looking at this world. To do that, and to also weave a tale, sometimes requires a certain amount of storytelling space not provided by the short-story format. After all, SF is the only genre in which the setting isn't (necessarily) real.

SF is also one of the few genres that still has a thriving short-fiction market. It's possible to have a writing career in SF that focuses primarily on less-than-novel-length works (indeed, some of the authors in this volume have such careers). Unfortunately, most short-fiction markets, limited as they are by space, the rising costs of paper, and the desire to include as much as possible, prefer the traditional short story (which usually averages 3000–8000 words) to those silly-sounding novelettes, which are about 8000–15,000 words, or to 15,000–40,000-word novellas. Such longer works still do get published, of course, but in much smaller numbers.

A pity, that, as some of the most influential and important stories in the field are novelette length: "The Bicentennial Man" by Isaac Asimov, "Blood Music" by Greg Bear, "Tower of Babylon" by Ted Chiang, "Buffalo Gals, Won't You Come Out Tonight" by Ursula K. Le Guin, "Sandkings" by George R.R. Martin, "The Screwfly Solution" by Raccoona Sheldon (better known under her other pseudonym, James Tiptree, Jr.), "Slow Sculpture" by Theodore Sturgeon, and so many more.

The book you hold in your hands is an attempt to provide a new source for these novelettes.

It all started in Framingham, Massachusetts.

It was Boskone, 1999. Boskone is a science-fiction convention that has been held in or near Boston for over four decades now. I was there, doing a panel on anthologies. Also present—either on the panel or in the audience—were Patrick Nielsen Hayden, Kathryn Cramer, Esther M. Freisner, and David G. Hartwell, all experienced anthologists. We got to discussing Patrick's *Starlight* series of original anthologies, and how it was a return to the old-fashioned anthology, à la Terry Carr's *Universe* series, where the only requisite was that a story be a good example of the genre, as opposed to the "theme" anthologies that proliferate these days (hell, I've edited a whole bunch of them).

Kathryn made a comment that there needed to be more books like that. And I said to myself, "Self," I said, "you should do that."

The catch was trying to make mine unique, and it didn't take long to hit on how to do that: length. I would do an anthology that would be home to the best new novelettes (silly word notwithstanding) in the genre. As a result, the two requirements for consideration in *Imaginings*—which was a totally open call, with no preselected stories or guaranteed spots—were that the story be in the science-fiction or fantasy genre (or horror, but only if the story contained SF elements), and that it be between 8000 and 15,000 words in length.

I received approximately 450 submissions over nine and a half months, and somehow managed to whittle it down to the ten in this volume. It wasn't easy—I could have filled two more volumes with excellent stories that I ultimately passed on. But in the end, I think we have the cream of the crop. The quality of the submissions certainly, to my mind, proved the ideal-length thesis to be corrrect.

What's more, we have variety. Within these pages are hard-science stories, fantasies, horror stories, superhero stories, funny stories, speculative stories, stories that couldn't have been written before the turn of the twenty-first century, stories that could just as easily have been written in the mid-twentieth, stories from acknowledged masters of the field, stories from relative unknowns.

They have only this in common: they show us the world we know, but with at least one important thing changed, and they are quality tales.

Well, at least *I* think so. I hope you feel likewise. If you do—or if you don't—please drop us an e-mail at imaginings@albeshiloh.com or send us a letter: *Imaginings*, PO Box 4976, New York, NY 10185-4976. I want to hear your thoughts, positive and negative. As of this writing, I have no idea if there will be an *Imaginings 2*, but if there is, I want to go in prepared. . . .

So enjoy your journey through ten authors' wildest *Imaginings*.

—Keith R.A. DeCandido
somewhere in
New York City

Imaginings

Next Year in Jerusalem

Harry Turtledove

Had the spysat been a man, it might have raised one eyebrow. Several hundred kilometers below, down in the wine-dark waters of the eastern Mediterranean, something, or rather a good many somethings, lurked under the surface. Lurk as they would, the somethings could not hide; the spysat's electronics duly noted the tiny distortions of the surface level their passage through the water produced.

The machine compared the magnitude and speed of those distortions to the ones in its capacious databank. They matched with almost perfect precision the changes to be expected from a pod of dolphins. The spysat watched out for a great many things, especially in the waters of the eastern Mediterranean. Dolphins, however, were not dangerous. With the emotionless computer equivalent of a sigh of relief, it dismissed them from its consideration.

Had the spysat been a human, it might have raised both eyebrows, or even exclaimed in concern, for the dolphins, by their course, seemed intent on beaching themselves just south of the ruins of Tel Aviv. But the spysat was not a human. It did not care whether the dolphins beached themselves. Dolphins were not dangerous. It went on looking for things that were.

Yakov looked at his wrist. "Twenty twenty-five," he said. "If our intelligence is good, the spysat should be safely below the horizon."

From where she lay just in front of her comrade, Miriam tried to shrug. In their cramped quarters, it wasn't easy. "If our intelligence is bad, we shall be dead before we have the chance to curse it."

That was so obviously true, Yakov did not bother answering. He hated having to depend on machines to tell him what he needed to know, to take him places where, if he tried to go without such aids, he would, as Miriam had said, die before he could do anything else. He wished for the old days, when it had been man against man, gun against gun. The terrorist's trade had never been easy, and technology made it tougher year by year.

Miriam touched a control. The sub in which she and Yakov rode emitted a sonar ping identical to the one an actual dolphin might have sent forth. The sub's instruments, however, drew vastly more information from it than a real dolphin's merely organic senses could have. Miriam grunted in satisfaction. "Beach just ahead."

"Good." Yakov could not keep the hunger from his voice. The Second Irgun had planned for years to make this day possible. "We raise the people, and then—"

"And then," Miriam agreed. "Israel once more." Her grandfather, like Yakov's, had gone into exile sooner than accept any flag over the Holy Land save the *Magen David*. Nor were they alone; they were two of tens of thousands. But hundreds of thousands— millions—had had to stay behind, and endure yet another chapter in God's never-ending trials of His Chosen People.

The dolphin sub's belly scraped sand. Waves slapped against it. Miriam checked the infrared cameras that saw through its eyes. No one was on the beach. She pulled a lever. The dolphin's mouth gaped open, farther than any natural beast's could. Miriam scrambled out onto the soil of the Holy Land.

Yakov was right behind her. His face worked with some fierce emotion compounded of love, hope, battle lust, and fear. "Next year in Jerusalem, Lord," he whispered.

"May it be so," Miriam said. "May we *make* it so."

Other dolphins were beaching, and other fighters of the Second Irgun wriggled free of them. Their stealthsuits seemed to be working: no searchlights turned the sand from night-gray to golden, no automatic weapons began their deadly chatter. The longer one counted on such immunity, though, the likelier it was to evaporate. Yakov knew that. "Come on!" he hissed urgently.

The men and women hurried over the sand. Once past the electronically patrolled beach, their chances for living long enough to do their cause some good increased dramatically. Sand flew under Yakov's boots as he dashed inland. Behind him and his comrades, the false dolphins that had borne them to the beach wriggled and splashed, as real beasts would have done in their efforts to return to the sea. The little subs were programmed to wait in twenty meters of water until the raiders summoned them. Yakov murmured a quick prayer that some of them would one day be called back to the sand.

Bushes grew behind the beach. The raiders split into four-person teams. Yakov and Miriam quickly stripped off their stealthsuits. So did their teammates, a dark-haired couple named Aryeh and Sarah. The discarded stealthsuits, no longer energized by body heat, began to dissolve. By morning, only a forensics expert would have been able to tell they'd been there. By next afternoon, all trace of them would be gone.

Some teams went north, some south. Yakov and his companions struck out for the road straight inland. Soft Hebrew farewells filled the air: *"Shalom aleikhem!" "Aleikhem shalom!" Peace to you. And to you also peace.* Yakov tasted the irony of the words even as he spoke them.

Away from the beach, the raiders' ground-eating trot turned into a slow, lazy walk. Yakov held Miriam's hand; Aryeh slid an arm around Sarah's waist. At a distance, they would look like two couples out enjoying an evening stroll. They had papers to prove that was just what they were. For the moment, though, Yakov knew those papers would not fool any thorough security man, for they also carried a great many massively illegal weapons. Best not to rouse suspicion until some of those weapons were expended.

A tall, straight shape, half seen, made Yakov whirl in alarm, ready to begin using up the pyrotechnics inconspicuously strapped under his clothes. But it was only a public phone and computer terminal, turned menacing by darkness and adrena-line. He grinned, drew a plastic card from his back pocket, and advanced on the terminal.

The card went smoothly into the slot. Somewhere inside the banking network, half a dinar disappeared from a dummy account. The drive muttered to itself and returned the card. Again, alarms stayed silent. Sarah chuckled. "It doesn't know it's swallowed poison."

"It will find out," Yakov said with grim enjoyment. The best couple of data saboteurs in the Second Irgun had labored long and lovingly to craft the virus in that card. By morning, big chunks of information in the infobanks would be so many ran-domly scattered electrons. Better yet, when techs from Jerusalem or Damascus or Cairo sought to trace the infection back to its source, they would find only a trail that led to a terminal in Eilat, many, many kilometers to the south. That card was a *lovely* toy.

More bushes lined the highway—oleanders, by their narrow, shiny leaves and the sickly-sweet scent that rose from their flow-ers even at night. The raiders wriggled though them until they got a clear look at the endless stream of little hydrogen-burning cars and electrics purring by. Every tenth or twentieth vehicle was a noisy old petroleum-eater, something out of another cen-tury to Yakov, who had grown to manhood in prosperous, pro-gressive Argentina. The rank exhaust fumes made him cough.

Beside him, Miriam held her nose. "The Arabs are filthy, to let those things stay on the road," she said. "I came here to fight, not to get lung cancer."

"The Arabs are filthy," Aryeh said, a complete sentence to him and his comrades in more ways than one.

A new set of headlights, higher and wider than most, came into view. "Here we are," Yakov said softly. He slid a magazine into his personal defense weapon, raised the PDW to his shoulder, and shot out the bus's tires. The oleanders and the flash suppressor on the muzzle kept him hidden; the smart bullets, programmed for rolling rubber, did their job. The bus slewed, straightened, and came to a stop on the soft shoulder almost in front of the raiders.

"Very neat work," Sarah said. She got to her feet, stepped out onto the shoulder herself. Her PDW was small enough to be inconspicuous as she approached the bus, whose driver stood scratching his head as he stared at his ruined tires. Aryeh and Miriam covered Sarah's approach: a lone woman was far less likely to be viewed as an object of suspicion than a solitary man. Yakov quickly switched to antipersonnel ammunition so he could also protect his teammate.

In fluent Arabic, Sarah called to the driver: "Can you help me, sir? My car's broken down."

The man ripped the air with a series of guttural curses before he calmed down enough to answer, "I am alive myself only by Allah's grace, fool of a woman! Can you not see that this bus will go no further until the repair team arrives? The way those lazy sons of sheep crawl, I may be here till morning."

"What is your trouble?" Sarah said, walking closer.

The bus driver clapped a melodramatic hand to his forehead. "Look at these tires! I cannot imagine what I must have rolled over, to destroy them so. I—" He got no further. From two meters away, Sarah pointed the PDW at his chest. She kept his body between the bus and her, so the passengers could not tell what was happening until it was too late.

Yakov and Miriam ran forward, shouting at the top of their lungs in Arabic and Hebrew: "Everybody off the bus! One at a time, hands on top of your heads! No funny business, don't do anything stupid, or everybody dies! Off! Now! Move! Move! Move!"

The first passenger off the bus was a middle-aged woman in a black dress. "Jew or Muslim?" Miriam snarled at her.

"J-Jew," she got out, her eyes wide and staring at the weapon in the raider's hand.

Miriam gestured with it. "Over here." The next person was an old man. "Jew or Muslim?" When he admitted to following Islam, she jerked the stubby barrel in the other direction. "Over there."

The fifth or sixth man off wore a khaki army uniform with a captain's collar tabs. "Jew or Muslim?" Yakov demanded.

"Jew," he answered.

Yakov shot him. "Neither traitors nor liars deserve to live." The people already outside and the ones still in the bus shrieked and wailed. "Shut up!" Yakov yelled, shouting them down. "Shut up, if you want to keep on breathing. Come on, God curse you all. Keep moving!"

Counting the driver, the bus held thirty-eight people. Nine of them, excluding the late captain, claimed to be Jews. Aryeh emerged from hiding. "Prove you are what you say," he demanded.

"How can we prove what we are?" a woman asked. The only answer she got was a bullet in the face. She spun backwards and toppled.

Amid more screams, biting their lips in terror, several of the people standing by the bus choked out, *"Sh'mah yisroayl, adonai elohaynu, adonai ekhod." Hear, O Israel, the Lord our God, the Lord is one.* Aryeh nodded in approval and shot the three who failed the test.

The Muslims who had been separated from the Jews saw their fate in what had happened to the three who dissembled. They broke and ran. PDWs purred and snarled. None of the Muslims got more than a few meters. The antipersonnel ammunition was as good as the clandestine broker who'd sold it to the Second Irgun claimed it would be. Less than three minutes after the raiders shot the tires out of the bus, they and the half-dozen truly Jewish passengers it had carried were the only ones left alive. On the highway a few meters away, cars unconcernedly kept going past.

Yakov turned to the shaking Jews. "Go," he said. "Tell our people the Lord has spoken unto the fish once more, and they have vomited us out onto the dry land again to build the new Israel." The language from the book of Jonah pleased him.

"That—you call building?" an old man asked, pointing to the sprawled and bleeding bodies.

"They took our land from us," Yakov growled. "We will take it back, with their blood as mortar for the bricks of the new Jerusalem, the Jewish Jerusalem. Go, elder of Zion; go, all of you; and let the children of Israel know we have brought deliverance with us."

"Or if you do not care to go," Miriam added with brutal practicality, "you can join those robbers there." She gestured with her PDW at the dead Muslims.

The Jews ran. The raiders let them go. Miriam fitted an incendiary grenade into the muzzle of her PDW, fired it at the rear of the bus. Fierce flames shot up, followed a moment later by a blue-white fireball as the pressurized hydrogen tank exploded. The blast blew furnace heat into Yakov's face. He and his comrades hid their weapons as they scurried along in the shelter of the oleanders.

Now cars pulled to a stop, to gape at the inferno the bus had become. A fire engine, blue lights blazing and siren awail, charged up to the blaze. Yakov's lips curled in a grim smile as he imagined what the crew would think when they found what lay beside the burning hulk.

By then, though, the raiders were already on the pedestrian overcrossing several hundred meters south of the bus. The television camera on the overcrossing might have been trouble, but they were ready for it. The card Aryeh fed into the access gate not only opened it—as any proper citizen's ID could—but also gave that camera several minutes' worth of amnesia, plenty of time for the raiders to get across. Grinning ferociously, Yakov plastered a blue-and-white *Magen David* sticker to the concrete side of the overcrossing. By itself, it was not enough to leave a trail, and it would give Arab security personnel one more thing to worry about.

It was after midnight when the team trotted into the town of Azor. Yakov felt an eerie sense of déjà vu. He had never been in Azor before; none of the raiders had ever set foot in *Eretz Yisroayl* till now. But he had studied this town with holovid shots and memory drugs. He could have gone down any street blindfolded with more confidence and certainty than he would have shown in his native Buenos Aires.

Yet even holovid training had its limits. His nostrils had never tasted this particular blend of dust, mutton fat, and sour garbage. His lip curled. In Argentina, as in the Israel that had been, garbage did not stay out long enough to go sour. "Filthy Arabs," he mouthed voicelessly.

But those Arabs were the cause of the other main difference

between holovid training and actually being here. In the training, he had traveled these streets to learn: he had been the observer. Now he was the observed. Every public computer terminal, every driver and bicyclist (though the hour was late, there were a few people on the road) seemed a potential betrayer. He looked now over one shoulder, now over the other, feeling very much like a computer virus himself.

Four winding blocks east, two blocks south . . . "Third house on the right," Miriam said quietly. Yakov nodded. He knew as well as she did. The house, in the way of Near Eastern houses from time immemorial, presented an almost blank face to the world, with two narrow windows and the door the only breaks in the whitewashed wall. Yakov strode up to that door, knocked twice, once, once again.

He knew a scanner inside watched him. From behind the door, a voice presently said, "Judah?"

"Maccabee," he answered.

The door opened. "Inside, quickly," said a tall, thin middle-aged woman. The raiders obeyed. As the woman shut the door behind them, Yakov found his hand itching to grab for his PDW. If this was a trap . . . if this was a trap, he was a dead man. He forced himself to relax.

"No one saw you on this street?" the woman demanded.

"No, Jael," he answered, calling her by the name he'd been given in his briefing.

A bit of strain eased from the woman's pinched features. "Then we will hide you. The security police will be crawling over Azor tomorrow like fleas on a dog of the streets. Come with me." She led them out of the entrance hall and into the main room. Her long black dress flapped about her ankles as she pushed past Yakov. But for going unveiled, she might have been a Muslim.

She reached up with a broom handle, caught it against one of the ceiling beams, tugged. Yakov expected her to have to grunt with effort, but the secret panel slid aside smoothly and silently. He nodded, impressed. "Very neat—no hole to give the snoopy bastards a clue. How do we get up there?"

"Climb on a chair." Jael dragged one up under the opening. "You're young and strong; you can pull yourselves up."

Yakov went first. Between ceiling and roof, he found close to a meter of space. He scrambled into it. Aryeh followed a moment later, then Miriam. Sarah was short; he had to reach down and help pull her into the hidey-hole.

Looking up from below, Jael said, "You can rest easy. Walls, roof, and ceiling will all give proper readings to cavity sensors, and this house has been decorated to make the ceiling look higher than it really is. There is a store of food and fresh water, and you will find the toilet arrangements. The Lord bless you and keep you; the Lord lift up his countenance to you and give you peace."

"And to you, Jael," Yakov called softly as the woman in black closed the panel. Even as he spoke, though, he knew he did not want the Lord to give him peace. He wanted combat; of themselves, his hands curled into fists. He wanted Arabs maimed, Arabs dead, Jews rising after a century of silence to reclaim yet again their twice-stolen homeland.

Through the wood and shielding of the ceiling, he heard Jael dragging the chair away from the opening that led up here. The darkness inside the low chamber was absolute; Yakov imagined walls closing in, imagined monsters that might do horrid things to him while he never saw them.

He was not the only one to conjure demons from the dark. He heard someone reach into a tunic. The output from a small electric torch seemed bright as the sun after that brief but absolute absence of light.

Yakov sat up in relief—and banged his head on the bottom of the roof. The hidey-hole was perfect—so long as one remembered to crawl. Miriam, who had been the first raider to pull out a flashlight, turned it this way and that. As Jael had said, off against one wall stood sealed jars of water and plastic-wrapped military rations that could be counted on to stay good forever, or possibly twenty minutes longer.

Further exploration revealed the toilet arrangements, which, if not elegant, were better than the simple plastic bucket Yakov had expected. Not far from one wall was a hole which, examination by flashlight showed, was connected to a pipe that led down, presumably, to the main plumbing system. The only real trouble was that using the hole required either nearly superhuman agility or a good deal of padding to protect one's head from the low ceiling above.

Military rations and warm distilled water in *Eretz Yisroayl* were as delicious as fine wine and steaks ten centimeters thick in Buenos Aires. Behind the water jars lay aluminized blankets, thin and light but very warm. Yakov stripped off trousers, tunic, and weapons, wrapped himself in one, and, hard floor notwithstanding, fell asleep in minutes.

The touch of a hand woke him. He started to jerk upright, but stopped just in time, remembering where he was. The hidey-hole was almost completely dark; Miriam had set her torch against one wall. "What time is it?" he whispered, careful to put as little strain as possible on the soundproofing in the walls around him—no telling whether an Arab with listening gear lurked outside in the street.

"It's 0630." The answer returned so softly that he needed a couple of seconds to be sure it came from Miriam. Her hand stayed on his shoulder for a moment, then slid under the blanket. "If we're very quiet, do you think we can—?"

The Second Irgun clung to the old Israeli tradition of female independence and initiative. Yakov reached out to Miriam in turn. His fingers found warm, soft, bare flesh. She drew him to her, guided his lips to her breast. After a moment, he murmured, "I think we probably can."

Her hand squeezed, almost to the point of pain. She laughed in his ear, her breath warm and moist. "By this, I'm sure we can."

They joined, moved together. Yakov found the need for quiet distracting and exciting at the same time. Excitement gained quickly. Beneath him, Miriam's breathing came fast and short. He was close to exploding when the hidden panel in the ceiling below suddenly slid open and Jael's head poked through, up into the hidey-hole.

The light that came with the opened panel was not much, but it was enough to make Yakov blink. It was also enough and more than enough to show him Jael's expression of horrified disgust. "Are you animals?" the woman exclaimed. "Even the Arabs are not so shameless. I came to warn you, and I see—this? Filthy, filthy."

Yakov slid out of and off of Miriam. "Warn us of what, Jael?"

"Have you not even the decency to cover yourself?" she demanded, and he belatedly slid a hand down over his groin. Jael went on, "The Arabs are going house to house here in Azor, looking for you. They have a Korean with them; I saw him when I went out with the garbage. Stay very still, if you value your lives or mine." Without waiting for any further response, she closed the panel.

"Miserable prude," Miriam snarled as darkness returned. "The Jews here have lived under Arab rule too long—they've taken on the manners of their masters." As if to prove she had not, she reached out and took hold of Yakov, though Aryeh and Sarah lay awake now beside them.

That, however, was not why he failed to rise to her fingers. "A Korean," he whispered. In spite of everything, he shivered. Korea and Japan had made the best military electronics in the world for a couple of generations. But while Japan was content just to sell hardware and software, the Koreans also exported secret policemen in technicians' clothing. A Korean was likelier to sniff them out of hiding than any half-assed Arab, and infinitely likelier to make them suffer if they were caught.

And now they had something else to worry about. "Fools," Sarah said, her voice the tiniest thread of whisper. "Did you have to pick that exact time to screw? Now this Jael is likely to give us away."

"Oh, shut up," Miriam hissed back. "We are free people; if we cannot act free, what good are we? Besides, how were we supposed to know the damned busybody would look in just then? It could have been you two—or you and me—as easily."

"Good thing it wasn't you and me this time," Sarah said, "or likely we'd be in the Korean's hands right now."

"Shut up, both of you," Yakov said, "or we *will* end up in the Korean's hands. We just have to wait this out."

He brought the words out one by one, almost as if by main force, knowing they needed saying even if he had trouble believing them at the moment. His own body still cried out for release. Members of the Second Irgun grew up free in free countries, and were used to pleasing themselves in all things when they cared to do so. Intellectually, he had known that was no longer true in *Eretz Yisroayl*. But he had not expected to have his nose rubbed in it so hard so soon.

He—the whole Second Irgun—had always counted on that freewheeling spirit, inherited from the old Israelis, as a major military asset, something the tradition-bound Arab security forces could never hope to duplicate. But the simple unwillingness to obey anything but one's own impulses could also be deadly dangerous, and none of the raiders, himself included, had thought enough about that.

Time in the darkness crawled past on hands and knees. A year or so after Jael had warned of the Arabs and the Korean, Yakov looked at his watch and found an hour and a half had gone by. The hidey-hole was not air-conditioned; that would have betrayed it. One way to gauge the slow stagger of seconds was by how hot it got. Sarah slithered over to the water jugs and brought a couple of them back. By its feel, the liquid might have been blood in Yakov's mouth. Sweat poured off him.

Then, abruptly, something thumped against the side of the house—a ladder. The raiders had not moved much before. Now they froze. Men in boots clumped about on the roof. Faintly, Yakov heard harsh Arabic oaths. If the security men decided to tear the place apart physically instead of trusting their instruments, the game was up. He knew how far away his PDW lay, and in which direction. If he went, some of them would go with him.

They were in the house, too; Jael's voice rose in convincingly whined protest. "Be still, Jewish whore," an Arab snapped. Yakov's fist closed in helpless fury, so tight his nails bit the flesh of his palms.

Another voice spoke, down below: "The sensors say the terrorists are not here. Let us go on." Yakov's Arabic was excellent, but he had to strain to understand the language when spoken with a Korean accent.

Things quieted down. The team from the Second Irgun did not relax. For all they knew, the Arabs were laying low and waiting for them to come out. Yakov's bladder filled to bursting; even crawling to the relief hole was too big a risk to take.

Finally, after a geological epoch that was just more than half a day, the sliding panel opened. Four PDWs aimed at it, but only Jael looked through. "They are gone for the day, God be thanked," she said. "Will you come down and see the news?"

Yakov wondered how safe coming down was, but before he could open his mouth Miriam had already descended. The others followed. Jael looked at Miriam with all the warmth she would have given a louse on her bedclothes. Miriam ostentatiously ignored her.

The newscaster had a sincere face and a black, bushy mustache. He spoke of foreign-inspired atrocities perpetrated against the peaceful people of Palestine; the holovid screen filled with a view of the bus Yakov's team had wrecked and the sprawled corpses beside it.

"Attempts by the murderers to divide our population on the basis of religious affiliation will surely fail," the announcer declared unctuously.

The screen cut away to an ancient bearded rabbi in black caftan and broad-brimmed black hat. "We Jews are and must remain a peaceful folk," he said in quavering Hebrew; Arabic subtitles translated his words into the speech of the rulers. "Our years of militancy here in Palestine brought only tragedy in their wake."

"Chaim Perelman, is he?" Yakov growled, reading the rabbi's name. "We'll settle with him soon enough, him and his thirty pieces of silver." Only after the words were out of his mouth did he realize they belonged to a faith not intimately concerned in this struggle . . . although some of the Lebanese Christian terrorist outfits were as dangerous as the Second Irgun.

The newsman's face returned for a moment, only to be replaced by a street scene with a handful of young men throwing rocks at Arab policemen in respirators. The police fired gas grenades. The young men fell, grinning foolishly. The newscaster said, "A few misguided individuals have chosen to riot against properly constituted authority. Psychotropic gases pacified them without the need for bloodshed. Because their numbers were small, no arrests were made."

Yakov ground his teeth. He had hoped for—the Second Irgun had counted on—massive demonstrations breaking out in occupied Israel against the Arab regime. Tens of thousands of people in the street would not have been dealt with so cavalierly as a handful of zealots—and in the chaos created by tens of thousands of people, the raider teams could have ranged freely, like piranhas in a school of pacu.

A new image filled the holovid screen: the Premier, black-haired and bearded and made up to look ten years younger than he really was. In a voice full of reason, he said, "I am confident my Jewish citizens will obey the laws in the same way and to the same degree as their Muslim neighbors. We do not fear foreign terrorists, not in the slightest." He switched from Arabic to Hebrew and repeated the same message.

Yakov wanted to kick in the holovid set; hearing Hebrew spew from the Premier's mouth made him feel dirty, feel betrayed. He needed a distinct effort of will to content himself with growling, "Turn those lies off!" The Premier's image spiraled into darkness. Yakov wished the man were as easy to cast down as his simulacrum.

"We've only begun," said Miriam, who might have picked that worried thought right out of his brain. He nodded gratefully.

"You know your safe houses for tomorrow?" Jael asked.

"Yes. God bless you for sheltering us as you have," Yakov said, fighting a different kind of unease. Jael was of the Second Irgun, had risked her life to shelter and protect the raider team. Yet their presence in her home did not excite her, did not make her want to join a rebellion. All she wanted was to have them gone—she had done her duty, and that was the end of it.

The next morning, the raiders left her house openly, as if they were two couples who had been over for breakfast. They split up,

Yakov and Miriam heading north, Aryeh and Sarah south. The raiders looked ordinary enough, with Yakov wearing a kaffiyeh on his head, a cotton tunic, and baggy wool trousers, while Miriam was in a black dress that might have been twin to Jael's. Once she was well away from the house, she even put on a veil.

Yakov got in line behind a couple of Arabs at a public computer terminal. After the fellow in front of him finished selling his goats or whatever he was doing, Yakov made his own transaction at the terminal. "Come on, woman," he growled to Miriam. She hung her head and submissively took her place at his side.

Though he strode on jauntily enough, he waited for alarms to go off behind him: the plastic he had fed into the network was not of the ordinary sort. But all remained quiet and serene. His respect for the virus designers back in Buenos Aires went up another notch. He'd certainly managed to get the change past the first level of electronic sensors. Soon enough, he would learn whether it had gone all the way through.

Men and women lined up at a newly erected street barricade. Yakov and Miriam took their places with the rest. The line inched forward, toward a couple of bored-looking soldiers. "Your papers," one of them said to Yakov, holding out his hand.

With a hidden snort of contempt, Yakov passed over his identity card: Arabic, he thought, was such a backward language that it couldn't even call things what they really were. The soldier fed the card into a portable terminal. A moment later, a green light flashed. Yakov had been confident his forged card would pass muster. The soldier gave it back to him, demanded Miriam's. Her bona fides also appeared bona fide.

The two raiders walked on. Now they were in the Muslim part of Azor, mostly newer buildings than those of the Jewish quarter. The big, impressive mosque, stark black and white in the slightly outmoded style of the twenty-first century, lay just ahead. Yakov looked down at his watch. It was almost time for morning prayers.

In ancient days, a muezzin in a minaret would have summoned the Muslim faithful to their devotions. Later, records and tapes made it unnecessary for a man to climb the stairs five times a day. These days, computerized speech synthesizers had largely supplanted tapes.

The first sound from the speakers made Arabs' heads turn expectantly, made every Muslim whom Yakov could see take half a step toward the mosque. But instead of the infinitely familiar *La illaha ill'Allah; Muhammadun rasulu'Allah—There is no God but God; Muhammad is the Prophet of God*—the minarets blared forth the *Sh'mah*, the basic creed of a faith older than Islam.

Arab men stood and stared and flared up at the speakers that were summoning them to the wrong sort of prayer. Before they could do more than that, the *Sh'mah* ended and "Hatikvah," the old Israeli anthem, took its place.

Yakov wanted to hug Miriam. That would have got him noticed, however; the oppressively puritanical local society frowned on public displays of affection. He also wanted to hug himself, for sheer glee. All over occupied Palestine—maybe as far away as Damascus and Beirut, depending on how the Arabs con-figured their computer networks and how adept their trouble-shooters were—minarets were calling the Arab faithful to Jewish prayer.

"Vile Jews," a man not far from Yakov said. "They insult the Prophet, peace be upon his name."

"Peace be upon his name indeed," another man said. "We must teach them a lesson, so that we need never fear such an affront again." He picked up a stout stick that was lying in the gutter not far away, then started purposefully toward Azor's Jewish quarter.

"Wait for me," called the man who had spoken first.

Yakov and Miriam went round a corner and headed back toward the Jewish quarter themselves. All over the remains of the state of Israel, Muslims would surely be moving against their Jewish neighbors. If the Jews here would not fight on their own, likely they could be provoked into doing so.

"You, there!" someone shouted at Yakov. "Yes, you! What are you doing here, dog of a Jew?" Nothing about Yakov's clothes or the way he carried himself marked him as a Jew. But he did not look familiar to the Arab, and that was the only thing necessary to become an object of suspicion in a small, clannish town like Azor. The fellow shouted more curses, then clenched his fists and rushed at Yakov. Several men started to form a circle around them, to watch the Jew get beaten and maybe to have some sport with his woman once he lay bleeding on the ground.

Had the Arab carried a sign with half-meter letters on it, he couldn't have telegraphed his moves more plainly. He was fat, past forty, and doubtless hadn't tried hitting anyone more ferocious than his wife in a good many years.

Yakov ducked under a clumsy right-handed swing, grabbed the Arab's outstretched arm, and flung him over his shoulder. The man's startled wail cut off abruptly when he slammed against the pavement. Yakov stomped on his chest, heard and felt breastbone crunch under his heel. Then he kicked him with careful precision below the right ear. After that, the Arab lay still. The whole fight had lasted perhaps ten seconds.

The rest of the men close by stared, as if they could not believe their eyes. Then one of them had what he thought was a good idea. Yakov had proven himself dangerous, but the woman with him was only a woman. Get hold of her, and they might as well have him by the balls. The Arab sprang at Miriam.

She whirled and kicked out, showing a lot of strongly muscled leg for a moment as her dress rode up to her thigh. Her toe smashed into the Arab's crotch. He folded in half, writhed in the street clutching at himself and howling like a dog.

Miriam's smile was all carnivore. "Who's next?" she asked sweetly. No one answered. When she took a sudden, sharp step toward a young man with a beard, he turned and fled. The rest of the crowd followed posthaste.

"Let's get away from here," Yakov muttered, glad the mob hadn't had anyone brave in it. A rush forward instead of back could have been unpleasant: they might have been swarmed over before they could get out their weapons. Even fierce Miriam only nodded. They headed back toward the Jewish part of town.

No sooner had they turned a corner than they came upon the body of a man who had been stomped to death—their own certain fate if they hadn't been trained fighters. His blood ran into the gutter. Flies buzzed around him. A scrawny dog scuttled forward to sniff at the corpse. Yakov shouted at it. It ran away.

That was not the only body he saw, but he and Miriam were the only two live Jews on the street (he hoped Aryeh and Sarah were safe, or at least causing mischief for the Arabs). The mob howled around the Jews' homes, shouting obscenities and bloodthirsty threats of vengeance for the blasphemy the Jews had committed. Stones flew through the air. Every now and then a small window smashed, but the houses were built to take more abuse than rocks could dish out.

In a civilized country, the police would have broken a few heads and run the rest of the rioters back to their own part of town. Here, men in the comic-opera uniforms of the local gendarmerie screamed slogans and threw rocks along with their friends and neighbors.

"Why won't our people fight back?" Yakov said.

Miriam's lip curled. She spoke a curse more hateful in Yakov's ears than any of the Arabs' cries: "Ghetto."

The men and women who had escaped from Israel as it fell carried with them their nation's tradition of freedom and ferocious resistance to oppression. Those who stayed behind and had to live under the boot heels of the Arabs quickly relearned another, more ancient Jewish tradition: walk small, don't give the conqueror any reason to be angry at you; don't fight back when he gets angry anyhow. That tradition had kept Jews alive before when they existed at the sufferance of Christian or Muslim overlords. It kept them alive in Palestine nowadays—but the cost to their manhood!

Miriam pointed to the shut-up homes and shops. "They're just going to wait it out until the stinking Arabs get bored and go away."

"That's what they think." Yakov ducked down an alley, then down another. He scrambled to the top of a back fence, pulled Miriam up after him. From there, getting to the roofs was a matter of a moment. The two raiders slithered on their bellies toward the street. The roof, like most roofs in *Eretz Yisroayl* down through the ages, was flat. The Arabs screaming through the streets below could not see them unless they got very close to the edge.

Miriam seemed to have just that in mind. She took out her PDW and got ready to fire a clip or two down into the mob. Yakov tapped her on the arm, shook his head. She looked daggers at him—until he reached under the waistband of his baggy trousers and drew forth a couple of apricot-sized fragmentation grenades. She grinned and nodded. Without showing himself, he lobbed the grenades down into the street.

The explosions were small, like popping balloons. The results were anything but small. The hypervelocity blast charges sent small, thin disks of industrial diamond ripping through flesh and bone like thousands of tiny circular saw blades. Shrieks of fury became howls of horror.

Yakov grabbed his own PDW. "Now!" he said. Miriam nodded again. She got up on one knee beside him. They hosed bullets into the mob, whose members were too busy with their own dead and wounded to hear the chatter of guns for a moment. Only when they noticed more of their number falling did they (or rather, those who still could) spin round to find out why.

By then, they were too late. Having emptied their weapons, the raiders speedily withdrew. The alley remained empty. Half a block down, it connected with another such byway, which led to a side street. From the side street, they dodged onto a way big enough for them to lose themselves in the crowd before any sort of pursuit could be mounted. From the moment they had opened fire, perhaps two and a half minutes had elapsed.

They spent the rest of the morning speaking Arabic and shouting slogans against the Jews. Ambulances marked with Red Crescents screamed back and forth, sirens warbling. Police and troops cordoned off the Jewish quarter. They checked Yakov's and Miriam's ID documents twice and sniffed them for weapons once. The team from the Second Irgun passed all tests.

"*Inshallah,* you will catch the wicked terrorists who disrupt the peace of our holy land," Miriam said, full of righteous wrath, to the fellow who ran the weapons sniffer. The man did not take off his goggles as he nodded. Along with his rather wide mouth, they made him look like a frog—a harassed frog.

Just then, the minarets that should have called the faithful to prayer cried out the *Sh'mah* and the banned Israeli anthem once more. The man at the sniffer swore several ripe Arabic oaths. So did Yakov, to keep from laughing.

The holovid was on when Miriam and Yakov got to their new safe house. The urbane Arab newscaster had lost a good deal of his urbanity. He seemed a man who had barely survived an earthquake. *"Afreet* are loose in our streets today," he declared. "Evil spirits spawned from senseless and antique nationalism. Along with the blasphemies that have defiled our mosques and cast filth on the name of Allah, blessed be He, we have endured outrages beyond counting. Let these pictures stand for the whole."

A helicopter swooped low over streets. After a moment, Yakov recognized the grid as Azor's. Blood streamed across the pavement, pooled in potholes. Some bodies lay still. Others thrashed and writhed. Doctors in old-fashioned white knelt by them, doing what they could. Yakov knew a moment's relief: The news helicopter had not been overhead while he and Miriam were at their work . . . although helicopters could be dealt with, too.

Other teams beside his own had been busy. He saw fires here, wrecked ground vehicles there, angry passengers in airport waiting rooms as security teams searched airplanes and dirigibles for explosives. More than once, they found them. Once, they did not; the wreckage of a light plane that had belonged to the vice chief of staff lay scattered over three fields not far from Jerusalem.

A few more Jewish rioters were in the streets in the holy city and in Jaffa, but only a few. The newscaster said, "The vast majority of Jews love peace and reject these acts of terrorism with the same shock and repugnance as the rest of our citizens. They are part of our nation, and would not be otherwise."

"Liar," Miriam snarled, as if the fellow could hear her.

And, as if in contradiction, Chaim Perelman's ancient, saintly face came onto the screen once more. Speaking again in Hebrew, he said, "Keeping the peace is God's chiefest law. Violence, no matter how noble the perpetrator reckons his purposes to be, surely transgresses against the will of the Holy One, blessed be His name. No good can spring from it, thus no good will spring from it. Bloodshed shall not yield justice."

"Mealymouthed old fart," Yakov said.

The safe house belonged to a fat butcher named Samuel. He said, "People listen to him, though, him and the rabbis like him. Not many Jews in Palestine are secular anymore; they learn in school how the old secular state caused war after war just by existing. Most of us are as pious as the Muslims in the rest of the country."

"Perelman looks damn near old enough to remember the real Israel, and to remember that what he's spouting is tripe," Yakov retorted.

"Tripe?" Miriam found a harsher word and proceeded to use it, following it with several more of a similar sort. Samuel seemed somewhat scandalized at a woman's swearing so fluently, but soon burst out laughing over her lewd speculations over what all the rabbi had abandoned to attain his old age, and how long ago. She finished, "For a quarter of a dinar, I'd hunt him down and pull off his pants just to see if he was born with one."

Laughing still, the butcher said, "If you want to that badly, you can. His synagogue is at Ashqelon, only twenty-five kilometers from here."

"*Is* it?" Miriam breathed. She looked at Yakov. He nodded—his thoughts were running in the same direction as hers. What better way to show Arabs and Jews alike the power—and the ruthlessness—of the Second Irgun than to have the government toady end up gruesomely dead?

"Tell me more," Yakov said to Samuel. "Do your people have a safe house for us in Ashqelon? We'll want to do this one at night, I think, for maximum psychological impact, but we'll travel in during the day, to make ourselves less conspicuous. That means we'll need somewhere to hole up until the time is right."

Samuel paused a while in thought, his lips moving. Then he nodded. "Yes, we can do that. As a matter of fact, our friend lives not far from the synagogue."

"Good," Yakov said. "We'll stay here tonight, then take the bus down the coast to Ashqelon. You'll need to give me the password and the backup, as we hadn't originally planned to go there at all. But if we can't be flexible, what good are we?"

"Not much," the butcher answered. "Now you'll probably want to bed down. Come with me." He led the raiders to the big refrigerator in the back of his shop, then inside it. They shivered until he pulled on a handle that seemed at first glance no different from those of the other meat lockers that lined the walls. But this locker, which was near ground level, had an unexpected amount of space behind it. Samuel chuckled. "It's hollowed out for several meters, with a false bottom in case a searcher is smarter than usual."

Yakov's teeth chattered. "I hope it's insulated."

"Of course, my friend, from cold and sensors both." Samuel's breath smoked from his mouth and nose, but the cold did not seem to bother him. "It has its own air vent, too, so you needn't worry about suffocating once I close the door. I'd keep you aboveground, truly I would, but . . ." His voice trailed away.

"We understand," Miriam said, giving him a look that came doubly warm in that frigid room. "We would not want to bring more danger down upon you than we must. When *Eretz Yisroayl* is free and Jewish once more, all those who helped will win their deserved reward."

By the way Samuel's eyes traveled up and down her body, Yakov thought he knew what reward the butcher would like. But Samuel said only, "Get in now, and may God keep you safe to do His holy work."

Climbing into the meat locker was like getting into a coffin, or into one of the refrigerated drawers of a morgue. Yakov was glad he had no tendency to claustrophobia. Even astronauts on their occasional visits to Mars and its moons had more room than he and Miriam did—and windows to see out of, as well.

He clicked on his flashlight. It showed him only how tiny and cramped the space in which he lay was. "Turn it off, " Miriam said. "I'd sooner imagine I had more room." He obeyed. In the pitch blackness, imaginary colors formed and twisted on his retinas. After a while, he put his hands under his head and tried to sleep.

He must have succeeded, for he thrashed like a cat hit by a car when Samuel opened the locker door. "Come on out," the butcher said. "Computer says the next bus to Ashqelon leaves in half an hour."

"Can't be too soon," Yakov answered with wrinkled nose. "Until you've spent a while in close company with a full slops bucket, you haven't lived life to the fullest."

Samuel laughed as he led the raiders to the door. "I'm just as well pleased my life is still partly empty, then. The bus station is two blocks east of here. God go with you, and with our *Eretz Yisroayl*."

The bus station was surrounded by security troops with scanners. Again Yakov and Miriam were examined with all the electronic ingenuity the Arabs had at their disposal; again their own gear, partly Argentine army issue, partly the product of the ingenuity of the Second Irgun, left them seeming altogether innocuous.

Innocuous they remained on the bus, a vehicle identical to the one they'd ambushed and destroyed just after they landed. Around them, Arab women in veils chattered about the price of chickens, old Jewish men complained about their health, and young men, Arab and Jew alike, bemoaned the inept performance of their American Football team in the Super Cup quarterfinals.

The bus rolled south toward Ashqelon. Some of the hills to the east remained green with tress planted during the days of Israeli rule. More were returning to desert. Yakov watched a herd of goats ambling over one of these, its Arab herder slowly following on foot. The scene could have belonged back in the twentieth century of the Common Era, or, as easily, back in the twentieth century before the Common Era. After the Arabs were driven out and Israel reestablished, Yakov itched to take a PDW and go hunting the sapling-munching goats. The land would have to be made to bloom yet again.

Yakov and Miriam got off the bus, made their way through the crowd pushing to get on. Rabbi Perelman's synagogue and home were only a few blocks from the bus station. They walked casually past, noting security troops in place here and there around them. They both nodded. The Arabs were enemies, but not fools—they knew a traitor like Perelman needed all the protection he could get. All the protection he could get, in fact, would not be nearly enough.

But proving that would come tonight. For the moment, the raiders needed a quiet place to wait. Benjamin the tailor's shop was not far away. When he walked in, Yakov again felt he had fallen back through time. Some of the clothes Benjamin made could have come straight out of a Polish ghetto. His tools were hardly more modern—tape measure, scissors, a sewing machine that differed from its earliest ancestors only by being powered.

He looked up from the pants he was hemming when Yakov and Miriam walked in. "How can I help you, my friends?" he asked with a smile that gleamed whitely through his thick, dark beard.

"Do you have the blouse ready for my cousin Esther?" Miriam asked.

Benjamin's smile disappeared. He rose from the sewing machine, took a step back from the newcomers, as if he was thinking about running away. That would have been stupid, fatally stupid. He seemed to realize it, and visibly pulled himself together. Still, his voice, firm and cheerful a moment before, quavered as he said, "Can you come back for it tomorrow? I'm not quite done."

"She'll be very unhappy unless she can wear it tonight," Yakov said.

"Tonight?" Benjamin sagged back to his chair. "Are you sure it has to be ready so soon?" Sweat sprang out on his forehead, though the shop was air-conditioned.

"Tonight," Yakov said firmly. He and Miriam exchanged a quick glance. This looked like the sort of fair-weather follower they'd been warned about in Buenos Aires: someone who talked like a patriot, and even acted like a patriot so long as acting like a patriot involved no risk, but got cold feet when the chips were down. He had to be watched even more closely than an out-and-out enemy, for he knew more about the Second Irgun than a mere foe could.

Miriam said, "Let me use your phone for a moment, Benjamin."

"It's over there." The tailor pointed. He said nervously, "Remember, the computer logs all the calls here. You don't want to call anyone who would draw suspicion onto, uh, you." *Onto me,* Yakov knew he meant.

"Don't worry," Miriam told him. "The number is guaranteed safe." She made the call, then made a face. "Anyway, the line's engaged." She put down the phone. "Maybe I'll try later."

"What do you plan to do—tonight?" Benjamin asked.

"What you don't know, you can't tell," Yakov said. "Doctrine." That was true, though he would have truthfully answered Samuel or even Jael: the latter might despise him personally, but he was sure she was loyal. Benjamin he did not trust. By the way Miriam paced back and forth, she was leery of the tailor, too. If he made her more than a little leery, he wouldn't last through the night any more than Rabbi Perelman.

Just then, a customer came in. Yakov busily examined a long, black, many-buttoned coat he wouldn't have bought for love or money. Even the plain white shirt and gray trousers he had on now struck him as boring; like any other Argentine male under forty, he was used to strutting in bright shimmersilks. The Jews who'd stayed behind after Israel fell were a dull lot, he thought, not for the first time.

Miriam played the shopper, too, exclaiming over the female equivalent of his ugly coat. Her true taste was even more flamboyant than his. Both of them spent more time watching Benjamin than really looking at clothes. If the customer was in fact a security man, their contact could betray them so they would never know until too late. But if he did, he would never do anything else again—Yakov promised himself that.

The customer bought a black felt hat that was to Yakov's eye the same as the one he was wearing. He gave Benjamin his plastic, checked the receipt, and walked out. Yakov breathed a little easier.

Benjamin said, "Shall I put you in the back room?"

"That's all right," Yakov answered. At the same time, Miriam vigorously shook her head, but he hadn't needed her signal to make his choice.

"You don't trust me," the tailor said in aggrieved tones.

Miriam tried to soothe him. "We've spent so much time

cooped up in hidey-holes that we're sick to death of them, that's all." Her words had the ring of sincerity. They were even, in large measure, true. That did not make them directly responsible to Benjamin's charge. Yakov worried harder than ever. If Benjamin thought the raiders didn't trust him, he was less likely to trust them.

The tailor closed his shop at 1800. Yakov and Miriam waited through twilight into darkness. Save for tea, their reluctant host offered them nothing. Miriam used the toilet in the back room. When she came out, she said, "Let's go do it."

"God go with you," Benjamin said, as he should have. "Will you come back here after—your mission?"

"Yes," Miriam said. Yakov looked at her sharply. He thought that was suicidally dangerous. Her face gave away nothing, to Benjamin or to him. The two raiders slipped into the dark, quiet streets. As soon as they were around the corner from the tailor's shop, Miriam said, "Of course we won't go back. Am I a fool, to trust myself to the likes of him? But if he thinks we may show up any minute, he'll think longer about calling security, if that's what he has in mind."

"What do we do about him if he does?" Yakov asked. Before he could answer, Miriam's wristwatch—or rather, what looked like a watch on Miriam's wrist and did, in fact, keep time—let out a beep, as if its alarm had gone off. And an alarm had gone off, though not the innocent sort that would have come from most watches.

Miriam said, "He didn't think *much* longer about calling security, that's for certain. Good thing I got my hands on his phone— at least we're forewarned." She touched a button on the rather-more-than-a-watch. "Now let's get a little farther away from here. He'll probably be so nervous about giving us away that he'll need to visit the toilet. And when he flushes—"

He must have flushed. The explosion sent rudely wakened birds indignantly twittering into the sky from rooftops and lamp-posts. People came rushing out of their houses, too, looking for the traffic accident. When they saw none, most of them went back inside.

Miriam's laugh held nothing but glee. "I got into the bath-room, too, remember? There goes one traitor. And the security people will come rushing from Perelman's over here, to see what happened, which should make our job easier."

"That would be nice." Yakov stood on a street corner for a moment, savoring the warbling wail of an ambulance. A couple of men hurried past him on foot, heading for Benjamin's shop, or however much of it was left after the bomb. He would have bet gold against radioactive waste that they belonged to security. They weren't curious about the blast—they were intent. They said nothing out of the ordinary, but their purposeful walk gave them away.

The raiders gave Rabbi Perelman's house by the synagogue another careful and discreet once-over. "What did it look like to you?" Miriam said. "I spotted two at the front door, one more at the back."

"That's what I saw, too," Yakov said. "Well, if there are more, we'll deal with them when we get there. Meanwhile—" He and Miriam put their heads together. They had run through enough computer simulations and live-action practices to make their planning quick and easy.

Yakov hung back while Miriam walked up to the guards at the front of Rabbi Perelman's house. They watched her approach with more appreciation than suspicion; even in the modern world, they had trouble taking seriously the idea that women could be fighters. The Second Irgun had exploited that blind spot before.

"Excuse me," Miriam said in Arabic. "I've just moved into town. Could you tell me how to get to Rashid's meat market?"

"It's right around the corner there." One of the guards pointed. "You turn left and then you . . ." His voice trailed away.

Miriam wore a scornful expression when she rejoined Yakov. "They never noticed me drop the gas capsule, and they weren't wearing nose filters. I don't know why they didn't die of terminal incompetence years ago."

Now she and Yakov walked right past the front of the rabbi's house. The two guards still looked alert, and no doubt thought they were, but their eyes did not track the raiders. There were psychotropics and psychotropics. This one ensured that they would be lost in their own private worlds for the next couple of hours.

The fellow in back posed a tougher problem. From well down the street, Yakov assembled a small contraption of plastic and rubber: a slingshot. He loaded it with what looked like a pebble, shot the load so it would land not far from the sentry. Then he checked his own not-quite wristwatch, grunting in satisfaction. The Arabs' electronic curtain around Perelman's house now had one corner lifted, and not in a way they were likely to notice. That left the sentry himself.

Confidence rising, Yakov crawled down the alley until he crouched behind the fence directly in back of Perelman's home. The fence was about a meter and a half high; the Arabs had strung razor wire atop it to inhibit climbers.

Yakov found a stone about the size of an egg. As with his slingshot, sometimes old ploys still worked, even in an age of constant computer scans. The Arab sentry was not a computer, and no computer could tell him what to do fast enough for him to be able to do it.

The raider tossed the stone over the fence, well away from his own position. He and Miriam popped up and fired silenced rounds from their PDWs. The sentry, who was still peering out to see what had made the noise when the stone landed, never knew what hit him.

Razor wire is an excellent deterrent against climbers. When no guards are left to watch raiders cut it, however, its value drastically diminishes. Yakov and Miriam swarmed over the fence, PDWs still at the ready. If more Arabs waited inside the house, they might have heard their comrade fall.

Silent as smoke, the two fighters from the Second Irgun drifted up to a window. It was undoubtedly wired in to the house's defense system, but the pseudo-pebble was supposed to keep anyone from noticing if it broke. Yakov was betting his life that pebble would do what it was supposed to.

He unreeled a couple of centimeters of monofilament wire, sliced through the windowpane, and caught the glass as it fell outward. It made not a sound, nor a peep on any detection system his quasi-watch could scent. He climbed into the house and reached out to help Miriam in after him.

In the darkness, she slipped what looked like ordinary if antiquated spectacles onto her nose. He followed suit. The light pumps turned night into day. Miriam pointed to the wall opposite the window. She whispered, "Have you ever seen so many books is your life?"

"Of course not," Yakov answered contemptuously. A player and a couple of disks would hold a greater library than all these papers and parchments put together, and give a reader instant access and cross-referencing features mere printed pages could not hope to match.

PDWs ready, the raiders glided into a hallway. Like the room from which they'd emerged, it was lined floor to ceiling with books. Yakov shook his head in bemused wonder at the waste of space and resources.

"I really don't think there are any guards inside here," Miriam said. Yakov nodded. Trust the Arabs to do a shoddy job of protecting Perelman, he thought—the rabbi was only a Jew, after all.

They found his bedroom. It, too, was filled, almost swallowed, by print on paper. A couple of books even lay beside him, as if in the quiet aftermath of love, on the narrow bed in which he slept.

"Perelman—wake up!" Yakov hissed. He wanted to shout it, but his electronic protections, good as they were, could not work miracles. Miriam was more direct. She gave the bed a good, hard kick. A book tumbled to the floor. Chaim Perelman sat up with a start.

In the darkness, the team from the Second Irgun could only have been a pair of indistinct shapes to him. Yakov's light-pump glasses let him see the rabbi's face as clearly as if it were daylight. "Say your prayers, traitor," Miriam said in Hebrew. "You are a dead man."

Yakov wanted to taste the old man's fear before he killed him. But Perelman only pulled up a corner of the sheet to cover his head and intoned, "Hear, O Israel, the Lord our God, the Lord is one. Blessed be His name—"

"Shut up, damn you," Yakov snarled. "How can you pretend to be a Jew on your deathbed when you spread your legs for your Arab masters all your life?"

Perelman seemed to realize he would not die in the next moment. But just as he had shown no fear before, now he revealed no sudden access of hope. He answered, "They are the rulers here. How can one not work with them? So long as we Jews live at peace with them, they are not harsh masters."

"They should not be masters here, fool," Miriam said angrily. "They should be subjects, or driven out altogether. This is *our* land—*Eretz Yisroayl.*"

"This is *Eretz Yisroayl* no matter whose flag flies over it," Perelman answered. Yakov watched his face in disbelief—by the way it came alive at the prospect of disputation, the old man might have been in a yeshiva instead of facing his executioners. He went on, "In God's scheme of things, a flag matters little. 'Next year in Jerusalem' is a matter of the spirit, not of the flesh. Where the flesh lives, and under whose rule, is of small concern."

"You're a liar as well as a fool," Yakov said. "Jerusalem was *ours*. It will be ours again, and the Arabs driven into the desert."

"As the Lord wills, and when the Lord wills," the rabbi said. "You shall not win the Lord's favor by slaughtering innocent women and children, no matter what they call the god they worship."

"I care nothing for the Lord's favor, so long as I win," Yakov said, and Perelman covered his head once more at the blasphemy. Yakov added, "History shows that terror is one of the best weapons to disrupt any state."

"The Marxist-Leninists believed history showed them this or that," Perelman retorted, showing that not all of his reading had been in the Talmud. "Where are the Marxist-Leninists now? Among the discarded things of the world, as is the state of Israel you hope to revive by fire and sword. It is gone; it shall not return until the Lord sends the Messiah in His own good time."

"What was here once can come again—*will* come again," Miriam said. "It happened once, after almost two thousand years of torment and oppression for Jews all over the world. Jews ruled their homeland; Hebrew was spoken in the streets. We stayed free for most of a hundred years. This time, we'll stay free forever."

"There were never enough Jews to hold this land free forever," Perelman said. Yakov heard both sadness and certainty in his voice, and hated him the more for them. "The Muslims all around *Eretz Yisroayl*—and in it—have been here a millennium and a half themselves, and outnumber us too badly to let us stand against them in the long run. They learned the soldier's trade as we beat them war by war, and we could not afford to lose even once. That is how it was; that is how it shall be."

"Liar," Yakov said again.

Perelman shook his head. "We are not even the first to learn this lesson. More than a thousand years ago, the *goyim* of Europe sent their Crusaders to free the Holy Land—theirs as well as ours—from the Muslims. They prospered here for a time, too. Some of their castles remain. In times of trouble, they make nests for guerrillas. But the Crusaders are gone. So is Israel. Gone it shall remain. Jews did without it for two thousand years; they can continue without it for as many more."

"What Jews can continue without is you." Miriam squeezed the trigger of her PDW. Bullets tore through the ancient flesh of Chaim Perelman. He writhed and thrashed, but only for a few seconds. One hand seemed to be trying to pull up the sheet so he could pray with his head covered. He died before the first word of the *Sh'mah* passed his lips.

Yakov spat on the rabbi's corpse. He knew that was stupid; if he was ever captured, forensics could link him to the killing. He did it anyhow, to show his utter scorn for everything Perelman represented. "Let's get out of here," he said.

Thousands—tens of thousands—of mourners snaked through the streets of Ashqelon, following the coffin that held the shattered remains of Chaim Perelman. Only the view from a hovering helicopter could take in even a good-sized part of the crowd. The wails and lamentations the mourners sent up were audible even through the growl and thutter of the copter's engine and rotor blades.

The smooth Arab newscaster said, "The Jewish community mourns the passing of its great spiritual leader, foully murdered by foreign factionalists. The tiny degree of support these fanatics have been able to stir up is well illustrated by the contrast between these two scenes."

The screen cut away from Perelman's funeral procession to show a few youths throwing stones at policemen. The slogans they shouted had echoed in Yakov's ears for as long as he could remember. Then the Arabs gassed the rioters, and they fell to the pavement with foolish grins.

"Which is the true picture of our Jewish citizens?" the newsman asked rhetorically. "Is it these few hotheads, or the great masses of the pious?"

The holovid cut back to Ashqelon. Jews in black were trying to clamber onto the bed of the truck that carried Perelman's coffin; other Jews in black were trying to hold them at bay, and not having much luck. The coffin rocked and swayed and almost fell off the truck.

Miriam swore horribly. "Better that snake should be run over and smashed flat in the road like a bug."

Samuel the butcher nodded his lips, but jerked a thumb at the holovid screen. "You know this and I know this, but those idiots—" He shook his head, pursed his lips as if he wanted to spit. "There are so many of those idiots. They would sooner pray than fight for their freedom."

"They didn't fight in Germany, either, or in Poland, not enough to keep the Nazis from making them into soap," Yakov said. "We thought those days of going like lambs to the slaughter were done forever." Bitterness threatened to rise up and choke him. The Second Irgun had spent so much, in time and money and lives and hope, to start the revolution, and what had the teams of raiders accomplished? Some terror, some confusion for the Arabs, the death of one major traitor—and an outpouring of sorrow at that death which made hash of everything they'd hoped to bring to fruition.

The frustration ate at Miriam, too. "We've lost," she said dully. Yakov had never imagined hearing those words from her lips.

Her spirit, he thought, was the strongest of any in the Second Irgun.

Samuel said, "I fear we have failed this time. There will be others. We Jews are a patient people. We will keep trying, again and again. One day *Eretz Yisroayl* will be free again."

"When?" Yakov said. When he was an old man? When his grandson—if he ever had a grandson—was an old man? In another nineteen hundred years? He had never considered the possibility of coming here and failing, or the consequences of failure.

"We have to think about getting you fighters out of the country," Samuel said with resolute practicality. "You are the ones who will keep the struggle alive."

"So we shall." Yakov did his best to make himself sound enthusiastic, to make himself feel that way. It was hard, so hard. He had hoped to storm into Jerusalem at the head of an army of Jews furiously fighting to regain the Israel of old. That was the dream of the Second Irgun, of all the Second Diaspora, though the refugees were now in their third and fourth generations. But it was no longer the dream of most of the Jews who had not fled when their country fell. And he would not spend next year in Jerusalem; he would spend it once more in Buenos Aires, once more in exile.

The sea slapped against the dark, quiet beach. Yakov threw what might have been a pebble into the water. It was not a pebble; it was a very special summoner. Unless the Arabs had exactly the right sensors in exactly the right place, they would never pick it up. Even if they did, they were unlikely to realize what it meant. And even if they knew just what it meant, they would have to be very good to get troops here in time to do anything about it.

The thought had hardly passed through Yakov's mind when a dolphin leaped into the air close to shore, fell back into the sea with a splash. "We have to hurry," Miriam said in a low voice. "The spysat will be over the horizon in a few minutes."

"Time enough," Yakov said. As he spoke, the dolphin beached

itself. Its mouth grinned wide, wider, widest. Down its throat, lights gleamed.

Yakov slid into the disguised sub feet first. Miriam followed. The dolphin's mouth closed, as if Jonah's whale, repenting of having spat him out, now decided to swallow him once more.

With an undolphinly jerk of its flippers, the sub freed itself from the beach. Palestine vanished behind Yakov. Securely innocent in international waters, the pickup boat waited. Turning his head toward the receding shore, he whispered, "We'll be back."

"Of course we will," Miriam said.

He wondered if either of them believed it.

Amends

H. Courreges LeBlanc

Ever had telekinetic sex?

A teek lover can reach your sweet spot from any position, even across the room, and never runs out of hands. And when two teeks go at it, they're always naked, even in their finest clothes.

Oh, sorry, Padre, I guess that's not how to start a confession, is it?

The words don't matter. What matters is what's in your heart.

But what's in my heart is so ugly, while words can be so beautiful. The Pope hires good poets—"Frig me farther, for I have skin. . . ."

That's quite enough. Confession is a sacrament. If you don't take it seriously, stop wasting my time.

Sorry, Padre, I am serious, really. I know I'm a smart-ass, but I need your help. And it is about skin, in a way.

Sex, per se, isn't necessarily sinful.

It's not sex. Hell, I love sex, and I don't think it's wrong, so don't even try to convince me of that.

I wasn't. You came to me, remember?

Yeah.

Why? Because you're convinced you're telekinetic?

Me? Naw. I couldn't bounce a check. No, I'm a telepath—two way, in fact. A tweep.

I see.

You don't believe me.

No, not really. What am I thinking right now?

Aw, not that tired parlor game, Padre. Okay, you're thinking of the number seven. Kinda cliché, Padre.

Easy enough to guess, then.

Yeah. But now you're thinking of a zebra, and now a cheese-burger, and now that god-awful Mac Davis song which I only inflict on hardcore skeptics. Believe me yet, Padre, or is it time for the Archies?

I believe you. You can stop now.

Oh, you're the one who's repeating that tune. I just got you started.

Hmm. So what's her name?

Who?

The telekinetic woman.

Damn, you're good. Makin' me jumpy, Padre.

I won't drag it out of you. Confess, if you're going to, or move aside for someone who will.

Amy. Her name is Amy.

And his?

Damn you, Padre. His name was Buck.

Was?

Yeah, he's dead.

Did you kill him?

Honest to God, Padre, I don't know. That's why I'm here.

It all started about a year back, just after I hit bottom and decided to fly blind for a while. All through college, and about three years after, I'd tweep my dates into putting out. But I got sick of it after a while. I could move 'em around for a while, but it never stuck. None of 'em would give me any unless I . . .

Unless you made them.

Yeah. What was the point? Might as well pay a hooker. At least I could relax and enjoy the show.

But you didn't.

No, damn you. How'd you know?

I know love.

Heh. Thought you guys never got any. Better not let the Pope know!

I'll take love over sex any day.

Yeah, well, me too. So, anyway, I stopped—went to a sex addicts' twelve-step program. All that Higher Power crap gives me the pip, if you want to know the truth, and I had to censor what I shared, even with my sponsor. But it worked.

Shouldn't have.

Well it did. So I started gigging again.

So you're a musician? Is that how you make your living?

Nah. Strictly coffeehouse stuff, real-book jazz, corn gigs. No money.

So how do you make a living?

I play poker. Easy money for a tweep. Hit the Indian casino once or twice a month, gives me all I need.

That's where I met Buck. Casinos are sugar for teeks too, though we played different games, natch. Buck was a craps man. I'd see him around on my casino circuit. Buck was a hard guy to miss—big redheaded lumberjack kind of guy, six foot plus, three hundred pounds plus. Looked like an Irish Sasquatch. But I had no idea he was a teek when I met him. Never paid much attention to him, to tell the truth, till he sidled up to me as I was liberating a paycheck from a siding salesman out of Owatonna.

"You got the gift, don't ya?" he muttered, breath hot against my ear and stinking of gin. "Every time I see you, you're up."

"Poker's a game of skill," I said. "I practice."

"You want to play, you need to ante," the dealer said. "Chairs are for players."

He vacated the chair, and the dealer laid out two hole cards and a deuce faceup. I didn't even look at the cards. I could feel Buck glaring at the back of my neck hard enough to give me sunburn. "Fold," I said, and got up too.

"Hey," the siding guy said. "Gimme a chance to win my money back." He was sweating, thinking about his kid. Hated his job, his nagging wife, his whole damn life, but loved that little girl. Had to get enough for that bike before her birthday this weekend. Hard to believe little Molly was seven. He was only down a yard.

I shoved my stack of chips in front of him, around three hundred bucks. "Here," I said. "Buy your kid a present."

He looked suspiciously at the chips. "What's the catch?"

"No catch, Herb. Just cash out and go home."

"C'mon." Buck grabbed my arm. The dealer slid the antes into the house hole, since Herb was the only player left—hell, it was two A.M. on a Tuesday. Herb scooped up the chips, still glaring at me, trying to figure my angle, and walked over to a blackjack table.

"You stupid fuck," I whispered. I tweeped him into cashing out, then propelled his sorry ass out into the parking lot, into his broken-down El Camino, and on down the road. What the hell, I'd have a bigger take on the weekend. I promised myself, not for the first time, to stay out of the casinos on weeknights.

Took me about two, three minutes, and Buck just stood there and watched. Maybe he was counting beads of sweat on my forehead, maybe wondering what came over me. Didn't know, had no extra to read him. But he waited just the same. But even though he was no telepath, it was like he was reading me. He watched me drag that siding salesman out of his own sewage, and just laughed. He had a great laugh.

"You a soft touch, brother," he said.

"You ain't my brother, brother."

"Buck's the name," he said. "As if you didn't know. And we're brothers, or maybe cousins." He leaned in and whispered. "We both got the gift. You can read people, and I can move things."

I shook loose. "You're nuts," I said, and walked to the casino's revolving door. But when I pushed the door, it pushed back. Behind me, I could hear Buck laughing, so I tweeped him into letting the door go. He knew what I was doing, and tried to fight, but I beat him down, stopped him from holding that door. Stopped him from laughing too. I ran to my car, with Buck strolling slow and easy up behind me. I hit the ignition, but Buck—I could feel him doing it—gapped the plugs wide enough to kill the motor. I tried to tweep him into fixing them, but I couldn't figure out how he did what he did. So I sat and waited for Buck to saunter up, pop the door lock, and sit beside me as an invisible doorman closed the door for him.

"I ain't crazy," he said.

"Okay. What do you want?"

"To get to know you. Compare notes. Maybe work together."

"Who you working for? CIA?"

He chuckled. "Dionne Warwick."

"Fuck you," I said, but I was laughing too.

So that's how you met Buck.

Yeah.

But you started to tell me about Amy.

But Buck leads to Amy. I'd've never met Amy except for Buck.

You're just avoiding the pain.

Look, whose confession is this? Let me tell it in my own way, Padre.

Okay. Tell me about Buck.

Buck. Buck was the king of scams. He knew every angle. Once we teamed up, casinos became small potatoes. A hobby. We had the perfect combination of talents for heisting banks. I was a telepath, and Buck was a telekinetic. He could feel things at a distance, as well as move them.

So we'd case a bank—I'd get the combination to the safe from the manager, and the location of all the security cameras too. Buck would find the cameras, scope them out. Then, on the day of the job, just before closing time, Buck would shatter the lenses of the security cameras, and I'd put all the bankers to sleep. Buck would open the vault remotely, and the money would just float into our bags. In and out, two minutes, no prints, no cameras, no witnesses.

The Poltergeist Heist.

Yeah, that got some play, didn't it? Too much, really, so we only did the one job. It was enough, though.

I'd say. Two million.

Two million my ass—we only got about eight hundred large. The bank scammed the FDIC for the rest—or maybe the manager scammed the bank.

Does that make your theft less wrong?

Sure it does. Well, maybe not, I guess. Don't matter, though; that ain't why I'm here.

So robbing a bank doesn't bother your conscience.

Don't change the subject, Padre. We were talking about Amy.

Were we.

Okay, okay. Jeez, what a ball buster you are.

Okay. Amy. Amy the Jinx. That's what Barb always called her. Stuff was always breaking around Amy; people got into accidents around her. She worked in that hippie coffee joint down on Thirty-fourth. The Grateful Brew. You know, the place with the giant stained-glass deadhead skull wreathed in roses? Two shifts a week, slowly driving the place under with the cost of replacing all the china that broke on her shift.

Buck and me were chilling after the heist, waiting for the media frenzy to die down before we tried another job. He met Barb down at the Pit, when I was sitting in on bass with Big Mary's blues combo. Buck was a master pickup artist. For a while I couldn't figure out how Buck scored with the ladies. He wasn't good-looking. He was three hundred pounds, plenty of muscle but even more fat. But he always had a honey on his arm, with two, three more waiting on the spike. After a while I realized it was his gift. You know, his teek gift. He could turn a woman on like a faucet, with feather touches wherever she'd like it best— nipples, earlobes, the back of her knees—all the while Buck smiling slow and easy. I watched him work on Barb as I thumped out one, four, five, one, four, five all night long. By last call, Barb was ready to spread like butter—Buck couldn't get her home, barely made it to the parking lot.

With you peeping the whole time.

Well, sure. That's one of the perks of telepathy. Buck didn't care. He was a dog.

And Barb?

She never knew. So who got hurt, Padre?

You know who. You did.

The hell I did. It was fun. Why do you keep changing the subject, Padre? I'm trying to get at the root of this.

So am I.

Well, let me get there, okay? Buck and Barb became an item, and the three of us would knock around together. Barb was great company. She could talk baseball, politics, movies, books, you name it. And she really knew how to tease Buck, get under his skin.

It was Barb who introduced me to Amy, early that spring. She took us round to the Grateful Brew. Soon Amy was ignoring the counter and hanging with us too.

"Barb talks about you all the time," she said. "I hear you're quite the musician."

"Yeah, I'm okay," I said.

"Okay, hell," Barb said. "Mac is a wizard."

"He plays four, five instruments," Buck said. "Can follow any tune, with or without charts, and never miss a change."

"Cool," Amy said. "How do you do that?"

"Telepathy." I scooted my chair closer to Amy. Damn, she was fine. Eyes green as jade, with black hair, and a spray of freckles over her pert nose. Sexy little overbite. And curves—she had a woman's body, and when she swiveled her hips she sparked magic like a Mesopotamian goddess. She thought she was fat, but as far as I can tell—and I've given the matter some research—every woman thinks she's fat. Woman built like a stick insect with an eating disorder thinks she's fat. Never met a woman who was happy with her body. But Amy's body sure made me happy.

And her mind?

What?

Never mind, keep going.

Anyway.

"You should play here," Amy said, reaching over to touch my forearm.

"Okay," I said.

"We don't pay much."

"I'm not in it for the money." I smiled wider, and she smiled back.

What was she thinking?

I wasn't listening. I told you, I was flying blind.

But it was all right to watch Buck and Barb have sex.

That's different. I just wanted to find a woman who would love me for who I was.

"You best watch out, Mac," Barb said. "Amy is a jinx."

"Barb!" Amy yelped.

"It's true," Barb insisted. "Her last boyfriend broke his leg after dumping her."

"We were just talking about a gig," I said.

"Yeah, Barb, he doesn't want to be my boyfriend."

"The hell he don't," Buck roared. Amy blushed, and I think I must have too.

But soon we were a foursome. We did everything together.

Everything?

Well, not that. I wanted to go slow with Amy. I wanted her to want me, like me as a person. A friend. I'd never been friends first. She was really into my music, came to every gig I played. Which was plenty.

Must be easy to book gigs when you're telepathic.

Fuck you, Padre! I'm good. I got a gift for music. I may not have monster chops on every ax, but I got something better. I can make a crowd dance, or weep, or shout for joy. And I don't fucking tweep them.

Not consciously, maybe.

Fuck you! You son of a bitch, you want to take the one thing I got left that's real and make it fake. Why you do this to me, Padre?

That's my job, Mac. To get you to see what you don't want to look at.

Oh man. Oh man. No wonder my CD never sold. Goddammit.

Maybe it doesn't matter. I mean the music isn't any less good. That's what all music does, convey feeling. You've just got your own built-in amplifier.

Oh, Padre. How could you do this to me? You've stolen something from me, all I had left.

Like Amy stole from you?

It wasn't Amy who stole from me, it was Buck.

Buck stole Amy.

Yeah.

Tell me about Amy.

I loved her, Padre. I loved that woman so much.

Tell me about her, not you.

What do you mean?

Who is she? She herself, other than being your object of desire.

I told you, I never read her.

So why did you love her, if you didn't know who she was?

Huh. I think I get you, Padre. Lemme think. Amy. Amy was lost. She drifted through life, and never found whatever it was she was looking for. I guess she was a frustrated musician or artist or something, because my music scratched an itch in her without really soothing it. All her boyfriends had been writers, painters, bohemian-type grunge boys. She lived in the upper half of a duplex owned by her drunk of a stepdad. Barb rented the lower half, but Amy didn't pay rent as long as she was a student.

What does she study?

Postcolonial women's studies, whatever that is. Her thesis is on the influence of British feminism on Indian pop music. Basically it was an excuse to indulge her obsession with Indi-pop. She was big into Bangra.

Camping. She liked camping too.

You don't know her at all.

Isn't that what I said? Why are you busting my chops? Who cares about all that computer-dating crap anyway? Long walks on the beach my ass. That bullshit doesn't matter. No one is who they pretend to be when they're dating. Nobody ever says they like trash novels, all-star wrestling, and fucking your best friend in the bar's parking lot while you're stuck onstage in the middle of the second set, watching helplessly.

Sorry, that just slipped out.

Mm hmm.

Stop changing the damn subject. I'm trying to tell you about Buck and Amy.

Okay. How did Buck tell Amy she was telekinetic?

It was in the spring, during exam week. Barb had a heavy course load, bio and chem stuff mostly, I think. Amy used to tease her about majoring in goop and slime.

Didn't Amy have finals?

Nah, Amy was ABD—All But Dissertation. She'd been diddling on her Bangra thesis for a whole semester, when she wasn't partying with Buck and me. So we were hanging out at the Grateful Brew, when some sleazeball management type, complete with comb-over, start hitting on her—right in front of me and everything.

So were you and Amy an item then?

No, not officially. I hadn't even kissed her. But she knew how I felt.

Read your mind, no doubt.

You're trying to rile me, aren't you, Padre? Well, it won't work. Anyway, Comb-Over Boy was leaning over the counter trying to look down her dress as he was saying, "I have to fly to the Caymans this weekend in the company jet for an international conference on arbitrage. I'd love if you could come with me."

"No thanks," Amy said, leaning away and twisting a dishrag in her hand. "I have to work."

"Call in sick, then, beautiful." Comb-Over didn't even know her name.

"I can't. I need the money."

"I've got plenty of money," Comb-Over said. "I'd cover your lost income, if you wanted."

I stood up and walked over. "The lady said no, buddy. Now take a hike."

Mr. Middle Management looked down his nose at me. "I wasn't speaking to you, uh, sir."

"Well, I'm talking to you, uh, dick."

"Mac." Amy had practically tied that rag into knots. "I can handle this."

"But this . . ."

"Please."

"Okay." I glared at Comb-Over. "I'll be right over here."

He turned to Amy. "That's not your boyfriend, is it?"

"Mac's a friend."

He smirked. "Well, then, how about this weekend? You'll love it, baby, I promise you."

"No. Really. I don't date customers."

He smirked more. "I can stop coming here. The coffee sucks anyway."

I started to get up again, but Buck touched my arm and shook his head.

"I'm trying to be polite about this," Amy said. "But I'm not interested."

"Fine," he said, picking up his cappuccino. "Bitch."

Amy's face grew dark, and the paper cup disintegrated in his sweaty little hand. Man, it was beautiful. Scalding, foamy cappuccino, all over his Brooks Brothers blues.

"Jinx strikes again!" said Carl, who was back baking in the kitchen.

"It's ruined!" Comb-Over screeched. "Do you have any idea how much this suit is worth?"

"You messed with the jinx," Carl crowed. "She puts the hoodoo an any man crosses her."

"Shut up, Carl," I said.

"You next, Mac!"

"I want to speak to the manager." Comb-Over was so busy pawing at his precious suit he didn't even notice the blisters on his hand. He was barking like a seal. "Get me the manager now!"

Buck stood up, walked over, and turned Comb-Over around by the shoulders. "Time to go, brother."

"You can't . . ."

"Sure I can," Buck said, absolutely placid as he propelled the man toward the door. "And you know it."

I stood up as he passed. "And if he won't, I will."

Comb-Over glared at us, back-stepping through the door. "You'll hear from my lawyer."

Amy was still wringing the rag, fighting back tears. I walked over to her. "Don't let that jerk get to you," I said, reaching over the counter to take the rag from her. "It wasn't your fault."

"Molly said she'd fire me if there was one more accident."

"You didn't do anything," I said. "It was a paper cup, you know how cheap they are; it just soaked through. Happens all the time."

"You a jinx!" Carl said.

"Carl, I'll jinx your teeth down your throat if you don't shut up."

"Jeez, I was just kidding."

"Can't you see Amy's upset?" I walked around the counter, and grabbed Amy's hand. "C'mon, Amy. Take a break. Carl will cover the counter." I put my arm around her shoulder and glared at Carl. "Won't you, Carl?"

"Sure," Carl said. "I didn't mean nothing, Amy."

Amy burst out crying. "Don't tell Molly, please?"

"Sure," Carl said. "Sure. Whatever you say. Jeez, don't cry."

"C'mon," I said, and walked her out to the parking lot. Comb-Over was just pulling away in his Porsche Carrera—a knockoff; I read that from him as he peeled out. Smugly thinking how Amy was eating her heart out over his car, and she was too dumb anyway to tell it wasn't real, and besides probably had crabs. He peeled out of the parking lot, and something small rattled from underneath his car and bounced right up to us. I bent down to pick it up. It was the drain plug from his oil pan.

I looked back at the coffeehouse door, and Buck was there, leaning against the stained-glass skull. He winked at me. I grinned back and tossed him the plug.

"What's that?" Amy asked.

"Plug from his oil pan," Buck said, tossing it into the air and catching it again, like he was flipping a coin.

Amy's face screwed tighter. "I'm such a jinx."

"Aw," I said. "No you aren't."

"Sure you are," Buck said.

"Shut up, Buck."

"What, Mac?" He kept tossing the plug up, down, up, down. "You gonna make it all better by telling her it ain't real? I'm'a give her some real help."

"Wh—what are you talking about?"

"Your jinx." He tossed the plug toward her; it stopped three inches from her astonished face and hooked back into Buck's palm.

Amy gaped. "How did you do that?"

He grinned. "I got a jinx too. Best damn thing ever happen to me." He leaned in and grew solemn. "Once I learned to control it."

"But that jinx stuff is just talk," Amy said. "I just have bad luck."

"You," Buck said, enunciating each word with a little pause in between, as if he was rolling them round on his tongue to moisten them with meaning before he spoke them, "have the gift. And so do I. But I know what to do with it."

"No way," Amy said, folding her arms and looking stubborn. "This is another one of your scams."

Buck shrugged, then turned over his open palm. The oil pan plug dropped halfway to the ground, stopped and hung in midair, then shot between Amy's ankles. She gave a little shout and jumped back, away from me. The plug looped around her, spiraling upward till it stopped right between her eyes, twirling slowly on its axis like a globe.

"It's not a jinx," Buck said in that slow liquid voice, "and it sure ain't bad luck. I don't know what it is, but I do know how to work it, and I can show you too."

She reached up, plucked the plug from the air in front of her. "Okay," she said. "I believe you."

"Okay, then."

Amy looked at me. "You too?"

I shook my head. "Nope."

"Mac's got a different gift," Buck said, but I shot a warning look at him.

"Music," I said. "I got my music."

"Yeah," Buck said. "That's what I meant."

Amy patted my arm. "That's a wonderful gift, Mac." Then she turned to Buck, all business, like I didn't even exist. "How does it work?"

And he showed her.

Yeah. Took her quite a while to get it. Sometimes I'd hang out while they practiced, and practice myself—guitar fingerings, sight reading, stuff like that.

Where were you?

At Amy's place. Her apartment was like an oven, but she had a porch. It was no bigger than a handkerchief, but it was a little cooler than inside. The maple in the front yard was far enough away that it really only gave shade after five. Usually we were there in the late afternoon, between Amy's shifts and my gigs. But early in June on Amy's day off, we decided to make a marathon session of it. I was working on a complex instrumental passage in Nat King Cole's "Nature Boy," and Amy was trying to roll boxcars. She wasn't allowed to touch the dice—Buck dumped them out of a Yahtzee cup.

Seven. A five and a deuce.

"Damn," Amy said.

"You gotta feel it." Buck curled his pinky and made a hooking motion, and the dice flipped themselves over to boxcars.

I muted the strings with a palm. "What's the pinky for?"

"Nothing," Buck said. "Style." The dice rolled across the folding table toward Buck, and hopped back into the Yahtzee cup. Something about that fourth chord wasn't working. I tried a G augment with an A bass.

Nine—five and a four.

"It's easy," Buck said to Amy. "You're trying too hard."

"What the hell does that mean?"

Buck touched his index finger to the side of his nose, looking for all the world like the Great and Powerful Oz dispensing a diploma. "Just let it flow naturally."

"Let what flow?"

"Can I make a suggestion?" I asked.

Amy rolled her eyes, but Buck nodded. "Sure. Why not?"

"Amy, have you ever dropped a pencil, and it was about to roll off the edge of the table?"

"I suppose," she conceded.

"And you reach to grab the pencil, but before your hand gets there, the pencil stops?"

"Uh-huh."

"Maybe it's like that."

Amy paused a moment, then she turned to Buck. "No, really, let what flow?"

I sighed and went back to my guitar. C seven, sharp nine?

Buck rolled again. Snake eyes.

B natural, with a D bass?

Eight.

A minor with a B flat up high?

Snake eyes again.

"Jesus, Mac!" Amy exploded. "Must you keep strumming those hideous chords?"

"I've got to find the one that fits."

"What about the one Nat King Cole used?"

"Dissonance gives it tension."

"But it's such a pretty song. Why do you have to twist it all around?"

"Jazz is the art of interpretation," I said. "Besides, I thought you liked my arrangement of this tune."

"I did the first thousand times."

"Fine," I said, and put my guitar back in its case. "I don't want to bore you, and I'll manage to live without the excitement of watching you try to roll boxcars."

"Hey, take it easy," Buck said.

"He gets on my nerves."

"Well, excuse me for failing in my duty to amuse you." I grabbed the case, stepped over the sill, and tripped down the stairs.

Amy jumped up. "Oh my God."

"Shit." Buck jumped up, too.

My left wrist hurt like hell, and I'd torn open the knees of my new pants. I climbed gingerly to my feet, then grabbed the guitar. It seemed undamaged.

Amy was at my elbow. "Are you all right?"

"No," I said, carrying my guitar case in my good hand. "But soon I'll be out of range." I regretted it the minute I said it, but I was too proud to take it back. Amy's face fell, and she turned away from me.

"Come on, Mac," Buck said. "It's not her fault."

"Oh, it's my fault. That's great." I limped down the stairs. "That's just perfect."

My wrist was sprained, so I canceled all my gigs for a week. A week sprawled on the couch, scowling and throwing paperbacks at the wall. It was another two weeks before I was back in form. And it was nearly a month till I saw Buck and Amy again.

They showed up at the Pit one night when I was sitting in with Eddie the Tree's jazz quintet. I was running the solo in Nat King Cole's "Nature Boy"—the very instrumental passage I'd been working on that day—when I saw her and Buck sitting at the bar. Damn near flubbed it, too. But I didn't.

At the set break, Buck and Amy wove between stools toward me. I could hear Amy's deck tennis shoes peeling away from the archaeological layers of Grain Belt and frat-boy vomit gumming up the floor.

"What's the matter with you?" Buck said. "Don't you put your friends on the list anymore?"

I looked at Amy. "Friends," I said. "Is that what we are?"

"Sure we are," she said. "Don't be mad anymore."

"Why should I be mad?" Boy, I was sweating like crazy. "It's not like you did anything wrong."

"That's right," Buck said. "You tripped your own self."

"Mm."

"But you are mad," Amy said.

"I just don't want to bore you."

"See, Buck? I told you he was mad." She stepped back. "Okay, I admit it. I got frustrated, and I snapped at you, which pissed you off, so you fell. I didn't make you fall, but I got you mad. I admit it, goddammit! Jesus fuck! I'm sorry! What the hell!"

I grinned. "That's the most gracious apology I've ever heard."

She punched my arm. "Fuck you, Mac. You could have cut me some slack too, so don't go all beatific on me."

"Okay, I could've cut you some slack, and I didn't. Jesus fuck!"

Buck threw an arm around each of our shoulders. "That was touching," he said. "Just like something out of *Little House on the Prairie*."

Amy grinned. *"Old Yeller."*

I grinned too. *"Casablanca."* I ducked from under Buck's embrace. "So," I said. "You ever figure out how to shoot craps?"

"Eventually," Amy said. "Hardest thing I ever learned." She wrapped her arm around Buck's waist.

I looked down and to the left. So that's how it was. I looked back up at them, forced a grin. "Harder than finishing your thesis?"

"Well, almost."

"So." I shifted from one foot to the other, audibly peeling away from the floor with each step. "You and Buck are . . ."

She hugged Buck tighter. "Isn't it great?"

"Maybe not so great for Barb."

"Hey," Buck said. "Barb and me were just casual, you know? She's cool with it."

"You should call Barb," Amy said. "She told me you were cute."

"Sure," I said. "Great. Gotta go now, get ready for the next set."

All that night, I kept breaking strings. Went through both sets of spares, and finished the night with only four strings left on the neck.

"You had a lousy night, Mac," Eddie said at three in the morning as he gave me my cut. Forty bucks. "You using razor blades for picks, or what?"

"Nah," I said. "I'm just jinxed." I pocketed the two twenties and walked out the door. I could feel Buck and Amy in the parking lot, waiting for me. I'd been feeling them out there for hours.

Didn't you tell Amy how you felt?

What for? For her pity?

For your self-respect.

I didn't have any left, Padre. How could I respect a self that couldn't be loved? I'd dropped every defense, opened myself up to her totally.

No you didn't. You lied to her.

Well, I couldn't tell her I was a tweep. She'd've never been able to trust me.

You told me.

Shit, Padre, the whole thing would make no sense without you knowing that.

So you trust a stranger, but not the woman you love.

I'm talking about love, Padre. Trust got nothing to do with it.

So I'm changing the subject again.

Yeah. I loved Amy, and she didn't love me in return. That's what matters.

She was your friend. Didn't that count for anything?

My friend. Jesus, Padre, don't you know anything about love? Ain't nothing more humiliating than to have the woman you love be your friend.

But friendship can lead to love.

The hell it can. Never has, and never will. You been watching too many chick flicks, Padre.

I thought that's what you wanted with Amy. To start as friends.

Yeah, and look what it got me.

So why didn't you tell her how you felt, then?

I couldn't. I had it bad, Padre. I had to have something. I couldn't quit Amy cold turkey.

So what did you do?

I called Barb, of course. Ain't nothing better for what ails a heartsick man like a good hate-fuck. Or a heartsick woman, for that matter. Barb needed it about as much as I did. Man, she was pissed at Buck.

She told you that?

Nah, she didn't need to. I didn't even need to tweep her. Quickest pickup I ever had. I called her up, said hello.

"Who's this?"

"Mac."

Pause. "Oh." Longer pause. "Come on over."

"Okay."

I drove over to her apartment, one flight under Amy. I knocked on her door. She opened up, handed me the bottle. I knocked back a slug, then I kissed her. Then I handed her the bottle.

"That bastard," she said.

"Yeah."

"Yeah." She pulled at the bottle. But when I reached for it, she shook her head and set the bottle on the floor. "Fuck me," she said, and pulled the sundress over her head. I took off my T-shirt, kicked off my shoes. She stood there, watching, waiting. I kicked the apartment door shut, unzipped my pants, stepped out of them, shucked my shorts. I reached out and squeezed her small upturned breast. She ran her thumbnail along the length of my penis.

I get the idea. You two made love.

No, Padre. We fucked. And all the while her legs were wrapped around me, her fists pummeled my back and arms. "Bastard," she kept saying. "Bastard. You fucking bastard."

Afterward, I lay on the carpet in the hall next to her, staring up at the smoke alarm. We lay there a long time, not saying any-thing. Finally Barb reached across my chest for the bottle. She took a long pull. "Get out," she said.

I reached for the bottle. "Gimme a drink first."

She shrugged and handed me the bottle. Then she sat up, back against the hall closet door, wrapped her arms around her knees, and watched me get dressed.

When I was completely dressed, hand on the knob, she looked at me, her face almost completely hidden, just her eyes peeping over her knees. "Don't go," she said.

I sat next to her on the floor. I could see her left breast, nipple pressed against thigh.

"You love her, don't you?"

I nodded, still looking at her breast.

"I wish it was me you loved."

I leaned over, kissed the ball of her shoulder. "Me too."

She turned her head sideways, like a bird, her wavy brown hair draping over her knees. "I aced the final for organic chem."

I turned my head to parallel hers. "I found a Wall fretless bass in a Bemidji pawnshop for four hundred bucks."

"Is that good?"

"It's an 'A' in chemistry."

"Are you hungry?"

"Ravenous."

"I can't cook."

"But I can." I stood up.

"I don't have much food."

"I'll find something." I went into the kitchen and inventoried her fridge. She was right—she didn't have much food. But there was enough for an omelet of sorts. I started melting butter in the skillet when Barb appeared in the doorway, back in her sundress. I rinsed off some mushrooms that were desiccated but still salvageable, threw them in the skillet, and started grating cheese.

"I wish I could cook," Barb said, leaning on the doorsill.

"No you don't."

She stuck her tongue out at me.

The omelet turned out pretty good, considering what I had to work with. I gave Barb half, and we dug in.

"Like it?"

"Ng," she said, mouth full. She only ate half of her food.

Afterward, we sat on the couch. We didn't talk. I was wondering whether we'd have sex again, and starting to consider what to do about it, when the noises from upstairs started. Springs squeaking. Moans.

Buck and Amy were fucking.

You mean they were making love.

Damn you, Padre. All right, they were making love. Barb looked at me, her eyes saucers of terror. I reached out to her. She drew back. "No," she said. "I can't."

"But . . ."

"You'd better leave, Mac." Her voice was soft, but she wouldn't meet my eye.

"Are you all right?"

"Please."

So I left Barb's apartment, and sat on the front steps. I couldn't hear Buck and Amy from there, but I could sure feel them. God. She was so gentle with Buck, so tender, so . . .

Loving.

Yeah. I'd never had a woman love me like that. I sat there for a while. A long while. Then I knocked on Barb's door. She opened it, started to say something. But I tweeped her, and she kissed me. She kissed me the way Amy was kissing Buck. I led Barb to her bed, pulled off that sundress, and stripped down again. I kissed her as Buck was kissing Amy, slow, lingering, moist kisses meandering down the length of her, till I reached her womb, and slid in two fingers and my tongue. It was Barb I touched, but Amy I felt. And when I climbed on top of her, she . . .

I get the general idea.

But it wasn't just sex, Padre. I'd had sex plenty of times before. Hell, Barb and I had fucked less than an hour ago. This was something totally different. It was paradise.

The gates of Hell, more likely.

Oh no, Padre. It was wonderful, better than anything. And

Barb was grooving on it too. Well, part of her, anyway. So I encouraged that part of her, nurtured that feeling like a tongue of flame. Soon Barb was falling for me. It was so easy. All this time I'd tweeped women with brute force. But when I just nudged Barb's natural feelings in my direction, it was so much more effective. Lasted longer too. Like judo, you know, using her energy to my advantage.

So you made Barb love you.

Not made, Padre. Helped. Finessed.

Did you love her too?

Aren't you listening, Padre? I loved Amy. I was just learning on Barb, perfecting my technique. It took a while before I got Barb into me enough so she was okay to hang out with Buck and Amy again.

Didn't you care at all how Barb felt?

Of course I did! I made Barb happy, Padre. She was miserable, and I made her happy. What's wrong with that? She was happy, and so was I.

Is Barb happy now?

Yeah, she is. I took good care of her.

You sound defensive.

Hell, you're attacking me. Let me finish, and then you can judge me, okay?

Okay. Tell me about the sex with Barb.

Padre, you dirty old man!

I don't want graphic details. But tell me, was all your sex with Barb just echoes of Buck's lovemaking with Amy?

It was at first. God, that was the best. I'd receive from Buck, and send to Barb, and the pleasure fed back in a loop.

But you didn't read Amy.

Didn't need to. And besides, I was still set on getting her to love me on her own.

Even though you knew she loved Buck.

Well, I knew that wouldn't last. And in the meanwhile, I was along for the ride.

Ah yes. Your feedback fucks.

Yeah. Not only were they fun, but I was learning to multitask. It pushed me to develop my gift, get finer control.

But soon they switched to telekinetic sex.

You're good, Padre.

That's where we started, remember? So tell me about it.

I don't know how to describe it. It was amazing. Buck could touch any part of her with his teek gift—and feel what he was touching, too. He had a thousand grasping hands, a million invisible fingertips. He'd ruffle her hair, tweak a nipple, tickle her on the back of her neck, massage her clit—that, and a hundred other things, if he wanted, all at once.

And Amy would do the same to him—she wasn't as skilled at first; she'd only be able to concentrate on one part at a time. But soon she had nearly as many hands as Buck did.

And you felt them all.

Yeah, but I couldn't echo with Barb. I could feel what Buck felt, but I couldn't do it myself. And Barb, of course, didn't have any idea about the gifts.

Didn't Buck and Amy have sex anymore?

Don't you get it, Padre? Buck and Amy were having sex continuously. They just stopped needing to physically touch. Once they outgrew that, their lovemaking was twice as intense.

They couldn't maintain that indefinitely.

You know a lot about sex for a priest, Padre.

Everyone knows that without valleys there are no peaks.

Well, yeah. Buck and Amy figured that out after a while. So they'd ebb and flow. They'd turn it down, but never completely off. Soon they made a game of it, trying to surprise the other one in public. We'd all be hanging out at the Grateful Brew, watching Amy work.

So you were socializing again.

Sure. We were the four musketeers. Amy was thrilled that Barb and I were together, and Buck was relieved. So there we were, hanging out at our usual table beneath the stained-glass skull. Barb was telling us about internships.

"I can't decide between Greenpeace or 3M for an internship," Barb said.

"That's an easy choice," Amy said.

"I don't know. The Greenpeace internship is closer to my career path," Barb said. "But the 3M gig could lead to a permanent job."

"That'd be nice," Buck said. Amy trailed invisible fingers across his scrotum. He grunted and crossed his legs.

"Yeah," Barb said. "If it led to a job, I could stay here in the cities." She put her hand on my knee, and Buck squeezed Amy's breast. I could see her breast rise beneath her halter top, indented with invisible fingers.

"What do you think, Mac?"

"Huh? Oh, that's up to you, baby."

Buck switched breasts, and winked at me.

"I mean," Barb said, "it'd be tough to have to choose between my work and"—she removed her hand from my knee—"my friends."

I put my hand on Barb's knee, and gave her a little tweep. "Follow your heart, Barb, and you'll get everything you need."

She smiled. "You're so sweet." Amy was tugging on Buck's penis, pinching the glans. I kissed Barb, and Buck spilled his latte.

So you were one big happy family.

Yeah, it was nice.

But you still didn't tweep Amy.

Nah, but by the middle of July I was starting to worry. What if Amy fell in love with Buck?

She already had.

Nah, it was just infatuation.

That's your opinion. Wishful thinking.

Well, Buck sure didn't love her. He was a dog.

Did he cheat on her?

I guess great minds think alike, Padre. I figured if Buck cheated on Amy, she'd dump him, and I could catch her on the rebound.

But did he?

Sure he did.

With help from you.

Damn little, Padre. I tell you, Buck was a dog. I just showed his true nature to Amy.

How thoughtful.

He didn't love her, Padre, not like I did. All I did at first was try an experiment—I'd wait for a pretty woman to come into the

Brew, and tweep her into scoping out Buck. She'd smile at Buck, and Buck would smile right back. One shift of that, and Amy was smoldering.

"I wish you wouldn't flirt with all those women," Amy said that night at the Pit, as I was setting up for sound check.

"Who?" Buck said.

"Well, that blonde in the tube top, for one."

"I just said hello."

"You were flirting," Amy said.

"Baby, I never touched her." Boy that was a mistake, and Buck knew it the minute he said it. Amy looked over at Barb, then back at Buck, and said nothing.

"Check, check," Eddie said into a mike. "One. Two. Buckle my shoe. Plosive. Three four, shut the door. Sibilant."

"Hey Mac, got a tuner?" asked Judy, the bassist. "Hey Mac, wake up."

"Oh," I said. "Sure, here." I tossed her my strobe tuner.

"What are you on?" Judy asked.

"And why ain't you sharing?" Eddie chimed in. We all fell out laughing, except Vinny the keyboard player, who was a twelve-stepper.

"That ain't funny," he said.

"Aw, lighten up, Vinny," Judy said.

Meanwhile, Buck was touching Amy up, but she was still scowling. It wasn't till halfway through the second set that she started touching him back. But she wouldn't let him come home with her.

That night, after we got back to Barb's place, we made love for the first time—just the two of us, I mean. We fucked, but Barb didn't come, so I went down on her till she did, and then I was hard again so we fucked some more, slowly this time. When I came again, she came with me. I lay on top of her, inside her, but shrinking fast. She crossed her ankles and squeezed, while wrapping her arms around my back and kissing me on the mouth.

"Mm," she said. "You are so sweet, Mac."

"Sweet on you." I kissed her again, and she unclenched her legs so I could lay beside her.

"Buck and Amy were fighting earlier," she said.

"Yeah, I heard."

"Is he cheating on her?"

I rolled onto my side, laid a hand between her breasts. "If he isn't yet, he will."

"How do you know?"

"I know Buck. He cheated on you, didn't he?"

Barb looked away. "Yeah."

I kissed her under her ear. "Lucky for me."

She turned her face back, and our cheeks grazed as I pulled my head back. "Are you over her?"

"Are you over him?"

"Yeah," she said. "Sure."

"Me too."

Barb brushed the hair back from my forehead, and twirled a lock around her finger, gazing deep into my eyes. I knew, at that moment, without needing to read her, that she loved me. She really loved me.

I was ready.

The next morning, when we were all hanging out at the Brew, before Amy's shift, I started my campaign of attrition.

"I'm getting restless," Buck said. "I think I'm gonna go to Vegas for a few days."

Not "Let's go," but "I'm gonna go."

Amy's eyes narrowed. "Fine. Have fun."

Too late, Buck realized his omission. "You can come too."

"No thanks." Amy was prim. "I have to work."

"Aw, come on, baby," Buck said. "You can call in sick."

"No she can't," Molly said from behind the counter.

"Then quit," Buck said. "I got plenty money. Besides, Vegas is fun. We'll shoot craps, make a killing. You'll love Vegas. The hotels are amazing."

"All-you-can-eat-crab-legs," Barb chimed in.

"Legalized prostitution," I said, and Barb kicked me underneath the table.

"Who cares about that," Buck said. "I ain't never needed to pay for it." I stared at him in amazement. He'd piped up with that little gem without any prompting from me. This was going to be easier than I'd thought.

"If you're quitting," Molly said, "tell me now so I can try to cover your shift."

"I'm not quitting," Amy said. "Buck can amuse himself in Vegas without me."

"It was just a thought," Buck said.

"No, I want you to go. Go on, have fun. God forbid you should get bored."

Buck shot me a look, but I shrugged and shook my head. All I'd done was put Vegas in Buck's head. All the rest fell out naturally.

So your hands were clean.

Hey, Padre, all's fair, you know?

Is it. How convenient.

Hey, it's not like I made Buck cheat. All I did was send some temptation his way.

So Buck cheated on Amy in Vegas?

Damn right he did.

Did you tell Amy?

No, how could I? "I know Buck cheated in Vegas because I read his mind"? No, Amy and Buck had to work it out on their own.

So you weren't "helping" Amy break up with Buck.

Nope.

What an elaborate set of rules you had.

No, Padre. It was very simple. I just created situations for Buck to be Buck. I didn't make him cheat. And I wouldn't tweep Amy at all till she broke up with Buck.

You weren't even reading her?

Sure I was. How else would I know if the moment was right?

Did she love Buck?

She thought she did.

But you knew better.

Sure I did. She had no business loving a dog like Buck.

When she could love you instead.

Yeah. It was amazing how little I had to do. Buck did all the dirty work for me. All I had to do was nudge him. It looked like

Amy would dump Buck by the end of summer, so I had to ditch Barb quick.

Was it easier to destroy love instead of creating it?

It wasn't like that, Padre. I really cared about Barb. I wouldn't hurt her. She got the Greenpeace internship, and the 3M one fell through.

With your help.

I'm not gonna let you rile me, Padre. You're making me out to be a monster. But you don't have all the facts.

Okay, give me the facts. Did you sabotage her internship at 3M?

Okay, yeah. But she might not have gotten it anyway. I just tweeped an HR wonk into misplacing her paperwork. Paperwork gets lost all the time. Afterward, I headed back to the Brew. Barb was already there, talking with Amy. Buck was in Vegas again.

"Where have you been?" Barb demanded, eyes red.

"I was out running errands," I said. "Did we have plans?"

"No."

"What's wrong, Barb? You look upset."

"She lost the 3M internship," Amy said.

"Oh no." I put my arm around Barb. "But you were so well qualified."

"They lost my application packet."

"What? But you sent it in months ago."

"Well, it's gone now."

"So send them another copy."

"Today's the deadline," Barb said. "It took me over a week to collect all those letters of recommendation, photocopies of my thesis, all my transcripts."

"Can't they give you an extension?"

"It's not like college, Mac," Amy said. "They've already selected someone."

"They picked Greg Reardon!" Barb growled.

"That dweeb?" Amy said. "I thought you said he paid some undergrad to finish his lab work while he was waterskiing in the Hampdens."

"Well, maybe that makes him managerial timber," I said.

"His skull, maybe," Barb muttered.

"Well," Amy said cheerily, "3M's loss, Greenpeace's gain."

There was a long pause. "Yeah," Barb finally said. "I suppose."

"Greenpeace will suit you better," I said.

"I'm not sure I still want the Greenpeace internship."

"Of course you do." I put my hand on her knee. "It's what you've worked so hard for, a chance to make a real difference."

"But it's deep in the woods of Oregon," Barb said. "It's so far away from you."

"Barb," I said, "I won't let you throw away your dream just to hang around and keep me company. I love you, and that means your happiness matters to me."

"So you want me to go."

"Instead of staying here, full of resentment and regret? Yes."

"You're right. I guess you're right." She put her hand on mine. "You could come with me."

I drew my hand back. "I'm a musician, Barb. I need a crowd. I need a city. If I went with you, I'd be giving up my dreams for you. Is that what you want me to do?"

"Damn you, Mac. How can you be so rational?"

"One of us has to be. I didn't say I liked it. It's tearing me up. But I've thought it through, and I can't come up with a better solution. Bad as it is, this seems least bad."

"He just wants what's best for you, Barb," Amy said.

"Is that what this is?"

"You know it is," Amy said. "Before you ever met Buck and Mac, you told me you didn't want to practice dirty science, spending your days calculating how much toxic waste you could legally pump into the river."

"Yeah." Barb's voice was tiny, practically a whisper.

"You applied to 3M as a fallback," Amy said. "Advocacy science is where you've always been headed." Amy looked down and away. "I wish I had such a sure goal in my own life."

"I wish I didn't," Barb said.

So you finessed her into leaving, just as you finessed her into loving you.

I did the right thing for Barb. She's happy in Oregon. I just talked to her yesterday.

Happy.

Well, her new boyfriend dumped her, but she loves her work.
Hmm. Tell me about Buck and Amy's breakup.

What, Padre? No more recriminations or accusations about Barb? You're losing your touch.
And you're changing the subject.

All right. All summer long, Buck dogged Amy more and more. It got to the point where I was just an observer. Amy knew he was cheating, but didn't want to face it. Well, one day in the middle of August, we were hanging out at the Brew when the air-conditioning went out. It started cranking out heat, right in the middle of lunch rush. The heat eventually drove away all the customers. By the time it emptied out enough for Amy to leave the counter, the whole coffee shop was roasting. After she figured out how to shut the system down, Amy called Molly, who of course blamed the breakdown on Amy's jinx. Amy hung up the phone. "She's gonna fire me for sure this time."

"For what?" I said. "For being in the building when her crappy air conditioner finally gave out?"

"She ain't gonna fire you, baby," Buck said.

"Yeah," I said. "Molly loves you."

Buck scowled at me, then smiled at Amy. "Anyway, what do you care what Molly thinks? You could make a month's salary on just one trip to the casino."

"I hate casinos," Amy said.

"Yeah, me too," Buck said. "But I like the money."

"I thought you had plenty of money."

"I'm doing all right," Buck said.

"Yet you spend more time at casinos than with me."

"Well, what do you want me to do? Hang out in this dump and live off your minimum wage?"

"Maybe I should go," I said.

"Don't go, Mac," Amy said.

"Yeah," Buck said savagely. "Why not watch us fight? You've seen us do everything else."

I shrugged. "With Barb gone, you guys are all the friends I got."

"You coulda gone with Barb."

"That's not fair," Amy said. "Mac's music is here. He'd have to start building his reputation from scratch in a new city, and Barb isn't anywhere near a decent music scene. It was a tough decision for the both of them."

Buck snorted.

"Whereas you would rather hang out in casinos—which you supposedly hate—than spend time with me—whom you supposedly love."

"I do love ya, baby. I just get sick of hanging around here, doing nothing day after day."

"This is me, Buck. This is my life. Who is it that you think you love? I work, I hang out with my friends. That's all there is, all I am."

"But don't you ever want more?"

"More what?" Amy wiped the sweat from her upper lip. God, it was hot in there. "What is it you want? To scam the casinos? The thrill of the big score? I don't want to live that life, Buck."

"You were pretty hot for it a couple months ago."

"I was interested in exploring who I was, learning to live with this—this jinx."

"It ain't a jinx," Buck said. "It's a gift, and you oughta be doing something with it."

"Some gift. I can cheat at craps, pick pockets. Great. Just the life I've always wanted."

"And this is better?" Buck gestured at the empty sweltering café.

"You've got your doctorate," I said.

"That crap!" Buck laughed. "Feminist Bangra, my ass. Like that matters to anyone."

"It matters to me."

"If it matters so damn much to you, why ain't you been working on it?"

Amy shrugged. "I don't know. I'm stuck."

"Academia is a bigger scam than anything I ever done." Buck said. "You told me that."

"Maybe I was wrong. Maybe I was wrong about a lot of things."

"Bullshit. You hated academia. Nothing but backbiting and inventing seven-syllable words."

Amy looked at me. "What do you think, Mac?"

I shrugged. "I'm a college dropout. I don't know anything about the academic life except what you told me."

"You know me," she said.

"Yeah. You like learning, you like reading, you like people. Maybe you would like academia, despite the politicking."

"But you hate your thesis advisor," Buck said. "He's a petty tyrant."

"So college life isn't perfect," I said. "But it suits you better than casino life."

"Fuck you, Mac," Buck said. "You just trying to break us up."

"He is not," Amy said. "Mac has always been a perfect gentleman, and a real friend to me."

"Huh. Yeah, right."

"Unlike you, who grabs every cute girl's ass when you think I don't see."

"You ever see me touch another woman?"

"You don't have to," Amy said. "I see the women sniffing round you. And I know how you do it." She turned to me. "Mac, he's always using his gift to grope me. He's touching me all the time."

I smiled. "Can't say as I blame him."

She blushed. "But how do I know he isn't doing the same to other women?"

This was the moment. I reached into Amy's heart, so gently, so deftly, and whispered to her deepest self: You can't trust Buck. But you can trust me. Buck is a dog, and I'm a perfect gentleman.

"I been faithful to you, baby," Buck was saying, and all the while I was whispering, No, don't believe him, he's lying, he's cheating on you.

"No," Amy said. "I don't believe you. You're lying. You're cheating on me."

"No I ain't," Buck said. "You don't know that."

"Of course I know," she said wearily. "You live for the chase, Buck. The thrill, the scam. Once you had me, you got bored."

"I'm not bored with you," Buck said. "I'm just bored with this penny-ante café."

"I'm a penny-ante gal," Amy said. "I'll never be big-time enough to keep you satisfied."

"You're dumping me? You are dumping me."

She looked away. "It's over, Buck."

Buck glared at me. "Thanks a lot, pal."

"I don't know why you want to blame Mac. You did this to yourself."

"Fine." Buck stood up, knocking his chair over. "Bitch."

Buck jutted out his chin, gave me one more dirty look, wheeled around, tripped over the chair he'd tipped, and fell face-first through the stained-glass skull.

"Oh my God," Amy said. "Oh my God, oh my God."

"Call 911!" I ran over to Buck. He flopped around in a widening puddle of blood and shattered roses. A dagger of skull glass pierced his neck, entering at the left front and exiting to the right. I flipped him onto his back, put my hand on his chest. "Hold still, dammit." He glared up at me, but held still. The blood sprayed from his neck wound in spurts. I pulled the glass out and clapped my hands over the two wounds. The blood squirted between my fingers. I clenched tighter, trying to choke the life back into him. His mouth worked open and closed, like a gasping fish. Finally I realized he was trying to say something. But no sound was coming out.

You didn't read him?

Oh no. Oh no, Padre. One time, when I was twelve, I read someone while they were dying. I was visiting my grandma in the hospital, and some woman in the next room, drowning in her own snot, checked out while I was in her head, and I stayed in her as she tunneled toward that place the dead go. I nearly died myself. I was in a coma for a week. Ain't never made that mistake again.

Wish I knew what Buck wanted to say, though.

You know.

No I don't, Padre. I wish I did.

Don't lie to me, Mac.

I'm not, Padre, I swear.

Why are you here?

I gotta know, Padre. Was Buck's death an accident, or something more?

I don't know, Mac.

But that's why I told you all this! You're supposed to know about this stuff.

I'm not a mind-reader, Mac. I don't know what was in Amy's heart at that moment.

Well, what's the point, then?

You're asking the wrong question, Mac.

What's the right question, then, Padre?

Are you morally culpable for the circumstances leading up to Buck's death?

I dunno.

For breaking up Buck and Amy?

Jeez . . .

For using Barb, without regard for her feelings?

I cared! I told you . . .

You erased the feelings you didn't like. You violated her, didn't you?

Fuck you, Padre!

That won't do, Mac. You need to answer me. That's why you're here. Did you alter and manipulate the thoughts and feelings of Buck, Amy, and Barb for your own ends?

But you don't understand.

Sure I understand. You want to justify your actions. You can do that if you want, and I won't stop you. But if you want forgiveness, you've got to own up to doing wrong.

I didn't do anything wrong.

It's a terrible burden, isn't it? Justifying sin. It would feel so good to lay that burden down, to receive the forgiveness you crave. But you can't have it both ways.

Oh Jesus, Padre, help me.

How?

Forgive me.

For what?

You fucking sadist.

No, Mac. I'm trying to heal you. But the only way out is through.

You can wash away my sins if you wanted, Padre.

Yes I can. If you repent, and promise to change.

Change. That's the whole problem ain't it? Changing what I don't like, all the painful bits on the cutting-room floor.

I meant you had to change yourself, not those around you.

Forgive me, Padre.

Are you heartily sorry for all your sins?

Damn it, forgive me.

Not like this, Mac. It wouldn't mean anything.

You'll forgive me, you son of a bitch.

True repentance is . . . forgive me, I lost my train of thought.

I'm the one who needs forgiveness.

Very well, then. Your sins are forgiven.

I'm forgiven?

Yes. I absolve you of all your sins, in the name of the Father, and the Son, and the Holy Ghost.

Oh damn. I'm so sorry, Padre.

It's all right, Mac.

Oh Jesus. Please forgive me.

Just let it go, Mac. It's in God's hands now. God knows when you truly repent. God sees you make amends.

Totem

Janet Berliner

Again and again on the two-moon journey from her home in Nzingaland across Inkanyala, the Cold Treeless Place, Nshesha Nyaloti renewed her promise to herself: *By the word of Queen Nzinga, Mother of my People, and of Tharu the Python, Father of my Tribe, I will have it all.*

Had she not heard the song of Nzinga and seen the scattering of bones form the head of a python with the symbol of her name superimposed upon it? "N." Nshesha.

The familiar anger rose in her and lodged like a rock in her heart. She had yet to meet her enemy, twin sister to the Lovedu Rain Queen, who lived in the Dragon Mountains. She recalled the words of *Umame*, her Chief's mother. "Guard the sister of the Rain Queen as closely as if she were joined to you by the head." It was she who had sent Nshesha to greet the usurper, Tandi, upon her arrival at Maseru Station and escort her back to Thotharu so that she could become First Royal Wife to Nshesha's lover and Chief, Mzimba. If anything should happen to Tandi or to any member of her party—

That fair-skinned daughter of a father who was also her uncle had no right to have Mzimba, even if he was promised to her in infancy and even though the law said that she, Nshesha, could not be both First Royal Wife and Chief Witchdoctor, High *Inyanga*.

Inside her head, she heard Mzimba's question, *"I will ask you one more time if you will be my second wife,"* and the echo of her response, *". . . I will answer one more time. I cannot."*

When *aloala,* the shadow of death, came to her grandfather, Vusama Nyaloti, High *Inyanga* to her people the Thotharu, and he returned to his ancestors, she would become the new High *Inyanga.* By then she would have befriended her enemy and learned the secrets of the usurper's ancestor, the Lovedu Queen, Ayesha, She-Who-Was-Immortal.

She would control her.
She would have it all.

Nshesha paced the concrete platform of Maseru Station. She felt unnerved, out of control, like an ant about to be devoured by an aardvark. Once a minute, she stopped to stare down the rails, expecting, dreading the sight of the oncoming train, which carried her rival for the heart of Mzimba the Chief.

Unlike the rest of the greeting party, who stood in a huddle at the far end of the platform, this was not the first time Nshesha stood at Maseru Station. She had done so twice before, once when she'd left to join her parents in Johannesburg, the City of Mines, and the second time when she'd returned to resume her studies under her grandfather the High Witchdoctor. She loathed having to spend any time at all around the town of Maseru, which lay within a mile of the border of Lesotho, one of the Republic of South Africa's many small independent nations. It bothered her that the Sothos chose to hold on to their umbilical attachment to the old establishment and that the Black population of the town of Maseru was diluted and governed by White traders and businessmen, technicians and government officials, missionaries and teachers.

Despite all of the changes that had come about in southern Africa since the advent of President Mandela, Maseru remained the end of the only railroad track that led into Lesotho. There were no other railway lines in Lesotho, nor any other real form of public transportation. There was a single main road that ran for a little more than two hundred miles along the country's western and southern boundaries, a mountain road that reached from Maseru into the interior, and short-distance roads that fed into the town from the villages. As for the nearly two thousand miles of bridle paths, such as the ones Nshesha and her party had used to get here, they could hardly be called roads and challenged even the hardiest of travelers.

In the distance she heard the rumbling of the train. Her stomach lurched.

"May she look like a toad of the Limpopo," she said.

She had no idea she had spoken aloud until she heard Dahodi laugh behind her. He placed his arm across her shoulder. She shrugged it off, like an errant mosquito.

"You had better be nice to me," he said. "Once the Princess has our Chief on the love-mat, you will need friends."

The hyenas are gathering, she thought. As if it weren't bad enough that Tandi was to become Mzimba's First Royal Wife, Dahodi was waiting like a predator to force himself on her and usurp her place as High *Inyanga*.

Enough, she thought. He will have neither. And Mzimba, too, will be mine. The trip across the mountains from their village had been arduous, but it would seem as nothing with the toll this first meeting with Tandi was going to take on her. At that moment, she felt something akin to hatred for Mzimba, and swore anew that she would control him, his bride, and the tribe over which they thought they were going to rule.

There was a sudden press of people around her and the train from the north labored into the station and screeched to a halt. She hitched up the multicolored blanket that was wrapped ceremoniously around her sweating body, set her conical reed hat in place, and glanced longingly at the banks of the Caledon River, which ran alongside the town. How much she'd rather be bathing in its cool waters right now, she thought, turning toward the train.

"This is it, isn't it, Nshesha," Dahodi said, making no effort to disguise the note of triumph in his voice. "Your days of playing First Royal Wife are over."

The passengers began to debark: White tourists coming to the casinos; a few Black students bound for the colleges and missionary schools, which contributed to Lesotho's having the highest literacy rate in Africa, though less than a third of the students were Sotho; absentee husbands starting their annual visits home, there to make babies and to help with fieldwork usually done by the women.

Mostly there were Whites, lots of them.

Many were renegades, tired of their orderly lives in the suburbs of the Republic. They came to work at milling, at brickmaking or furniture making, or hoping to mine Lesotho's small supply of diamonds and iron ore and gypsum, quartz and calcite, and make a quick fortune for their retirement. And there were the do-gooders, too, those who, sooner than they thought, would grow tired of food deficiency, venereal disease, chronic rheumatism, respiratory infections, and dyspepsia. Lesotho was a country of fewer than twenty hospitals and only one medical doctor for every two thousand or more people, though shamans were plentiful as the trout in the streams stocked for the weekend pleasure of the tourists.

When the platform was almost clear, the conductor wiped his sweating head with the edge of a red flag, settled his cap on his head, and hollered his first "All aboard." There was no sign of the Lovedu party and Nshesha felt a rising sense of optimism.

Perhaps Tandi had decided not to come after all.

Then she remembered the drums that had confirmed her rival's departure from home. What foolishness, to keep her hopes alive. She touched the shoes that were tied together and slung around her neck and debated putting them on. Deciding that she would rather endure the heat of the concrete platform and that it was enough if Tandi saw that she owned shoes, she continued walking toward Dahodi, who stood at the door that opened into the end carriage of the train.

"Welcome Tandi, sister of the Rain Queen," he said.

He bowed and Nshesha cursed. Mzimba was right. He always said that she moved too slowly, even in bare feet. She had been so busy contemplating Lesotho, the value of wearing shoes, and Dahodi's attitude that she'd given the man-eater a chance to ingratiate himself with the Lovedu princess.

Squinting against the sun and standing tall so that she could see her rival over the heads of two elderly women who chose that moment to block her path, Nshesha tried to see Tandi more clearly.

If she had hoped that her rival would be old and ugly, her illusions were quickly shattered.

The usurper was, at most, her own age. She was not as tall as Nshesha but her bearing was regal. The design of her blanket was as complex as Nshesha's own, but the colors were more subdued. What hair escaped the confines of her sapphire turban gleamed copper against skin that was a pale shade of mocha.

As for her traveling party, they were as dark as any Tharu. There were six bearers, each with the carriage of a warrior, and two handmaidens, who looked down modestly at the ground.

What a pity she could not see into the woman's heart, Nshesha thought, noting that nothing about her body was imperious. Still, looking into her eyes would help her gain the knowledge that she needed, and there would be plenty of time for that on the journey home.

"Dahodi?"

The stranger's voice was low and sweet as she repeated the name of Nshesha's enemy and tried to pronounce it in the correct manner. "Forgive me if at first I do not say your words as you do. Perhaps you will help me to become familiar with the music of my new language?"

Nshesha was close enough now to hear that Tandi's speech was free of the clicks of the Thotharu, but nevertheless easy to understand. Before Dahodi could answer, she was there.

She bowed, but not too low. "Welcome, Tandi, Royal Princess of the House of Lovedu. I am Nshesha, granddaughter of Vusama Nyaloti. I have been sent to take you to our people and to your husband."

"Forgive me, I assumed Dahodi here . . . ?" The stranger cut herself short. "We are most grateful that the granddaughter of Vusama Nyaloti has come to greet us," she said, changing direction with ease. "Your grandfather's fame has become part of the songs of our elders, and our storytellers speak warmly of his stay with us in the days of my infancy."

She smiled at Nshesha, her manner that of one seeking a friend. "Nshesha. The name sings, but I know not what song. What is its meaning?"

"It sings of the dew on the flowers of the morning," Nshesha said, responding in kind. Nor did she stop smiling when she remembered that Tandi was her enemy. It would be helpful to gain the Lovedu's confidence, she thought.

"We have been told that the journey to our new home will be difficult. I trust I will have energy left to devote to learning about my new husband and our new people."

My husband. *Our* people.

The words reminded Nshesha again that this was the usurper. Under other circumstances she might truly have befriended this young woman, who was of her age and had a brightness in her and a strength in her gentleness, even after the long train ride from the Drakensberg Mountains. There had been times in Nshesha's life when she had longed for the one thing her status as Vusama's granddaughter had denied her: a female friend, a confidante. It was too late for that now. She must never allow herself to forget that this woman was her enemy, for to forget would be to open herself up to the greatest danger of all. Feeling kindness to one she must destroy was a weakness she could not afford.

Immediately upon their return to the village, and once *Umame* had satisfied the rites of virginity, ceremony piled upon ceremony. There was Mzimba's public asking for the hand of Tandi, the dispatch of much *Lobola*, and finally the wedding itself.

Four years passed from the time Nshesha had lain with Mzimba. In that time, he fathered two daughters by the proxy Tandi had chosen for him when it seemed that she was not destined to bear him children. That he lay with proxies did not seem in any way to distress her, as long as the choice of the women was hers and he lay with her, too, and accorded her the dignity due his First High Royal Wife.

"This is also the way of my people," she explained to Nshesha, when the subject of an heir was first openly broached between them.

At first, she and the First Wife were seen together often in earnest conversation, or laughing like any two young women might at some private joke. The first strain in their apparent friendship came when Dahodi, returning from a foray with his cronies, suggested loudly enough to be overheard by the two women that Mzimba might prefer to return to his old ways and share the sleeping mat of his High *Inyanga*'s granddaughter. As if this were not enough, he repeated the words once spoken by Ziko, Father-of-the-Chief, to his old friend and advisor, Vusama.

Talking of Nshesha, Ziko had said, "If she could play both the role of High *Inyanga* and that of First Royal Wife, I would delay my departure from this world to see what manner of heir Nshesha and Mzimba could produce."

"What manner of comment is that from a Chief?" Tandi asked.

"We knew each other from childhood, as the two of them had known each other always," Nshesha said. "It was merely the speculation of two old men."

Tandi spoke no more of the subject, but she began to watch Nshesha warily when Mzimba was around. It did not take her long to realize that whatever had been between the two of them still pulled at their hearts and bodies. She confided in Nshesha less and less and soon avoided her company completely, except when she had no choice.

Now Tandi was at last beautiful with child.

"It is time, Nshesha," Vusama Nyaloti said gently, opening his rheumy eyes one morning as the birthing of the heir approached. "I am old and tired; I hear the call of our ancestors."

"I am not yet ready to take your place."

Nshesha's protest was a required courtesy. They both knew that. Still the courtesies had to be carefully observed. In truth, she was as ready to take Vusama's place as she would ever be. She could taste the flavor of power on her tongue and it was more aromatic than the meat she had eaten with her evening meal, though that had been biltong, dried buck, and highly salted.

Vusama looked at his granddaughter and smiled. His eyes were fathomless as the waters of the Tugela, brown as the mud of its tributaries, and as filled with hidden wisdom as rivers were crowded with crocodiles, but Nshesha knew he was not so old that he could not remember the impatience of his youth when he had longed for the mantle of power to be draped around his shoulders.

"When you were an infant, strapped to your mother's back, I knew one day you would take over from me; you have only known it fully since the night you last led the Dance of the Python."

Holding one hand within the other, Nshesha examined her palm as if it held the thorn of her love for Mzimba. She remembered how the python had stirred, responding to the sound of her voice as she sat in the clearing, waiting for a sign. Inside her head and her heart she heard again the song of the minstrel—the song of Thoto—and felt again the power of the snake's muscles as he twisted around her arm and constricted to make sure of his hold.

"It will fall to you to help with the birthing, Nshesha," Vusama said. "Your training has been rigorous. You have been through the Ceremony of Purification and I have proclaimed you Custodian of the Sacred Tribal Relics. I have taught you all I can. There is nothing left for me to do except to throw the *amadolo* and *mazinyo-endlovu*, the bones, one final time before I go on my journey." Slowly and with great care, Vusama struggled to the cross-legged position he had once assumed as easily as a young leopard climbs a tree. "Bring me my pouch, Nshesha," he ordered. "I will look into your future and show it to you before you begin your service."

Without waiting to be invited, Nshesha sat at her grandfather's side. She betrayed no sign of emotion, said not a word while the old man performed the ritual throwing of the bones, a collection of carved pieces of ivory and cowrie shells and the dried heels of the sacrificial black mountain goats, which haunted the caves of the surrounding hills.

"The *idlozi* have spoken," Vusama said, as the bones settled into a design more intricate than any Nshesha had ever seen. "They have chosen a totem for you. Look closely at it, Nshesha, for within its curves lies the story of your past and the challenge of your future."

Nshesha stared at the outline that had formed on the mud floor, its body curved and resting, its eyes watchful and waiting.

"Will you read the prediction of the bones?" Vusama asked.

Nshesha shook her head. "I cannot speak the words," she said.

"Then I will say them for you." Her grandfather bent closer to the floor. "Listen and remember."

Vusama spoke and Nshesha listened. He told of what she would have to do to gain power, of what would happen to her if she did not maintain it, and of the storytellers who would talk of her around the night fires if she fulfilled the predictions of the bones. She listened while darkness descended and through the hailstorm that sang on the thatch of their hut, listened until, reverently, Vusama gathered up the bones and replaced them in his snakeskin pouch.

"Never forget that you are the daughter of the son of the son of Vamba Nyaloti, Witchdoctor to Malandela." Vusama held out his hand for assistance.

Sadly, for it was the first time he had openly asked her for such help, Nshesha gave him her hand and he straightened his gnarled body to its full height. Bowing to her as to a high priestess, he said: "Be sure that you use your power well. It will not always be easy."

"I will serve my people as you have taught me."

"Do that, *Inyanga*," Vusama said. Raising his head as he called her Witchdoctor, he handed over the snakeskin pouch that had been his father's and *his* father's before him. "While you serve your people, you serve yourself. Abuse that power, and it will turn on you as surely as the sun follows the moon."

With that, he turned and lowered himself onto his sleeping kaross. Nshesha, too, lay down. Though she could not imagine finding sleep, it found her. For how long, she did not know, but she was awakened by a scream.

"Aaiee!" Mzimba's fair-skinned Royal Wife cried out in pain. "Aaiee!"

On the other side of the hut, the men's side, Vusama moaned once but he did not stir.

"Grandfather?"

Nshesha's tone was urgent, but her grandfather lay silent. She did not have to look at him to know that his long journey had begun. They had said their farewells while he was alive and warm and she could tell him of her love and gratitude, so she shed no tears now. They would serve only to slow him down on the journey he had been ready to make. Instead she prayed to the *idlozi* to speed him on his way and to guide her in the days ahead.

"Aaiee!"

As the holder of the bones, it was Nshesha's duty to take care of Tandi, even though, in the end, she would use her as she saw fit. Stumbling to her feet, she went outside and breathed in the dawn. There was one omen that would assure her success, and it was that she sought, but the eastern ridge of hills was lost in clouds. They hid from her the moment of the day's rebirth, that instant the rim of the African sun showed the edge of its face to the morning, and she did not have time to wait for the wind to blow the clouds away. She had delayed too long and would have to hurry if she was not to anger Mzimba. Nor was there time to search for another omen, not if she was to prepare properly for her first test as High *Inyanga*.

She went back inside the hut.

Carefully, trying to ignore the increasing frequency of Tandi's screams, she plaited cowrie shells and coins into her hair and placed goatskin strips around her breasts to identify her status. Having surrounded her throat with beads and necklaces and suspended the tail of a goat and several dried gallbladders from the belt that she'd fastened about her waist, she applied a generous amount of red ochre to her cheeks. Then she looped Vusama's snakeskin pouch into her belt and stood before the body that lay cold and stiffening on its kaross.

"Go well on your journey," she said, stooping to kiss her grandfather.

His flesh was cold against her lips and she was grateful when another urgent cry from Tandi forced an end to the moment. Still there was one more thing left to do before she could go to the hut of her Chief: she must keep the promise she had made to her grandfather, who had asked to be speeded on his journey in the way of all great *Inyanga*s.

When she was sure that the fire she had promised to light was burning, Nshesha left her grandfather's hut and all of its child-hood memories behind her. There was no point in looking back. It would soon be a pyre and, seeing the flames, everyone would know that Vusama was gone and that she was the new High *Inyanga*. By the time the birthing was over, they would be halfway through building a new hut for her next to the ashes of the old one.

Moving quickly, Nshesha trod the path that led to the Great Hut of her Chief. The soles of her bare feet tingled with the low rumble of drums and her ears filled with the chanting of the Council of Elders, whose gentle tone told her their songs of hope and comfort and prayer had only just begun. Their voices would grow stronger later, after Mzimba ordered the village maidens to perform the Python Dance. Together, the voices and the fertility dance would help Tandi bear the pain of childbirth.

Shaking her head so that the cowrie shells and coins she had plaited into her hair could make the sound of warning that she was coming, Nshesha passed through the drummers and Elders and the waiting maidens, and entered the Great Hut of the Chief. In the dim light, she could see Tandi, flanked as always by her two silent handmaidens and crouching on her love-mat on the women's side of the hut. The sight of the *Inyanga* quieted Tandi's screams, but it could not still the pain that kept her hands clasped in support beneath the huge swell of her belly. It was clear that soon she would rise to her haunches in readiness for the fall of the child she had been carrying for nine moons and more—the child that should have been hers, Nshesha thought. She waited for the flow and ebb of envy to subside and prayed for the relief of hatred.

"Greetings, *Inyanga*," Chief Mzimba said. "Where is Vusama?"

Nshesha bowed her head in greeting, low enough to show her respect and grateful for the custom that allowed her time to disguise her longing for this man whom she had never ceased to love.

"My grandfather, the High *Inyanga*, has gone to meet his ancestors, Great Chief," she said, looking up to meet his gaze as befitted her new status.

Mzimba accepted the death of his advisor as naturally as he did the changing seasons and signaled her toward the women's side of the hut, where Tandi continued to crouch on her love-mat, her eyes modestly downcast in the way befitting a woman in the presence of power. Damn her strength, Nshesha thought, seeing that Tandi's back was straight and firm, though her face shone from the sweat of pain.

As if she could read Nshesha's thoughts, Tandi held out her sweating palms, not in supplication but for her handmaidens to fan. Nshesha's own hands were none too dry or cool; she had not been this close to her lover since the night of their last lovemaking, and the pain of being so near to him was far harder to bear than she might have foretold. He who knew her so well must not see in her eyes a hurt and vulnerable woman or he would not acknowledge her publicly as his High *Inyanga*.

Remembering the lessons she had been so carefully taught for this occasion, she bowed. Then, standing tall, she did again what none of her tribe would have dared; she looked her Chief directly in his eyes. In them she saw the hardness of power and the warning that, for him, their past could not exist.

"Let the ritual begin," Mzimba said at last, granting her acceptance with his words. "My wife, Tandi, has long been beautiful with child. It is fitting that the bones be thrown now. You shall read what the *idlozi* plan for her."

Taking her cue, Nshesha looked away from her Chief and began to sway. At first it was as if the ice she had seen in Mzimba's eyes had frozen the blood in her veins and her body was cold and stiff, but the music of the drummers could not be ignored. As it entered her and she kept time with its beat, her movements changed. They became slow and sinuous, daring Mzimba to watch and ignore her fire. The longer she danced, the more she knew that Mzimba was as he had always been, and that the coldness of his eyes was a warrior's shield. She felt warm, sensual, in command.

Changing the rhythm of her body until it outpaced the drummers and moved only to the pounding of her own heart, Nshesha caused her breathing to become shallow and her eyes to take on the look of Tharu the Python, Father of the Tribe. Hooded and glazed. Then, knowing it was enough, she placed the balls of her feet firmly upon the ground and, raising her hands above her head, stood deathly still.

The effect was as she had wanted it to be: the necklaces and the beads, the goat's tail and the dried gallbladders suspended from her waist continued to dance as if of their own volition.

Glancing quickly at Mzimba she saw that the drama of her choreography pleased him.

"Let the Python Dance begin in the *lekhotla*," he ordered, his voice less stern than it had been before.

Remembering what she had learned from the bone-throwing ceremony of the night before and mentally rehearsing what she had to tell Mzimba and his Royal Wife, Nshesha prepared to complete her part of the ritual.

Stepping into the opening of the hut, she lifted her hand. Instantly the beat of the drums changed. The voices of the Elders grew louder and Nshesha dropped her hand and turned from the daylight to face Mzimba, who leaned against the mud wall of the hut.

Tandi, who had been quiet, whimpered.

"Be still, wife," Mzimba said, "else how can we hear what the *Inyanga* has to say."

Nshesha waited, hoping he would be seated, but he merely repositioned his body more comfortably, making it clear that he intended to remain standing.

"Why do you wait, *Inyanga*?"

Asking him to sit would have been an admission that she was aware of him when only her duty should concern her, so Nshesha removed the snakeskin pouch from her belt and closed her fingers around it. She had hardly done so when something took hold of her and sent the blood flowing through her veins with such force that her body became as feeble as a raft being buffeted through the rapids of the Tugela. When it reached the shallows, she ceased to be aware of Mzimba's presence. Nothing mattered except her hand. Like the limb of a tree that had survived the storm alone, it took on a life of its own, lifting itself into the air, twisting and cupping its fingers around the bag of bones to circle them over head—once, twice, thrice—until at last it lowered itself to her side and Nshesha sank to the ground.

With the feel of the earth under her came a sense of calm and power such as she had never before experienced. The complex knot that held the pouch together fell open at her touch. Her hand was sure as she scattered the bones and their design created a python. As she read the tales that lay within its curves, she knew exactly what she could safely tell the royal couple and what must be kept hidden from them.

Taking her time, she bent low over the *amadolo* and muttered a series of deliberately low sounds. When Mzimba leaned forward to listen, she gathered up the contents of the pouch and prepared to throw the bones for a second time, as if what she had seen was far too important to divulge without confirmation. She could hear Tandi's breathing, heavy with the strain of keeping silent, and it was not difficult to sense Mzimba's growing impatience.

Spitting upon the bones, she rattled them several times and spread them once more upon the earth, where they danced to the chanting of the Council of Elders, whose voices were raised to the *idlozi* and to their ancestors, who were always listening:

> "Bring a son to our Chief-of-Many-Daughters and
> Ai, what celebrations there will be tonight."

Nshesha lowered her eyelids and waited. "I have seen," she said at last. "You have begotten . . . sons." She hesitated just long enough between the words to make certain that the import of what she was saying was not lost on Mzimba, who stamped his foot with the annoyance of a small child and drove the tip of his spear into the ground.

"None of my other wives are beautiful with child. How can there be more than one?"

"As the First Royal Wife Tandi has a sister who is her twin, so she will give birth to two boys. Blessed ones—"

"Two Blessed Ones?"

Mzimba's voice filled the hut and overflowed to the ears of the Elders and from there to the drummers.

"Though the children will both be Blessed Ones, born with the caul," Nshesha said, thinking of all that she knew and had not told and feeling again the surge of energy that had come to her with the throwing of the bones, "the law must be obeyed. Your father, Ziko the Great, carried a piece of Maieg from the Zambezi and placed it at the feet of Maiegawana, the Mother of all Children, before he descended the Mont-aux-Source and found his way to this place which is now our home. Your secondborn must be carried up the Tugela River to Maiegawana and—"

"No!"

It was the first time Tandi had spoken and it was only one word, yet it was too much for her husband the Chief, who looked at her sternly. "You would dare to break protocol?" he said.

"Maiegawana watched the Sun Dragon devour all of her own children," Nshesha said for the benefit of Tandi, for the sake of ritual, and to cement her own purposes. "Do not be saddened that she awaits the gift of your son, for when his small earthly shape has been buried at her feet, she will help his spirit rise to the heavens. He will play as a star among the stars and bring hope into your heart and into the hearts of all who see him there."

Tandi's eyes were filled with both the pain of her defiance and with the labor of childbirth, which sent her nails digging holes into her palms, but she spoke on, this time addressing Nshesha directly. "I was warned of your barbarous custom," she said. "I will not push a pebble down the throat of my own child."

"The spirit of my son *will* shine from the sky, not creep like a lizard upon the ground with the spirits of ordinary children," Mzimba bellowed, his voice as ominous as the thunder which heralded a storm. "I myself will search for the smoothest white pebble." Mzimba's voice was kinder now than Nshesha had ever heard it. "When it is time, our High *Inyanga* will do what must be done."

"You must bring two pebbles, O Chief," Nshesha said. "What one son receives, so must the other in equal measure."

"You have said, *Inyanga*, that our sons will be Blessed Ones," Tandi said. "If that is so, they are destined to be wise and famous and must drink of the fluid from the caul. What child can drink if its throat is filled with stone?"

"Your sons will be given one ivory spoonful of the fluid before I prepare the *gri-gri*, the rolls of calfskin containing the cauls and dried navel strings. Once each child has a *gri-gri* fastened around his neck, what must be done will be done and your secondborn will be carried to Maiegawana or much evil will befall us all."

Tandi opened her mouth to speak but choked back further words of protest. She bit down on her lower lip to stifle that which would serve no purpose and, as the odor of her fresh blood filled the hut, she rose to her haunches in anticipation of the birth of her sons.

"It is best that you go now, O Chief, and that the First High Royal Wife's women leave to prepare a leopard-skin bag for your star-son," Nshesha said. "It will take two days of journeying in our canoes and many days of walking before we reach Maiegawana and we dare not anger her by delaying. Dispatch a messenger to Ntonu the gravedigger so that he may begin his search for the sacrificial black-eared goat."

The two handmaidens made no move to leave the hut.

"I wish my servants to remain with me," Tandi said.

Nshesha shook her head. "They are mutes. No one who is not whole should be with you at the moment of birthing."

"Leave!" Mzimba pointed at the handmaidens. His voice was harsh now, threatening, with none of the kindness that had been there before. "Nothing must happen to my heir."

Nshesha looked up so that she could read her Chief's face, but he had left the hut. Where he had been only the sun shone. It illuminated the snake crafted by the bones left to her by Vusama—the tail a point of painted ivory, the eyes two cowrie shells, the mouth the hairless heel of a black mountain goat.

She could hear the drums outside and knew that the dance of the village maidens quickened to its climax. Their excitement was in her blood. She could feel its throb in her fingers as she caressed the reptile image, tracing its length and imagining that it responded to her touch. Her woman's body, invaded by the drumbeat and the voices of the elders, ached to dance, and she began to sway. Then, from the corner of the hut, she heard Tandi take in a deep and frightened breath, and she remembered.

Bidding the image of the python to rise into the air and join with the unfulfilled needs of her own flesh, she gathered the bones and replaced them in their pouch. Moving toward Tandi, she knelt before her and gently, tenderly, using sweet-smelling grasses, stroked her face and comforted her.

She did not have to look to know that the spirit-image of her totem, the python, hovered at her side. At her command, it would enter the First High Royal Wife and draw from her the soul of the child that would give it life. For now, her attention must be given to Tandi. It was a good thing, she thought, that her grandfather had schooled her well. She had assisted him at many births, beginning with calves in the valley and graduating to the women in the fields. This was her first time with twins, human twins, but she was not afraid. Queen Nzinga would guide her spirit, and her grandfather's voice would speak inside her head and guide her hands.

"You will have to help me, First Wife of the Chief," she said.

Tandi obeyed, screaming as her sons entered the world. Then, crying softly, she named her first son Karesu, and his brother, who was identical except for a small blemish in his right eye, she named Kadesi.

When the babies had been birthed and cleansed, after the Ceremony of the Blessed Ones and while Tandi slept, Nshesha ordered that the basket containing Tharu the snake of the Python Dance be brought to her. She carried the basket into the hut and removed the lid. Glancing over her shoulder to make sure that she was unobserved, she took the infant Kadesi from his place beside his sleeping mother and gave the spirit of the child to the body of Tharu for safekeeping.

She emerged from the birthing hut with the python wound about her. In her hand, she carried the basket and its new contents, a leopard-skin bag containing what appeared to be the small form of Tandi's secondborn son, Kadesi, an ivory spoon, and a smooth white pebble to represent Karesu.

Dahodi, standing again with his cronies, looked up and smiled, and Nshesha felt the icy presentiment of things to come.

The litter that led the funeral procession was not much larger than the small leopard-skin-wrapped bundle that lay in its center, its edges tightly sewn together with rawhide strips. Karesu, the child who would live, was fastened to Tandi's back. Though the litter could well have been carried by one person, Mzimba, wishing to make it clear to the mother goddess, Maiegawana, that Kadesi was the son of a Chief, had ordered four bearers.

Nshesha walked at the head of the litter, balancing the outermost corner upon her palm.

Opposite her, much to Dahodi's disgust, since he thought he should be the one so honored, was one of Ntonu's apprentice gravediggers. Having traveled back to the kraal with Mzimba's messenger to assure the Chief that proper preparations were being made for the party's arrival, it was only fitting that he represent Ntonu at the front of the procession.

Behind Nshesha, carrying a third corner of the litter, walked the father of the infant, the Great Chief Mzimba. Aside from his one moment of sympathy shortly before the birth of his sons, Karesu and Kadesi, and despite his Royal Wife's pleadings, Mzimba had not softened in his determination to obey the law. The fourth bearer was the Royal Wife Tandi, whose weeping had barely decreased in the more than two days since her secondborn son had been torn from her bosom. Once the burial was over she would have to be reminded that tears dishonored her son's spirit, which lived as surely as that of Karesu.

Suddenly Nshesha felt a stirring against her arm, a movement so subtle that for an instant she did not remember what it was that caused a ripple through her body like the kiss of the lover for whom she longed. She looked down and her glance caressed the python curled around her free arm, the totem she had brought forth to be seen after she had sent Tharu's spirit to its freedom and sewn together the leopard-skin shroud. Smiling down at her totem, she admired the symmetry of the whorls on the python's skin, their colors so bright they dulled the copper of her beads. From a distance, he looked no different from the others who made their homes in this part of the land, and no one would venture close enough to notice the small black mark that distinguished him from them, the mark that lay in the center of the pattern closest to his right eye. Nor could they guess at its meaning if they did.

Only she and he knew that.

"Do not grow too swiftly, little one," she murmured, enjoying the sensation of strength against her flesh.

Though most of his kind were docile by nature, this python would be different; she would have to feed him well and often to hide his liveliness. She had best not become too fond of the pressure of his body for he would soon become too long and heavy to be carried entwined about her person.

"It is almost sunset, *Inyanga*," Ntonu's apprentice said, leaning across the litter.

This was his way of telling Nshesha that she was holding up the pace of the litter and of the retinue of mourners who followed behind, among them Tandi's people from whom the First High Royal Wife would not be parted.

For the rest, most of them were warriors selected from those who had been left to guard the canoes at the shores of the Tugela. Their job, all but the two who carried a portable stone altar upon which the black-eared goat and the leopard-skin bundle would be offered up to the mother goddess, was to protect the royal procession should they meet with trouble en route.

Nshesha did not slow down again until the party came within sight of Ntonu, who guarded the towering granite rock inside of which rested the spirit of Maiegawana. Tandi's cries had softened to an acceptably low keening. She had traveled all of the way with her eyes downcast, so that she might delay her first view of the hungry mother goddess, but she no longer protested. To have done so would simply have angered her husband. Besides, it was too late for argument. Her secondborn would never suckle at her breast.

"Welcome, Great Chief!"

Ntonu greeted Mzimba but he did not bow before he had raised himself slightly to look over the heads of the walkers to see for himself the old man who, straggling some distance away, led the red cow demanded by the gravedigger as payment for his services. Only then did he bend ceremoniously, hiding a face that was old and shriveled as untanned leather and eyes filled with the avarice of his profession.

"We wish to leave before the sun has gone to sleep," Mzimba said. "Have all of the preparations been completed?"

Tandi's keening grew louder and she reached across the litter to touch the bundle that had been her second son. Nshesha watched her movements.

"Let us proceed," Mzimba said.

The litter was placed on the ground near the hole that had been dug for the burial and the altar was brought forth. When Ntonu and his assistant had trussed the live goat and placed it in position, Nshesha stepped forward.

Taking a short, sharp knife from her belt, she slit the neck of the complaining goat and allowed its blood to flow into her medicine horn, while Mzimba took up the leopard-skin bundle and cradled it in his huge hands. Lifting it high into the air, he held it where it seemed to catch the flame of the sun lying low upon the horizon.

"Kadesi, my son," he said, "I give you to the mother goddess, Maiegawana."

Kneeling, he placed the leopard-skin bag into the hole that Ntonu had dug.

"The sky is cloudless." Nshesha moved to the edge of the grave. "That is a good omen. Tonight the heavens will be filled with stars. Kadesi will receive a warm welcome."

Slowly, drop by drop, she poured the contents of the medicine horn into the hole and onto the leopard-skin shroud. When she had finished, she lit the fire beneath the altar and Mzimba gave the order to depart.

Leaving the litter to be destroyed by Ntonu, the party began a slow retreat, walking backward along the path by which it had come. Once the first star could be seen in the heavens they would turn to face the river and truly commence their journey home.

"Kadesi." Tandi, her face gray with the labor of walking backward with an infant strapped to her back, pointed a finger at the dusk sky.

"I, too, can see your son," Nshesha said. "He lies in the arms of the evening star. Let us honor him."

One by one the party fell to the ground, until only Kadesi's parents and Nshesha stood upright, their eyes directed at the sky.

Quickly, now that the change had begun, the soft African dusk became night. Soon the heavens were filled with stars and even Tandi ceased her keening. No one moved and nothing disturbed the silence until the infant on Tandi's back began to whimper.

Mzimba looked at his wife sternly, his eyes commanding her to quiet the child.

"Karesu must be fed," she said,

"Do not neglect to also offer food to Kadesi," Nshesha said. "His spirit will be troubled if our tradition is not observed. Everything one son receives must be given the other equally, be it food or gifts or love."

Lifting the infant gently from his pouch, she handed him to his mother. Tandi, seated and resting against a rock, held him to her right breast and crooned to him as she looked down at his suckling. Then she turned her head to the left and, crooking her arm, sang to both of her sons of the love that lay in her heart.

"Kadesi my beloved son," she sang. "Though to others you may seem to be cold, I feel you warm and lively against my skin."

When Tandi had finished her song, Karesu was once more firmly strapped to her back and the party continued on its way home to the kraal. The boy is good-natured and eager to please, Nshesha thought. He will grow strong and plump.

Then she stroked Kadesi-the-Python. "You will drink of the dew of the flowers of the morning and *we will have it all*," she whispered in the moonlight.

Mzimba took great pride in the growth of his son, and in the increasing prosperity of his tribe since Nshesha had become his advisor. His only sorrow, echoed in the songs of the Elders and the drummers, was that he begot no more sons. Fearful that something might happen to Karesu, he checked on the boy's welfare many times each day; every night he prayed for the birth of a second son. He carved a phallus on a flat stone, created a bezel and a band out of plaited grasses, and wore the fertility ring on his right thumb. Regularly, Nshesha was instructed to prepare potions for Tandi and his other Royal Wives, for who knew which one of them the *idlozi* wished to favor. While Tandi did not show signs of objecting to sharing her husband's body, she objected strenuously to drinking the *Inyanga's* brew.

In all other things, Tandi remained outwardly quiet and respectful. The only time she stiffened was when Mzimba and the Elders spoke eagerly of the day when they could begin training Karesu as a warrior. "We of the Lovedu nation do not believe in making war," she said, arguing with the other wives, whose eagerness matched Mzimba's own.

Nshesha was astonished at how quickly Tandi had learned to adopt the language and dialect of her new People. Though Tandi rarely addressed her directly it was obvious to Nshesha that the woman had not forgiven her for having been the instrument of Kadesi's death. Often, when Tandi thought Nshesha was not within earshot, she sang to Karesu of her sadness and of her determination to keep him safe from Nshesha's evil eye. Nshesha, hearing her, was not happy, but she did not interfere.

Nurtured by his mother and doted upon by his father, Karesu grew. At birth he had shown himself to be the more docile of the twins and so he remained, good-natured and eager to please.

As the child grew, so did Nshesha's totem. There was no lack of live rodents to satisfy his predatory instincts and when that was not enough, Nshesha murmured to him in the low voice a mother would use to soothe her child. In her whisperings, she taught him the ways of her people and shared with him the secrets of the future. No ceremony was conducted without him at her side, and her power was soon such that no one could see her without trembling at the influence of the High *Inyanga* and her totem over the gods and over their Chief. There was no one seeing him look at her, who could doubt that he still felt the admiration of a man for a woman.

Nor was Nshesha unaware of his desire for her, or that hers for him had not diminished. Unfortunately, not all the mutual desire in the world could overcome the Law of the Tribe.

Not yet. Not until it was the anniversary of her grandfather's death and the time came for Nshesha to begin the fulfillment of his predictions.

Waiting, Nshesha grew restless. She had not left the immediate confines of her village since their journey to Maiegawana. In need of a change and of advice from her grandfather, she headed toward the river to address his spirit, which surely, like her other ancestors, resided in the body of a crocodile. When she reached the banks of the river, she settled down to sleep, for the best time to be heard was at the moment when the sun ate the moon.

But it was not the rising sun that awakened Nshesha. It was Dahodi.

"I know what you have done," he said, his body upon hers and his mouth next to her ear. "I watched you do it."

You watched as the tsetse fly watches its next victim, Nshesha thought. She struggled against his strength, drawing blood with her nails; he laughed at her struggles, puny against his brawny form.

She relaxed and stopped fighting him. "You win," she said softly. "I will take you as my husband and we will be High *Inyanga* together."

He sat up, taken off guard. His face wore an expression that was more puzzlement than victory. Nshesha resisted the impulse to chuckle and took his hand. "Let us first cleanse ourselves in the river," she said.

"The river is filled with crocodiles." His voice carried an edge of fear which pleased Nshesha.

"They carry the spirits of our ancestors and we are *Inyangas*," she said. "Surely you are not afraid of your own relatives? Surely you cannot think that *they* would eat your flesh?"

They had reached the edge of the river. Nshesha held her head high and boldly entered the water. Protect me, Grandfather, she thought.

Predictably, Dahodi could not resist the challenge. He entered the water, came level with Nshesha, and moved ahead. As she had known they would, the crocodiles quickly smelled blood. They were upon Dahodi before he knew what had happened. She backed out of the water, her movements gentle enough not to draw the attention of the crocodiles.

"Now I am the one watching," she called out from the shore. "It does not amuse me. I trust that you will forgive me if I leave."

When she walked away, she did not look back.

Returning to the village, she gave instructions that she was not to be disturbed until the following evening. Having done that, she retired to her hut and the companionship of her totem to await the anniversary of Vusama's death.

As the sun faded from her hut the following morning, Nshesha fed her python. Then she lifted his head and summoned a strong man to help her carry him outside and place him near Karesu.

Stretched out, her totem was now five feet in length and his girth was almost that of Mzimba's lean thigh; when he was coiled into a tight ball, as was his habit when he was resting, Nshesha could have rolled him outside herself. She generally preferred to do so, taking pleasure in leading him ceremoniously into the last rays of the descending sun. It was something she did frequently enough that her people were not surprised to see the two of them appear at the end of that day, though familiarity had not lessened their respect and they described wide circles about the pair as they went about their business.

Only the boy, Karesu, never displayed any fear of the python. Today was no different. Guarded by his mother, to whom Nshesha felt he was overly attached, he continued to play contentedly in the dirt.

"Come to us, Karesu," Nshesha said, her voice soft, her hand resting gently on her totem.

Karesu was but one sunrise short of his first birthday; digging holes was of great importance to him. Besides, thanks to his mother, he had never shown warmth toward Nshesha.

"Karesu!"

This time Nshesha's voice contained a command. The boy stopped his play and looked at the python, as if the snake and not the High *Inyanga* had called out to him.

The bones had long since told Nshesha what the child would do next. It was no chance event that she had ordered her totem carried outside today; no coincidence that Karesu chose this moment to clutch at his mother's arm and pull himself up to a standing position; no accident that he seemed to be aware of nothing other than the python.

Tandi laid aside the black calfskin skirt to which she had been attaching cowrie shells and copper beads. Placing her hands over her son's, she raised her head and looked at Nshesha. Karesu struggled to free himself, but Tandi held firm.

"Let him go," Nshesha said, her voice quiet but insistent.

Tandi hesitated. Her eyes were filled with the wariness of a deer whose thirst had driven her to a river where she knew crocodiles lurked below the surface.

"Let him go," Nshesha repeated.

Though Tandi obeyed, she made no attempt to hide her hatred as Karesu took a faltering step toward the snake, then a second and a third. When he lost his balance and fell, she lunged toward him and scooped him into her arms. The boy laughed, enjoying this new game.

Nshesha moved closer to the snake and stroked him tenderly, taking his energy into her body and her soul. She would need that and more for what was to come.

"Karesu has taken his first steps," she called out. "We must throw the bones and prepare him for the Sun-baby Ceremony. The little Sun-god Shati must be asked to bless him and make him strong and unafraid. This is our custom, as it is the custom of the Lovedu."

A messenger was sent to Mzimba, who was overseeing the training of a group of young *induna*s. When the Chief arrived, Karesu was made to repeat his performance for his father.

"The infant has become a child." Mzimba placed the boy on his broad shoulder. "Let us send runners far and wide to invite guests to the Sun-baby Ceremony and let each one be reminded that all gifts must be brought in twos."

"Two identical calves must be found for the feast," Nshesha warned him. "That may take some time."

"I will lead the search myself," the Chief said. "I promise you that no one will be able to tell them apart."

"They may look the same to you but their mother will be able to distinguish between them," Tandi said quietly.

Nshesha frowned. Motherhood was a stranger to her, so she could not understand the meaning behind Tandi's words. She would have to find out what Tandi had meant but she could not ask her openly, not in front of others who believed there was nothing their High *Inyanga* did not know.

Hiding her interest in his mother's words, Nshesha took the boy from his father's shoulder. Though he could not yet form words and he went to her without protest, as he did to everyone, his eyes were filled with speech. Nshesha knew he would have refused to come to her, had he only dared.

"It is time for my son to eat." Tandi held out her arms.

Nshesa released the boy to his mother, who held him a little too closely. The curve of her body around the child spoke of an instinctive fear that he needed protection. "Soon you will be able to speak to me, my Karesu," she said.

"Be sure he always talks of himself as 'the two of us,' " Nshesha said, "or his brother's spirit will be displeased."

The woman bowed her head in acknowledgment of Nshesha's warning and turned to go. Though outwardly Tandi's behavior was perfectly normal, Nshesha's intuition again told her that the woman should be watched and questioned. She thought about following her, but instead retired again to her own hut with only the companionship of her totem to divert her. There she prepared herself mentally for the crisis surrounding Karesu for which she had been waiting since Vusama's final throwing of the bones.

While Nshesha remained in seclusion, an air of festivity prevailed in the kraal. Guests arrived from many miles away; warriors rehearsed the stick dances of their ancestors; maidens primped and practiced the dances most likely to attract the warriors.

All of this Nshesha ignored.

By the time the night before the morning of the Sun-baby Ceremony arrived, she was ready. With her totem curled beside her on her mat, she watched the darkness slip away and waited to be called to Karesu's side. She had not even tried to sleep, yet she felt fully rested when the moment was finally upon her.

"Come quickly, *Inyanga*." Tandi stood in the opening to Nshesha's hut, her voice filled with terror. "Our son, Karesu, is most ill. His flesh burns my fingers and—"

"I will come as soon as you send two men to carry my totem," Nshesa interrupted, anxious to waste no time in meeting the challenge which lay before her. "I will need his help in this."

When Tandi had left, Nshesha bent over the sleeping python. Overwhelmed by a love greater than she had yet felt for any man, even Mzimba, the sight of whose limbs stirred the blood in her veins, she kissed the snake full on the mouth.

"Thanks to you, Kadesi-son-of-a-Chief, my deeds will be recounted by generations of storytellers," she whispered, granting him for the first time the spoken gift of his birthright. Then, using the dried bone of the shin of a goat, she scraped the juices of her totem's palate into her medicine horn and waited for the men to come for him.

In full regalia, balancing the medicine horn containing the spittle of the python who was being carried close behind her, Nshesha approached the Great Hut of the Chief. There, the Elders were gathering to plead with the gods for the life of their Chief's only son. As she entered the hut, she heard the boy's shallow breathing, and she could see the tall figure of her Chief, bent low over Karesu's restless body.

"Can you heal my son?" Mzimba drew himself erect and turned to face his High *Inyanga*.

"I can, O Great Chief." Nshesha sounded sure and calm, though her heart was beating with the wings of a caged hawk.

As if for reassurance, she glanced down at the python who lay coiled at her feet; he was living proof that she had already done what no one had done before.

Nshesha knelt at the dying boy's side. She put her hand on his forehead. It was like a rock that had been lying all day in the summer sun. His color and the heat of his flesh told her that death was fast approaching.

"What ails our son?" Tandi's voice rose like a reed flute. "It is as if his blood boils within him."

Nshesha had her answer ready. "His brother is calling him. I must persuade Karesu that it is not yet time to join Kadesi."

"Should you not throw the bones and consult the *idlozi*?" Mzimba asked.

"There is no time." Nshesha felt the eyes of the Chief boring into her back. "The moon will soon be disappearing into the arms of the sun. Your son must be cured before the heat of the day or it will be too late."

"What of the Sun-baby Ceremony?"

"Let the Elders cease their chanting so your guests will remain unaware of what is happening. The Sun-baby Ceremony will take place as promised, so there is no need to alarm them."

"Will the *idlozi* and our ancestors not be angered if the Elders do not honor them with prayers?"

"They will be angry if you do not leave the hut. I can do nothing while you are here. And have Tandi cease her weeping. It distracts me from what must be done."

Nshesha turned to make certain that Mzimba and Tandi had obeyed her instructions. The boy had contracted a disease for which death was the only cure unless she could lower the temperature of his blood beyond normal human endurance. For what she had to do to achieve that, there could be no witnesses.

Having made certain that she was alone, Nshesha wedged her medicine horn tightly in her belt and took hold of the boy's jaw to force it open. When she had done so, she collected several drops of his saliva on her palm and mixed it with the tiniest drop of the excretions she had taken from her python. Pushing aside the fear of failure, for which she had no time, she opened the python's mouth. With the tip of one finger, she rubbed some of the mixture into the snake's palate. Then she repeated the process with the boy, holding him down firmly in case he began to convulse.

The first step over, Nshesha leaned against the mud wall of the hut and waited for Karesu's temperature to drop in proportion to the rising heat within the body of the python, which thrashed dangerously against the earthen floor of the hut.

"Be careful, my little one," Nshesha cooed, leaning forward to place a comforting hand on his head. His eyes had become milky; as long as nothing disturbed the python's equilibrium, in less than fifteen minutes the process for which she was waiting would have begun and ended. "You must shed your skin, not your life."

Without warning, there was a shuffling at the door. Nshesha jumped and twisted around, pulling her hand away from the snake as if she had been caught stealing from the altar of the gods. Mzimba and Tandi had returned unbidden. Nshesha sighed and gathered her strength, reminding herself that they were not *Inyanga*s. They could not see the spirits of the two boys trading forms, but only the body of their son, arching his back before he sank to his kaross, where he lay still and stiff as death.

"I told you, I must be left alone with Karesu," Nshesha said, shifting to block their view of the python.

"You also gave your word that our son would live." Mzimba's voice cut like the wind in the dead of winter. "Now he lies there like one whose spirit has already joined our ancestors."

"If *you* will not leave, *I* must," Nshesha said. "The spirits will not listen while you are here."

"If you allow my son to die . . ." Mzimba backed out of the hut. What he would do to his High *Inyanga* if she failed him was written on his face and Nshesha shuddered and bowed her head to show respect. In truth she did not fear his wrath; it was as just as his punishments were predictable.

"Come, wife."

Nshesha waited for Tandi to obey her husband. Driven by something more powerful than the command of her Chief, the First Royal Wife did not immediately follow him outside. Instead, she turned to face the coming dawn. Standing framed in the doorway and speaking softly so as not to disturb Karesu, she begged her spirit to leave her body and stand sentinel over her firstborn son.

When both of Karesu's parents had gone, Nshesha started a small fire near the doorway of the hut. Once the flames burned steadily, she reached out and felt the boy's flesh and the snake's.

Sure now that the boy was growing colder and that the python was becoming warm to the touch, she knelt beside Karesu. Wedging her medicine horn between her thighs, she took her knife from its beaded sheath and, using its point, cut lightly into the fleshiest part of the boy's ankle so that she might fill the tip of her horn with his blood. Having wedged the horn firmly back in place between her knees, she applied pressure to stem the bleeding, and only when the wound was dry did she pick up her knife once more. Wielding it with a surgeon's precision, she took a thin stripping of the boy's flesh and of the python's skin and added those to the contents of the horn. Finally, she lifted the child's small hand. Carefully, this time using the flat edge of her knife, she scraped the tips of three of his tiny fingernails and let the fine, white powder float down into the medicine horn. That done, she replaced his arm gently at his side, stirred the mixture, and dribbled it onto the fire.

During all of this, Karesu gave no sign of life, but Nshesha had felt the faint beating of his heart in his wrist. She could do no more than rest and wait. Outside, the morning sun rose higher in the heavens and began to fill the hut; inside, the fire hissed and crackled and burned low. Nshesha was soothed into a half-sleep filled with creatures neither snake nor human but resembling both. Yet it was not the dreams which awakened her, it was the sensation that she was being observed.

She was.

The child, either because he had sensed that it was time for her to awaken or because he was no longer amused by lying around, had turned to look at her. He was smiling at her from his Royal leopard-skin kaross and appeared relaxed and fully recovered.

Smiling back at him, Nshesha moved toward the kaross. She searched his eye for the blemish the gods had placed there at birth to distinguish him from his brother, but it was not only that which convinced her that he was Kadesi. The boy's eyes were so filled with wisdom far beyond his years that she knew at once she had succeeded. She had brought forth Mzimba's secondborn son from his temporary home within the body of her totem, and the python, which lay curled into a ball and content at the boy's side, now sheltered his brother, Karesu.

"You shall never again be called Kadesi," Nshesha said to the boy. "They will know you as Karesu. If you wish someday to be the Chief of a tribe restored to greatness, you will respond to your brother's name as if it were yours."

The boy's hand reached out to stroke the head of his brother, Karesu-the-python. The python, having taken on Karesu's docile nature, lay unmoving. Nshesha watched for a moment in wonder. Then, having for the time being nothing more to say to her student, she stood and walked to the entrance of the hut.

Mzimba and Tandi, seeing her there, approached at once.

"Your son is well and may be prepared for the ceremony. When we are gathered I will throw the bones and give thanks," Nshesha said, pleased that she was able to speak so calmly to them.

Tenderly, the parents bent over their child and embraced him. He responded as any child would, hugging first one parent and then the other, but showing no sign of fatigue from his ordeal.

"You shall be rewarded." Mzimba's voice and face and body were a song of gratitude for the return of his son from the arms of death, but Tandi remained silent, her eyes cold and shadowed with unasked questions.

"Are *you* not pleased, mother of Karesu?"

Tandi bowed. "I am most grateful for your skills, O High *Inyanga*."

Nshesha could feel the sounds of trouble quavering between each of the requisite words. Though she wanted to return to her hut where she could rest and examine her triumph in private, she chose to stay where she was.

"I must rejoin our guests," Mzimba said, addressing his wife. "Do you wish your servants to be sent to you?"

"It is not necessary." Tandi removed two clay pots from the corner of the hut where they had been stored in readiness for this moment. "The preparations are simple and will not take long. Let my servants enjoy the festivities with the others."

When Mzimba had left the hut, Tandi stirred the contents of both pots. Using her fingers, she began to daub the mixtures onto her son's sturdy body, painting it with broad black and white stripes of soot and clay.

At first the child seemed quite himself, docile as ever and smiling at his mother to show that he was enjoying the attention. It was not until she took out a light, round calfskin mask and placed it over his face that he began to fuss, wailing and pulling at the grass fringes that surrounded the ceremonial mask.

"Perhaps Karesu is not fully recovered after all," Tandi said. "It is not like him to complain."

"The mask is stiff; it scratches his skin," Nshesha said.

Tandi shook her head. "He would not have complained before his illness."

Nshesha took the boy's hands firmly in her own and removed them from the mask. "You must wear this, Karesu," she said. "It is the face of the Sun-god Shati. While you wear it, you will be strong as he is." She picked up a second mask, different from the boy's, and held it up to her own face. "See. I have a mask, too."

The child stiffened. His eyes glittered angrily through the slits in the mask, but he did not shrink away from her and he kept his hands where she had placed them. "He is ready now," she said, turning away from him toward his mother and deliberately setting her body in an attitude of challenge that dared Tandi to comment further on the boy's behavior.

Tandi held her silence. She picked up her child, and carried him outdoors into the gathering of people anxiously awaiting his appearance. No amount of discretion had been able to keep the news of his illness from the guests. When he appeared in their midst, ready for the ceremony, they joined the warriors in a frenetic dance of thanksgiving for his recovery, toasting him with beer from each of the two containers with which every one of them had been provided.

Before long, Nshesha clapped her hands for attention. "We must give thanks to the *idlozi* for Karesu's recovery," she said. "Bring me my totem and I shall throw the bones and call upon the Sun-god Shati to bless the son of our Chief with health and wisdom."

While Nshesha held up her hand for silence, two men carried the python into the center of a circle which had been cleared for the ceremony. When they had set him carefully upon the ground, Nshesha took up her position at his side. Stroking him gently, she bent her head to his as if to listen to his advice.

Those closest to her shuffled uneasily.

"If you cannot tie your feet to the earth my totem may grow restive," she said brusquely to the worst offender. "If that happens, I shall give you to him as a playmate, and it will not only be your feet that are stilled."

A few people in the crowd giggled and the man, one of Tandi's bearers, glanced over at his mistress and narrowed his eyes with anger at having been shamed in public. He dug his heels into the ground and stood unmoving as Maiegawana herself.

Nshesha followed his glance and Tandi, her face filled with hatred, tightened her grip on the boy in her arms.

"Let the child, Karesu, be made to join me," Nshesha said, addressing the Royal Wife directly.

Tandi stepped forward from her place next to Mzimba but did not release her son.

"Put him down," Nshesha ordered.

Still Tandi hesitated.

Even the most drunken of the guests fell silent. The drummers held their hands at their sides and the warriors and maidens ceased their dancing. Nothing moved except Nshesha's fingers as they stretched out toward the boy.

Seeing that she was left with no choice, Tandi lowered her son to the ground. Though she stood him on his feet, she had no sooner let go than he bent his knees and sat down. Unconcerned at being the center of attention, he reached for a handful of earth, examined it closely, and began to eat it.

At the back of the crowd, a woman laughed. Nshesha raised her head and stared in the direction of the sound. She was met by silence.

"Stand, Karesu," she commanded. "Stand and walk to me."

Tandi moved forward as if to help her son onto his feet. Nshesha waved her imperiously away. The boy looked around for something upon which he could pull himself upright and with an expression of triumph on his face, slid toward a small bush. Using it as a lever he stood, balanced himself, and took a step forward and another and another.

The crowd held its breath, but with each step the child's balance grew firmer until, sure of himself, he reached Nshesha's side.

The watchers raised their fists and cheered. The child stood for a moment, accepting their adulation; then he began to wobble. His knees buckled. To the tune of friendly laughter, he dropped to the ground next to Nshesha, who, though no one else must know it, was now flanked by both of the twins to whom Tandi had given birth. With one hand she fondled Karesu-the-snake and with the other hand she stroked the head of Kadesi-the-secondborn, who had once been a snake and must from this time onward answer to the name Karesu.

"Well done," Nshesha crooned. She smiled down at the boy. He squirmed with pleasure at hearing again the familiar tone with which she had addressed him so often during the past year.

Removing her right hand from the python, Nshesha held it up for silence. She kept it there until the only sounds that could be heard were the rustling of lizards in the long grasses and the coughing of wild dogs in the distance.

"Tell us of my son Karesu, O High *Inyanga*," Mzimba said into the silence. "Scatter the *amadolo* and tell us how to give thanks to the *idlozi* and honor the Sun-god Shati."

Bowing her head toward her Chief, Nshesha put on the mask she had shown the boy, the same one her grandfather had worn during ceremonial occasions. It sat loosely on her face, but it was nonetheless uncomfortable and limited her peripheral vision. She did not like wearing it any more than the boy liked wearing his, but she had no choice. Her people believed that it helped their High *Inyanga* to communicate with the dead and, above all, she needed their belief to be intact.

Adjusting the mask as best she could for maximum vision, she removed the pouch containing the bones from her belt. She circled the pouch three times above her head, and scattered its contents upon the earth. The boy next to her fidgeted impatiently but the python did not stir.

"The son, Karesu, will grow up to be as brave and strong as the father, Mzimba, Chief of the Thotharu, Killer of Lions and Protector of his People," Nshesha intoned, telling Mzimba what he wanted to hear. She had not yet examined the pattern of the bones, but the grand design would be as always, her totem. As for the rest, it did not matter.

Whatever she saw, she would have said the same thing. "He will be a great leader, with the cunning and the wisdom of his father, the great Chief Mzimba."

Again, the crowd cheered. Nshesha took the opportunity to examine the bones. Her glance was casual, in the manner of a wife hearing her lover's steps behind her and knowing what she would see if she turned around.

As always, Mzimba had been watching her closely. "Is the Sun-god Shati not sufficiently honored by our feast of the two cows?" he asked.

Automatically, Nshesha nodded and said the words that were expected of her. "The Sun-god is greatly honored. Your son, Kadesi-the-Star, too, is pleased. He takes pleasure in the same-ness of the cows for the feast and he smiles because we have provided every one of our guests with two bowls of food, each filled with an identical quantity of food."

The boy next to Nshesha, he who still thought of himself as Kadesi, raised his head at the mention of his given name. Nshesha's glance flew quickly across the faces of the crowd to see if anyone had noticed, but their expressions remained as they had been. She relaxed. After all, the child was expected to be attached to the spirit of his twin, so why should it be thought strange for him to respond to his brother's name.

Then she scanned the face of the First Royal Wife. What she saw washed rivers of fear up her spine and into her brain, where they splashed against the hollows like echoes bouncing around the caverns of the Dragon Mountains.

Closing her eyes, Nshesha allowed the echoes to carry her back to the day of Karesu's first walking: Mzimba, tall and handsome in the sunlight, his heir balanced easily on his broad shoulders; Tandi, standing silently in their shadow, and though she could not see herself, she could hear her own voice as it issued instructions for the Sun-baby Ceremony. *"Two identical calves must be found for the feast."*

"I will lead the search myself," Mzimba said again, continuing the pattern as if he had seen into her reprisal of the memory. *"I promise you that no one will be able to tell them apart."*

Tandi, too, opened her mouth to speak. Knowing what was to come, Nshesha tried not to listen, but the echoes were insistent. Though Tandi spoke as quietly now as she had done then, the words rose above the roaring in Nshesha's ears: *"They may look the same to you, but their mother will be able to distinguish between them."*

The first time around, Tandi's words had sounded in Nshesha's head like the warning drums of battle, but she had ignored them. She could no longer afford to do so.

Opening her eyes, she stared at Tandi and tried to pierce the barrier of her mind. Surely the woman's short time with her secondborn son had been too filled with blinding sorrow for her to have noticed the tiny blemish in his eye, the stain placed there by the gods to help guide Nshesha—

"How do the *idlozi* wish to be thanked for restoring life to our son?" Mzimba asked.

Nshesha cursed herself for being foolish enough to open her eyes, for while they were closed Mzimba would not have disturbed her. Now that she was aware of his gaze upon her, her concentration was broken, and she could no longer hope to penetrate Tandi's thoughts.

How much simpler it would all be if she could tell Mzimba that she had been directed by the gods to save his secondborn son from the arms of Maiegawana by hiding his infant soul in the body of her totem.

That she had loved him and begun to teach him to use his mind and to know the ways of his people.

As certainly as the man before her had once, long ago, shown her she was the wife of his heart, so she was the true mother of this secondborn son, who would soon begin to learn the lessons of the Son-of-a-Chief from his father. She could not tell him, though, not only because he would know that she had disobeyed Tribal Law, but because he would know that her power over the child was absolute.

Besides, power over the boy was not enough to achieve her ends.

If she was to choreograph the renewed greatness of her nation and place her own name forever on the lips of the storytellers, she must find a way to become his mother and Mzimba's wife in the eyes of her people. Only then could she fulfill the prediction of the bones and return to her tribe the power and wealth they had known in the warrior days of their supremacy.

Only then would the son of the sister of the Rain Queen share the way to eternal life, known only to the descendants of She-Who-Must-Be-Obeyed.

It was all possible.

The *idlozi* had told her so through the mouths of the *amadolo*. But it could all come to pass only if the secret of what she had done, of what was still to be done, remained hers alone.

She looked at Tandi and felt the wound in the woman's eyes, so filled with hatred that there was no room for this celebration of her son's return from the arms of death, no sign of happiness in her face. An ache came over Nshesha, the loneliness of knowing that if she had obeyed her heart they could have had a true and abiding friendship.

"Will you speak, *Inyanga?*"

Mzimba's voice was darkening with impatience; he was unused to being kept waiting, even by so powerful a person as his High Witchdoctor.

Knowing what it was that she must do, Nshesha gathered the bones. "Let us examine the further wishes of the *idlozi*," she said, scattering the bones once more on the ground before her and bending low over them in the way that was expected of her.

"Aaiee!"

The cry that came from Nshesha's throat sent wild dogs and children scurrying. Even Mzimba trembled as she began to moan, tearing at her hair and rolling her eyes around as one might who had witnessed the disemboweling of her own father.

"What is it you see?" Mzimba asked, when she stopped to take a breath. "Our hearts are warm now that Karesu is well. What is it that will warm the hearts of the *idlozi*?"

Nshesha looked up at the clouds. As always at this time, they chased each other playfully across the heavens.

Praying to the gods to come to her aid, she held out her hand palm-upward. Sure enough, to her delight, she felt a drop of rain dampen her skin.

"The *idlozi* called Karesu to them because his brother, Kadesi-the-Star, pleaded for a companion," she said, raising her voice to be sure it would carry to the outermost fringes of the crowd. "Karesu has been returned to us because you, who are a great and powerful Chief, desired it. Now Kadesi-the-Star cries with loneliness, and his tears distress the *idlozi*. Put out your hands and you will feel his tears."

Mzimba reached out into the drizzle. He looked at the drops of water in his palm and, like a small child, dipped into them with his tongue. Nshesha could almost taste the salt from the sweat on his skin.

"My son, Kadesi, weeps," he said. "Which one among us is willing to go keep him company and tell him stories through the long days and nights?"

The Chief's words were no sooner spoken than a warrior stepped forward. Somewhere in the crowd a woman . . . wife, sweetheart, sister, mother . . . screamed. Ignoring her cry, or perhaps not even hearing it in his anxiety to prove his manhood and join his ancestors in triumph, the warrior bowed to his Chief. Turning his eyes to the heavens, he fell on his spear. It pierced him in the stomach and emerged at the other side as he dropped to the earth.

"There," Mzimba said. "It is done."

"If only that were so, O Chief." Standing up, as if with great effort, Nshesha began again to tear at her hair and to roll her eyes. All the while, she emitted sounds that spoke from her throat of a sorrow and tragedy too great to be framed in words.

"The *idlozi* are not yet satisfied. There is someone in our midst who will not allow your son, Kadesi, to rest. That person must die or be sent far enough away that your sons will not hear sounds of mourning, for if Kadesi remains unhappy, Karesu will become unhappy too. He will grow thin and miserable and be without the strength for his warrior training."

"Shall we gather your helpers for a smelling-out or have the *idlozi* named a name?"

Nshesha removed the tail of the goat from her belt. "They were too saddened by your son's tears to say more," she answered. "I must perform the smelling-out myself." Closing her eyes, she began to dance around the edge of the crowd. The drums picked up the beat of her soles and, instinctively, those closest to her took a step backward. "It is a woman they seek," Nshesha moaned as, circling, dancing, her shoulders hunched and her eyes shut, she continued her charade. "A woman."

The men in the crowd relaxed and held on to their women, who slumped into their arms. Some, at the back, tried to sneak away. They were stopped by others who held fast to their arms. At last, silent now, Nshesha began to move among the people, snaking her way through them and out again until, finally, it seemed that no woman dared breathe in case attention be drawn to her.

"Aaiee!" Nshesha broke her silence and stood still. She opened her eyes and a gasp of horror went up from the crowd. The drums ceased their beating and there followed a silence so ominous and brooding that it was as if the Mother of all Lightning Birds, Negwenya, was hovering overhead. The gathering could do no more than stand frozen and even Mzimba, who stood within easy range of Nshesha's vision, covered his eyes as he would have done in the presence of *Luzwi-Muundi,* the as yet unborn savior of the Bantu People.

Knowing that the moment had come, Nshesha lifted her goat's tail high into the air. Then she flicked its tip across the burning cheek of the woman who threatened to keep her from fulfilling her destiny.

"How dare you!" Reflex action had sent Tandi's hand to her

cheek. She held it there for a moment, then drew herself to her full height. "You may be High *Inyanga* of this village," she said, glaring at Nshesha and apparently unafraid, "but I am a Princess of the Lovedu Nation. I will not be treated in this manner."

For the first time since her arrival in their midst, Nshesha saw in Tandi the full bearing and manner of a member of a Royal household. Mzimba stared at his First Wife, then at Nshesha, who could feel his fury. To her relief it was directed at the *idlozi*.

Nshesha felt suddenly very tired. "I am merely the messenger of the *idlozi*," she said quietly.

"And I am the servant of my husband, the Chief," Tandi said, calm now. "Do you wish me to leave, O Chief?"

"The *idlozi* have spoken," Mzimba answered.

"*She* has spoken. The one you call your High *Inyanga*."

"The *idlozi* speak through her mouth," Mzimba said. "It is the way of our people."

Tandi inclined her head. "I will gather my bearers and my handmaidens for the long journey," she said. Looking first at the totem, then into Nshesha's eyes, she raised her voice and sent it out across the land toward Dragon Mountain. "I know you as I know myself. I will not beg to stay, but hear me well. I will protect my sons from you, even unto my death."

Your death is closer than you think. It will come when I have learned your secret. As for your sons, they are yours no longer, Nshesha thought. They are mine now, as Mzimba is mine.

She waited in vain for a sense of triumph to flow through her being, but she felt nothing. Only sadness for the woman who could have been her friend.

The Thalatta Thesis

Charles L. Harness

It started with the selection of a subject for his Ph.D. thesis. The six best topics (and money) had already been snapped up: Search for Lunar Oil (Texas Petroleum Institute), Spectral Lines of Extra-Solar Planets (NASA), Faster-than-Light Velocities (Naval Research Institute), C-14 in Pre-Cambrian DNA (Gesellschaft fuer Lebensforschung), Visitors from Kuiper and Oort (Nova Propulsion Society), and Durable Venusian Probe (Dorfman Enterprises).

Nicholas Renfield had got into the program late, and only the rather minimal grant offered by the Terraformers Administration was left, topic open. He took it. His thesis advisor, old Max Stoner, pretty much made the selection of topic for him: Find a microbe capable of flourishing at 460 degrees Centigrade, in an atmosphere 96.5 percent carbon dioxide, at a pressure of ninety atmospheres, and last, but perhaps the most important of all, capable of replacing that carbon dioxide with oxygen.

This was for use on the planet Venus, of course. Nick laughed mournfully and took the grant.

With great pride, a colleague, Sam Baxter, showed Nick his own thesis product, half-finished and already attracting attention outside the university: the Dorfman Probe. "Previous probes lasted only a couple of hours—couldn't take the heat or the CO_2 pressure. Mine uses special insulation, special heat-resistant alloys. Working life, we estimate at six months. At least. Dr. Dorfman has personally approved my design."

Nick duly admired the growing assembly. He read the engraving on the waist-high cover shell, which sat next to the internals: BAXTER.

The candidate explained, "Dr. Dorfman suggested it. Great guy." He added casually, "He's offered me a job on graduation—in six figures. I'm thinking about it. How many offers you got?"

"None yet."

"Oh. Sorry I asked. But after all, Nick, who gives a damn whether bugs grow on Venus?"

Nick shrugged.

"And you're saddled with old Stoner. God take pity on you, Nick."

Nick was the last of the Renfields. He had buried his father, paid off the debts of the estate, and found himself broke. He had finally squeezed through college with a B.S. in biology and had looked for a teaching job. A brief exposure to the job market convinced him that he would need a Ph.D.

"Just two years," he explained to Muriel. She had looked at him in silence for a full sixty seconds. Nick was a good-looking kid, tall, a bit gangly. But there was something ragged and unformed about him, something he had futilely tried to improve.

He had read the sad announcement in her eyes: "Nick, you are a sure loser. I will not wait for you." In silence she returned the ring. He pawned it for bus fare to the university.

Max Stoner used to come into the lab at night when Nick was working late. Whether to help or to scold, the young candidate could never decide. Both, probably.

Nick could always tell when the old man was near. The savant's feet hurt, and he wore oversized padded moccasins that slapped the concrete floor with ambiguous authority as he shuffled about the lab.

Stoner was a semiretired substitute lecturer in biology (emergencies only). Otherwise his sole academic responsibility was Nicholas Renfield. The candidate turned now and watched the approach of his designated mentor.

Professor Stoner stopped and began patting his pockets absently. Nick studied the approximately shaven face, which appeared to him to resemble a bowl of bristly potatoes. "They're on your nose."

The visitor grunted and pushed the lost spectacles farther up on his nose. Meanwhile he examined Nick's bench setup. "Let's *not* be *stupid*, Renfield. Your bug must *make* oxygen, not *consume* it." The old man emphasized every other word, whether or not the emphasis made sense. Heavy bags under his eyes jiggled as he spoke.

"I know that," Nick said. "This particular bug doesn't."

"Okay, wrong bug. Try another one. Try several at once. A dozen, fifty, a hundred. You're a big boy, you can do it."

Another time Stoner commented on an equation Nick had written on the blackboard.

$$6CO_2 + 6H_2O \rightarrow C_6(H_2O)_6 + 6O_2$$

"Sure, that's the standard chlorophyll synthesis, for glucose, with by-product oxygen. Forget it. Your oxygen producer won't be a plant with water coming up from the roots. And it certainly won't be like photoplankton, floating in the ocean. The only water where that bug is going will be traces of water vapor in the atmosphere. Oh, maybe a teensy bit in the crust." He gave Nick a very serious look. "It may be you'll have to design your own little microbe, a hardy little beast, one that needs very little water. And you can be sure it won't make anything as juicy as glucose or any other carbohydrate."

Another time the relentless savant declared: "Let's back up. Everything you do, every new microbe you try, keep in mind the fundamentals." He would tick them off on flabby fingers. "One, your microlife has to function at a temperature of at least 460 Centigrade. Why? Because, my forgetful young aspirant, that's the surface temperature of yon Witch World. Two, your microlife has got to consume carbon dioxide, absolutely gobs of it, and simultaneously produce oxygen." He leered at the candidate. "But, if the poor thirsty little thing needs water, it's got to find its own. Somewhere. Air, desert crust, anywhere, nowhere." He shook his head in mock sadness. "You want to change your thesis, Nicholas?"

"Didn't you leave out a couple of requirements?" Nick observed mildly.

"Mayhap I did. Such as?"

"It ought to lower the pressure enough for normal breathing, no space suit needed."

"Well, that would be very fine."

"And be cool and wet enough to produce occasional snow?"

"Mr. Renfield, are you being impertinent?"

"I don't think so. I read your paper 'Terraforming Our Sister Planet.' You said if Venus could lick the greenhouse effect, its cloud cover would reflect enough incoming solar radiation to make it even cooler than the Earth."

"If . . . if . . . if. Now look, Nick, when I wrote that I was young and arrogant. And impertinent. Get back to work."

Nick watched the old scientist stomp away, moccasins flapping, and was thoughtful. Of course, in a thesis it was supposed not to matter whether the project succeeded or failed, just how you did the work. Out of the seven candidates that year, six could reasonably expect success. One could reasonably expect failure. Himself. It wasn't supposed to matter? The hell it didn't. (Already, "Hey, Nick, are the bugs biting?" And behind his back, the snickers.)

Still, the deeper he got into it, the more fascinating it became. A bug . . . one little microbe. Could a speck of life you needed a microscope to see convert a poisonous atmosphere into breathable air? Terraform an entire planet? No. It was asking too much of any existing life-form. No bug on the planet Earth could long endure a temperature of 460 plus—which was the temperature on the Venusian surface on an average day. That was even hotter than the interior of most sterilization autoclaves.

"So make your own bug," Stoner had suggested. Nay, commanded.

So he had acquired and tested certain interesting possibilities: bacteria taken from boiling springs and geysers in Yellowstone

National Park, hardy at 110 degrees Centigrade. But dead at 200. Keep looking. Thermophilic bacteria taken from sulfur vents deep in the ocean, flourishing at 250 degrees Centigrade and 265 atmospheres—three times the atmospheric pressure on Venus, which in turn was ninety times the atmospheric pressure on Earth at sea level.

Stoner said, "You're on the right track. Let's see how far we can push the heat envelope. Try accelerated sequential evolution."

He cultured colony after colony of the deep-sea bacteria, raising incubation temperature ten degrees in each new run. This killed off nearly all the population, but there were always a few survivors, available for the next temperature jump.

He got thermophiles up to 475 degrees. As seen under the optical microscope, the heat-bred microbe was not merely Gram-negative, with a double cell wall: the little cell was Gram-double-negative, with a quadruple wall.

Max Stoner came by, shrugged, mumbled, "Okay, next step. If your little fella is going to replace carbon dioxide with oxygen . . . ?"

"Photosynthesis in a *dry* world? I thought you said it was impossible."

"You believe everything you hear?" He searched for his glasses, found them. "I do believe you'll need a heat-hardy photosynthetic microbe. Let's see if we can get an inheritable chloroplast into your current microcell. A tricky bit of genetic engineering."

Nick researched the literature and decided on chlorophyll genes from cells of the barrel cactus, one of the hardiest known desert flora. It was reported to be able to extract traces of moisture from the driest desert floors. Stoner had contacts at the University of Arizona, and viable samples were duly forthcoming.

The rest was routine. First, he extracted the plasmid circlet from the waiting thermophile cell. The plasmid contained DNA separate from the thermophile cell's chromosomal DNA and, when coaxed with the proper enzymes, readily accepted chloroplast DNA taken from a cell of the cactus. This done, he placed the altered plasmid back into the thermophile cell with a micropipette. All standard technique. Several replications proved the new chimera was breeding true.

He examined the now much-modified cell under the microscope. It appeared to be a typical plant cell, with very thick cell walls, plus all the organelles of the original deep-sea thermophile, and in addition a great many chloroplasts. There was a vague resemblance in appearance and behavior to the blue-green photobacteria. The chloroplasts in the new cell took their energy from the red and blue wavelengths of visible sunlight. There should be plenty of both on Venus. Once the photons struck the chlorophyll, everything was supposed to proceed with robotic efficiency. The cell was supposed to find a water molecule—pull it out of the air, maybe. An enzyme was then supposed to split the water molecule into two protons and an oxygen atom, and the protons were then supposed to latch on to the carbon-dioxide molecules.

Theoretically.

"Brand-new species," Stoner said. "You need a name for it. What'll you call it?"

"Wait until we're sure it works. Then I'll think of something."

To test the new cell he put some of the culture in a chamber filled with carbon dioxide heated to 460 degrees Centigrade. Nothing.

Max Stoner came by. "You added a little water?"

"No. It's supposed to draw it out of the air. Or maybe the crust."

"Well, add some crust. Dirt. Here." He scooped a handful of dirt from a nearby pot of African violets and tossed it into the chamber. "Seal up, try again."

The next day the old man was back. "Get a little O_2?"

"Some."

"And used up a little CO_2?"

"Yeah, a little."

"Well then, why so gloomy?"

Nick pointed to the equation on the blackboard.

$$2CO_2 + H_2O \rightarrow HO-C(:O)-C(:O)-OH + 1/2\ O_2$$

Stoner frowned. "Hmm. Oxalic acid—one of our deadliest poisons."

"Yep." After a moment Nick added morosely, "It's all over, isn't it?"

"Now you're being stupid again. You didn't use ninety atmospheres pressure?"

"No, of course not, just ambient. We don't have the apparatus. We need field conditions, Doc. . . . "

"Oxalic. Hm. Well, can't be helped. When is your midterm review with the dean?"

"Tomorrow. Any advice?"

"Just be polite."

Dr. Vass, dean of the Graduate School, was skilled in the uses of autocratic ceremony. He kept Nick waiting two hours, and after calling him into his office he ignored him and continued dictating to his secretary for several minutes. After dismissing her, he adjusted his monocle and looked up at Nick.

Vass knew—and Nick knew—that this man held the power of life or death over Nick's thesis, and consequently over Nick's future in academia. While the dean didn't exactly *flaunt* his power, neither did he make any effort to conceal it. He liked the feel of it and it gave him a peculiar satisfaction when others felt it.

He began in the middle. "You've created a heat-resistant bug that makes a poison. You call that progress?" He stared across his desk at Nick.

This was too sudden. Nick stared back at the monocle for a moment, then recovered his voice. He stammered, "I think it might work under field conditions, sir."

"Field conditions . . . hm. Venus? But we'll never know, will we?" He examined papers on his desk. "Terraformers Administration is apparently content to let the work continue forever, but the regents are not. The Graduate School is not a charitable institution, Mr. Renfield. They expect me to maintain a certain discipline, a certain reputation. Your project is hopeless. Still,

I'm inclined to give you the benefit of the doubt." His face contorted into something resembling a smile. "I'll give you another week."

The next day Nick heard a very unsettling rumor. It was hard to believe. He caught Stoner in the hall, headed away.

"Max?"

The old man stopped but didn't turn around. His answer was flat, noncommittal. "Yeah?"

"The *Morningstar* heads out for Venus next week."

Again the monotone. "Yeah."

"Dammit, Max, turn around and look at me."

The scientist took a deep breath and faced the candidate. "Shoot." There was a harsh edge on the monosyllable.

Nick continued evenly. "I hear by the grapevine that Terraformers Administration wants to put an observer on board. They asked for you, you turned it down." He glared at the older man. "Then they asked about *me,* and you turned that down too. The story I get, Terraformers would give me three days on the planet, three days to test my microbe. Full field conditions. I could get an extension from Vass. I could finish my thesis. You turned it down. What the hell were you thinking of?" He could hardly speak.

The old man stifled a groan. "It would be—very dangerous."

"Max, they have special space suits. Full protection against heat and pressure. For God's sake! There's no—"

"Nick, shut up and listen. I'll spell it out. Those suits offer no protection against the real danger—which is Derek Dorfman."

"*That* Dorfman?"

"Him. It goes way back. He and I were both under consideration for science director here at the university. He manufactured certain evidence—exhibits, photos—seeming to show I had had affairs with various young females in the student body . . . including the daughter of the President of the World Congress. All very cleverly done. All false. I was passed over, of course. A wonder I wasn't fired. He got the job. But I had friends. We finally dug up the people who had faked his exhibits. He left, joined the science staff of one of the emerging Arabian states. And now this new venture. The Dorfman terraforming process is his big chance. His backers are financing this Venus junket for the Congressional Colonization Committee. I truly believe that he would stop at nothing"—here he took the young man by the shoulders and looked into his eyes—"*absolutely nothing*—to push his project through Congress."

The youth stared at the old man in amazed concern. "Max! Lighten up! You're not making any sense. Is it something about my thesis?"

The semipensioner snorted. "Which the entire scientific community—yes, even the Terraformers—thinks is a loser?" He dropped his hands. "No, your thesis has nothing to do with it. Your bug won't bother Dorfman, not in the slightest."

"So what's the problem?"

Stoner inhaled in several sharp gasps, let it out slowly. "Nick, Terraformers could put you on that ship, and you could test your microbe under field conditions. But in return they would want you to check out Dorfman's process. He knows you'd be reporting back to them, and he'll be wondering what you are going to tell them."

"All that's a bit premature, isn't it? I have yet to see his demonstration plant. For all we know, his process is perfect for the planet."

"Nick, do you hear what I'm telling you?"

"I hear you, Max." He shrugged. "I'd still like to go."

"Oh God." The old man dropped his hands. After a time he said, "All right. I'll set it up. Just avoid him whenever possible."

"It's a small ship, Max."

"I know. He'll probably come to you. It will happen after the plant inspection. You'll be alone with him. He'll want to know what you're going to tell Terraformers. Be smart. You don't have to tell him anything."

"I understand."

The savant took a deep breath; it sounded like a moan. "Okay. Here's the layout. Terraformers has built an underground station on Aphrodite Terra, one of the big plateaus. It's air-conditioned, pressure-proof, well stocked. Dorfman's pilot plant is nearby.

"Basically he proposes to create a breathable oxygen-nitrogen atmosphere out of Venus's carbon dioxide. He'll crack the CO_2 into CO and oxygen, and absorb the CO. He'll need nitrogen, of course. He has a nuclear fission process for making that nitrogen, but they will also look for subcrustal pockets of nitrogen gas. They'll do this by seismic exploration in a three-day tour of the planet. You'll have to complete your tests within that time. Then the ship returns to the station, picks you up, then home again." He gave his protégé a grim look. "You got that?"

"Sure, Max. That's great. And don't worry. What can he do? What can go wrong? A full crew, six committee observers. I'll be perfectly safe. You're worse than Mom sending me off to camp. Relax!"

Professor Stoner walked away, moccasins slapping slowly, sadly. His back was bent as though he was carrying a heavy load.

Nick met Dorfman soon after takeoff, when the passengers were circulating and getting acquainted and exploring the little ship. As far as Nick could tell, the entrepreneur was average-size, with close-cropped blond hair, mustache, and goatee. He had a pleasant voice and a ready smile. He seemed far too mild and debonaire to pose any threat to anyone. Maybe (thought the student) old Max had misjudged his onetime rival.

Early in the flight he decided that he couldn't get used to being weightless. He performed the recommended daily three hours of physical exercise but even so he lost several grams of muscle and bone and was often disoriented and had spells of motion sickness. His only sense of "down" was where his feet happened to be. It was cold comfort that most of the members of the Congressional Committee shared his physical problems.

The committee makeup puzzled him. There was one senator, who was here mainly because he wanted a space trip before retiring. The five others were young men in their thirties, clerks to senators and representatives—mostly lawyers. Not a science degree in the lot.

There were various pastimes to relieve tedium, mostly games, solo, duo, group. Eventually they all drifted into their own individual routines.

The *Morningstar* set down on schedule on the torrid planet's station launchpad. The visitors suited up in the ship's airlock and made their slow awkward descents down the fold-down steps and then into the waiting electric Rover, driven by one of the land crew. Nick and two others rode in the trailer cart.

He looked up into the semilight. A hundred miles of thick upper atmosphere filtered out most of the incoming sunlight. The reds came through, vaguely and ambiguously, with perhaps a bit of orange. His bugs would work with that. He wondered whether these skies had ever been blue, or ever would be. Probably neither. He twisted around and looked behind him. Beyond the cliff everything was flat, an ancient dust-covered lava flow that stretched to the horizon.

The pilot plant, a formidable array of tanks, tubes, and instruments, appeared to conform to photographs and flowsheets that Nick had seen and studied before and during the trip.

Dorfman got out of the Rover, turned back to the group, and pointed to an intricate piece of nearby apparatus. From where he sat in the trailer cart, despite the insulation in his suit, Nick could feel the heat radiated by the unit.

"The Dorfman Process starts here," said the host. "This is the heater. At high temperatures carbon dioxide breaks down into carbon monoxide and free oxygen. Actually, we are more familiar with the reaction when it is going the other way, with oxygen burning the monoxide to dioxide with the release of heat. We recover the effluent, a gaseous mixture of carbon dioxide, carbon monoxide, and oxygen. We run the mixture through absorbers— first nickel metal, to pick up carbon monoxide as nickel carbonyl, then alkali to pick up carbon dioxide. That leaves fairly pure oxygen, which we discharge into the atmosphere, far away from the generating plant." He indicated a pipe leading away from the pilot plant. "We may decide to take a side stream from our oxygen product line. I'll explain about that later."

He waved his metal-cased hand toward another unit. "We heat the nickel carbonyl to recover CO. In the number-two heater, there, we heat the CO, and it converts to carbon dioxide and carbon. We discard the carbon, and the mix of CO_2 and CO is recycled back to the separation units. At this point the end products are oxygen and carbon. One molecule of carbon dioxide gives one molecule of oxygen and one atom of carbon. Simple, but it works." He paused and look around the cluster of helmets in the Rover. Nick couldn't see the man's expression, but he suspected Dorfman was smiling.

The lecturer continued, "Now, gentlemen, I know you have questions. I suggest at this time that we adjourn to the conference room in the station, which is a nice cool cave dug into the side of the plateau below us. There we can desuit and relax with something wet and cool, and I'll try to answer all your questions."

It was a fair-size oak table. One of the land crew took orders for drinks. Nick asked for iced tea. He felt out of place. He knew it was possible that the rest of the group, despite youth, inexperience, and lack of scientific knowledge, might well decide the fate of a planet. He took one of the seats farthest from Dorfman.

One of the younger men spoke. "Dr. Dorfman, I'm troubled by that nickel carbonyl. Isn't that stuff pretty poisonous?"

"It is indeed, Mr. York. We will have to use extreme caution."

Another asked, "Couldn't you absorb the carbon monoxide in something else? Water, maybe?"

"Good question, Mr. Zimmer. We tried that. However, water absorbs both monoxide and oxygen. The separation is poor. And we tried several other monoxide solvents. For a while, cuprous chloride looked good, but we found the oxygen was oxidizing it to the cupric form, which wouldn't work."

"How about nitrogen, Doctor?"

"I'm glad you brought that up, Mr. Munson. For here we see the most ingenious unit of the entire plant at work. I mentioned a side stream to be taken from the oxygen product line. This side stream goes to our nuclear cracker, still under construction. Here each atom of oxygen is stripped of one proton, one neutron, and one electron, all of which come together as deuterium, which is vented and eventually vanishes into outer space. What's left is nitrogen. The nitrogen stream joins the oxygen stream. The mixture of nitrogen and oxygen is about four to one by volume and approximates Earth's atmosphere."

"Pity you have to use up all that oxygen just to make nitrogen. Can't you get your nitrogen some other way?"

"We completely agree with you, Mr. Lee. You'll be pleased to learn that we are indeed looking into alternate sources. We may find extensive underground bubbles of nitrogen gas, and we have an extensive seismographic program under way, using spaced explosives."

"Bottom line, Doctor. What would the whole schmear cost?"

Dorfman smiled. "Over ten billion, Senator."

"Ouch. Can you beak that down?"

"One million per plant. Ten thousand plants."

"Well . . ."

"Actually, Senator, that's considerably less than the aggregate assessed taxable value of the world's golf courses."

"Hm. Well, assuming we do it, build all those plants, how long will it take to give Venus an atmosphere similar to Earth's?"

"Thirty-eight years, Senator, plus or minus three months."

Nick started. He had seen the raw data in an ultrasecret Dorfman corporation report. He had used the data in a very rough approximation on his laptop, and the figure he had come up with was close to four hundred years.

The speaker gave Nick a curious look. "Of course," he added pleasantly, "if we can find some underground nitrogen, we may reduce the time considerably. At present, though, in the interests of caution, we offer the outside estimate." He looked around the table. "Any more questions? No? Well, gentlemen, you have seen the Dorfman process at work. I hope I have demonstrated to you that it deals completely and competently with the problems of terraforming this planet." He looked one by one at each of the seated men. His gaze came back to the senator. "Is this the process to choose for terraforming Venus? The answer—I think you'll agree with me—is yes." He looked around the table again, smiling.

BS, thought Nick. But he kept his mouth shut and his face

blank, and the speaker continued. "Now, as you know, we have on our program a three-day tour of the planet. During that time Mr. Renfield will remain here at the station and will conduct certain experiments relating to his Ph.D. thesis. He'll be alone here, no other personnel, no distractions. We'll pick him up on our return, and then *Morningstar* will head for our beautiful Terra."

Nick and Dorfman sat alone at the station conference table drinking iced tea. The others had returned to the ship. The executive gave the guest a friendly smile. "Before I leave, I just want to make sure you have everything you need for your research. I'm afraid we don't have an incubator. Can you improvise?"

"No problem, sir. A capsule under my armpit, with several capped tubes." He looked around the room. Shelves along the walls were loaded with tinned goods, little bags of flour, powdered milk, powdered eggs. A freezer in the corner was supposed to contain frozen meats and fresh vegetables. Above the freezer, a medicine cabinet and first-aid kit. The dormitory was down the hall to the rear.

"Looks like it's all here," he said. And he was thinking, This chap is a great con artist, but otherwise he's harmless. Certainly no personal danger to me. I'll tease Max about him when I get back home.

He blinked several times in succession, then shook his head as though to clear it.

Dorfman watched this with narrowed eyes. He said quietly, "I see you seem to have the usual symptoms, recovering from a long period of weightlessness. If you stand for a few minutes, you feel faint. The space medics have a name for it: 'orthostatic intolerance.' And when your head moves, you have the illusion your surroundings move. A simple pushup exhausts you. Don't worry, in forty-eight hours you'll be fully recovered."

Two Earth days? he thought. Will it interfere with my research? He said, "It doesn't seem to bother you."

"I barely feel it. As host for the group I have to keep a clear head. I use one cc of dimenhydrinate, in my tea, coffee, whatever. A modified Dramamine, only faster. Clears up everything in a few minutes." He took a vial from a jacket pocket and pushed it over. "Highly recommended for your particular situation. The plastic stopper measures one cc."

"Well, thanks." Nick unscrewed the lid, squirted a measured dose of oily liquid into his tea, returned the vial.

Dorfman lifted his eyes and seemed to study the foam glass insulation in the ceiling as Nick sipped his tea. Finally he said: "Nick, I have the impression that you perceive, shall we say, certain flaws in my process?"

Nick sat up very straight. Now wait a minute, he thought. Seeing probable flaws was one thing, but telling a man of Dorfman's stature what you saw was quite another. He thought about Max Stoner's lurid warning. His mouth was suddenly dry. He took a long swig of his tea.

Dorfman noted the gesture and seemed to smile faintly. Nick thought, Okay, so now you know what I think about your process. So what?

"Talk to me, Nick. What flaws did you see?"

His head didn't feel exactly right. He hoped the medication would kick in soon. "Not exactly *flaws,* Dr. Dorfman. Actually, so far as I was able to tell, each of your unit processes would work exactly as you have described."

"That's good to hear. Ah—you were hired by the Terraformers Administration to examine the process and report back to them?"

"It wasn't all that formal, sir. The Administration arranged a berth on the ship and a chance to test my microbe under field conditions. In return I am supposed to tell them what I think of your process."

"So what do you think of my process?"

Nick twisted uneasily in his chair. He finished off the tea and stared for a moment at the shrunken ice cubes. "Just as I said, sir, technically, it should work."

"Hm. Nick, are you being evasive? Or perhaps I'm not asking the right question. Let's explore this a bit. As you know, our prospectus claims the Dorfman Process can put a full Earth atmosphere on Venus in under forty years."

Nick was having trouble focusing on the interrogator. He wiped his eyes with a handkerchief.

Dorfman continued. "We say one Earth atmosphere is 5.194×10^{15} metric tons of air. Would you agree?"

"Yeah, that sounds about right."

"And we claim that ten thousand plants spread over the planet will give a total of about 3.6×10^{11} tons of air per day. You agree?"

Nick thought out each word before answering. He wished he felt better. He wished this were over. "If your plants operate at design capacity, I guess you would get that total."

"So, at least theoretically we meet the specifications?"

"In numbers, yes, but it's still not quite right. The air won't be breathable, Dr. Dorfman." He knew he should shut up. "One problem would be atmospheric pressure. Atmospheric pressure on the surface of Venus is ninety times the air pressure on Earth, over 1,300 PSI, and it would still be over 1,300 PSI after you deliver your one full atmosphere to the surface here, and the surface would still be hot enough to melt lead."

Dorfman's eyes seemed to harden.

Now I've done it, Nick thought. What happened, Max? Why couldn't I listen to you? Everything is so fuzzy. Well, finish up. "Even if your process works, after forty years, the atmosphere here would still be about eighty percent carbon dioxide, and it would still be unbreathable."

He realized that Dorfman was watching him intently. Something was wrong. The tea . . . His tormentor was going in and out of focus. He was seeing double.

Dorfman continued evenly, almost monotonously. "Nick, I'd like for you to stop a moment and consider the magnitude of the crime you were about to commit. A crime from which I am going to save you. Can you hear me? Ten thousand converter plants at one million dollars each. That's ten billion dollars, Nick, just for the hardware. Add personnel, that's another ten billion—*annually*, my young friend. If you were permitted, you would kill all that. You would say misleading things in your report to Terraformers, and the whole magnificent project would come crashing down. But you're not going to turn in that report, are you?"

And why not? thought Nick dreamily. He couldn't voice the question. He could only think it. And Max had been right. Dorfman would do *anything*. Question: What was this *anything*?

He couldn't keep his eyes open. He seemed paralyzed. At first everything was gray. Then black. Then nothing.

When he regained consciousness he thought at first he was simply waking up on the ship with the beginning of another artificial day. But then he realized everything was wrong. He was lying on the floor, not on his cot. And he remembered things . . . Dorfman . . . they had been talking . . . arguing. His head hurt. His mouth was dry. He tried to identify the taste. Vinegar? Detergent? Battery acid? All of the above?

The bastard had drugged him—"modified Dramamine," like hell. But was that all? No, something had kicked him out of his stupor. Had knocked him to the floor. Where was he? Ah, still in the station conference room. He groaned, pulled himself up on a chair, and looked around. Things were all over the floor. He tried to think. Earthquake? No, of course not. Venus had no tectonic plates. What then? An exploratory seismic explosion? Had to be. Searching for subterranean nitrogen chambers. And near, too near. Not supposed to be any around here. But this one, practically under the station. Somebody had made a mistake. A big one. Or had they? Dorfman? Where was the executive?

He staggered to his feet and walked unsteadily toward the exit corridor. His voice rattled querulously. "Dorfman? Dorfman? Hey? Anybody?"

No answer. He entered the airlock that opened into the tunnel exit and peered through the heavy glass window. He could see very little. A broken shaft of dim sunlight just outside revealed that the door was pretty well blocked by shards of shattered mineral. He thought about that for a moment. Gypsum, probably. Maybe the obstruction was manageable—just a meter or so. He might be able to work his way through it. Surely the ship crew knew about this, and men were even now digging strenuously at the other end. He might be able to help.

He went back inside the conference room and looked around.

His suit and helmet were still there, hanging from a peg on the bulkhead. Dorfman's was gone.

Only then did the full enormity of his predicament hit him. He had been sealed in, left to die. Nobody was coming to dig him out. Oh, Max, you were so right. I should have listened. The wily adventurer had intended to kill him and simultaneously and permanently seal off the station entrance.

The World Congress would approve the Dorfman Project without a single dissenting vote.

Because of one cc of liquid in his tea. Knockout drops. Mickey Finn. Dorfman wouldn't have taken the little bottle with him. Still here somewhere. He fished around in the wastebasket. There. He pulled the stopper and sniffed. His nose wrinkled. Chloral . . . CCl_3CHO. He felt very stupid. He should have recognized the odor. "You bastard," he muttered. "You were just stalling, making sure I passed out before you left."

Well, Dorfie, prince of scoundrels, I intend to be a terrible disappointment to you. I am not going to die. Not for a long time, anyway. I am going to get out of here, and you are going down for attempted murder.

How will I do this? Not too clear just yet. It'll come to me.

First, what does my armory hold?

He walked to the blackboard and wrote:

INVENTORY
1. Me. Physically, mentally in fair working order, despite all.
2. Station. Shell still intact. Nuclear generator and utilities still functional.
3. Air tanks—60 days.
4. Water—45 days; 60 with waste treatment.
5. Food—60 days.
6. One suit.
7. My microcultures.
8. And all wrapped in a superpressured death-dealing outer atmosphere.

•   •   •

Sixty days of life. A ship would probably not come in for several months, possibly not before the next Earth-Venus opposition, some eighteen months hence.

He laid the chalk aside and stared at his list. No escape. No ray of light.

No, that wasn't quite right. There was a ray of light. It was coming straight down through the tumble of rocks just outside the air lock. Reddish orange, vaguely luminous, filtered through miles of atmosphere. And my microbe is photosynthetic. And I've never tried it under field conditions . . . 460 Centigrade . . . 1,325 PSI pressure. But that's why I'm here, isn't it? Let's go!

He suited up, took a culture tube from his collection, and shuffled to the airlock. He spun the second wheel, opened the hatch, and looked out. The shaft of sunlight seemed surprisingly bright. He turned on his shades. The beam seemed to spread and multiply as it reflected in a million directions within and around the rock fragments. Crystals, he thought. Maybe I can climb out through this mess.

But first things first.

He pulled the seal from the culture tube and upended the liquid over the nearest sunlit rock.

The little cream-colored culture was immobile on the mineral surface for a few seconds. Then it began to flow, and to spread out. Slowly at first, the way (he thought) a pool of oil might spread—then faster. And faster. It covered the first piece of rock, then moved along points of contact with adjacent crystals.

He watched in awe. "Huh? No, not possible. CO_2, okay, plenty of that. But you have to have hydrogen, too. From water. But I didn't give you any water. Surely not that much as water vapor in the atmosphere. So where are you getting the H_2O? The crust? From gypsum? Maybe. $CaSO_4.2H_2O$."

There was no other explanation. The microbe was taking H_2O from the mineral. Like a terrestrial lichen on a rock, it was extracting nutrition from the mineral host.

He took a deep breath. He chortled. A gold mine! Only better, much better.

He visualized the equation.

$$4CO_2 + 2H_2O \rightarrow O_2 + 2HO-(C=O)-(C=O)-OH$$

Exactly as predicted, copious oxygen, with by-product oxalic acid. Four volumes of carbon dioxide were disappearing for every volume of oxygen he made.

He watched in spellbound fascination as the affected crystals, divested of two-thirds of their molecules, began to crumble and collapse. He had to jump back against the cavern wall as a mass of overhanging rock tumbled into the area. This greatly expanded the rock surface exposed to sunlight. As he watched, marveling, the mass of rocks in his immediate area was soon reduced to powder, and the sunlight spread again.

He heard a faint hissing. Gas escaping somewhere? There, coming up from below the rocks. Had the explosion actually found—and tapped—a nitrogen reservoir? Sure looked that way. Well, thank you very much, Dorfie, I may need that.

He watched with great interest as the culture moved quickly into the light, followed by clouds of steam. He was surprised to see the steam, but soon realized what was happening. The oxalic acid molecules were condensing, splitting out H_2O and polymerizing. Which meant, after the first oxalic, condensation of every new oxalic would give a molecule of water.

But could it be? This was *too* good! In sum, the little microbe was pulling CO_2 out of the air, H_2O out of the crust and spewing O_2 and H_2O into the atmosphere. Make that water vapor, for the little beads of liquid boiled away as soon as they came into existence. Still it was *liquid* water, something these vast lava flows hadn't seen in hundreds of millions of years.

More carbon dioxide was disappearing than the oxygen and water he was creating, and that meant air pressure would soon show a measurable drop.

He clambered up the resulting slope and out into the open.

Through the semilight he looked over at the launch site. No ship. Of course. Nothing but the little electric Rover. They had even taken the trailing cart.

He was alone on the planet.

The ground seemed to move slightly. He looked down, managed a weird chuckle. The culture had caught up with him, had shattered the stratum of gypsum near his feet. Why hadn't he been able to get results like this back home? Must be the combination of high temperature and high pressure here. Somebody's law: Raise the temperature ten degrees, the reaction rate doubles. So when we raise the temperature many times ten degrees and the pressure by ninety times Earth pressure, what happens to the culture propagation rate? Right off the scale!

The living layer eddied around his heels for a moment, as though tasting the titanium alloy of his boots, then withdrew and spread rapidly outward. He watched the movement with a curious detachment. The thing was beyond wonder. "Bon appetite, little fellow!"

He turned slowly, in a complete circle, and then he stood there, just looking, watching, thinking. The culture had spread away in patches and arms as far as he could see, out to all horizons. Anywhere there were adjoining outcrops of gypsum, the microbe was there, or soon would be.

As long as the sunlight and gypsum lasted, his little darlings would feast. And the Venusian day was incredibly long, with over sixty Earth days still to go before the terminator brought darkness over the station. So for the time being at least, sunlight would not be a problem. But the local supply of gypsum was probably limited. Sunlight or not, the bugs would have to quit when the gypsum and its $2H_2O$ was used up.

Was this the only gypsum deposit on the planet? Surely not. Other seas must have dried up, just like the lowlands surrounding this Aphrodite Terra plateau; lime and sulfur must have left their hydrated calling cards in many other locales. Where?

He knew there were some geological charts in the station. Spend a little time with them.

But first . . .

He strode off toward the launchpad, got into the Rover, checked the dials, turned the key; the little engine jerked once, then began purring. He smiled. Leaving a dusty trail of gypsum particles floating in the thick air behind him, he headed back to the station.

As he drove up, he wondered about the ultimate consequences of his highly educated, if ravenous, microbe. So far, so good. Even very good. He ran the photosynthesis equations through his mental computer. First you get oxygen gas, with by-product oxalic acid. Oxalic is poison, but with high heat and pressure it dimerizes, splits out water, then trimerizes, splits out more water, and soon it's a harmless long-chain polymer. The water condensed out doesn't hang around. It boils away instantly as steam. I am making one humongous mess of steam, he thought. Where's it going?

He looked up, but saw only the usual high overcast. Sulfur dust gave the clouds a yellowish tinge. But no water.

They said that Venus once had had a lot of water. Volcanic outgassing and billions of cometary snowballs had perhaps given it as much as Earth. But proximity to the sun eventually boiled it away as water vapor, and then the sun's ultraviolet radiation had broken up the water molecules into hydrogen and oxygen. Hydrogen was too light for the planet's gravity to hold, and it had slowly frittered away into space. And the free oxygen had combined with free metals—iron, aluminum, silicon, calcium—and made the oxides and silicates of the crust. And with sulfur it made sulfates, including gypsum. And all while the volcanoes were pouring our their gases and their lavas, so that much of the original crust now lay under many meters of basalt. This world was now total desert, far dryer than any like place on Earth. Death Valley was a lush oasis by comparison.

But *that,* he thought, is about to change. In sixty days, or I am a dead man.

Just then he sensed that something was—*different.* Wind direction? He knew that weak winds had probably been moving over the plateau for the last couple of billion years. When he had emerged from the station the wind pressure on his suit had been barely perceptible, but constant. He took note of it now because it had stopped.

He stood up in the Rover, flipped on his helmet binoculars and panned the area. There, toward the horizon, dust clouds had come out of nowhere and were moving in steady strata along the surface. In the north, the streams were moving east; in the east, movement was southward; toward the south, movement was west. He didn't need to look west. He knew what had happened. The microbe had extracted enough carbon dioxide from the local atmosphere to create a low-pressure zone, and air was whirlpooling in to fill it. He was standing in the center of a rapidly developing vortex. He had to get out of there fast, or he might soon have the rare privilege of observing a Venusian tornado from within.

He jumped down and ran for the entrance to the airlock. Isolated bolts of lightning were beginning to strike around him. He looked behind him. The funnel had formed, and it had picked up something. Yes, the Rover was tumbling around, about a hundred meters up the funnel shaft, which at this moment was roaring toward him.

He dove into the airlock crevice, grabbed the hatch handle, held on, and looked up. Sight and sound shook him like a leaf. He watched in awe as the massive funnel screamed across the plateau and finally broke up as it approached the eastern horizon.

I did that? he thought. Am I Froh, the old Norse storm god? Or maybe even Zeus, with his thunderbolts?

He shook his head in wonder. And of course, nobody around to see. Only then did he recall the video system in his helmet. Story of my life.

A brief survey of the locale showed that the storm had wrecked several units of the Dorfman pilot plant. Not to worry, Dorfie, it would never have worked anyway. And I'll bet you have it insured for twice what it was worth.

Everything was now still and silent. But only for a moment. Suddenly hundreds, thousands of small white balls began to pelt his suit. But they sizzled and vanished into puffs of vapor almost as soon as they struck the hot ground.

Hail! Of course! Formed way overhead, from water vapor *he* had made from the gypsum deposit. The tornado had pushed the vapor into the distant clouds, where temperatures were below freezing. And this time he remembered the video.

He pressed the temperature and pressure buttons in his chest panel and studied the numbers that flashed on his helmet visor. Temperature, 445. Down fifteen degrees. Pressure, 1,249 PSI, down seventy-four PSI. Just local, of course, but nice going anyway. If gypsum and the station food locker held out, think of the possibilities! Or was he fantasizing?

He looked around. Everything was quiet. Not a breath of air. The Rover? Yes, over there, on its side. Hardy little beast. Very likely still operable, or at least repairable. He'd need it for what he planned next. He walked the half kilometer to the machine, got it back on its wheels, and tested the ignition. Everything worked. Amazing.

Next, a visit to the conference room.

He dug out all the maps he could find. There appeared to be only one gypsum outcrop here on the great Aphrodite Terra plateau, but there were several others indicated in smaller neighboring plateaus.

And there was an interesting alternative, right here on the home plateau: bauxite, $Al_2O_3.2H_2O$. *Hah!* A vast dome of bauxite had pushed through sheltering beds of granite and its igneous cousins. Terraformer geologists had even left a sample, here on the shelf. Red stuff, probably traces of iron. I'll take the whole jar.

First, though, a full meal. And then recharge the air, water, and liquid food canisters in his backpack, enough for forty-eight hours. Now, suit up, and out we go, into the heat and sunlight.

Next, the bauxite. He sprinkled a little of the powdered alumina mineral onto a flat culture-covered crystal. For a moment, nothing. Then the reddish powder began to jump. And then to froth.

Ah! He was very happy. He loaded his backpack with culture-covered fragments of gypsum and bauxite into the back of the Rover and set forth, rolling west along the equator.

He found the bauxite deposit without difficulty. Again, everything worked. He inoculated alternating outcrops: gypsum, bauxite, gypsum, bauxite . . .

Sometimes he stopped and thought about the ultimate consequences. Suppose the bug covers the whole planet? Well, let it. It would keep spreading and making oxygen as long as it could find hydrated minerals and carbon dioxide. So, keep at it, nameless little bug!

From time to time he looked overhead, but could see or hear nothing. Actually there were supposed to be at least twenty satellites in present orbit, most with radar and various equipment for keeping Earth informed about conditions here. With the radio gone, there was no way for him to contact them. But what was going to happen if and when they started reporting strange changes in pressure, temperature, and air composition?

He grinned.

On his return journey he made experimental side trips. From the maps he recalled outcrops of other hydrated aluminas: diaspore, gibbsite, halloysite. And then there was brucite, $Mg0.H_2O$. He gleefully dosed them all and gleefully outraced a score of churning tornadoes. Once his long-suffering suit endured hail as big as baseballs. He stayed away too long, and toward the end of the trip he realized that he was getting dangerously low on air and that he was singing into his helmet silly songs from his high-school days.

Safely back in the station kitchen he microwaved and ate two steaks in succession and was content. Before he turned in for a long nap he checked the external dials. Temperature was down another fifty degrees, pressure was down an additional 150 PSI. If this keeps up . . . But he was asleep.

Some time during the third week he stopped shaving. It wasn't a question of forgetting, nor the inconvenience of running the water recycler. He just decided it had stopped being relevant. The beard grew well; he never trimmed it.

As he explored and inoculated new deposits, he watched the time carefully. In this phase of its 225-Earth-day solar orbit, the planet's axis of rotation was substantially coplanar with the ecliptic. Currently the planet was in its "autumn" mode, and the station side now had about twenty Earth-days of full solar exposure remaining. After that the station would be in intermittent darkness and light until it moved into its "spring" position, where it would bask in full sunlight once more, and the microbes would thrive again. Like Johnny Appleseed following the frontier west, he'd have to keep ahead of the terminator, which at the equator moved along at a leisurely eight miles an hour. With the Rover, no problem.

September 30, 1659. I, poor miserable Robinson Crusoe, being ship-wrecked, during a dreadful storm, in the offing, came on shore on this dismal, unfortunate island, which I called the Island of Despair, all the rest of the ship's company being drowned, and myself almost dead.

He laid the e-reader aside. And so, he thought, you begin your famous journal, which you kept more or less faithfully for some twenty-eight years. For company you had goats, a dog, cats, birds. And finally that footprint in the sand.

Well, Robbie old friend, our situations aren't exactly identical, but if you can endure for twenty-eight years, maybe I can hang on for a few more weeks.

The "days" passed. By the end of the thirtieth day external temperature was down to 110 Centigrade, pressure was down to 21 PSI. Still high, but looking better and better. He ran a sample of dry air through the microanalyzer and wrote the results on the blackboard:

	Now	Before	Goal
CO_2	23	96.5	<0.1
O_2	15	0	21
N_2	60	2.7	78
Other gases	2	0.8	1

At this rate, in another week he'd have the CO_2 down to a fraction of one percent. With no CO_2, no greenhouse effect. The outer cloud cover would reflect most incoming solar energy. Condensation of his by-product oxalic polymer had created vast tonnages of water, but it was all in vapor form. The planet was still too hot to let the vapor condense as water but was cooling off rapidly.

On the thirty-fifth day the rains began. They continued steadily for ten days, then became intermittent, then stopped altogether. At first the raindrops were scalding hot; even so they were cooler than the surfaces they struck, where they changed into clouds of steam. But the steam didn't last. The deserts surrendered. Rain no longer evaporated the instant it hit the surface. He could already see little pools—*hot* little pools, to be sure, but there they were. He caught a spoonful of hot rain in a saucepan, let it cool, rolled it around his tongue. It tasted as pure as distilled water—which, considering its history of evaporation and condensation, it was.

He discarded his space suit.

After several more days the plateau was noticeably cooler. Pools collected on the surface and made rivulets that cascaded prettily down the cliffside. Water covered the great plain below the ridge. And the skies were no longer a hazy orange yellow. They were blue. They had been washed clean. The sun was blindingly visible though the haze as a big yellow orb. Later that day he saw a rainbow.

He looked about in wonder. *I did this?*

He felt like Balboa, looking out over the Pacific "with a wild surmise." He felt like a newly born Greek god, suddenly discovering his Hellenic inheritance.

And if this beautiful stuff is liquid at sea level, he thought, what is it at 38,000 feet? He lifted his binoculars to the southwest, and he gasped. Maxwell Montes was capped with white. As pretty as a postcard snow-covered Fuji. Prettier. And all mine. For now, anyway.

He had a sudden urge to run around and scream and yell and howl. So he did. His domain was so vast no echo returned to measure him.

On the fifty-fifth day his O_2:N_2:CO_2 gauges read: 21:78:0.03. Pressure, 14.7 PSI; temperature twenty degrees Centigrade. And now, with diminished CO_2, diminished heat, and diminished pressure, his darling little bugs were beginning to go dormant. He sealed off the nitrogen vent under the airlock.

He had now reached the goals for oxygen, nitrogen, and carbon dioxide. He hadn't worn his space suit in ten days. At this point, he was certain the planet had the purest, most breathable air in the solar system. It still had a little dust in the upper troposphere, but that was necessary as nuclei for the formation of rain-drops.

All the lowlands were now covered with water. There was a real sea out there, with real surf. And it was irresistible. He walked down to the cliff bottom, stripped buck naked, and waded out into the nearest lagoon. The bottom here was mostly clay, and it was soft and squishy between his toes. He ventured farther out. The water was transparent as glass. It rose to his knees, then to his waist.

He jerked. Something wiggly had brushed past his ankle. He looked down. There it was, gray, about the size and shape of a young catfish. He took a breath, ducked down and picked it up with both hands. When he got it up in the air it began to squirm and flog about. He noted the gills. A hibernating *fish*? Buried for eons in the Venusian equivalent of pre-Cambrian mud? Just waiting for the seas to return?

He thought of Adam, naming the creatures of Eden. Fish hadn't been included there. Big mistake. It was high time. "I hereby dub thee, *Pisces ostracodermis.*" He tossed it back into the water and watched it as it wriggled to the bottom a few feet away. From where he stood it appeared that the creature's mouth was working rhythmically. It was eating. Some sort of plankton? Is the water awakening an entire planet? Like rain on the desert, where seeds sprout and flowers bloom overnight?

He waded out into the sea, where a light surf was breaking. Even out here the water was fresh and sparkling. He swam out beyond the surf, made a few turns parallel to the shore, then returned. "Out of shape," he grumbled. "Do this more often."

The temperature was fine just now, in sunlight, but how about ultimate mean temperature? He worked out the final equilibrium on the computer. There were a lot of very complex variables: location on the planet, peculiar season of the planet's peculiar orbital year, incoming solar radiation, reflectance of outer atmosphere, continuing loss of heat stored by billennia of the greenhouse effect. Yet, some reasonable estimates could be made. Eventually, sunside might be a little cool, yet reasonably comfortable. For about fifty days out of the 225-day Venusian year, temperatures might occasionally dip below freezing. Max, he thought, you were right.

So—now he had plenty of air and water. But how about something to eat?

It was the sixtieth day. The station larder was approximately empty.

He decided it was well that he liked seafood.

Sometimes he drove the Rover a hundred kilometers or so into the darkness beyond the terminator, just to look at the third planet, hanging there like an emerald jewel, with her pendant pearl, Luna. With the telescopic lenses in his helmet turned to maximum he could make out cloud-dappled continents, sparkling seas.

Home. After such outings he always returned to the station with mixed feelings. Oh, he'd eventually get back to Earth. He had no doubts about that. He could guess what Dorfman had told everybody. There had been a bad accident. The young intern was dead. And by now, long dead.

Of course, maybe somewhere they had already landed. Venus was a big planet, nearly Earth-size. Not likely, though. When they came, they'd land at the station site.

He had listened to all the music, watched all the movie crystals. Many many times. He had played thousands of games against the chess computer, won some, lost some. He had found a three-octave keyboard and after much trial hunt-and-pecking, taught himself a little Bach, simple Beethoven (including of course, "Fuer Elise"), Schubert's "Serenade." It helped.

He knew he had done a tremendous thing. He was certain that the orbiting satellites had noted the change in atmospheric composition, the tremendous drops in temperature and pressure. He wondered what the Earth-bound savants thought about it. Could they conceive that he, a mere doctoral candidate, had done this thing? He thought about the professorial mind, shook his head. It would be beyond them. Even Max Stoner. They would think their instruments were flawed, probably corroded and dysfunctional.

They would have to come in person and verify. Even then they might not believe. He didn't really care.

Sometimes he was lonely. He would sit at the cliff edge with his chin cupped in his hands, staring out over the waves and listening to the breakers as they rolled musically into the shore below. At such times he felt very sorry for himself. Nick the Nomad, doomed to wander forever. His eyes would dim, he would blink. Control. Never lose control. He would think of painful things. Dorfman. He imagined intricate schemes for bringing the rogue to justice. The day must come.

At such times he would give much to hear a human voice. He thought of Max. He wondered what Dean Vass would say to all this. And the other candidates in the doctoral group. He'd even be glad to hear from Sam Baxter, the arrogant probe-maker. He thought about—what's-her-name—Muriel. Lately he was having trouble remembering her face. Muriel had been right. It would never have worked.

Some days later as he stood on the cliff, looking out over the sea—*his* sea—he knew the time had come to name his microbe. He thought of Xenophon's Greek mercenaries, and their shouts of joy as they neared the sea, which meant life and home. *"Thalatta! Thalatta!"* The sea, the sea! O beautiful word—and now my name for you, my marvelous life-giving little friend.

Thalatta.

On the next-to-last day before the terminator overtook the station, a probe fell out of the skies. Nick watched the descent in amazement. It had a tiny parachute, evidently designed to slow descent in the anticipated high-pressure atmosphere, but of no use at all in the new Earthlike troposphere. Fortunately it retrofired just before it landed near the station entry.

Nick dropped what he was doing, ran over, noted the Terraformers insignia, and under that, BAXTER. He knew how Robinson Crusoe felt on encountering that footprint in the sand.

He noted a glassy protuberance on the side of the cylinder. He took this to be a camera lens, and he waved at it. Though Venus and Earth were approaching opposition, they were still over fifty million miles apart, and signals from the probe back to Earth would take over four minutes.

Meanwhile he examined the new arrival. He could see that it was heavily insulated against the expected heat, and save for the camera lens all exposed parts appeared to be thick, probably acid-resistant sapphire. Several side ports had opened to permit entry of ambient air, Nick presumed for chemical analyses, temperature, pressure, and maybe some new properties.

He had to smile. This was indeed Sam Baxter's pride and joy, brainchild, masterpiece, and the crowning glory of Venusian probes. It was certainly better protected than prior assemblies, most of which had lasted only a few hours before yielding to the once ferocious Venusian atmosphere.

Could they recognize him? Probably no microphone or two-way audio. Unless—perhaps somebody back home thought he might still be alive? He called out: "I'm Nicholas Renfield. Alive and well. Who are you?"

He waited. A few seconds passed. Then: "Nick! Nick! Oh thank God! They told us you were dead!"

"Oh, hi, Max. Glad to hear from you. That was fast. Are you nearby?"

"Yes, we'll soon be down in orbit."

"Max, you were right about Dorfman. He tried to blow up the station with me in it, but he miscalculated. How is he, anyway?"

"He's been arrested, Nick, held without bail, pending a complete investigation. Several of his own crew turned on him. They wanted no part of it. But back to you. And Nick, I'm afraid parts of Baxter's probe have already broken down. Pressure, temp, gas analysis. None of the gauges are working properly. We're getting impossible readings."

"Yeah, I guess that's the way they would read. A bit low?"

"Impossibly low. And, uh, Nick—maybe you're a little out of focus. Can't see you too good. You *are* suited up properly, aren't you?"

"I'm very comfortable, Max."

"My eyes, not so good—or maybe it's the video. I see a hairy face, but no space suit. Wait—now, yes, there it is. No—just the helmet on that white shiny creature. *He's* wearing a helmet. *Aliens,* Nick?"

"He's a snowman, Max. I didn't have a hat. Hence the helmet. It's on his head."

"Snow? Some sort of powdered mineral, you mean?"

"No, Max. Real snow. White fluffy stuff. Falls in flakes from the skies. Beautiful hexagonal ice crystals, no two alike. You ball it up, make a snowman."

"Nick, I'm an old man with high blood pressure, off-the-scale cholesterol, an incipient ulcer, and our probe is obviously totally screwed. Tell me, please, what is going on?"

The candidate relented. "It's *Thalatta,* Max—our bug. I spread her all over the planet. She ate up the CO_2, and gave back oxygen. Pressure, temperature dropped. Oxygen-nitrogen ratio now like Earth's, about 20:80. The greenhouse problem disappeared with the CO_2. Max, this air is so pure, until you get used to it, it could actually make you slightly sick."

A long pause.

"Nick, I believe. I just don't know what to say."

"You think Vass will accept *Thalatta* as my thesis?"

"The regents will. What a question! And you'll get the Nobel, all that crazy stuff. You'll have cities, countries, continents named after you."

"Well, that'll be very nice. Up to now, you know, except for Maxwell Montes, everything has been named for women. How soon can you get here?"

"We plan to dock in fourteen hours."

"Great. Tomorrow, just in time for supper."

"Can we bring you anything special?"

"Lemons, Max."

"Lemons, of course. For the vitamins? Anti-scurvy?"

"No. I have vitamin pills for that. I need lemons for the fish."

"They left fish?"

"No—I catch them in the lagoon, not far from the station."

"Fish? Lagoon?"

"Sort of fish, Max. When the lagoon filled up, the mud softened, and up they came. Out of hibernation, I guess. Dormant for

a billion years or so. Like the mud puppies in our pre-Cambrian. Just needed a little water. Even bigger ones out in the ocean. Marvelous filets. You and I'll go surf fishing. Lots of microscopic water life, too. They dote on our oxalic polymer. Uh, Max, who'll be on the examining committee for my doctor's oral?"

Long pause.

"Max?"

One million kilometers away the old man was thinking. Ah yes, the dissertation jury. There are certain impossible things, which if done, are nevertheless still impossible, an affront to logic. Who shall be competent to critique this impossible ultra-mortal thesis? Who is knowledgeable in the creation of worlds? Chronos? Brahma? Ammon-Ra? The giants that built Valhalla? Does Dean Vass number himself among these immortals? No. He dare not.

Stoner said gravely, "Under the circumstances, I think the regents will probably waive jury examination."

"Whatever. And also bring green veggies and some dinner rolls, okay? And if you have any ice cream . . ."

A Planet Called Elvis

Craig Shaw Gardner

1

Once you got used to showing up naked, the rest was easy. At least that's what they said back at the academy. Jerome Smith-Seven supposed that someday he might actually get used to it. But every jump he'd taken, from the first tentative student journey to the four he'd made during his internship, ended up the same. He just couldn't think when he wasn't wearing clothes.

"Set relays!"

"Bank one is go!"

"Bank two is go!"

"Bank three—searching—bank three is go!"

"Destination is confirmed!"

The jump technicians' chatter did a lot to calm him. The way they announced their readiness seemed like a chant, not so much scientific jargon as a mystical mantra, a magical spell that propelled you to your destination.

Not that he'd ever say something like that to the other members of the team. There was a lot Jerome didn't share.

"SmithSeven!" the lead tech called sharply. "To your mark!"

He had no more time for beginner's nerves. This jump was for real. He moved across the dark floor to the bright circle that began his journey.

"Ethel?" the lead tech asked in a much gentler tone.

His partner nodded as she stepped forward. "I'm there already."

Their boss's face filled the wall screen before them. He smiled much too warmly for this chilly room.

The jump stations were always cold. Something about keeping the transfer equipment at peak efficiency. Jerome really should have paid more attention to the theory when he was in class. Or maybe he should have gotten a little more sleep. Sometimes he wondered why his dad had pulled all those strings to get him this job in the first place. Jerome shivered while he waited for his boss to give them the official go-ahead.

"Greetings volunteers!" the image of Maurice OneO'Leary called heartily. "This is a quick in, quick out situation. But your speed must be tempered with a certain caution. Remember, we are dealing with Gert Durston, with all that implies. Your implants have been briefed to answer any questions."

Gert Durston? Jerome didn't remember the name. He quickly keyed a download. "Gert Durston is well known to law-enforcement personnel as a career criminal and notorious free-thinker—"

He paused the inner voice. Their boss had started speaking again.

"You should never forget," the image continued, "that with someone like Durston, any sort of slip could mean life or death. But you've already studied all that in your downloads."

Jerome did his best not to frown. He should have taken a little while to review this, rather than going for that final night on the town. Especially after what had happened with Mona. Who knew she would be so afraid of lampreys?

He blinked. He had to keep his mind on their assignment. The boss's image had faded out, and the techs were calling out their best instructions.

He was glad Ethel was going out with him.

On most of the independent worlds, they were less suspicious of tourists if they traveled in pairs. That was all there was to it, really. And Ethel was always so cheerful. Their boss OneO'Leary said he could learn a lot from her. She was the senior agent on the case.

Except she wasn't smiling now. She wasn't even looking at him. Her face was frozen in a disapproving frown.

"Okay, Nine," Jerome heard faintly.

Ethel looked up, then she was gone. Her thin white robe fluttered to the floor.

"We're ready, Seven," a tech called over his subliminal speaker. "Or should I call you Elvis?"

Very funny, he thought. The tingling came and went. And then he was there.

Jerome blinked. It was far too bright.

"Uh-huh," someone said in front of him.

He shook his head and did his best to focus. All the techs on this end seemed to be dressed in leather, either basic black or white with rhinestone trim.

"Uh-huh," somebody else replied.

Oh, yeah, this was in his program somewhere. On this world, everyone was Elvis.

Somebody handed him a fluffy bathrobe with "EAP" embroidered in gold on the breast. Ethel stood next to him, similarly attired. Jerome realized he was so surprised by his surroundings that he hadn't even thought about his nakedness.

A bored young woman in black leather barely looked at the two of them.

"Welcome to Elvis. Young or old?"

"Pardon?" Jerome keyed his datafeed to active, trying in vain to understand the question.

"The planet Elvis—" the inner voice began.

"Uh-huh," the woman replied dryly. She glanced at a young man, also dressed all in black. "Note that they forfeited their choice. Gal's a definite young. Guy could go either way."

"Looks like an old to me," the man in black replied. He frowned as his fingers flashed across the keyboard.

Jerome had the feeling something important was being decided here. He pointed to the keyboard. "What are you doing there?"

One corner of the man's mouth flicked up in a smile. "TCB, baby."

Jerome nodded uncomprehendingly. "Uh—TCB?"

"Taking care of business! TCB!" The man's smile turned to a sneer.

"Tourists!" the woman at his side agreed. Everybody else in the room turned to nod. They all had the sneer down.

Lights flashed on a five-foot-high, avocado door set in the wall. A silver script above the handle read AMANA. The door emitted a series of melodic beeps.

" 'Heartbreak Hotel,' isn't it?" Ethel asked.

"Well, yes." The tech's sneer opened into a grin. "Maybe there's a little Elvis in these folks after all."

The TCB guy opened the door and pulled out two packages wrapped in plastic. After a quick check of the labels, he handed one to each of the newcomers.

Ethel tore hers open first. It contained a black leather jumpsuit. Jerome pulled the plastic off a white outfit made from some fabric he had never seen before. His inner voice said it was something called polyester, "one of the miracle fibers of the fifties." Jerome had no idea what that meant. He needed a program to explain his program.

Underneath the polyester suit was a large rhinestone belt.

"You'll thank me for it later," said the female tech as Jerome studied his clothes. She slapped at her skintight leather pants. "The rhinestones are so much easier on the waist."

Ethel smiled at the locals. "This is so overwhelming!" she said, perhaps a bit too enthusiastically. "I've read about it in the literature, of course, but to actually see it around me. On this world, everybody's Elvis?"

"Well, yeah." The male technician returned her grin. "Well, we have a couple of Colonels, a handful of Priscillas. But you gotta apply for those in writing."

"I mean," the woman added, "who else would anyone want to be?"

"But doesn't that get a little confusing?" Jerome asked.

"I see your point," Ethel cut in. She shot Jerome a withering look. Was he asking too many questions? He was a tourist. Weren't tourists supposed to ask questions?

"On the contrary," the woman replied, "it makes for a totally harmonious society."

The man nodded. "Do not ask for whom the Elvis frugs, he frugs for thee."

"Besides," the woman continued, "there are those who take on other roles. Go-go girls and beach bunnies. The occasional French race-car driver. Our version of national service. It wouldn't be Elvis without them."

"Go-go girls?" Jerome asked. "Beach bunnies? But if everyone, male and female, is Elvis—"

"Don't pay any attention to my husband," Ethel interrupted. "He wanted to go to Monty's World."

Both the technician's looked shocked.

"Oh, dear."

"You have our sympathies."

The woman smiled tentatively. "Maybe now that you have come to Elvis, he will see the light."

Ethel grinned back. "Perhaps we don't know as much about your planet as we should. Can you recommend someplace we can stay?"

Both techs frowned at Jerome.

"Especially for someone with—special needs?" the female tech asked softly. She picked up a glossy disc from a nearby counter. "It's a little pricey, but it is Elvis."

Jerome looked down at the label as she handed it over. The disc was a brochure for someplace called Graceland Towers.

"This is Elvis," the brochure announced. "The coolest planet out there. And Graceland Towers is the most way-out—"

Jerome quickly hit the brochure's pause button.

"Why don't you go to the hotel and study up?" the female tech asked. She frowned slightly. "But where are our manners?"

Her male counterpart slapped his forehead. "The welcome wagon! If you'll just follow us to the lounge?"

Jerome nodded. Now that the initial shock was past, he was hungry. A jump always left you famished, since whatever was in your stomach prejump got left behind. Generally, then, a little snack was offered as you became acclimated to your new surroundings. He was glad this was one custom Elvis still observed.

The tech led them over to one corner of the room in which a number of couches and overstuffed chairs were sunk into the floor. The tech waved for them to take the steps down, then removed the lid from a large silver tray.

"Fried peanut butter and banana sandwiches," he said proudly. "The official food of Elvis."

"It's an honor," Ethel agreed as she accepted one. Jerome did the same.

Grease oozed between his fingers. His stomach growled. Fried bananas. And peanut butter. What an interesting smell. And they would probably get kicked off the planet if he even thought about refusing it.

Jerome took a small bite. The taste was every bit as interesting. He swallowed quickly. He really would have to review the information so he wouldn't get any more surprises. Jerome and his implant were going to have to spend some time together.

"My," Ethel said between bites. "This is certainly different."

Quick in, quick out, their boss had said. Jerome swallowed again. Right now, he couldn't agree more.

2

Rock and roll filled the air.

Jerome recognized the sound immediately. The twanging guitars, the pounding drums, the bass line that shook the ground beneath their feet. He had been exposed to it during his Rebellion Rotation; another requirement of the academy. He had never cared for the stuff, even in its purest form. And the music that blared through the streets was far from pure. He and his partner had been assaulted by it as soon as they had left the safety of the jump station. Jerome took a deep breath and told himself he would not get a headache.

The whole world conspired against him. It was night outside the station, but it was far from dark and anything but still. A faint but insistent pounding tickled the back of Jerome's skull. It was not just the music. Lights strobed above a dozen different establishments. The Heartbreak Hotel. A delivery service called Return to Sender. A theater named Letts Playhouse. The street before them was broad but crowded. People jostled each other, rushing in a dozen different directions. And almost everybody on the crowded streets was dressed like Elvis: young and old, fat and thin, leather and polyester; most with dark hair, with a sprinkling of dirty blondes; men, women, children, even the family pets. Jerome realized this was the first time he'd ever seen a poodle with sideburns.

He looked around for his partner. "We're not going to Graceland Towers?"

According to the technicians, the hotel was only a short left turn from the jump station. But once out the door, Ethel had immediately led them the other way.

"We'll get there eventually," Ethel explained. "But we have to talk with our contact first."

Contact? He should know about a contact. Jerome checked in again with his inner voice.

"The Protectorate has no official standing on many of the outer civilized worlds, and must therefore use paid operatives to supply information. The operative on the planet—" A pause, and then, with a different voice: "Elvis is—" Another pause. "Elvis Ivan Barishnikov."

Jerome understood. "We're going to see—"

She cautioned him to silence.

"We are sightseeing. That's what we're here for. We're just sightseeing in a very specific direction."

Ethel led the way forcefully through the crowd. Jerome hurried after her. He guessed it was okay to gawk. It played in with being a tourist. And there was plenty to gawk at: bikers, doctors, cowboys, race-car drivers—yet almost all of them unmistakably Elvis.

A long, black limousine pushed its way through the crowd. He wondered if it was transporting a Colonel.

They turned another corner and the crowd thinned out a bit. He caught up with Ethel. A funny thing about Ethel. From the back of her black leather jacket, she looked pretty much like everybody else. If they ever got separated . . .

On second thought, that wasn't funny at all.

Jerome smiled weakly at his partner. "Is everybody here named Elvis?" he asked.

She nodded. "Just about everybody. Ourselves included, Elvis Jerome."

She paused, perhaps checking with her own inner voice, then pointed to their right.

"I think we need to sightsee down this street."

She led the way down a lane considerably narrower that the road they had just left. Despite its smaller size, it managed to be even more garish than the avenue in front of the jump station. One bright pink establishment appeared to stretch the entire length of the street. A sign at its center flashed:

VIVA LAS VEGAS.

The letters were pink, too, in sharp contrast to the blue-outlined palm trees that covered a place on the opposite corner called Blue Hawaii. But both the pink and blue tubes had something in common. Whatever was inside those glowing pipes seemed to buzz like a living thing.

"Neon," his inner voice explained. "An archaic form of lighting especially popular during the twentieth—"

Jerome shut it off. He could catch up later.

"There!" Ethel called triumphantly. The stores on this end of the street were far smaller and less well lit than anything out on the boulevard. She pointed to a tiny storefront, even shabbier than those around it, wedged between a King's Dry Cleaning Shop and a place called Everything Elvis for a Dollar. At first, Jerome didn't even think the place in the middle had a sign. But as he followed his partner across the street, he saw faded letters painted on the dirty glass.

CADILLAC TOURS, the chipped gold letters read. VISIT ELVIS, AND BEYOND.

Ethel pushed open the door. A single electric guitar chord echoed through the air. Jerome realized it was some sort of doorchime.

The place looked even grubbier inside. A single desk was piled high with clutter, which also spread over two of the three chairs jammed into the tiny room. And there didn't seem to be any sort of storekeeper, real or virtual.

"This is our contact?" Jerome asked. His partner frowned and shook her head.

"Hello!" Ethel called.

After a moment's silence, a gold lamé curtain was thrust aside at the very back of the establishment to reveal a very short, elderly man in a bad Elvis wig.

"You're in the wrong place," snapped the short man.

Ethel nodded pleasantly. "We want to see Elvis."

The short man sneered. "You're seeing it, all around you." He stepped back and began to reclose the curtain.

"No," Ethel insisted, "we want to get down to the roots."

The man stopped and stared at her. "What's that?"

"You know—the blue suede shoes."

He pushed the curtain away for good. "It'll cost you."

"Anything for the king."

The small man nodded. The light in the tiny room changed abruptly, perhaps because of those steel shutters that suddenly clanged into place over the front windows. With most of the illumination gone, the shadowy clutter looked a little sinister.

"We must have our privacy," the small man said with a toothless grin. "Call me Elvis."

Ethel nodded again. "You can call us Elvis, too."

"Uh-huh," the small Elvis agreed. "You're learning." He swept a hand across his desk. Papers and discs went flying to the floor. "Look here."

A screen was set flat in the desk top. The short Elvis pressed what looked like a torn bag of potato chips. The screen came to life.

"The last known picture of Gert Durston." A heavyset man with bright red hair and a beard stared out at them. "Not that he'll look like that now. Let me engage the local reconstruct program." He reached into a box that read MOON PIES. The image on the screen shifted. The beard vanished, the red hair became slicked-back black. He looked like Elvis. Well, actually, he sort of looked like Gert Durston, trying to look like Elvis. Or maybe like

Jerome, trying to look like Elvis. Or even a little like Ethel, trying to look like Elvis.

Ethel grunted. "This isn't going to be easy."

"Nothing ever is, around here."

Maybe this guy could tell them something they could use. Jerome cleared his throat. "Then Elvis—the world—is different?"

The little guy sneered.

"He's a raw recruit, isn't he? If you had seen half as much of the known universe as I have . . ." He snorted. "Elvis is different, but not that different. You know what this place really is?"

"A tourist trap?" Jerome replied.

"Nine-tenths of the universe is a tourist trap. The other tenth—well, you wouldn't want to go there. No, Elvis is one of those worlds where you've got to know your way around. Durston's no fool. He will have studied this place, found ways to blend in, go with the rock-and-roll flow. Which you, recruit, better remember." He waved a bony finger in Jerome's direction. "One false move on this world and you end up as a chicken fried steak!"

That didn't sound at all pleasant. Chicken fried steak? When things quieted down, Jerome would have to ask his inner voice what that meant.

"Yes, we've come with a full program—both of us." Ethel was beginning to sound the slightest bit annoyed. "Do you have any idea where we might find Durston?"

"Well, now that you mention it . . ." Their contact pressed what looked like a rotting apple core.

For an instant, Jerome thought his head was exploding—from the inside, where someone had misplaced a large bell from a gothic cathedral. Even Ethel took a step away.

"Do you hear it?" the small Elvis called.

How could he help but hear anything else? Right next to the inner voice, the techs back at headquarters had installed the inner alarm, specifically programmed for this mission.

Jerome grabbed the sides of his skull. It didn't help the internal clanging one bit. Durston was near.

Their contact hit the rotten apple a second time. The alarm faded.

The contact shrugged. "If I didn't keep the damper on—always gives me a headache." He waved his hands at the steel shutters. "Durston's almost on top of us. He's got to be working in one of the two clubs up the street."

"You don't know which one?"

"That's your job, not mine." He squinted at Ethel and tugged at his wig, which seemed to have slipped a bit during the alarm. "They've given you both programs. Study them. You'll need all your wits and all that information if you're going to catch Durston."

"But—the alarm," Jerome managed, his voice little more than a croak. While the ringing was gone, his head still shook.

Elvis Ivan nodded his loose-wigged head. "I'll set it so that it will only ring when Durston is in your line of sight. When you look straight at him, the alarm will get faster and louder. What could be easier? Perhaps you'll have time to catch your breath before you pursue him."

Ethel shook her head. "Speed is of the essence. Durston might decide to move."

Their contact sighed and backed away.

"Suit yourself," he replied, turning toward the back of the shop, "so long as that suit looks like Elvis."

He disappeared behind the curtain as the steel shutters rolled away from the windows.

"That's it?" Jerome cried. "That's our local help? He reset the alarm? For one of the two places down the street? What about providing us with helpful local information? What about providing us with some helpful local weapons?"

Ethel looked at him sharply. "Save it for when we're finished—Elvis."

3

Ethel led the way back onto the street. Jerome's head was still pounding. Any attempt to access his inner voice only made the headache worse.

He had thought the alarms were automatic. How could Elvis

Ivan have muffled them? Jerome never knew he could have so many questions. He had too much to learn to be stopped by a throbbing skull.

He took a deep breath and cued his inner voice.

"The fugitive alarm function is triggered automatically when said fugitive is within range, generally five hundred meters," the voice explained, "unless an interrupt is programmed into the planetary parent circuitry. This interrupt is now activated more often than the planners cursbuzz anticipated. Since the alarm razburt sometimes be extremely disruptive, some only advocate its use in combination with sunfluzz buzzmumble gerble snik—"

He stopped the voice abruptly. The headache was so bad, the words were beginning to sound like random noise. He'd have to review everything first break they got. They would get a break, wouldn't they? Jerome realized the only way he could find out was by cueing his inner voice.

"Here," Ethel said, pointing to Blue Hawaii, the much smaller of the two clubs on the street.

"Okay," Jerome managed.

"What do you think?" his partner asked. "The smaller place will be easier to investigate."

"Makes sense to me." Jerome swallowed. That hurt, too. "Let's get it over with."

He let his eyes close for a moment as Ethel opened the door. This headache came from more than the alarm. It was his body's reaction to the night before the jump. If only Mona hadn't gotten so angry. If only he hadn't started to pop those StimJims™.

Jerome would not let this overwhelm him. They trained them at the academy to deal with pain. There. He took deep breaths, and recited the first mantra of release. His neck muscles relaxed; the pressure eased in his temples. Maybe the headache would actually go away.

"Elvis!" Ethel called. Jerome's eyes snapped open. His partner was waiting for him in a hallway bathed in blue light. Her stumbled after her. The boots they'd given him pinched his toes. Maybe he'd concentrate on that for a change.

But the gently undulating light, combined with a soft breeze from who knew where, even made him forget about his boots. Yes, this was much better. The music was almost soothing. Soft guitar, melodic vibes, the occasional birdcall. The hallway opened up ahead into a large, high-ceilinged room, still filled with blue light.

He saw something else that was different about this place. The room was jammed with women. Jerome had seen a few females on the street, but there were a lot more in here. What's more, a lot of the women actually looked like women. Rather than hiding their differences behind their Elvis-wear, these women seemed to do their best to accentuate their more unique qualities.

As the gentle music played, the many women upon the dance floor bobbed up and down in their grass skirts and colorful bikini tops. The dozen or so women gyrating in the hanging cages seemed to prefer fur bikinis, dyed in numerous pastel shades. No matter what their attire, various parts of all these women bounced more than others. Jerome winced. His eyes still weren't quite capable of following something as complex as bouncing.

The mantra, he reminded himself. The mantra.

Jerome cringed a bit as a voice boomed over the gentle music.

"I hope everybody enjoyed that little breather! A bit of that soothing music from the islands. But we know what we like to do on Elvis! Let's rock!"

The room exploded with sound.

BOMP DE BOMP DE BOMP, DE BOMP BOMP!
BOMP DE BOMP DE BOMP, DE BOMP BOMP!

Jerome realized he had stopped breathing. The beat was so loud it almost pushed him off his feet. For a moment, he felt like the massive noise had shocked the headache clear out of him.

With the start of the bass-heavy beat, all the women and the various Elvises scattered about the dance floor before him really started to move; an odd shimmying dance punctuated by everyone jerking their elbows up and down. Lights flashed on and off, making the dance whirl about him in great waves. He would become lost in the sea of dancers. There were already half a dozen of them writhing between him and Ethel. If he wasn't careful, he'd lose his partner in the throng. He tried to control his breathing, find the center he'd been shown in all his training.

The music only grew louder.

Everyone was dancing. Some made motions with their arms as if they were swimming, while others made fists and stuck out their thumbs. Was this some ritual of the planet's inhabitants—the moves symbolic of some deeper meaning? He thought about asking Ethel or keying his inner voice, but he wouldn't be able to hear either of them.

BOMP DE BOMP DE BOMP, DE BOMP BOMP!

Women were smiling at him everywhere. They gathered around him, bouncing suggestively, as if they expected him to join the dance!

BOMP DE BOMP DE BOMP, DE BOMP BOMP!

They pressed in, everywhere he turned. He was surrounded by blondes! He could no longer stand the pressure!

"What is this?" Jerome cried aloud.

"The frug," a passing Elvis replied.

Whatever that meant. Yet the women all continued to smile. BOMP DE BOMP! He had no reason to panic. He would have to make the best of his situation. BOMP DE BOMP! That was one of the most important lessons they taught back at the academy, after all. Perhaps, if he were to study those closest to him, he could discern valuable information that would help him in his mission. DE BOMP BOMP!

Many in his immediate vicinity wore long hair styled in what his inner voice referred to as a "flip." Yeah. His inner voice. It seemed to have adjusted itself within his skull to be heard over the music. Excellent. Now that his headache was gone—

"Do you want more?" the disembodied voice somehow called over the music.

"Yeah!" everybody cheered.

"I can't hear you!" the first voice replied.

"Yeah!" everybody cheered louder.

"DO YOU WANT MORE?"

"YEAH!"

"DO YOU WANT IT LOUDER?"

"YEAH!"

"I CAN'T HEAR YOU!"

The crowd noise became so loud it almost forced Jerome to his knees.

But that was nothing compared to what happened next.

The music grew louder than anything Jerome had ever heard in his entire life.

BOMP DE BOMP DE BOMP, DE BOMP BOMP!

Whammo. Jerome gasped, and barely prevented himself from falling to his knees. Last time, he had stopped breathing. This time, for an instant he forgot how to use his lungs. Jerome screamed. Not that anybody heard.

BOMP DE BOMP DE BOMP, DE BOMP BOMP!

Headache? He could no longer call what went on his head anything so simple. He realized that all the things banging around in his head hadn't vanished; rather they had just been marshaling their forces for a new attack. What had once been a headache graduated to a pain beyond words.

He grabbed his head and howled.

"Way gone, guy!" somebody nearby called in admiration. "That's the way to rock!"

BOMP DE BOMP DE BOMP, DE BOMP BOMP!

Pound de pound pound, his head replied. Jerome only howled some more. His knees were getting weak, wobbling back and forth. Some fool slapped him on the back. He almost fell on the floor.

"Hey! Buddy!"

Jerome peered through his pain and saw a curtain move nearby. Somebody was waving to him from a corner of the room.

"What?" he managed over the earsplitting din.

The hand beckoned him forward. "Come on over."

Even through his pain, this seemed suspicious. Why weren't they calling him Elvis? Wasn't Buddy some other rock-and-roll guy? Still, this could be a lead. Jerome stumbled toward the curtain.

The other man frowned as Jerome approached. Jerome squinted, trying to bring the man behind the curtain into focus. The other man's gray hair would have made him look distinguished, if he hadn't been wearing a sport coat with checks so loud that Jerome's brain wanted to reject the pattern outright.

Jerome stopped a few feet away from the stranger. The curtain closed behind Jerome's back, cutting them off from the rest of the crowd. Belatedly, Jerome thought of Ethel. It might have been a good idea to tell her where he was going.

The older man smiled. "You look like you're in need of a little help."

"Help?" Jerome managed, the syllable sounding more like a burp than a word. The checks of the sport coat danced before his eyes. Was this another example of the frug? It made him feel even worse than before.

"Take a couple deep breaths." The other man spoke soothingly. "It's darker here, and quieter."

Was his condition that obvious? Maybe it was because he was constantly swaying. Or the sweat that plastered his hair to his head. Or the no-doubt painful scowl he wore on his face. The older man unbuttoned his sport coat, and opened the jacket to show what was hidden inside. The coat's lining was jammed with transparent pockets, each pocket holding tubes filled with liquids or vials of tablets or assorted hypos of every conceivable color.

Jerome knew what those were.

"Drugs," he managed.

The other man smiled encouragingly. "See? You're not that far gone. But these are not just drugs. These are wonder drugs."

The other man pointed at a few of the tubes and vials.

"These are uppers. Those are downers. These take you in some other directions."

Jerome thought he'd be more interested if all the colors didn't hurt his eyes. And something else about them was bothering Jerome.

Oh, yeah.

"Aren't they illegal?"

The checkered man smiled. "Are you kidding? Drugs are what makes Elvis run."

Jerome didn't know what to say. He certainly needed something if he was going to be of any use at all.

"But—"

"Say no more. I'm a trained professional." The older man studied the pockets to his left, then pulled one of the hypos free of its transparent pocket. "I know just what you need."

"But—" Jerome tried again.

"Just think of this as another little highlight to your visit." The other man reached for Jerome's arm. "Sooner or later, everything happens on Elvis."

"But—"

"You won't feel a thing." He pressed the colored hypo against Jerome's skin. "It's instantly absorbed through the skin, right into the bloodstream."

Jerome felt the slightest tingle just above his elbow. "Whoa! But these aren't free—"

The other man nodded agreeably.

"We give you the first one at a discount. Our way of welcoming the tourist trade. Hey, they're already charged to your account." He leaned back and grinned. "It'll take a minute or two for them to hit your brain."

"Brain—" Jerome pondered. "But won't I feel—"

The other fellow chuckled. "Hey, once those are done with you, you won't feel a thing." He waved. "You can thank me later. I'll find you when you need to—renew your prescription."

Jerome realized the curtain had closed behind him, and he was back out on the dance floor. How did that happen?

"Elvis!"

He looked around to see who was talking to him. Maybe his headache *was* a little bit better. Ethel stood by his side. She tugged at his sleeve,

"Don't you hear it?" she insisted.

The beat was so loud, it took a minute for him to identify the underlying ringing.

"The alarm," his inner voice remarked.

The alarm—reset so that it would only ring when their objective was right before them. Gert Durston was somewhere in the room! And what had that little Ivan Elvis said? Oh, yeah! He had to be looking right at him!

But he was looking at a hundred or more in the crowd before

him, a vast mass of frugging flesh! How could they hope to apprehend him in this kind of a crowd? How could he hope to do anything with this sort of headache? No doubt his inner voice had an
answer to all this as well.

Jerome blinked as he realized three things:

He could actually hear his inner voice.

The headache was gone.

And this place was rocking!

The music was a part of him, the bass line his pulse, the wailing guitar his dancing feet, the drums his pounding fists. He *was*
rock and roll!

BOMP DE BOMP DE BOMP, DE BOMP BOMP!

Why hadn't he felt this way before?

Jerome started shaking. The Elvises around him danced and
nodded in approval. And look at the way those go-go girls smiled
his way!

"What are you doing?" Ethel demanded. "What about Gert
Durston?"

Yeah! Gert Durston! He could take on Gert Durston, with one
polyester hand tied behind his back! Heck, he could take on all of
Elvis!

BOMP DE BOMP DE BOMP, DE BOMP BOMP!

This wasn't a job. It was a party! The crowd surged around them.
Hey, this music really swung. That's what they said, wasn't it?

"Rocks," his inner voice corrected him. "That is the proper
term. Although this might not be the ideal time to discuss propriety. Man, this music is solid gone!"

He'd never heard his inner voice sound so enthusiastic.

BOMP DE BOMP DE BOMP, DE BOMP BOMP!

His body might be rockin', but his mind was totally clear. As
good as he felt, he needed a plan. And now that he could access
his inner voice, he actually could formulate a course of action.

"So what can you tell me about Gert Durston?"

The inner voice obliged: "Gert Durston was born thirty-seven
years ago into a disadvantaged home on the planet Sven. At an
early age, he decided he would never be disadvantaged again—"

Jerome shook his head to stop the flow. While this might be

valuable information under other circumstances, he needed something more immediate.

"How about something more recent?" he asked. "Modes of operation, suspected crimes, that sort of thing."

"Oh, well, why didn't you say so? My banks hold sixteen minor and eleven major infractions that Durston is wanted for. From the most recent, these include: On Monty's World, he's wanted for unlawful cavorting. Within the sea of Kebbob, he has been suspected of consorting with ameboids. On the desiccated plains of High Cavatt, he is accused of decompressing—"

No, that wasn't it either. "Aren't there any more *serious* crimes?"

"Well, he is suspected of ruining an entire planet's economy. Boy, this place is really rockin'! And then there are those three murders—"

"Murders?"

"Whoopie!" his inner voice replied.

"I need some specifics."

"Specifics spemicus! Whoopie! I'm takin' care of business, baby!"

Taking care of business? Jerome's feet were moving with the beat. He had to focus. "I gave you a direct command!"

"I mean, gosh darn, who can concentrate with all that music going on? Whoopie!"

Gosh darn? Whoopie? Jerome didn't know what to say.

"*Whoopie* is a perfectly good word," the inner voice sounded the slightest bit defensive. "It indicates excitement, enjoyment, and well—it rocks. Whoopie!"

Perhaps he couldn't depend on his inner voice after all.

Ethel was at his side. Oh yeah, Ethel. Attractive. Especially the way that jumpsuit emphasized her curves. And the way her slicked-back hair made her look just like Elvis.

He found Elvis attractive? Maybe the drugs were affecting more than just Jerome's inner voice.

"Look!" said somebody—maybe Ethel, maybe his inner voice, maybe even Jerome. "It's Durston!"

He turned to see a heavyset man take the stage as his personal alarm mixed with the noise around him.

"Height, weight, general physical characteristics all check," his inner voice chimed in. "Ninety-eight-point-six percent confirmation. Whoopie!"

Ethel tugged at his polyester sleeve, pointing at their goal. He managed a nod. Somehow, they had to corner Durston long enough to subdue him. But how could they do it in this crowd?

Durston raised his arms to quiet the noise of the crowd. "Thank you very much," he drawled. "You remember such great songs as 'Rock-a-Hula-Baby,' 'It's Carnival Time,' and 'You Can't Say No to Acapulco'?" The crowd cheered at the mention of each title. "Well, I'm going to sing a brand-new song—" The crowd was suddenly very still. "—but its style is pure Elvis!"

The crowd went wild as the music surged again. Durston swiveled his hips as he belted out the words:

"Well, I'm new here, I'm a guest."
BOMP DE BOMP DE BOMP, DE BOMP BOMP!
"But this planet is the best."
BOMP DE BOMP DE BOMP, DE BOMP BOMP!
"How can anybody stroll,"
BOMP DE BOMP DE BOMP, DE BOMP BOMP!
"When you can choose to rock and roll!"

His words were driving the room into a frenzy! Jerome had to control himself. But his feet were moving along with all the rest!

Inner voice! he thought, forcing himself to concentrate despite the pounding beat. How can I get through this crowd?

His inner voice appeared to be singing along with Durston. Jerome felt his elbows twitch with the power of the music. Yeah! The frug! Why think, when you could dance?

He was almost jerked from his feet. His partner had a firm grip on his arm and was taking him with her.

"Jerk," his inner voice rambled. "Along with the frug, the hitchhike, the swim—"

Jerome realized they were headed straight for the stage, shoving aside anyone who got in their way. Ethel and Jerome were going to apprehend the felon, no matter what Jerome or his feet had planned.

But the crowd grew ever thicker as they approached the stage.

Their way was blocked by a surging mass of dancers. And some of the dancers were objecting to Ethel's forceful advance.

"Hey," shouted one portly, older Elvis, "be cool, baby!"

She elbowed him in the face. He crumpled to the dance floor. But the half-dozen Elvises in the immediate vicinity looked very angry.

"Nobody treats Elvis like that!"

"You don't lay a hand on the King!"

"There's a riot goin' on!" Jerome's inner voice announced. "Remember your hand-to-hand training."

Oh, yeah, now that the inner voice reminded him, it all came back. He could use those Elvis-approved kung fu moves! He let his inner voice guide his form as he swung arms and legs in the air.

"Hi-ya!" Jerome screamed. "Whoopie!" This was fun, even though it didn't look all that different from the dancing. And while his chops and kicks weren't connecting with any of their opponents, the other Elvises had all backed a few feet away to properly admire his moves.

"Everything's hip on Elvis!" his inner voice assured him.

A hundred faces danced around him, then swirled around him, then turned upside down around him.

"Whoa!" Jerome shouted. "What's going on?"

His inner voice sounded even more enthusiastic. "Now the drugs are *really* kicking in!"

He looked up to see a tall, overmuscled Elvis standing above him.

"Who's messing with my performance?"

Oh. That's what that ringing alarm meant. He was staring straight at Gert Durston!

"Whoopie!" warned his inner voice.

Now he was staring straight at Gert Durston's fist!

A hundred miles away, that fist connected with Jerome's jaw. Another fifty miles distant, another fist got him in the stomach. Jerome thought he felt pain, very far away. But the first fist was coming back again, straight for Jerome's nose.

This pain was considerably closer.

"Ladies and gentlemen!" his inner voice called. "Elvis has left the building!"

After that, Jerome couldn't remember a thing.

4

Jerome opened his eyes and saw Elvis.

"Tee hee," Elvis replied in a high, girlish voice. The sound hurt his head. On closer inspection, this Elvis was wearing somewhat more mascara than one would regularly expect from the King. Jerome shifted his gaze—that hurt, too—to see that his head rested on a pillow covered with leopard spots. Not that the spots would stay in one place. Jerome closed his eyes so he could focus on the pain. He groaned.

"Tee hee," Elvis repeated. She pulled her arms free of the tangle of spotted sheets. Apparently, she was naked. "A little the worse for wear, are we, tiger? Well, I shouldn't wonder, after last night—"

"Night?" Jerome managed. It hurt to talk, too, in so many ways, sore teeth, sore tongue, stiff vocal cords, aching lungs and beyond. So this must be the next day. Whoa. If he had thought he had been hungover before . . . Yesterday had been the economy size—today, he was sporting the super jumbo. The thought hurt his brain.

"I've never seen anybody with more of the spirit of Elvis!" the other, apparently female Elvis continued. "Wild, crazy, unafraid of death or any consequences. When you took on that black-leather Elvis gang after the moonshine drinking contest—" She whistled in admiration.

"Gang? Moonshine?" Jerome couldn't remember any of this. Or much of anything else.

"And then when you won the prize for Bacon Fat Wrestling—"

No. He did remember something. Gert Durston's fist. And his partner. What had happened to his partner?

"And I've never seen anybody do *that* with a guitar—"

He squinted at his surroundings. The walls were done in tiger stripes. The ceiling was one huge mirror.

"What is this place?"

"Tee hee. You insisted on the Jungle Room. And then you really showed what an animal—"

"But where's Ethel?" Jerome blurted. That's what he was really worried about. The last thing he remembered, she had him by the arm. And then?

The other Elvis looked shocked. "Ethel? Who's Ethel?"

Jerome frowned, even with the pounding, throbbing, and jackhammering that was going on in his skull, he still remembered that he was on a clandestine mission. So what could he tell a native Elvisean? Worse, what had he told her already?

"She's—uh—the woman I came here with."

His bedmate recoiled in distaste. "What? After everything you told me last night? I should have known—this was just another Elvis One Night Stand!"

"Wait!" Jerome called as she leapt off the bed. "No! I didn't mean—" But what did he mean? And what had he done with this woman anyway?

"Well, you'll be the one who's lonesome tonight! Good-bye!" She grabbed her black leather outfit and ran from the room. A moment later, he heard an outer door slam.

Jerome was confused. Well, he'd been confused since he'd gotten here. What could he do without his partner? He had never really paid attention in the briefings, always figuring Ethel would carry the ball. She always knew enough for both of them.

But he still wasn't alone. The jump police had supplied an answer in his own skull—a device that was with him throughout everything that happened, no doubt recording all that was beyond his somewhat addled senses, a device that would help him put everything back together for good.

Jerome pressed his temples. "What am I going to do?" he wailed.

"Oooh," his inner voice moaned. "Don't talk to me."

"But—" Jerome protested.

"Go away," his inner voice added. "I'm not talking to anyone. I may never talk again."

For an instant, Jerome forgot his own headache. "So last night got to you, too? I didn't think that was possible."

"Never happened before." The inner voice groaned. "Not in the entire history of inner-voice technology. Apparently, I never experienced the kind of drugs you get on Elvis. Apparently, no inner voice ever experienced those kind of drugs. Now shut up, and let me degenerate in peace."

This was impossible. Wasn't it? Jerome wished now he had stayed awake in more of those inner-voice classes.

"There's got to be some way I can get out of this."

Someone coughed behind him. "I thought you'd never ask."

Jerome screamed. A man stood by the side of the bed.

He was dressed somewhat formally for this planet, what with the tie and sport coat and all. And didn't Jerome remember those checks from somewhere?

"Sorry. You startled—I'm not quite myself—"

"I've got just the thing for you." The man pulled something from the inside of his sport coat—a long tube filled with swirling colors. Jerome had a vague memory that this guy was some kind of doctor.

The man leaned down to lift Jerome's arm and press the tube against his skin. The contents sparkled as they flowed into his arm.

"Wait!" Jerome called. What did this guy think he was— "Whoa!" He felt like somebody had just turned on the air-conditioning in his head. "Whee!" What was he worried about, anyway?

"That cute little Elvis let me in as she was leaving," the doc explained as he tucked the empty vial into the lining of his coat. "I knew you needed me."

"You were there—last night."

"Always at your service," the doctor agreed.

"Have you seen my partner?"

The doc thought for a moment. "Oh, that other female Elvis? She went off with that big, beefy singer. Who wouldn't? I mean, that guy could rock! Hey. I wouldn't worry. If you can pick up chicks like that little number that just ran out of here—"

"But no—" Jerome interrupted, worried again about how

much he might reveal. "She's my—business partner—we had meetings—"

"I wouldn't worry. Everybody runs into everybody else on Elvis again. I found you, didn't I?"

Well, yeah, Jerome thought. In fact, he suddenly felt as though he could do anything. He'd find Durston, rescue Ethel, win the day, get a handful of medals, and date another three or four of those cute chicks!

Jerome frowned. Well, he would, unless—

"But, if this wears off—"

"I'll know before you do. It's my business. And don't worry now, you've got a long way to go. The new batch hasn't even really kicked in yet." He waved jauntily as he left the room.

"What? What have you given me?"

"You'll know in a minute or two," the doctor called as he disappeared. "Glad to be of service!"

The outer door slammed again.

"I'm back," his inner voice announced in a much firmer tone. "And I'm clear."

"Not for long. You heard what the doc said?"

"There must be ways to minimize the effects. Eat something, drink water, walk around the room. Let's get moving."

"Okay. But let's call Ethel first." Now that the inner voice was back, they should have a direct line of communication.

"Can't get through," the voice announced after a moment. "Something's in the way."

"Her inner voice is giving you a busy signal?"

"Not busy. More like it's—clogged. Don't ask me—I'm on drugs. We'd better move."

Jerome stood at last. No problem there. Well, maybe he was a little light-headed. And look at that wallpaper! He had never realized how intricate a tiger-stripe pattern could be. What fascinating detail—the way the jagged black swept across the orange! He could stare at the wall for hours.

"Wait a minute!" his inner voice warned.

Jerome blinked. The stripes were moving.

"Down, man, down!" his inner voice shrieked.

He looked down. No, actually, he was moving. His pointy-toed boots were floating, six feet above the green carpet! ("Astroturf," his inner voice informed him.)

"Out of sight!" his inner voice exclaimed.

Jerome's ears were filled with music. ("'Hound Dog,'" his inner voice explained.) Pounding drums, ringing guitars, and the voice of the King with highly professional vocal backing. ("The Jordanaires," the inner voice added.) It was pretty cosmic.

The music shifted. ("'Baby, Let's Play House,'" the inner voice amended.) As did the scene around them. They were no longer in the jungle room. In fact, Jerome wondered if they were even still on the planet Elvis.

He appeared to be floating in a great dark cavern of some sort, a huge space whose edges were lost in shadow. The air around him was filled with hundreds of spinning golden discs. But the center of the place held an even stranger sight.

Three small, wrinkled creatures stared at him from a column of light. While the three bore little resemblance to humans, Jerome did find something oddly familiar about them. Perhaps it was the Elvis wig that each of them wore.

What? Who? When? Jerome thought.

"I have no idea," his inner voice confessed.

One of the three spoke, or maybe he sang. *Welcome, Jerome. You do us honor.*

"How did I get here?" Jerome asked. "How did you find me?"

We have done nothing. The singing voice, though deep, was very far away, and sometimes faded beneath a burst of static. *It was you who have reached us.*

You have a special gift, a second voice sang, in a voice that might be deeper still. *It is found in the combination of your normal mind, that device you call the inner voice, and the magic pharmaceuticals of Elvis. Alone, each is ordinary, unremarkable, mundane. But together—*

Much like dual carburetors, Jerome thought a third added. With the static, it was difficult to tell. *Elvis greatly admired dual carbs.*

As I was saying. Together, they form all that is Elvis.

A higher state of Elvisness.

The three together. That would be like triple carbs. The King would have liked that.

We are the AEC. The Alien Elvis Consciousness.

We seek the perfection of Elvis.

Elvis transcends simple musical genres, simple worlds, even simple species.

You have sought us out for a reason.

"I have?" Jerome asked.

Gert Durston.

He is the playboy trying to steal Elvis's girl, the French race-car driver with his eye on Ann-Margret, the evil slumlord trying to shut down Dr. Elvis's ghetto clinic!

He is everything unElvis. His music must end.

And only your Elvisness may end it!

Go now, Jerome SmithSeven! the first sang.

Swivel the hips, the second added.

Find the chord, the third chorused.

Take care of business! sang the three in perfect harmony.

"But—" Jerome began.

It was already too late. The three creatures were lost in the swirling mists as softer music ("Can't Help Falling in Love") faded away.

"Was any of that real?" Jerome whispered as he found himself lost in darkness.

"Don't ask me," the inner voice whispered back. "I'm in here with you."

The world took shape around them.

They still weren't in the Jungle Room. Instead, they were on the nighttime streets of Elvis.

Jerome looked at the plethora of neon before him. "I'm guessing this is where we find Ethel."

He stood before a great building that stretched in either direction as far as he could see. The largest of the seemingly infinite number of the building's glowing signs announced its name.

ELVIS-O-RAMA.

The place was so gaudy it made the nightclubs from the night before seem tasteful and refined. Smaller neon spelled out types of music and brands of beer. The largest of the signs appeared to be a fifty-foot-high Elvis, swinging white spangled hips left and right.

"Modeled after Elvis's Las Vegas period." The inner voice used Jerome's hand to point at a door marked DELIVERIES.

"Why not?" the voice added. "We're here to deliver."

Jerome pushed open the door and stopped dead in his boots.

He stood at the edge of a large storage area. Ethel sat in the middle of the room. He barely recognized his partner with her puffy cheeks and wild eyes. She was strapped into a large machine that repeatedly opened and closed her mouth, pushing some deep brown mush inside. The machine relentlessly pushed food into her mouth and forced her to chew. She must have been trapped like this for hours. The seams of her black jumpsuit were already showing signs of strain.

She stared at Jerome as he approached.

"Jmmfff! Thmm gmm yrr hrrrr!"

"What?" Jerome whispered.

A large man stepped from the shadows.

" 'Jerome,' she says. 'Thank god you're here.' " Gert Durston grinned. "I have a lot of experience interpreting for those in the chompamatic."

He patted the side of the machine as it continued Ethel's force-feeding. "It's ingenious, really. We keep her throat open with regular squirts of root beer as the machinery encourages constant chewing and swallowing action. And of course, a never-ending supply of fried peanut butter and banana sandwiches. In a matter of days, every major vein and artery, muscle and organ in her entire body will be clogged with fat! And so she will expire—pale, bloated, peanut butter dripping from every orifice . . ." Durston sighed happily. "It's an Elvis kind of death."

"Ethel!" Jerome called. "What do you want me to do?"

"Mrrfflll!" She replied urgently. "Drff smmll crxxx lbbll!"

" 'Give up,' she says," Durston interjected. " 'Fried peanut butter is tasty.' "

Jerome frowned. "She's not saying that!"

"How can you tell? Her mouth is full."

A red light went on overhead.

Durston glanced at the interruption. "A shame we can't continue this pleasant discourse. And even more of a shame you jump cops got in my way."

"Wttchuutt!" Ethel moaned.

Too late. Jerome was roughly grabbed from behind by some other fiendish mechanical device. Before he could react, he was clamped firmly against the wall!

Durston grinned. "I just want the simple things in life—money, women, flashy clothes, the adoration of huge crowds. I finally found them all on Elvis."

The red light overhead began to flash.

"But you'll have to excuse me. It's showtime!"

Jerome panicked. He didn't want to be left, trapped like this.

"How would you know?" he blurted.

"Excuse me?" One corner of Durston's smile turned down.

Jerome tried on his best Elvis sneer. "I saw that pitiful excuse for a song you did over at Blue Hawaii."

"I occasionally perform at the lesser clubs as a form of advertising." Durston's smile disappeared. "What do you mean—pitiful?"

"I don't know. Maybe it was your squeaky voice. And the way you move. It's like you've got two left hips. And you call yourself Elvis?"

Durston's face twisted into a very unElvis rage. "That's it! No chompamatic for you! I'll find some *really* disgusting way for you to die."

He strode quickly from the room.

Jerome sighed. "That didn't work."

But it set the stage.

Jerome frowned at the sudden snatch of music.

"I think our friends are still with us," his inner voice said.

No, you *are still with us,* sang the reply.

In mere minutes, you will enter a state of Elvis.

And Gert Durston will learn the meaning of showtime!

"But I'm stuck here!" Jerome pointed out. "Strapped against the wall!"

The true Elvis is never stuck anywhere.

You know what is required.

"We do," his inner voice replied, "don't we?"

Jerome knew indeed. He had to swivel the hips. He had to find the chord. He had to take care of business!

He sang a single note. His inner voice added harmony. And somewhere in the static-filled distance, three other voices joined in.

The pressure was gone from his arms. He looked down, and saw that his restraints had popped open, hanging off his wrists. He was free.

"Did I do that?" he said in wonder.

No, that was done by something greater.

"Greater?"

Nothing can stand before the true *power of Elvis.*

"Mrrffllsttll!" came the cry from the constantly feeding machine.

"Ethel!" Jerome ran across the room. "I'll stop this!" He pulled a large red lever. The machine ground to a halt, and he quickly pulled apart the restraints surrounding his partner's head. She coughed as he freed her from the mechanism.

Jerome was more than happy to put her in charge. "Can you talk?" he asked. Ethel would tell him what to do! She put a hand to her peanut-butter-smeared chest, and took long, shallow breaths.

"We have to get Durston!" Jerome urged.

She looked at him with some dismay.

"Pardon me—*burp*—*urp*. I have to find the facilities."

"But—"

"Sorry—*burp*—I ate two hundred and forty-three sandwiches—*urp*—and then I lost count—*urp*—not to mention—*burp*—root beer. I'll catch up when I can."

She staggered back into the dark recesses of the room.

Jerome realized he couldn't wait for her. Someone had to apprehend Gert Durston before he could escape once more.

He would have to be Elvis all alone.

"Not alone!" his inner voice reminded him. "Remember what the aliens said? There are three of us!"

"Uh-huh," Jerome replied. No. Not Jerome.

The aliens had been right.

Now he was Elvis.

5

"Ladies and gentlemen! Elvis-O-Rama is proud to present—Elvis!"

The crowd was screaming as Jerome entered the back of the club. At the far end of the room, Gert Durston stood on a stage, bathed in a single spotlight. He started out with "Blue Suede Shoes." He put a lot of energy behind it, and everyone swung to the beat. But while he might have had energy, he wasn't Elvis.

"Thank you very much!" Durston called to the adulation of the crowd. He signaled to the band to begin another number.

But Jerome had heard enough.

"Hey, baby!" he called over a suddenly silent crowd. "You call that—Elvis?"

The drugs were with him now. His inner voice was humming "Blue Moon of Kentucky." Or maybe it was "Do the Clam." Elvis had sung hundreds, maybe thousands of songs. And Jerome knew them all.

He strode forward, aware of every muscle in his body, the roll of the hips, the twitch of the sneer. He was being driven by something larger than himself. He was being driven by Elvis.

The crowd could sense it, too. No one was paying attention to Durston anymore. And Durston was furious.

"You?" he shouted from the stage. "How did you get out? There's no place for the likes of you at Elvis-O-Rama!"

Jerome showed his sneer to the crowd. "That doesn't sound much like Elvis. It sounds like the greedy club owner out to cheat Elvis, the college-educated know-it-all trying to put Elvis down, the guy with too much money who's stealing Elvis's girl!"

The crowd roared with him. "El-vis!" they chanted as one. "El-vis! El-vis! El-vis!"

Durston backed away as Jerome approached the stage.

"I'll show you how it's done." He waved to the crowd. "When I sing it, you just won't see those blue suede shoes, you'll be wearing them!"

As he climbed onto the stage he saw that both Ethel and Elvis Ivan stood in the wings. And they were carrying submission guns. This was the endgame, as long as Jerome could do his part.

But what could Elvis do but sing?

"Well, it's one for the money, two for the show . . ."

He sang, but he was beyond song. His hips swiveled with the rhythm of the stars. His white polyester jumpsuit shone like a beacon of truth, and his golden belt shone as though it had captured a piece of the sun.

He sang with everything that was Jerome, topped by the power of his inner voice and the wonder chemicals of the planet Elvis. The music welled around him, until he felt he was floating upon the power of rock and roll, accompanied by perfect, if slightly static-filled, vocal backing.

Out of the corner of his eye, he saw Durston backing behind the curtains and a flash that meant someone had used one of the guns. Durston fell heavily to the floor. The music was so loud his fall made no discernible noise.

Jerome segued into "Jailhouse Rock." The band shifted effortlessly, as though they had backed this particular singer forever. But they had, because now he truly was Elvis.

If the crowd had been wild before, they went absolutely crazy now. Durston was gone, spirited away during Jerome's last chorus. Nobody noticed.

Jerome resisted the urge to sing another song. He had had his moment of pure Elvis. He waved to crowd, then quickly retreated as he heard the announcer's voice behind him.

"Ladies and gentlemen. Elvis has left the building!"

And this time, Elvis had done it his way.

6

"—despite certain irregularities, you are to be commended for your actions."

Jerome's attention snapped back to Jump Officer OneO'Leary. They had been in this debriefing for well over an hour, despite the fact that neither Ethel nor Jerome had anything to add to their reports. He just wished he felt a little better. It had been a day and a half since they had brought Durston back, and Jerome's throbbing skull had reminded him of every minute—no, every nanosecond—of that time. If jump technology couldn't take your clothes, why did it have to bring your hangover?

"We've already explained about the problems with Jerome SmithSeven's inner voice—" Ethel said for perhaps the fifth time.

"Yes, I have it all here, Agent NineThompson—the necessity to go underground, the unfortunate encounter with certain foreign substances, which appeared to have temporarily disrupted the voice's recording mechanism. It is all noted. And we can piece together what happened from your testimony, as well as your inner voice, augmented by the report from our field agent. And SmithSeven seems to have overcome the loss of his inner voice in the field with both courage and integrity. Still, this office does not appreciate loose ends—" OneO'Leary hesitated. "But Durston is back in custody. In the end, that's what matters most."

Jerome nodded—which of course hurt. Actually, he hadn't lost his inner voice. What with all that it had been through, the device simply refused to talk to anybody. But that was one more thing the jump authorities didn't need to know. He hummed to himself—a little piece of "Paradise, Hawaiian Style." He imagined—or did he?—that he could hear some faint, static-filled vocal accompaniment. "Uh-huh," he said to himself.

Maybe a little bit of Elvis was still with him.

Maurice OneO'Leary was talking about commendations for both of them and how the team might graduate to even more sensitive missions. Ethel seemed to be actually paying attention. Jerome would have to ask her what their boss really said once he felt a little better.

This hangover couldn't last forever. He wondered if Mona was free this weekend. He looked up to see Ethel standing by his side, and realized they were dismissed at last. He stood and followed Ethel into the corridor.

Even with the headache he felt like he had more spring in his step, a certain rhythm to his walk. Maybe he would always have a bit of Elvis in him. But then the headache stabbed back in. He groaned and frowned.

"Still not feeling up to par?" Ethel asked. She waved at a doorway down the hall. "Why don't you visit the infirmary?"

"Uh-huh," Jerome murmured. No doubt, he was still feeling the last effects of the Elvis superdrugs; but the jump docs had probably seen much worse than that before. As usual, Ethel knew exactly what to do.

She called out that she'd see him next week—after she had gone on a diet. He laughed and opened the infirmary door.

The nurse immediately ushered him into an examination room.

"Don't worry, Mr. SmithSeven!" the doctor's voice preceded him as he pushed open the door. "We'll fix you up like new."

Better than new, Jerome thought, because now I have a piece of Elvis. But all thoughts of Elvis left him as he looked up at the man who entered the room.

Why was the doctor wearing a checkered suit?

Great White Hope

Daniel Pearlman

1

"They lost our luggage," said Angie, applying dark red lipstick while looking into the mirror of the compact she dug out of her alligator bag. "Fuckin' Aeronaves is totally full of shit and you believe 'em."

Jason slumped against the back of the stone bench and resisted the urge to disagree. Angie's bag was the same shade as her Acapulco tan. The shellacked head of the alligator fixed him with its red-beaded eyes. It reminded him of the snake heads at the base of the serpent columns flanking the portal of the Temple of the Jaguars. Stony eyes glaring, still guarding sacred mysteries. That was at—where? Uxmal? No. Chichén Itzá. Two weeks ago in Yucatán. He'd like to have stayed longer, but ruins bored Angie, and besides it almost never stopped raining.

"Just a simple, ordinary flight from Acapulco to Mexico City, and those morons—I bet they stole them," she said, switching from lipstick to hairbrush as she spoke. It was warm and sunny and dry, and the late-afternoon breeze whipped her hair against her lips. "I'm a mess. Why we ever took that bus full of chickens to get here instead of the plane—"

"We wanted to see Morelia."

"A total bust!" said Angie.

If Jason were to name Angie's one outstanding feature—

177

leaving aside her slinky hips and melon-breasted torso—it would be those glistening waves of hair that flowed like black gold down to the middle of her back. The raggedy kids and the neatly dressed adults who occupied separate stone benches in the square were united at least in their stares, which Jason had learned to ignore in the States but seemed triply intrusive in Mexico. After three weeks of travel, he still felt the mosquito-like buzz of those eyes, whereas gawkers never bothered Angie.

"You're supposed to know Spanish," said Angie. "Well how come you couldn't *demand* that we get our stuff back—*before* we left Mexico City? Three days' delay so far! How we gonna enjoy Guadalajara now without our fucking luggage?"

"Fortunately," said Jason, patting a red leather bag on the bench beside him, "our carry-on has basics for three or four days."

"One dress! Only one dress, just what I'm wearing."

"And they promised to notify American Express as soon it arrives by bus."

"You should've yelled at them in English, Jay. As soon as they heard you fumfering in Spanish, they knew they had you over a barrel." Angie put away her toiletries and snapped her handbag shut. "If my father'd been there—"

"I don't want to hear about your father."

"If my father'd been there, that clerk would have shit his pants so hard he'd have catapulted off to Acapulco—and back the same day—with our bags, and with shit to spare."

"Gee," said Jason, "maybe we should've invited your father to come with us. I guess it's not enough being in each other's faces, the three of us, all day long, five days a week, all year long. And that's not to *mention* the weekends I've spent running rush jobs off for him."

"What's your problem, Jay? He gave you all the overtime you wanted. In the two years we've been married—"

"He piled on the overtime because he thought I couldn't handle it."

"What?"

"Do you think he really gave a crap about my wanting to save up money so I could go back to school?"

"Of course! He's even given us this vacation—so you can practice your freakin' Spanish and be a better teacher for it."

"You're about as eager for me to quit working for him as he is."

"You're a good worker. You know all the offset presses as well as he does. In another year you'd make manager."

"In another year we'd all be in jail if he carried out his plan to print *money*."

"That's a lot of crap, his way of joking," she said, turning around, feigning interest in the market behind the square. They hadn't explored that sprawling market yet. They first had to find lodgings they could agree on. After a cab dropped them off in the city center, near the cathedral, they had wandered around on foot, looking for an acceptable, medium-priced hotel, then stopped for a rest where they now sat and argued, in the Plaza San Juan de Diós.

"You never acted positive about my wanting to go back to school. All it'll take me is three semesters to finish my Ed degree. One more lousy year and a half."

"I'm positive, I'm positive! But meanwhile, what's in it for me, Jay? Another couple of years as Dad's bookkeeper, that's what in it for me."

"Instead of?"

"What do you mean, 'instead of'?"

"I mean, instead of what he and your mother want you to do, stay home and pump out a baby."

"Have I ever told you I wanted to have a baby?"

"I don't know, Anj. It's like they're always hinting, putting pressure on us, on *me*, to sacrifice my career goals so that—"

"If it happens, it happens."

"What's that supposed to mean? You're on the Pill."

"It's not one hundred percent effective."

Jason grew suddenly anxious. "You do have them on you, right? You didn't leave them in the luggage?"

Frowning, Angie unsnapped her bag, poked around, and drew forth the compactlike container of her month's supply. Jason felt both embarrassed and relieved. One slip could ruin his greatest hope.

"Seen enough?" She thrust the pale green disc back into her purse. "There are rumors that they're not even safe," she muttered, looking off at the wind-ruffled trees of the plaza. "They only came out a couple years ago, you know."

2

"Got the time, fella?"

The gruff American voice descended from Jason's left. He looked up into a weathered face, into iron-gray eyes beneath a stormy, bushy brow. As they sized each other up, the old guy stood there tall and ramrod-straight. His pinstripe suit and yellow tie showed hardly a wrinkle. It took Jason a few seconds to switch gears and glance at his watch.

"Six-fifteen," he said.

"Thanks. Americans?"

"Yes. From New York."

"Pittsburgh for me. Mind if I sit down?"

"There's plenty of room," said Jason, pointing to the space beside him. The elderly stranger patted his tie and tugged at the lapels of his suit. As far as Jason could judge, the intruder was in his seventies and looked pretty hale for his age.

"Do I have the lady's permission?" he asked with a courtly-comical bow. His abundant white hair, streaked with yellow and combed straight back, was not covered with a hat, but if he'd worn one, Jason thought, he'd have doffed it.

"Feel free," said Angie.

As he eased down next to Jason, the oldster thrust out a big, knobby hand and pulled back the sleeve. "Frank Moran wore a gold Rolex, right on that wrist," he said, "up till last week, when some jackass where I go dancing decided to insult me. So I gave him the old one-two—"

"And you lost your watch in the scuffle?" Angie offered.

"No, ma'am. My watch paid the cops to let me go. A very undignified scene, let me tell you, for a man with an M.D.—not to mention four other degrees."

"That's very impressive," said Jason, imagining two old farts flailing at each other over a sixty-something babe in some geriatric Mexican version of Roseland. "I'm working toward a college degree myself."

"Education's what matters," the old man said. "Not that I regret those interests in oil that I have in California."

"Nice to have some backup," Jason agreed.

"Well, if I hadn't been a broker on the New York Stock Exchange I'd have easily been burnt. Can't trust those oil stocks, you know."

"I'll take your word for it."

"California's crazy. Did a lot of acting out there in the old days—for the movies. *That* was the gold rush!"

"I'm Angie," said Angie, "and this is my husband, Jason. So you were an actor, Mister . . . ?"

"Frank Walter Moran," he said, crushing Jason's hand in a boa-constrictor grip. "You've heard of Frank Moran?" Lighting no spark of recognition, the old guy tried to hide his disappointment. "Long before your time," he mumbled.

"Wait," said Angie. "The boxer?"

"You knew? I'll be damned!"

"My older brother fought in the Golden Gloves. He used to talk boxing all the time. Taught *me* how to box, too. Used to beat the shit out of me. I loved it."

"Well Frank Moran would have loved to have a sparring partner like you, young lady." The old man smiled, and the tip of his rugged nose turned pink. "Might have helped him flatten out Johnson."

"Jack Johnson?" said Angie.

"Exacto!" Moran gazed at Angie in silent admiration. "Ever hear of the Great White Hope? No? Well Frank was the Great White Hope who fought Jackie Johnson to a standstill. Stayed the course, a full twenty rounds on his feet."

"Jackie Johnson?" said Jason, looking at Angie, who frowned as if he should know.

"Never heard of Jack Johnson, fella? He was the Negro heavyweight champion of the world. No white man ever went the limit with him—except for Frank Walter Moran."

"As far as boxing goes," said Jason, "my knowledge doesn't go back before Joe Louis."

"The Negro heavyweights who came after Johnson were pussies by comparison. Pardon, miss. No offense meant."

"None taken," said Angie, leaning over Jason as if drawn by a magnet. "My brother told me all about boxing in the old days. No gloves, endless rounds."

"Who goes twenty with anybody these days?" Frank asked rhetorically.

"I bet you still could," said Angie.

A faint blush colored Moran's leathery cheeks. "Thank you kindly—Angie, is it? Well, Angie, I didn't settle in Guadalajara to look for a fight, but to court the beautiful women for which this town is famed."

Jason smirked.

"You doubt I'm still virile?"

"Of course not," said Jason, his eye on that meat-hook that Moran waved palm-up right under his nose.

"Don't make any mistake. I'm searching for *love.* I'm gonna marry a young señorita. I've been fooled, I've been used, but I'm still trying."

"Great fighters never give up," said Angie.

This is getting bizarre, thought Jason.

"I want a family. I want children. I still got a nice few rounds to go—if you know what I mean." The old man winked and clenched his fists. Feinting with his left, he grazed Jason's midriff with a rack of stony knuckles.

"Older sperm makes smarter babies," said Angie.

Where the fuck did she ever hear that? thought Jason, his stomach in a knot.

"In the meantime, till Frank Moran and his true love are united, a man's got to settle for whatever entertainment he can get."

"Yes, we noticed there are plenty of movie houses," said Jason, hoping to change the subject.

Ignoring the remark, Moran looked right past Jason. "Some of the cantinas are taxi-dance joints," he said. "A dance costs less than one American nickel."

"Is that how you meet girls?" asked Angie.

"Not the nice ones. These are the ones for sale. You dance to arrange a quickie, or an all-night shack job. . . . Excuse me if I'm being too 'frank.' " He smiled at his own pun. Angie laughed appreciatively. Jason did not smile. He thought that Angie *should* have looked offended. "There are other places to meet women, though. Have you been to the Woolworth's lunch counter?"

"We've just got into town," said Jason.

"The girls that work there are beautiful, really exotic. Do either of you read Spanish?"

"Jason does."

Moran whipped out a letter from his inside jacket pocket. "Can you do me a favor and tell me what this says? I got it today from my favorite waitress at Woolworth's. She's very interested in me, you know." He searched Jason's eyes for the least flicker of doubt. "I asked her to be my bride."

"That's so romantic," said Angie.

"Be glad to translate if I had the time, but it's getting late," said Jason, "and we still haven't found a hotel."

"Hotel? Your worries are over. An American friend of mine runs a great place—cheap and clean—only a few blocks down past the Mercado here. Harry Baker. Used to spar in his prime. Do you mind?" he said, shoving the letter at Jason.

Between the opening "*Atento Señor*" and the closing "*Su servidora,*" the page-and-a-half letter was riddled with errors in spelling and punctuation. But the message was clear. The girl's parents would not hear of it and would not allow her to have anything more to do with that very kind and generous *norteamericano.* Jason looked up at Frank Moran, wondering how a man with five degrees couldn't read simple Spanish. Moran eyed him with mounting suspicion while grinding his fist into his palm.

"I can't really make this out," said Jason, watching Moran's hands. "The handwriting isn't too clear, and it's full of bad spelling."

"I can't much follow her conversation either. I just kinda look into her eyes and guess." Moran grabbed the letter and tucked it back into his pocket. He even seemed relieved not to know.

"If she accepted your offer, she'd tell you in person," said Angie.

"Angie, keep your opinions to—"

"She's right," said Moran. "It's a TKO. They flatten you while you're still on your feet."

"There's plenty of fish in the sea," said Angie.

"You're absolutely right. Hey, I like that wife of yours. She don't pull any punches!"

"We really have to go," said Jason.

"I know. I'll introduce you to Harry Baker."

"Don't trouble yourself," said Jason. "We have a list of recommended hotels."

"You don't think I get a commission, do you?"

"Of course not," said Angie. "Lead the way, Frank. It's late, Jay, and we're tired."

Shrugging his shoulders, Jason went along. Moran walked between him and Angie, occasionally draping his hands around their backs. Jason thought the old guy's arm slipped down once or twice and strafed Angie's buttocks, but he couldn't be sure. She'll be pissed, thought Jason, when she sees this dump he's taking us to. Then she'll take it out on me because we won't have the guts to turn it down.

3

Only two blocks past the Mercado Libertad and a block to the left of Mina, the Hotel La Coronada, "The Crowned Lady," nestled short and squat between two gray apartment buildings. Jason noticed that the second o of the glued-on letters that made up the word "Coronada" was missing, resulting in "Cor nada," meaning "a wound inflicted by the horn of a bull." He thought this worth mentioning, so he mentioned it.

"Is that supposed to be funny?" said Angie.

"Not particularly." She was probably already sorry, he thought, that she hadn't resisted Moran's offer to help. "You lodge here too, Mr. Moran?" he asked, still hesitant about going in.

"Me? No, I board by the month in a house a few blocks away."

The small lobby consisted of a registration desk, a frayed brown sofa, armchairs, and a television. The stained beige wallpaper was covered with little gold crowns. A heavyset man of about fifty lurched up from his seat behind the counter and stared at them. "Well, if it isn't Frank Moran! Where you been these past few weeks?"

"Been out knockin' 'em down."

"The bottles or the ladies?"

"None of the above. Just those bastards who keep lookin' at me cross-eyed. Harry, meet a couple American friends of mine. Angie and—and—"

"Jason," said Jason.

"Angie and Jason, from New York," said Moran. "Told 'em you had great rooms at rock-bottom prices."

"And that's no lie," said Harry, reaching a beefy hand to Jason that a lifetime of sparring must have pounded into jelly—the way Mexican chefs treated steaks. "How long you folks staying?" His heavy-lidded eyes locked on Angie, reverted to Jason, then swiveled back to Angie.

"Two-three days, I guess," said Jason.

"Possibly as much as a week," said Angie. "We have a reservation to fly home from Mexico City."

"Hey, you might like it here enough to change your flight, maybe stay even longer," said Harry.

"Could be," said Angie. "Depends."

Jason looked at her, eyed the dreary lobby, and wondered whether she had lost her judgment or was cannily lying about a possibly extended stay to snare the guy's best room.

"Well, we're a pretty popular establishment, but—"

Jason scanned the grid of pigeonholes on the wall behind the desk. Every little box had a key dangling beneath it.

"—it just happens you're in luck. Big tour group just moved out. One of my best rooms is yours. Shower and *cama matrimonial*. Number Three down the hall, second door on your left." He pointed to his right, at the entrance to the dim hallway beside the desk. "Does twenty pesos a night sound agreeable?"

Jason was stunned. Only a buck sixty a night? What was wrong with this picture? He glanced at Angie, to catch the wince he fully expected.

"Fine, we'll take it" was all she said.

"Angie, shouldn't we first take a look—"

"I'm sure it'll be adequate," she said, cutting him off.

Plucking a key wired to a clumsy wooden block, Harry handed it to Jason. "You can sign in later. That all your luggage?"

"American Express said they'll notify us when it arrives at the bus station," said Angie. "We'll call them from our room and tell them where we are."

"You can call them from out here. No charge."

"No, that's okay," said Angie.

"No phones in the rooms. Keeps costs down," said Harry.

"Look," said Jason, prepared to beat a retreat and only waiting for a sign from Angie, "I think we'd better—"

"No problem; thanks," said Angie.

"You'll like it here," said Moran, sidling up between them and draping his big hands over their shoulders. "Would you two like to join me for lunch tomorrow at the Mercado?"

While Jason searched for a polite way out, Angie said, "Sure, we've got shopping to do anyway."

Jason watched the tall ex-boxer leave the hotel. He could not help admiring that sturdy frame; he took note of his stride, oddly rigid, almost wooden. Determined. As he and Angie headed for the hallway, he glanced at the sagging sofa against the lobby wall to the left. It was bookended by tables decked with oval-leafed rubber plants (probably *made* of rubber), and on the wall above the sofa hung a framed poster of the *Cenote de Sacrificio* that they'd actually seen in Yucatán—the "Well of Sacrifice," an enormous circular limestone pit carved out naturally by water over the aeons, a hole down which the ancient Mayans threw the occasional sacred virgin and respected enemy warrior and anyone else they decided to honor to death.

Their room came furnished with a double bed, a seedy armchair, a tall wardrobe that tilted forward on the uneven floor, and a writing desk with chair opposite the bed. Except for the light-green flower-pattern wallpaper, everything seemed brown, including the stained old carpeting that made Jason yearn for the slippers still to come in their luggage.

"Well," said Angie, with a shrug of the shoulders, "what do you think?"

Jason watched her toss her handbag onto the desk, then pull out the empty drawers and snap them back in place as if expecting to find abandoned underwear or a shriveled condom or two. "It's okay. It'll do," he said. He knew that if he were to voice any obvious displeasure—which meant criticizing her judgment—she would accuse him of failing to take a forceful stand earlier, when they still had a chance to back out.

"You're sure?" she said, testing him.

"The basics are all here," he said, trying to sound cheerful. He dropped their red leather bag next to the bed, then strode up to the window against the far wall, parted the thick beige curtains, bent back the dusty venetian-blind slats, and peered out at the cement-block wall of the adjoining building. "Not much of a view," he said. "Let me check out the bathroom."

The bathroom door was a step away from the window, between window and bed. He flicked on the light. The toilet yawned open. Soundlessly, he lowered the seat. A green plastic curtain hung over a lion-clawed bathtub. He parted the curtain, heard a whir, saw something shoot past his head, looked at the tile floor, and spotted a giant roach skittering for shelter in the direction of the toilet. Abdominals stiffening, he stepped on it, squashing it, and kicked the carcass behind the toilet, out of sight. There was no sense telling Angie. She'd never forgive him for failing to object to her impulsive decision to stay here. He shook the white towels folded over a bar on the door, making sure that nothing else lay in ambush.

"Anything wrong, Jay?"

"No. Just testing the shower." Behind the bathtub curtain there were the usual two knobs, American-made because labeled H and C. Gingerly, he reached and turned the knob with the "C" on it, the one that should signify "cold" but here in Mexico usually stood for *caliente*, hot. Good, there was plenty of hot water, hot enough to fry a roach. Fortunately, he could see no others.

"That's what I could use right now, a shower," said Angie.

"Don't you want to eat first? We haven't had dinner. On the way here we passed that Hotel Gerente that looked like it had a nice restaurant."

"The Gerente can wait, don't you think?" She smiled at him and unbuttoned her blouse. He sat at the desk across from the bed and watched her undress. When she was down to bra and panties, she sauntered over, took his hands, and slipped his arms around her. After he unhooked her bra and peeled her breasts out of the stretched cups, she stared into his eyes and placed his thumbs under the edge of her peach-colored panties. "You take them off so much better than I do," she said in that throaty way that never failed to arouse. The sweaty-sweet smell of her breasts made his scalp crawl. He felt as if his hair were on fire. "You need a shower too, don't you think?"

He nodded. But he was tired and hungry.

"You'll just have to get back into practice, Jay."

"For what?"

Her eyelids fluttered. "For how to spend your spare time once you start school again."

"You really don't mind that I'm going back to . . . ?"

With her underthings strewn at his feet, she ground herself into him, then turned away as soon as she felt him swell. She'd known exactly what to say to dispel his lingering inertia. His was a knee-jerk resistance, born of habit, of anticipating her countless turnings away, of remembering their innumerable late-night quarrels back home—often over their plans for the future, over the hopes he had to finish his degree.

She picked up her purse and wended her way to the bathroom with a pronounced lurch of the hips. They were both so tired, he thought. Where did she find the energy? Back home she was never so constantly seductive, so sexually imperious, as she'd been so far for all three weeks of this monthlong trip of theirs. At home, in fact, she was often so indifferent to him that they didn't make love for two weeks at a time, and when she did want him to accommodate her, in the middle of the night sometimes, her approach was passionless, crude, mechanical, as if scratching an itch that wouldn't let her sleep. Often, when he did want her, overcome by the warmth and fragrance of the smooth, soft body beside him, she would push him away, even punch him with her elbow, so that negotiating for sex had become a nerve-racking issue and he had progressively shied away from being the initiator. Now, however, all vacation long, it was almost like in the early days before they got married—almost, not quite. Her sexual hunger was genuine all right, but she seemed to feel she had to be theatrical in order to excite him. Her advances sometimes turned him off, but more often than not they succeeded. He guessed that her job, and the boring routine of their lives at home, had done much to dampen her libido. And the effect on both of them of constant exposure to her father couldn't be discounted either. Did she expect to make up in one single month for all she'd held back for two years? Jason wondered.

The heady aroma of Maja soap wafted out of the bathroom in a cloud of steam. The name of the soap, not its black-and-red, sexless, Flamenco-dancer wrapper, conjured up for Jason Goya's *Maja desnuda* posed bare-assed on a couch, and the *Maja* in turn took the shape and odor of Angie. Unbuttoning his shirt, Jason looked up at the wall above the desk and noticed, for the first time, the framed print hanging there. It was a large photo of the *chacmool* they'd encountered at Chichén Itzá, among carved columns at the top of the Temple of the Warriors. The reclining stone figure with cylindrical head gazed blankly off to the left as it rested on its elbows and extended a flat stomach, shaped like a plate, that had served the Mayans as an altar of human sacrifice. He remembered how he had clowned around, posing on the *chacmool* like a victim waiting for slaughter. Angie had laughed, but the memory of his mockery, even now, sent a mild *frisson* coursing through him.

As he contemplated the image, he was distracted by what appeared to be a defect in the wall near the top of the frame, on the right. Jason planted himself on his knees on top of the desk. In that position he was at eye level with what turned out to be a hole in the wall—in a section of the wall thin enough that, with one eye pressed up against it, he could see a large portion of the room behind it. For there *was* a room behind it, room Number One, thought Jason. A room very similar to their own. The mirror image of their own, in fact, judging from what he could see, which included the entire bed and a few feet to either side. There appeared to be no one in the room just then, but it was furnished with the same bed, the same light green wallpaper, the same ugly wardrobe to the left of the bed (corresponding to Jason's right if he were to turn and look back at their own room), and on the floor to the right of the bed . . . *a piece of red luggage.*

A volley of darts stung Jason's neck. He spun his head around. Their own red bag still lay where he had dropped it, in exactly the same position—between bed and bathroom—as in the room behind the wall. Surely, he thought, it couldn't be precisely the same type of luggage. But before he could look through the hole again, Angie had turned off the shower. She'd be out in a minute. If she saw him up there and figured out why, she'd place all the blame—for an ugly situation he could no longer keep under wraps—on *him*. He looked frantically around for something to serve as a plug. He tried tipping the *chacmool* picture, but that wouldn't work. Then he dug around in his pants pocket and came up with a crumpled Kleenex. Measuring off a piece, he stuffed it into the hole. It would do for the time being.

He had just slid down off the dresser when Angie called out to him. "I thought you were getting ready to shower, dear." Her voice was as sweet as her incipient anger would allow.

"I thought I should go out front first—and sign us in, and call American Express."

"Can't that wait?"

"I suppose it can," he said, relenting. He gauged that her lust was greater than her anger, and that as soon as he'd washed off the grime of their long day, he'd be ready to snuffle the *Maja*-smell of her flesh, magical flesh which, night after night, managed to slough off the stale dry skin of their marriage.

4

In the morning Jason got up early to pee. Angie still slept soundly, her covers kicked aside, her naked ass facing him in rosy contentment. Remembering the peephole, hoping he'd only dreamt it, he slipped out of bed and blinked repeatedly, focusing on the wall opposite the bed. There it still flickered, like an irregularity in the wallpaper alongside the *chacmool*. The Kleenex plug was gone. It had fallen out—or been *pushed* out—and lay on top of the desk. A cold vise gripped Jason's testicles. They had made love with his bedside lamp on. Angie could not sleep without a light on.

Jason picked up the plug again, moistening it this time with saliva. Climbing up and planting his knees on the desktop veneer—as he imagined the *other* must have done during the night—he placed his right eye up against the hole. He saw motion, bodies in violent motion in the light of a familiar-looking bedside lamp. The room looked just as it had last night, a replica of their own. The red bag had been moved, though. It lay at the foot of the bed. He focused on the arching bodies of the woman and the man on top of her. He did not recognize the woman, but the man, even from the back, he identified as Frank Moran. Moran had said he boarded elsewhere, but he must have had a landlady with a restrictive visiting policy. There was no doubt that it was Moran— the same shock of gray-white hair, the big bony shoulders and hands. The skin of his ass was wrinkled and gray, Jason noted with disgust. He looked like a fornicating lizard. But why did they make so little noise? Either the bed did not squeak much, or the sounds they made were baffled by the wall, a thick enough partition except, probably, only in the vicinity of the peephole.

So the peeping Tom was either Moran or Harry Baker! But what could they have seen through a plugged-up hole? *But*, thought Jason, how could he know when the plug had been dislodged?

Jason shuddered at a sound from behind him. He turned around, fearing the worst. But all Angie had done was roll over onto her right side. She was still sound asleep.

Their red bag too, he noted, had migrated to the foot of the bed!

He wanted to peer through the wall again, distrusting his memory, but Angie might spring up any moment. He replugged the hole, unable to come up with any better idea, and quietly descended from the desk. One thing he knew: for the time being, not to tell Angie. And that meant keeping what he knew to himself.

5

"Where you guys off to?" asked Harry. "I've got coffee and brioches in the breakfast room."

"Thanks, but we're in kind of a hurry," said Jason. By way of tacit agreement, they both felt the need to start the day in a more cheerful setting, perhaps with a touch of class.

The nearby Gerente served Continental breakfast on a spotless linen tablecloth with napkins shaped like hats. They slathered their rolls with imported preserves as if to balance the energy budget raided by last night's lovemaking.

At what seemed an appropriate moment, Jason tried to dissuade Angie from keeping their date with Moran. "We don't have much time left in Mexico, and there's so much we want to see here on our own. He'll understand."

"But Frank is part of the *fun* of being here. He's what makes our trip out of the ordinary. We actually met someone famous!"

"A has-been."

"What's your problem, Jason?"

"Wouldn't you rather have lunch right here? Look, they've got *pozole* on the menu. It's a local Jalisco specialty."

"They'll have it at the market too," said Angie.

She was beginning to show displeasure, so Jason decided to drop it. After walking around the city center, from the Plaza de Armas to the Parque de la Revolución, they returned to La Cor(o)nada about eleven. Harry Baker greeted them. In a talkative mood, he asked them how they'd happened to hook up with Moran. "He and I have a special relationship," he said.

I'll bet you do, Jason thought.

"Have a seat," said Baker, pointing to the sofa. Exiting from behind the *Recepción*, he settled into an armchair opposite them where he could still keep his eye on the lobby.

"He tells us he was the 'Great White Hope,' " said Jason, balancing on the edge of the lumpy couch. No less uncomfortable, Angie perched to his left.

Baker waved his hand dismissively. "There were dozens of Great White Hopes. Jack Johnson beat 'em all."

"But he says he was the only one who fought him to a draw."

"A standstill," Angie corrected.

"That's right. He went a full twenty with smilin' Jack and fought him to a *standstill*. He's not telling you that he *lost*."

"He's accentuating the positive," said Angie.

"At the cost of a great deal of truth," said Baker.

"Like what?" Jason asked.

"Is it any of our business?" said Angie.

"I'm curious. What's wrong with that?"

Baker smiled and shook his head and patted his stubby fingers together. "Frank'll never tell you, but that fight was fixed. It's a part of boxing history, but Frank hasn't read the books."

"Hasn't read the books? A man with five degrees?"

"He told you that?"

"Among other things," said Jason.

Baker clucked his tongue.

"Even if the fight was fixed," said Angie, "it still doesn't mean it was Frank who fixed it."

"They fought in Paris in the summer of 1914. It was the biggest sporting event on the eve of World War One. It was such a big attraction, in fact, that their managers arranged to have it filmed—so they all agreed to make it go at least ten rounds. It was all a question of money."

"So it was as corrupt back then as it is now?" said Jason.

"Frank played the game just like everyone else," sniffed Angie.

Why, Jason wondered, was Baker bad-mouthing Moran? To appear not so chummy with the Great Lost Hope? To avoid being eventually suspected of collaborative voyeurism? He imagined the two at the peephole, leering, switching off with each other, sometimes lucky, sometimes not. "I thought you two were good friends," he said.

"We are, but I wouldn't want him to mislead you."

"He says he doesn't board here, but I was just wondering," said Jason, looking pointedly to his left down the hallway, "does he sometimes happen to sleep here?"

"On rare occasions. Why?"

Jason stared right at him, but Baker didn't blink. "Just curious."

"Few months ago he got blind drunk. Landlady threw him out, so I put him up."

"It must be very frustrating for him to live alone with just memories," said Angie.

"Very selective memories," Jason added. "Speaking of which, how recently did you say Frank slept here, Mr. Baker?"

"How recently? How the hell would I—"

"Jay, who the fuck cares?"

"Speaking of the devil," Baker whispered.

Jason glanced first down the hallway, but Frank Moran entered from the street, dapper in gray suit and solid red tie.

6

At the open-sided, two-tiered Mercado Libertad—the biggest, newest market in Guadalajara, said Moran—Jason and Angie were overwhelmed by the scope and variety of goods displayed for sale. Handicrafts shouted bright colors at them, and foodstuffs whispered alien scents from teeming wicker baskets and groaning wooden tables that stretched for acres in row after twisting row of individual concessions. Pyramids of beans mingled with cages full of squawking birds in a dizzying panorama of sights and sounds as the three of them sashayed through bustling aisles barely wide enough to navigate. Vendors of food and embroidered garments, furniture and paper flowers, clamored for their attention. Guitars, leather purses, hats and huaraches called out, flirting, whirling around them, as Jason tagged behind Angie with Moran holding up the rear.

"Here's what I need," said Angie, stopping at a table loaded with underwear—bras, panties, stockings. As she picked up pairs of skimpy panties, stretching them across her waist—and thereby causing a traffic jam—Moran didn't hesitate to offer his opinion as Angie dangled them in front of him. Jason thought she was being a bit crude.

"Try the black ones," Moran urged. "Black drives *me* wild, I'll tell ya."

Who gives a shit what drives you wild? thought Jason, nudging Angie toward a section of sensible white cotton undies. But Angie twisted away. "You don't think black's too daring?" she said.

"For a girl like you?" said Moran, raising his brows.

"Well, if there's matching bras my size . . ." Self-absorbed, Angie stretched pair after pair over her blouse.

"There, that's a fit," said Moran.

"Think so?"

Jason couldn't believe that her decisions about underwear could be influenced by the opinions of a drooling old lecher like Moran—who undoubtedly fantasized seeing her wearing them, especially seeing her take them off. She wound up buying five pairs of panties and an equal number of bras. "Damn luggage may never arrive," she said. Jason bought a couple of T-shirts, some socks, and two pairs of briefs.

"How about a couple dried hummingbirds?" Moran said with a wink. "Mexican ladies stick 'em in their bras for good luck."

Jason spun around to the table behind him and picked up one of the bowie knives he'd been eyeing off and on. Slipping it in and out of its sheath of tooled Mexican leather, he admired the heft of the blade, sniffed the fresh, earthy scent of the scabbard, then raised the bared blade above his head in both hands the way those Mayan or Aztec priests must have done, he thought, when performing a sacrifice. "Popocatépetl Teotihuacán Quetzalcoatl," he intoned.

"You nuts?" said Angie, flinching. Moran watched him without even blinking.

"I'm getting it for your father. We haven't gotten a present for him the whole trip, remember?" Not waiting for a reply, Jason haggled for a while then bought the knife for the equivalent of about twelve U.S. dollars.

"I'm hungry," said Angie.

"Where do we eat?" asked Jason, tired of watching neck after neck craning in her direction.

"Upper deck." Moran pointed to a wide central staircase.

The open floor was sectioned into a series of competing restaurants, each a rectangle bordered all around by long counters crowded with patrons who seemed to talk more than they ate. Moran found them three seats together, and they studied the blackboard menu on the post behind the counter.

"I like the *cuerdo con pipián*," said Moran.

The prices, Jason noted, were ridiculously low. "Look, Angie, they've got *pozole*."

"Great. I'll taste yours," said Angie. "Order me the—what'd you call it, peepee, Frank?" Moran broke into counter-slapping laughter.

The *cuerdo* was a sorry-looking pork dish, a slab of fatty meat sunk under a thin brown sauce. Jason offered Angie some of his *pozole*—an aromatic stew of shredded pork and chicken steeped in an oniony tomato broth thick with beans. Angie wound up eating more of Jason's lunch than her own.

"Excuse me," said Moran, sauntering off to the right, to the end of the counter. Jason watched him chitchat with a pair of señoritas whose butts and bosoms strained against their dresses.

"He seems to know everybody," said Angie.

"He's probably offering to marry them," said Jason.

"What's your gripe, Jay?"

"You seem to think he knows everything, but he sure as hell doesn't know food."

"So? What's wrong with trying new things?"

"*Pozole* is new. We said we wanted to try it, didn't we?"

"Oh, we could get that anywhere. If not for Frank, I'd never have heard of peepee."

"The only Spanish he can read is from a menu."

"For a guy who doesn't know the language, he seems to be making out pretty well," she said with a nod to the right.

Jason managed to pay the small bill just before Moran came back.

"Gotta ask you guys a favor," said Moran. "It's kind of embarrassing. You still going to the picture show?"

"As soon as we drop off our purchases at the hotel—and go peepee," Angie said, laughing.

"We're going to see *Spartacus*, with Kirk Douglas," said Jason. "We missed it back in the States."

"Well . . . I wonder if you'd mind lending me your room while you're gone."

"For what?" said Jason.

"See the cutie in the red dress I was talking to?"

"Don't *tell* me!" said Angie, clapping her hand to her mouth.

Jason peered again down the counter. He saw her in profile. It was *she*! He'd swear it was the same "hot tamale" he'd seen Moran thumping in the morning.

"My landlady's the strict kind, you know," said Moran. "If my sainted mother were to drop down from heaven, she wouldn't get past that old witch."

There had to be a rational explanation, thought Jason. He couldn't have seen an event that had *not yet happened*. Anyway, could he swear she was *exactly the same one*? These sexy young *pepitas* looked so much alike. For sure, though, the old goat *had* been bopping someone. But twice in one day? And at his age? And why couldn't he just use the same room again? (Unless, of course, it was booked.)

"Walk back with us and we'll give you the key," said Angie, the Good Samaritan.

"But," Jason feebly protested, "we really don't know when we'll get—"

"It'll take us at least two hours," said Angie.

"You'll come back to clean sheets. Scout's honor," said Moran. He hurried back to his red chili pepper to let her know where to find him.

"See? To survive in Mexico," said Angie, "you really don't need any Spanish."

"This is unbelievable!" said Jason.

"What? That we'd do an old warhorse a favor?"

"No, I meant . . ." His scalp felt creepy. He ran his hands through his hair as if chasing after ants.

"You meant?" she said as if gearing up for a fight.

"Nothing. I mean—it's all so weird. That's all."

"It makes things that much more exciting, doesn't it?" she said.

7

The paper plug had dropped out—or so it seemed—once again. Chastened by the afternoon's uncanniness, Jason resisted the temptation to peek. This time, while Angie showered, he plugged up the hole with a wad of gum he'd been chewing. But there was no closing his eyes to the temptation posed by Angie when she emerged from the bathroom in slinky black panties and tight-fitting bra and danced à la go-go while unbuttoning his shirt and unbuckling his belt. Arousing him, she continued to disrobe him while Jason removed her bra and sunk his face in the slick groove between her breasts. Drawing him back toward the bed, she suddenly yanked him down on top of her. "Take me," she commanded.

"I—I want to, but the Pill! You haven't taken your—"

"One fuckin' pill won't matter, Jay."

"Maybe not, Angie, but to put in jeopardy everything we've been planning for . . ."

"All right, no problem. I'll show you I'm taking my pill." She dashed into the bathroom for water from the plastic container of *agua purificada* they always carried with them. Last thing they needed was a case of Montezuma's revenge. Emerging with water glass in hand, she deposited it on the desk, rummaged in her handbag, and extracted a little white tablet. Waving it grandly in the air, she flicked it onto her tongue and downed it with a swig from the glass. Alligator eyes glared fiercely at Jason in reproach for his boorish caution.

"Wanna peek into your parlor?" she said, opening her mouth

and vibrating her tongue. She got him to laugh. And then it all became silly and unendurably sweet again.

8

Jason awoke from a horrifying dream. On putting his eye to the hole, he met another eye gazing back. He sprang up in bed, but Angie, unperturbed, kept right on sleeping. The light of early morning filtered in through the blinds. Edging out of bed, he tip-toed to the writing desk and examined the wall. The plug had once again "fallen" from where he had squeezed it the night before. *When* had it fallen? he wondered. When they were making love? What if the gum had just dried up, and then dropped out on its own?

Climbing up on the desk, careful to minimize noise, Jason placed his eye at the peephole. No other eye met his, but he'd rather one had—as opposed to what he did see. He was peering into the same room, no doubt about that, and again there were two actors naked in bed . . . but this time the couple at foreplay— Jason bit down on his lower lip—were *Angie and himself!* The insuck of his breath was enough to rattle the desk. But he couldn't keep his eyes off what unfolded.

While Angie fondled his genitals, stroking and kissing them, this other Jason looked away—even gazed up at the peephole, as though aware that he was watching himself—and the only thing to harden was his unsmiling face despite all his wife's efforts to excite him. Was this still the dream, and he hadn't really awakened? he wondered.

Fascinated, he followed Angie's every industrious move.

"What am I doing wrong, Jay?" she said, peering up from his belly. He watched himself, thin-lipped, refusing to respond. Then Angie sat up, folded her arms, and said, "I fuckin' give up. I've tried everything I know to stiffen that 'Jack Johnson' of yours, but—"

Then he heard himself reply, "I can't believe you'd do this to me. All this time, using me as if . . . as if . . ."

And then he saw Angie jump out of bed, pull off her ring, and toss it at him.

At this point, his head pounding, Jason had to back away from the peephole. Glancing back at the "real" Angie, he let out a troubled sigh. Still sound asleep! And was he, in fact, right there beside her, dreaming all he was "seeing"?

Jason had had enough peeping. He descended from the desk, knees aching in a very real way from pressing against wood. Physically, nothing felt dreamlike at all. He needed to use the bathroom. Peeing felt absolutely lifelike, and he was not inclined to test its reality by spraying the floor and the shower curtains and trying to fly through the wall. Maybe it was only when he peered through the hole that his mind entered a dreamlike state, he reasoned. A prophetic state? Ridiculous! It was a warning. His unconscious was showing him a *possible* future if he—if he *what?* he wondered. He never got into snits like that, spurning Angie at a time like that. That was not him. He vowed to be affectionate to her all day. He mustn't allow anything to come between them that could sour their intimacy at bedtime. When he crept back beside her again, he leaned against the headboard, his whole body throbbing. The vibrations woke her.

"Up already?" she said, rubbing swirls of black hair from her eyes. "What time is it?"

His watch lay next to his bedside lamp. "Seven-fifteen." He heard her stomach grumbling.

"I'm hungry," she said. "But first . . ."

Jason felt a warm hand cup his testicles. His body's instant response was proof enough of the absurdity of the scene he had just seemed to witness.

9

This time their hôtelier insisted. They must stay for a Continental breakfast on the house. "The coffee's fresh-brewed, and the rolls are just in from the bakery."

Jason wanted an absolute minimum of Harry's hospitality. The sooner he left the Cor(o)nada, the better he would feel. "Thanks, Harry, but it's a bit too early for breakfast."

"C'mon, Jason, we're both out of energy," Angie said with a broad wink. Jason cringed on seeing Harry grin back—at both of them, like some sort of privileged insider. It was almost as if she *knew* about the peephole—as if she knew *Harry* knew, and as if she knew that Harry knew *she* knew, and that she didn't give a damn. "A little breakfast before breakfast?" she persisted.

"I don't see any breakfast nook," said Jason.

"Follow me," said Harry, taking them into the hallway. He stopped in front of the first door on the left.

Room Number One! Jason stiffened. "I thought this was a guest room, Harry."

"It's been used for various things."

"I'll bet," said Jason, staring straight at Baker, who played oblivious.

The door opened upon a bright, clean space furnished with several sets of cheap wooden tables and chairs. An aluminum coffeepot and a wicker tray of rolls occupied a cart to the left. No bed, no desk, no wardrobe. All that seemed unchanged was the light green, pink-flowered wallpaper. Jason felt dizzy. Angie pushed him forward, giving him a pissed-off look as Harry guided them to a table. While Harry did the honors, pouring them their coffee, Jason stared at the wall—the wall behind which lay their own room. Over the peephole—over the spot where the peephole *had to be*—there hung a framed poster.

"What are you looking at, Jay?"

"That poster. Looks like a festival."

"That's the big fiesta at Tlaquepaque," said Harry. "It lasts for days. In fact, it's going on now."

"Why don't we go see it?" said Jason.

"I'm festivaled out," said Angie. "Dad always drags us to the San Giovanni feast on Mott Street. Calzones there, tacos here, what's the difference?"

"One of you should go," said Harry. "Didn't your wife say she needed to do more shopping?"

"If I go, she goes," said Jason.

"Of course, I only meant . . ."

"What the hell, so we'll go," said Angie.

"Good plan," said Harry. "By the way, I have a message from Frank. He wants to take you to dinner tonight at a favorite restaurant of his."

"Really?" said Jason. "Tell him thanks, but we doubt if we can make it."

"He says you took him out for lunch, and he insists on treating you to dinner."

"We'll be delighted," said Angie. "Tell Frank we look forward to his company."

"Says he'll pick you up at eight sharp."

"We'll be back in plenty of time."

"Good. I'll tell him that. May I join you two for coffee?"

"Of course," said Angie.

To Jason's extreme annoyance, Harry stuck with them till they finished. Business must be booming at La Cor nada, thought Jason. They all walked out together. He did not get the chance he was hoping for to peek under the picture frame. Nor could he understand how, in the brief time it took them to fool around, shower, and dress, Harry could have switched all the furniture—and without lots of noise, at that! Why make such an effort? To cause him to doubt his sanity? But maybe the furniture had *never* been switched, and this was the décor he *should* have been seeing with every peek he had taken. What, then, would account for the visions he had been having? The only explanation he could fall back on was some peculiar state between waking and dreaming wherein his mind projected, as onto a movie screen, his own deepest fears and anxieties. That peephole triggered it all, acting on his brain like a lens. Even that earlier vision—of Frank getting laid—was it "prophetic," was he seeing the actual future, or was it, as seemed more likely, an extrapolative reaction by his unconscious mind to the old goat's primitive vitality?

10

He and Angie bussed out to nearby Tlaquepaque, only to discover that the fiesta had been over for weeks. Angie was pissed and blamed Jason for not double-checking. Jason now had twice as much reason to be highly suspicious of Harry. "Did you notice he was angling for you to stay while I came out here alone?" he said.

"What's that supposed to mean?"

"I don't know. Nothing, I guess." He was determined, in light of what he'd "seen" through the peephole, not to do or say a thing that might further dampen their spirits. Since Angie looked forward to dinner with Moran, he avoided grousing about the coming evening either. They saved the day by having lunch at a little place serving Bírria, a tasty dish of goat meat in tomato sauce that they'd never tried before. Later, back at the Mercado Libertad, Jason insisted on Angie's buying a new dress. Still no word from American Express, and he knew how much a change of clothes would please her. Especially now that they were going out.

Moran appeared exactly on time, in a neat blue suit with a handkerchief in the jacket pocket. In a show of gallantry, he extended a fresh red rose to Angie, which she pinned to her new black dress. The cotton dress showed plenty of cleavage and fit her ass like a glove. Since Angie was unconcerned, Jason decided not to let it bother him either.

11

Frank had made reservations at the not-very-fancy La Roca, where they were seated at an upstairs table for four, Jason across from Angie, Frank to Jason's right. A handsome waiter of about thirty paid them close, even finicky, attention. When Frank proposed shrimp cocktails for starters, the waiter leaned over Angie's shoulder, studied her menu with his head close to hers, and whispered a countersuggestion directly in her ear. Angie paid no attention and went along with Frank. Jason was undecided whether to attribute the waiter's behavior to discourtesy or to the Hispanic proclivity for close conversational distance. Returning with the cocktails, the waiter set them down with a disapproving smirk and then, gratuitously, reached for Angie's napkin. Draping his arms over her shoulders with a caressing familiarity that left Jason speechless, he placed his cheek against her hair and proceeded, with a fussy ceremoniousness, to arrange the cloth napkin across her lap. Normally unflappable, Angie flinched.

"I would suggest the steaks," said Frank, narrowing his eyes at the waiter. Still bent over Angie, the waiter whispered again. This time Angie jerked away, as if pestered by a mosquito.

"This man is making me uncomfortable," said Angie, looking straight at Jason.

Glaring at the waiter, Jason searched for the Spanish equivalent of "Stop making an ass of yourself," but his brain froze. The words wouldn't come.

"What's your problem, muchacho?" said Frank.

Ignoring Frank's comment, the waiter brought his face within an inch of Angie's cleavage and pretended to be smelling her rose. Angry and humiliated, Jason strained for just the right phrase to put the slimy bastard in his place. "*Oye, camarero*," "Listen, waiter," was all he managed to shout before Frank rose to his feet—shot up, rather, knocking his chair behind him to the floor. A pink flush overspread his stony gray cheeks. He took a step forward, grabbed the waiter's left arm, and yanked him away from Angie. What Jason next saw occurred in a flash, a blur. Moran's left fist flew forward. The waiter tumbled to the floor. A hush descended over tables all around. Forks hung suspended in midair.

"Lucky you didn't meet the famous Mary Ann," said Frank, this time holding up his clenched right fist. "But if you want an introduction, I'll oblige you."

The waiter, leaning on an elbow, rubbed his chin and scuttled backward, retreating over the tiles with his eyes fixed on Frank. As coworkers inched near and asked him what had happened, he muttered a little and shrugged his shoulders. Picking himself up, he retreated like a peacock minus a tail. Moran, meanwhile, crooked his finger at one of the newly arrived waiters.

"Hey, you!" he said.

"Sí, sí, Señor, momentito!"

"Maybe we should go," said Jason.

"Why?" said Frank. "I told you the steaks are good here. They hammer the hell out of them, true, but they're tasty and tender. Waiter, three steaks, *por favor.*"

No one mentioned the incident all through dinner, but Frank did regale them with stories of fights in which his famous *right*-hand punch, which used to be known as Mary Ann, brought him victory. Each tale of conquest affected Jason like another kick in the scrotum.

12

"I think you should take your clothes off in the bathroom," said Jason, watching Angie, in the middle of the floor, wriggle out of her dress. Standing in front of the chest of drawers, he turned and stole a glance at the naked peephole at his back. He hadn't had the chance to plug it up again, and not being eight feet tall, he couldn't block the line of sight between Angie and that hole.

"Why the bathroom? Don't you like what you see?" She curved her hands over her bra cups and down around her thighs.

"It's just that . . . we shouldn't be stepping barefoot on this rug."

"Whatever disease is there, we've caught it already," said Angie, unhooking her bra and tossing it onto the bed.

In spite of his suspicions about the extent of Angie's audience, he couldn't keep his eyes off her as she enacted her nightly ritual. All that was missing was the music.

"I would've whacked that fucking waiter myself, you know," said Jason.

"What for?" said Angie, slipping out of her panties. "It was no big deal."

"I wasn't close enough. Frank was right next to him."

"I'll never forget the look on the guy's face," Angie said with a distant smile.

"It also crossed my mind that I could've wound up in jail."

"It's a thought that didn't seem to occur to Frank."

"It damn well should have!"

"I'm glad *you* didn't do anything stupid, dear."

"I think Frank is crazy, don't you?"

"It *was* kind of exciting when you think about it, wasn't it?"

"To me?" said Jason. "I wouldn't call it exciting."

"It was stupid, of course. But also exciting."

"Exciting?"

Angie backed into him, smiling at him over her shoulder, grinding her bare cheeks into his pelvis. "What's the matter?" she said. "I'm knocking and I don't hear a hello."

"Your friend is speechless with admiration."

"Oh, he'll be talking soon. I'll have him singing like Frankie."

"Like Frank?"

"Sinatra," she said, sauntering off to the bathroom.

As soon as he heard her taking a shower, he balled up a wad of tissue, moistened it with saliva, and stuck it in the hole. Wishing he had a strip of tape to hold it in place, he wondered if Angie had Band-Aids in her purse. He didn't like rummaging in a woman's purse. It was like violating some unspoken taboo. He flinched at the alligator's beady red stare, but the purse lay on the desktop in front of him and he looked inside and began to poke around. There was too much junk for him to see what was there, so he spilled out the contents. Among hairbrushes, lipsticks, makeup, and tampons, her plastic folder of traveler's checks fell out. Jason had recently counted his own—those that could be counter-signed only by him—and he now thumbed through Angie's, sat-isfying himself that together they had enough left to last the rest of the trip.

Strewn among the spilled objects were a bottle of aspirins and her contraceptive compact. For no particular reason, Jason opened the little green clam.

Not a pill missing!

With shaking hands, he stuffed everything back into the

beast's dark belly. He wanted to run in and scream at her, right in the middle of her shower. Not now, though, he cautioned himself. Not tonight. Perhaps there was an explanation. She didn't like the way the pills made her feel? So fucking what! He thought of the consequences of her having a baby—Angie quitting her job, the ruination of his career hopes and dreams, his return to the prison of working for her father. They had planned to trick him, the three of them together, Angie, her mother, and her father!

Sick to his stomach, he undressed for a shower. A shower might dampen his anger, he thought. Angie came out, sweet-smelling and warm, toweling herself down. He brushed swiftly by her. But she grabbed him by the elbow and pulled him to the bed.

"Fuck the shower," she said, thrusting him down and kneeling beside him. "I want it to taste like Mexico—sweaty, with all the local flavors intact." Lying on top of him, she slithered along his chest, kissing him as she descended, her breasts sweeping a warm path down his body, tickling as they rode his thighs. Part of him wanted to forget that little green clamshell as she took him in her mouth, but the other part flowed like ice through his veins, and he wondered if she could literally taste the coldness that he felt coming over him. His blood refused to flow where she directed it. He felt his face stiffening. Nothing but his face.

After a while she looked up at him. "Jay, is something the matter?"

"I don't know, Angie." He tried to stay calm. "Maybe . . . if you hadn't stopped taking your pills . . ."

"Am I doing something wrong? I've tried every trick on that Johnson of yours—"

"Didn't you hear me?" he said, raising his voice. "You haven't been taking your pills."

"Once in a while it's okay to skip one. I told you they make me feel ill."

"One? Who's talking about one? You haven't taken any the whole fucking month!"

"How the hell do *you* know?" Her face turning red, she pushed herself up into a kneeling position, straddling him.

"I checked. I can't believe you'd do this to me. All this time, using me, making a damn fool out of me, you and your parents, planning to fuck me over!"

"You checked? You went through my purse, you son of a bitch? I fuckin' give up." Backing off the bed, she stood up and, to Jason's horror, proceeded to twist off her wedding ring.

"Wait!" said Jason, hoping even now to change the scenario he had vowed all day to prevent. "I'm sorry. You don't have to do that."

She tossed her ring at him. It hit him in the thigh and he picked it up. *No!* he said to himself. *This is not happening!*

"All you do is worry about your own fucking self. You never gave a shit about me," she said.

"You said you would help me. You promised!" said Jason, his tone more hurt now than angry.

Angie stood with her back toward him, saying nothing, rubbing her forehead. Suddenly, spinning around, she placed her hands on her hips. "You checked my purse? Okay, and what did you find?"

"You know what I found," Jason whispered, avoiding her angry stare. "Look, Angie, I'm not against having children. It's all a matter of timing."

"I'll tell you what you found. You found a completely unused pill pack, that's what you found."

"Isn't that enough?"

"Isn't it possible that I only just recently used up the old pack?"

Jason looked her in the eye. He knew she was lying. What if he asked her directly, *Did you?*—and she admitted she was lying? Would he have the courage to follow through and announce, there and then, that they were through? Did Angie want it to be over? Surely not. If she was lying, she was lying for his sake, for both their sakes, for the sake of their marriage. She'd been playing the forgot-to-take-the-pill game for at least six months now, but he had allowed himself to overlook those little "mistakes" of hers because they'd hardly got it on all those months anyway. But these past few weeks of nightly and sometimes daily copulation, all this time with nothing to guard against pregnancy, amounted to an all-out assault on his hopes for a meaningful future—a campaign of sabotage to which he'd been utterly blind. What if she was already pregnant? What if she had promised her mother, her father, her Golden-Gloved brother, that she would come back pregnant no matter what, and that they'd better scout for a good sale on a crib and accessories in the interim?

"Isn't it possible?" she repeated.

"It's possible. Sure, sure it's possible."

"Asshole!" she said. "Give me that fucking ring." She snatched it away from him and slipped it back on her finger.

For a long time Jason was unable to sleep. He tried to persuade himself that the morning's vision had not come true. They had not split up after all—in spite of that hole-in-the-wall's apparent prediction! Even better: Now fully alert, he was not likely to fall for any new tricks of hers in that department any time soon. As the night wore on and he thought more about all that had happened, a further notion obtruded itself: If he had watched through the peephole long enough, he would have *seen* that their quarrel would resolve itself as peacefully as it did. But that would be to accept that a mere hole in the wall *could* be a window onto the future! He finally fell asleep, awakening at the end of a troubling dream in which Frank Moran hammered him with his trusty Mary Ann, knocking him over the ropes into—his erstwhile bedroom in his parents' house in Brooklyn.

13

Disoriented, Jason was startled to see a tangled cascade of ink black hair sprawled over the pillow beside him, almost touching his nose, exuding an earthy perfume. It took a couple of seconds before reality kicked back in. The indirect light of another bright morning in Guadalajara seeped through the heavily curtained window to his right. Rolling away from Angie, he stared at the photo of the *chacmool* and focused on the peephole beside it. It just then occurred to him that now, having seen through Angie's game of deception, he might very possibly have simultaneously cured himself of the tendency to "see" beyond that wall only his own darkest thoughts. The paper plug had "dropped" out again. Still and all, he knew quite well that the room behind that wall was a breakfast nook. The hole was probably covered by that picture of Tlaquepaque.

Slipping out of bed, he tiptoed to the desk, slid the alligator bag aside, and supported himself on his knees while putting his eye to the hole. What he saw brought hot, blurring tears to his eyes. He could barely contain the cry that filled his lungs.

Again, their own bed faced him. On it lay a naked Angie, her legs spread wide, her suntanned skin aglow in the light of her bedside lamp. Between her legs she cradled the bobbing head of a man, whose white hair she stroked in rhythm with the gurgling that spilled from her lips. Eyes half closed, lips pouting, she rocked back and forth, in time with the motion of the head between her legs. The crack between the cheeks of her partner's wizened ass moved back and forth also, looking up at Jason like a lizard blowing kisses.

Jason turned away, blood pounding in his ears, his throat closing to strangle a shriek that threatened to burst through his chest. Descending from the desk, he stole a glance at Angie—his sleepyhead wife still sunk in blissful slumber. Squeezing his head between his hands, he closed his eyes and reproached himself. How could he be so paranoid? he asked himself. Why did he persist in torturing himself? Why didn't his nightmares cease to pursue him the instant he awoke? Was it possible that what he was perceiving was a projection, not of his own mind, but of *Angie's* dreaming brain—that Angie had been transmitting *her* fears and desires into his own highly susceptible unconscious? There he was, doing it again, looking for some sort of "rational" explanation for nothing but his own sick fancies.

How stupid he was to dwell on all this! There was no way in hell that the scene he had just witnessed could ever achieve real-world embodiment. He was going to be with Angie all day—and all night. Apart from a trip to the bathroom, there'd be no reason for either of them to leave the other's side.

14

"Coffee and a roll?" Baker offered, addressing Angie.

"What kind of 'roll'?" said Angie, arching her brow.

"Any kind you like, dear."

"Not this morning. Thanks," said Jason, facing the lobby door as he tugged at Angie's arm. She shrugged her shoulders but didn't resist. He didn't want to set foot again in that room that was—and then wasn't—there. He didn't want to spend another unnecessary second in the hotel. "By the way, Harry, any word from American Express?" asked Jason, fully resolved that they would sign out of The Crowned Lady as soon as they'd recovered their bags.

"Called 'em half an hour ago. Still no word, but don't worry, I'm keeping on top of it."

"Thanks. Shit!" said Angie.

"Double shit," said Jason.

They toured a couple of churches recommended in the brochures, had lunch at the Gerente, and then returned to their hotel, expecting to go out again to take in another afternoon movie. What Jason didn't expect was that old scaly-ass would be lying in wait. Dapper in blue pinstripe and solid red tie, Moran sat on the sofa playing cards with Harry Baker. Harry occupied an armchair across from Moran. On the coffee table between them stood a liqueur bottle and shot glasses.

"Top o' the day to you," said Moran, rising and making a theatrical bow. "Join us for some seven-card stud?"

"I don't think so," said Jason.

"Oh, c'mon. We can for a little while," coaxed Angie.

"We have to freshen up."

"You go freshen up, Jay." She sat down next to Moran although she could—as Jason noted—even more easily have taken the armchair next to Baker. "A little stud is just what Momma needs," she said, making the two men smile.

Jason wanted to take a leak, but instead he parked himself in the vacant chair. They were playing for loose change. Angie dumped a bunch out of her purse. The various denominations of centavo coins felt weightless to Jason; unreal, as though made of air; phantom money not worth bothering about, like the recent coinages of his mind. Harry got up and was back in seconds with another pair of shot glasses. The brown bottle with yellow label said KAHLÚA. It was a Mexican coffee liqueur that Jason remembered enjoying. Harry filled their glasses, refilled his and Frank's, and offered a toast: "May the best man win!"

"Or woman," Angie corrected.

"Absolutely," said Frank, clicking Angie's glass. When the round of clicks was over, Moran dealt the cards, two buried and one open for each. Jason liked the Kahlúa more than he liked playing cards. He wondered if this was how Frank and Harry spent much of their time with each other. It was relaxing, seductive, like dozing under a mental sombrero. Meanwhile, he and Angie—especially Angie—were winning most of the hands. Jason felt certain that Moran was throwing games—for Angie's sake, of course. Baker had to attend to the front desk only once. That was when Jason found it convenient to go to the bathroom. Baker kept topping off everyone's glass, and Jason didn't even remember seeing him leave and return with a whole new bottle of the same.

"You're not so tough if I can beat you in one round," said Angie, playfully jabbing Moran with a soft right to the ribs.

Moran bent over and winced as if hurt. "So you think you can land one on Frank Moran and survive, young lady?" he said.

"I can beat you with one hand tied around this glass," said Angie, taking a quick swig and handing the glass to Harry for a refill.

"Tell you what, missie. I'll double that pile of winnings of yours if you can land one legitimate punch on old Frank Walter Moran." So saying, he lurched off the couch, barely steadying himself, and stepped out past the armchairs. "I'm not hitting back, you unnerstand, but I'll block anything you can throw."

"You're fooling with the Girl with the Golden Gloves," said Angie, rising with fists circling in front of her and stepping around the table.

"A woman can throw a fit, but never a punch," said Moran.

"Oh yeah? You'll wish you were facing Jackie Johnson."

"Angie," said Jason, "will you please sit down? This is kind of stupid." In spite of himself, though, he started laughing, joining Harry Baker in a fit of snorts and sputters as Moran waved her on and Angie squared off, her right fist thwacking the cushion of an open palm.

Angie grew red in the face. Jason knew that mood change, recognized the stubbornness that gripped her when she felt she was being bested. She lashed out with a left, followed that with a quick right, but Moran's magic landing pods proved quicker—in spite of the fact that he seemed a little shaky on his feet. Face flushed pink, eyes bright with cunning, he quaked with soundless mirth, grinning as he kept on blocking Angie's flailing fists.

"Enough, Angie!" Jason managed to shout between hiccups of laughter. But Angie wouldn't listen. Finally, she landed a one-two punch to Moran's oaken chest, withdrawing in pain while the old man pretended to slump. Following up on her apparent advantage, Angie pounded Moran's chest another couple of times—until the old codger caught her in a clinch. Jason watched them stagger back and forth, whispering, neither seeming to want to let go. When Angie started giggling against the old man's neck, Jason grew uncomfortable.

"I'll bet you didn't clinch as much with Johnson," said Angie.

"Got that right, baby."

"Angie, will you sit down!"

"The winner is—Angie!" declared Harry, lifting his glass. Angie finally released Moran, and they both sank red-faced back on the couch.

Moran whipped a ten-peso note out of his pocket. "Here! I never welsh on a bet," he said, laughing. "Someday, Angie, tell this to your grandchildren: You're the only woman who ever spanked the stuffing out of Frank Walter Moran."

Everyone laughed again, and Baker dealt the cards for another round of poker. "Shit!" said Baker, slapping himself. "I forgot to tell you. American Express called. You can now pick up your luggage at the bus station."

"Great!" said Angie. "Be a sweetheart, Jay, and go get it."

"Come with me," said Jason.

"Can't you see I'm a little tired?" she said, rubbing her fists and grinning at Moran.

"We can go together later, then."

"The *consigna* may not stay open for more than another hour or so," said Harry.

"If we're going out tonight, I need another dress, Jay."

He knew his resistance to leaving had to sound petty and unreasonable, so he quickly came to his senses. What in the world could happen, he reasoned, in the hour or two he'd be absent? Old reptile-butt had got as close to Angie as he ever was going to get. It was Baker who bothered him. How come Baker "suddenly" remembered the call about the luggage? All along, Harry had been extremely conscientious, letting them know whenever he made a call to American Express, reassuring them he was on top of things. It was the Kahlua, Jason figured. Enough of that stuff could drill a hole in anyone's memory. As woozy as he himself felt at this point, Baker and Moran had started tippling much earlier.

15

"You must be mistaken," said Jason.

"I make no mistake, Señor."

"It has to be here! They called me from American Express to tell me it had arrived." Jason leaned over the narrow counter and checked out the snaky line of tagged bags and parcels that wound over the floor behind it. "You have more in your office," he said, seeing other pieces of luggage through the open door of the *oficina* to the left.

"I know what's in there. Your luggage is not in there."

"Let me in. I'll look for myself."

"I'm sorry, Señor. Unauthorized personnel are not allowed in my office."

Officious little prick! Thought Jason. He stood back, scratched his head, and stared blankly at the rot-green wall of the *consigna*.

What was wrong with those idiots at American Express? he wondered. How could they make such a stupid mistake?

"Do you know who you spoke to at American Express, Señor?"

Jason shook his head. Only Baker had been dealing with them. Baker couldn't have misunderstood them. The agents there all spoke English.

"I will call them for you," said the official, retreating into his inviolable little cubicle.

"Thank you."

"De na'."

While Jason waited for some explanation, a slyly smiling Harry Baker popped into his head. As Jason left the hotel lobby to try to grab a taxi, he had turned around and looked at Baker, catching that sneaky grin—then instantly dismissing it from his mind.

Jason now already knew what the clerk would come back and tell him. Blood rushed to his head like a surge of electricity. His face and neck prickled as if breaking into hives.

"I'm sorry, Señor. The agent I spoke to—"

"I know, I know," said Jason.

"The agent I spoke to was there all day and he is sure that no one could have called you because your—"

"Those fucking bastards!" Jason shouted, breaking into English. "They set me up, the three of them!"

"Señor?"

Jason could see them: Harry the pimp looking the other way as Frank and Angie disappeared into the hallway. He could see Angie stripping, Frank's pants molting to the floor, Angie stretching back on the bed . . .

Jason checked his watch. He hadn't been away very long. Yet how long would it take her, them? If he hurried . . .

The shortest path to the exit found him leaping from side to side to slip through lines of human traffic that interwove and eddied like a clutch of mating snakes. A dozen taxis lay in wait, lined up like a yellow cobra lusting to strike. He hopped into the first in line.

"You are in a hurry, Señor?"

"In a hurry?" Jason sat back against the wrinkled leather seat. He stared into space and took several deep breaths.

"Where to, Señor?"

"*Adonde*?" Jason repeated. It seemed quite clear where he wanted to go—where he *had* to go. "Are there planes still flying to Mexico City today?"

"Sí, Señor. You have plenty of time."

Jason had no doubt that, once in Mexico City, he could quickly connect with a flight to New York.

"Very well. *Al aeropuerto, por favor.*"

As the taxi entered the outskirts of the city, Jason began to feel queasy. His palms grew sweaty, and his breathing grew erratic. The sight of those green expanses outside the cab window afflicted him with a kind of agoraphobia. He wished the windows had blinds, wished he could shut out the suffocating light of the sky.

"Driver," he said, "I changed my mind. Turn around and go back, please."

"To the bus station?"

"No, not to the bus station."

"*Adonde*, Señor?"

"Do you know what they use to fill up holes in . . . in wood?"

"*Masilla*?"

"Yes, putty, exactly. Could you take me to a store where I can buy a little can of putty?"

"Sure. And if you will excuse me for asking, for what do you need this putty?"

"I live in an apartment that has a hole in the wall, and terrible smells keep coming in from the apartment next door. I want something to plug it up."

"I see. May I make an observation, Señor?"

"Of course."

"You will not keep the smells from coming in by plugging up one little hole."

"Why not?"

"Because it is likely that there are many other holes that you can't even see, all around the moldings and where the wall joins the ceiling, and that the smells are coming in from all those cracks at once."

"Makes no difference," said Jason. "In a couple of days we're moving out of that damned place anyway."

"If I may say so, Señor, you are a martyr. As for me, I wouldn't have lived in such a place even for a day."

Jason caught the grin in the rearview mirror. The man seemed to be mocking him. The cabbie made a couple of turns and drove back into the city. As the taxi pulled up beside some nondescript store, Jason spoke up again. "Driver, I've changed my mind."

16

Jason pushed open the lobby door expecting to see Baker, but a young Mexican with a trim mustache stood behind the counter in his place. "Where's the boss?" asked Jason.

"He left, Señor. I will be here all night. Do you need your key?"

"Yes, Number Three." Son of a bitch! thought Jason, frustrated at being denied the pleasure of calling Harry a liar to his fat pasty face.

The clerk cast him an ironical stare as Jason swiped the key from his hand and rushed on into the hallway. Tiptoeing up to his room, he put his ear against the door, inserted the key as quietly as he could, then kicked the door open.

No one was there. The bed was made. Jason was not surprised. But the air smelled sweaty, salty-sweet. It smelled of Angie. He wondered if maybe it always smelled of Angie, always smelled of sex, and he normally didn't notice. He paced around the room, clenching his fists, pressing them to his forehead, shaking his head. He examined the bathroom, found nothing amiss, then stopped in front of the bed, where he stood like a statue for several minutes, unable to take another pointless step.

Collapsing face-forward onto the bed, he began to sigh heavily, then found himself sniffing at Angie's pillow. When he looked at where he sniffed, he froze, as if he had nuzzled the beard of a dragon.

There were hairs on the pillow. Several black ones—and a couple that were iron gray.

Jason seized the pillow and flung it with all his might against the framed *chacmool*, which clattered to the desktop. Springing forward, he grabbed the print by its sides, but he could not follow through on the impulse to smash it to pieces. Theatrics were just not his style. Breaking things and punching walls would not cure the ache in his chest. His hands shook uncontrollably as he climbed up onto the desk. It took him several tries to get the picture wire to finally snag the hook.

Jason now stared at that winking, unpluggable peephole again. It drew his eye and easily conquered his will.

The sight of Angie stopped his breath. Emerging from the bathroom, she sauntered across the floor, toasty-warm and glowing from her shower, as though coming straight at *him*—but not looking up as high as she'd have to if she suspected he was there. As she approached, her hands made love to her breasts and slipped down over her glistening thighs. Her familiar smile and heavy-lidded gaze were directed to someone just below Jason's field of view, someone standing in front of that chest that was just like the one on which he knelt. As she approached him (for it had to be a "him," Jason knew), she exaggerated the sway of her hips and stroked her wet bush with lacquered fingertips.

"Hiding something?" she said with a grin, tongue-tip cruising her upper lip, staring down at the lower half of the man who remained out of sight. "Oh, you want *me* to find the Easter egg?" she said.

No sound came from the invisible man. Instead, a pair of arms swung up, visible down to the elbows. The hands, joined like the head of a bird, cupped a beak of steel.

"Jay!" she shouted in disbelief. (How could she know he was up there, behind the wall, observing? But what could he do, Jason asked himself, perched like a parrot, high off the ground, to stop those arms from descending?)

The movement was swift, allowing her no time to counter with a forearm block. The blade swooped down between her breasts and Jason heard the crunch of metal on bone. Cheek to the wall, he could not stop watching. Absurd! he thought. Absolutely impossible! he said to himself as the hands, raised again, plunged down for a second time in a smear of red the color of Angie's nail polish.

"What the hell are you doing?"

Angie's voice, coming from right behind him, ripped through his spine like a saw. Jason lowered himself carefully to the floor, leaning on the dresser to support his buckling knees.

"The *chacmool*," he said, pretending to straighten the picture frame.

"What about it?" Angie's face sported a deep rosy flush as if she'd just stepped out victorious from the ring.

"We're leaving the hotel right now," he said, picking up the sheathed knife from the dresser top and stuffing it into their red leather bag.

"The hell we are."

"We're leaving *Mexico* right now!" he said.

"Are you nuts? It just so happens that we have a date with Frank tonight."

"We are *not* going to see Frank tonight—nor ever again." His voice was shrill. He would not back down.

"Okay," Angie pouted, her eyes liquid-bright. "Then *I* have a date with Frank tonight. If you don't want to keep us company . . . well, you do what *you* have to do, dear."

Insider

Sarah Zettel

The voices intruded into Jani's environment in staccato bursts of nonsense.

Gay go up and gay go down, to ring the bells of London Town,
I said go away!
Mad Maudlin goes on dirty toes to save her shoes from gravel.

Jani shot up straight in her chair. Her eyes swept the virtual room. All the open windows looked out onto network-space from under the logo of Lockmaster, Inc., and their images played on, undisturbed by the new voice. The augmented realism inherited from Europe and the garish experiments from North America showed through the northern windows. The myriad stylizations from Asia shone through the east. Abstracts and fragments from the shifting worlds of Arabia and Africa filled the western windows. Near the ceiling, two dozen windows let in the signals from the off-world net-spaces with their combination of stark realism and brilliant colors.

But the signal didn't come through any of the links that the windows represented. It seeped in through the cracks in the room's corners, full of white noise between the poetry and pleading.

I won't let you stop me!
I'll come and go by Caterhaugh and ask no leave of thee.

"Control!" Jani jumped to her feet. "Get me a trace! I've got a live one!"

"Running!" responded Control's steady, tenor voice.

Let me go!

Mother, may I go out to swim? Yes my darling-daughter, but don't go near the water.

"Who are you?" Jani turned around in a tight circle, scanning all the windows intently. "What's your name?"

What are the twin born spirits, and they'll answer love and death.

I hear you!

"Keep talking. We'll find you." The pleading voice and the nonsense rejoinders sent a chill through Jani's mind.

If you don't . . . said the first voice.

If all the trees were beans and peas, what would we do for water?

The voices fell silent. Jani slammed her fist into her palm.

"Control, did you get anything?"

Control's response came from the northern window. Its frame now surrounded a hardworking crew typing frantically at antique keypads, their eyes glued to freestanding monitors. With Control's characteristic humor, the crew consisted entirely of monkeys.

"No more than a confirmation, Jani. It's a live one all right," said Control over the scene. "And it's two separate signals."

"Wonderful." Jani suppressed a shudder. There were still hackers and cowboys in net-space who had preferred things when the net had been their private realm of anarchy. Some of them created trouble for pay. Some of them just tried to scare out the pernicious influences of the outside world, like the corporations, net-space security, and the licensed guides. The taming of net-space had been a war, and the other side wasn't yet convinced they'd lost.

"Did you at least get a continent?"

"We didn't even get a world." The scene broke into a dozen representations of the planets of the solar system, plus the moons.

"Damn." Jani folded her arms and stared at the ceiling. Willows trailed their branches in the water overhead, making rings in the rippling, greenish brown water. "That one sounded really scared."

"Can you blame them?"

Jani sighed and shook her head. She'd been lost her first trip into net-space. For forty-eight hours she'd whirled through a hurricane world without shape or end. The memory still gave her screaming nightmares. "Get all the monitors on. I want total recall and I want the tracers standing by."

"We already are."

"Good enough. Keep every ear open. We may get another blip."

"You leave it to us, Jani. You've got to go meet the newbies from San Salvador."

"Fifteen demerits and an hour's pay for calling potential clients 'newbies' in company space." Jani glowered at the northern window with mock sternness.

"We're Corporate's liaisons here, Jani, thank you very much. If there's demerits to be handed out, we'll take care of it."

Jani chuckled. "I'll believe that when I see it. Thanks, Control."

"Our pleasure."

The northern window swirled like oil on pond water and the scenes from Control mutated into the New Dehli skyline. The transmitting buildings lit up as if they were candles.

Control's handling, she told herself. *Nothing else you can do without a trace of another blip.*

Jani sighed and forced her mind back to business. Corporate had been impressing the importance of this deal on her for a month. The spin-off contracts alone could push Lockmaster's profit margins to new highs for a year.

Jani faced the door that appeared next to the western window. Through the frosted glass, she could hear Esdras Delgado, Lockmaster's sales representative for the El Salvador territory, trotting out the introductory speech in his flawless Spanish.

"When our grandparents started building the networks, communication took on a third dimension. 'Networks' became 'net-space,' another territory. Some people say another planet." Esdras waited for his audience's chuckle and got it.

Jani resisted the urge to lip-synch the rest of the spicl. "And there's no denying it, net-space is huge and, what's more, like the real universe, it's constantly expanding." Jani made a gesture near her throat as if she were straightening a neck tie. A precisely tailored business suit replaced her trousers and shirt.

In the back of her mind, Jani knew her body was really encased in a VR outfit and suspended in an exoskeleton. When she moved inside net-space, her body moved in the skeleton, so she stayed exercised. A contracted medical service monitored and maintained her health, but after twenty years inside net-space she had ceased to think about the arrangement consciously.

She pulled the door open and stepped into the corridor.

Outside her work environment waited a hallway tapestried with silent simulations of the work being transacted through the net. Jani passed a symphony narrowcast, a hospital laboratory, a board meeting, and a holographically enhanced lecture on the fall of Rome. She kept on walking and Esdras's voice got louder, but the decorations on the walls got progressively simpler.

"In addition, net-space is constantly changing its shape. It's a dynamic system with a very high chaotic element." The simulations faded to become mahogany-paneled walls decorated with oil paintings of Lockmaster's founders. "What Lockmaster will do, while creating and stabilizing your own environment, is provide you with a trainer, a native guide, so to speak."

The paintings and panelings passed behind her and left white painted walls. *God we are starting these guys at the low end*, thought Jani. Full sensory interface with net-space had been technically and culturally possible for over thirty years, but because it had evolved in chaotic bursts, using it had never been simple or reliable. Most businesses, especially in the early days, couldn't afford the expense of equipment and training simply to have their employees roaming aimlessly about the net looking for information, or worse, getting lost in the shifting maze of links and channels that knit the separate environments together.

It had taken Jani a year and three psychiatrists to get the nerve together to force herself back into net-space after she had been lost. If she hadn't been so far in love with the idea of helping to explore and tame the world inside the net, she never would have done it. One of her psychiatrists said she overcompensated. He had been right. She hadn't let that stop her.

Jani stopped in front of a doorway that was nothing more than a well-lit opening in the wall and waited for her cue.

"I'd like to introduce you to the senior trainer who will be handling your account, should you decide to use Lockmaster to design your environment and interface capabilities."

Jani fixed her expression into her professional smile and stepped through the doorway. She and Esdras had rehearsed this timing carefully.

"Gentlemen, may I introduce our senior trainer, Madame Guide Jani Renard."

You're on, Jani.

The office-space was a comfortable simulation of a conference room overlooking the sprawl of San Salvador. The clients were three middle-aged men in stiff dark suits. They all looked vaguely uncomfortable.

"Good afternoon, gentlemen." Jani's Spanish was not as good as Esdras's but she really did speak the language, making it unnecessary to compensate for translator delay. "Welcome Inside." She swept her hand around the room. "Not much different from a real conference room, hm? Or a localized virtual-reality simulation?" She rapped her knuckles on the table. "A perfectly stabilized environment for your work. Now, the difference," she stepped briskly up to the nearest window, "is access." She tugged down on an imaginary string and a window pulled down like a video screen, blanking out the cityscape in a three-foot square. The view through the new window panned across shelves filled with plastic-cased optical disks. "And control." Jani reached through the window and pulled out a disk case. She flipped it open, extracted the disk, put the disk back on the shelf. She caught Esdras's eye and he nodded. *Keep shoveling,* she almost heard him thinking. *Make them forget the other side of it. Make them forget there's still chaos under the order we've created.*

Cut it out, Jani. You're on stage. Keep your mind on the job.

With a motion like opening a zipper, she undid a drive slot under the window. "The environment we design for you will make use of familiar tools and situations." She slid the disk into its slot and closed it. The view through the window shifted to become a stylized spider's web with dots of light gliding across its threads. "To produce a—"

Get away from me!

Jani's head jerked up. The voice had gained some measure of control. The signal was much stronger. So was the fear.

I must away, 'ere break of day . . .

Leave me alone!

Jani glanced at her clients. She remembered Corporate's emphasis on the profits and the importance of closing this deal. She remembered her limited store of currency and her eternal bills for medical maintenance.

She remembered screaming in the hospital for three days after she'd been pulled out of net-space. She remembered how close she'd come to murdering the hacker who'd cut her connection to the outside.

"I hear you!" Jani shouted to thin air. "Keep talking!" She bolted out the door. "Control! Home!"

The world became a blur of color and Dopplered noise. Then, Jani stood on a roofed-in veranda overlooking a silver river sliding between wooded banks.

Jani caught her balance against the veranda rail. "Come on!" she called out. "Talk to me! Where are you?"

But it was Control's voice that answered. "Lost it again, Jani. The trace slid right off."

Jani rubbed her forehead. "Have you told the net-secs we got a hacker yet?"

"Yes, and they've got somebody monitoring your work-space links."

Jani sighed and walked down the steps to the river side. The river itself was her visual reference for the myriad channels that made the paths between the environments of net-space.

"Print out unidentified voice transmission," she said to the river. In response, it smoothed its surface and printed out the words from the live one.

Jani chewed on her lower lip and considered the gold, glowing text.

Found me twice, even with hacker interference. Whoever the live one is, they're very good at what they're doing. So's the hacker, if even Control can't trace them.

"Can you hear me?"

The plea came directly from the river. The text burst apart in a shower of sparks. There were still no visuals, just a voice riding the surface of the water.

"What's your name?" Jani asked quickly. "Control!" she hollered back toward the porch.

"Ninon Dale, twenty-seven H, eight-four-one-nine, twelve-forty-six." Jani didn't dare take the time to wonder about the string of numbers.

"I'm Jani Renard, Ninon." She knelt on spongy ground of the river bank. "Can you see me?" Jani smoothed the water down with her palm, making a clear, flat screen. "I'm a guide. Talk to me. Help me find you."

"I don't know how," the voice whispered. "I've got nothing to work with. How do I—"

How does your garden grow?

Jani dove headfirst into the river.

A thousand fragments of sight and sound flashed past her. Apples ripening on the trees. Nebulae swirling in the void. Protozoa swimming by with their organelles stained red and blue. Lions and tigers and bears, oh my. The torque's wrong on that rivet but the approach vector's right on that shuttle.

"Ninon!" she shouted into the thick waters.

"Signal's gone again, Jani," said Control.

Jani swore until she ran out of breath. "I don't suppose you got the trace that time?" she inquired.

"No." The tone of Control's voice told Jani this was no time for additional sarcasm.

Jani bit her lip. *If I find the database the quotes are coming from and I might get a handle on Ninon's signal, even if it is just being shuffled through.*

The river had no current. Jani swam through a morass of images. She smelled cinnamon and anise and coffee. She felt electrodes probe a valve in a heart. She watched spheres turn inside out and outside in again in time to a lecture on abstraction in simulation. Somebody set off a model of Mount Vesuvius.

Nothing like what she needed. She needed pure sound. She needed a store of words. Jani jackknifed her body and plowed down toward the river bottom, where the thick silt was composed of nothing but words.

Jani skimmed the uneven surface. Her passage kicked up lazy clouds of dust. A dozen languages she didn't know swirled behind her. She heard some words she did know, but couldn't translate without Control. Eventually, she stirred up some fragments of English.

Those are pearls that were his eyes . . .

Why pullest thou the rose? Why breakest thou the wand?

Gay go up and gay go down to ring . . .

Gotcha! Jani changed her stroke so that she was treading water. "System, mark this database," she said to the net-space. "Give me a red post as a sensory representation." The environment responded and a pillar of scarlet wood sprouted out of the river bottom.

Jani grabbed hold of the pillar to keep from floating away. She bobbed in place, searching the sandy brown bottom for any indication of recent digging, but saw nothing except some fluffy seaweed swaying in the current.

This was no place she'd ever been, then. "System," she said. "Where am I?"

"Public archives 561-A. British Heritage Foundation. Physical location, Manhattan Island, the Republic of New York," said the flat, default voice of the net-space.

Home sweet home, thought Jani. *Which means I've voice access.* "Access authority Guide Jani Renard 159045." She rattled off her license number. "Locate data-storage units containing the phrases 'I'll come and go by Caterhaugh,' 'to ring the bells of London town,' and 'I must way 'ere break of day.' Additional criteria: Locate only the sources that have received a signal from user Ninon Dale in the last four hours. Open access channel. Sensory representation, stairway to reading room with books marked at the relevant sections on a desk. Secure and hold channels and apply personal link J2 to my home environment." That would let her see the data's environment from her back porch.

A square hole opened in the river bottom to reveal a stark white staircase. Jani expelled her breath and let herself sink down until her shoes touched the first stair.

Walking into the new environment was like walking into a room of black-and-white cardboard cutouts. The light cast no shadows on the outlines of the desk or on the three fat books resting on its surface. Jani picked the volumes up one at a time. They felt like nothing but dry paper in her hands.

"You getting this, Control?" she asked as she scanned the titles. *Childe's Ballads. Bartlett's Familiar Quotations. A Little Treasury of Great Poetry.* "Anybody home in any of these?"

"Loads of people, on and off," Control answered. "But none of them's our live one. We got a file to go with the name though."

"Great." The book of poems made no noise as Jani set it back on the desk.

"Ninon Dale, fifteen-year-old female—"

Jani growled. "Who let a kid in here without a leash?"

"Her mother," said Control. "Simona Dale. Ninon's an insider. Her mother registered five years ago and checked the kid in at the same time."

Jani nodded. That was becoming more common. Some of the medical services were even beginning to specialize in taking care of insider children.

"Is her mother available?"

"We just made contact. She's waiting for you." Control paused. "We've also got Esdras on hold, and he's madder than a whole hive of hornets. He's not the only one either. Corporate's discussing your . . . behavior. At length and in detail." Pause. "We're not at the UN Comm office anymore, Jani."

"I'd noticed," Jani grumbled. "Quote regulations at them. The paragraph where is says a registered insider is legally obligated to assist anybody who's lost. And then tell them that goes double for a licensed guide. Take me to Simona." Jani raced up the staircase. "And while you're at it, try to find out if those numbers Ninon was spouting mean anything."

"Done and done, Jani."

The staircase broke the surface of the river. The environment on the bank had been set to represent a lawn of perfectly trimmed grass surrounding a ruthlessly organized forest of rose trees. Spaced three feet apart, they grew in straight lines that stretched to the horizon, a tree of red blossoms, then a white one, a pink one, and a yellow one. The air was thick with the smell of the flowers.

In the middle of the scene stood a tall woman with all her brown hair pulled back into a tidy bun.

"Jani Renard?" The woman stepped forward. "I'm Simona Dale. I was told you've heard from Ninon."

"I've been picking up a stray signal." Jani stepped onto the bank. The river vanished into the expanse of trimmed grass. "The name the originator gave me was Ninon Dale."

Simona's lips moved, but no sound came out. She pressed her palm against her eyes.

"Excuse me, I'll be all right in a moment."

"Allow me," said Jani. She had no links operative in Simona's space, so the environment wouldn't respond to her voice or Control's, but the system defaults would allow her limited capabilities. With a deft motion, Jani signed the word *chair*. A basic, wooden piece of furniture appeared. Simona lowered herself into it.

"Thank you," she whispered. "You'll have to excuse me. I've been awake for a long time."

Jani signed for another chair. She sat down and waited.

"My ex-husband has kidnapped my daughter," Simona said at last. "She's been missing for three months. He's trying to keep her outside."

Jani clenched her jaw. An outburst would not help. Not now.

"I divorced Derek about five years ago. I got custody of Ninon. I'm an industrial environment engineer." Simona rubbed her thighs, as if trying to smooth down the fabric of her trousers, which were as perfect as her hairstyle and her rose trees. "I had to spend weeks at a time inside. I decided that instead of leaving her in child care, I'd bring Ninon in with me." Her voice began to take on a vaguely singsong quality. "Derek decided I was raising Ninon in an unnatural environment and went to court to get the custody order reversed. That dragged out for three years. I won and got a restraining order, but two months ago he broke into my physical residence and took Ninon. I've been in and out ever since, looking for her. The net-secs have been working with the outsider police, but they haven't . . . I'm not supposed to be contacting you but . . ."

"What's been keeping security from tracing her signal?"

"He's hired somebody to lock her out. You know, to scramble her orientation if she gets in, to yank her signal as soon as it's traced and to keep traces off her—" Simona's sentence broke off.

Jani licked her lips. "I wish I had some news for you," she said. "I've picked up a couple of blips from Ninon. My Control's found the space that the hacker's probably operating through. We're dumping everything we've got down to the net-secs. I've got my ears open, believe me, but whoever's scrambling her is doing a very good job. I'm amazed she's getting in at all." *And I'm amazed she's trying to contact a guide rather than her mother.*

"Ninon took to being inside like she was born here. She wanted to be a environment engineer when she grew up . . ." Simona's gaze drifted across her spreading field of rose trees. "Or maybe even a guide."

Leaning forward, Jani said, "What I can't understand is how she got back in at all, if her father's holding on to her."

"Security thinks she may have gotten away from him. That she may be trying to use public-access terminals to get inside, or that she might have even made herself a patch somehow. Of course for her, working under those conditions would be like an astronaut trying to fly the Wright brothers' airplane."

Jani nodded. *I haven't got anything to work with*, Ninon had said. Now, that, at least, made sense.

Simona raised her eyes and her voice took on a steely edge. "I want my daughter back, Madame Guide," she said. "I am not going to let that man turn her into a narrow-minded outsider who can't cope with the way the world is changing. Please, help me find her."

"I'll report to security," Jani told her, "and give them permission to put a trace directly on me. If I can follow either Ninon or the hacker, they may be able to get a physical location on her."

"Thank you." For the first time, hope sounded in Simona's voice.

Jani stood up and signed *card*. A white square of cardboard appeared in her hand. "My space and emergency call numbers are here."

"Thank you." Simona accepted the card and snapped her fingers. It vanished into wherever she kept her data environment. She stood smoothly and waved her hand in a dismissive gesture. The chairs vanished from the tidy lawn. "Please let me know when you hear anything more."

"I think I'd better stick to telling security, " said Jani, eyeing Simona carefully. "If too much gets around, we could be feeding the hacker information without even knowing it."

She was able to count to five before Simona answered. "Yes, of course. You're right."

Jani turned around and signed for an open passage to net-security. In response, her river flowed down the middle of the smooth grass. A rowboat floated on its surface and beached itself on the bank.

Jani stepped in the boat and settled onto the cushioned seat. As she did, she cast a last look at Simona Dale surrounded by her endless stretch of uniform trees. "I hope we all get this straightened out soon."

Simona nodded and raised her hand as the boat slid into the river's current.

Because it was a solid route with a stable destination, Jani's river flowed swiftly through black space. Possible alternate channels manifested themselves as a scattering of stars on all sides of her.

"Control? Did you hear any of that?"

"Jani, eavesdropping on you is part of our job. We think the net-secs should get a leash on Simona Dale."

"So do I. If she was telling the whole story, I'm the King of Jordan." She rubbed her eyes. "Have you got anything on Ninon's father?"

"His name's Derek Guinsburg," Control said. "He's a commodities broker. A big one. Runs an agency that buys and sells channels and links in net-space. He handles the outside work and leaves the inside jobs to his employees. Corporate's got some data on him. He's one of the ruthless kind, apparently. Lives off his reputation for getting the job done no matter what. And, Jani, speaking of Corporate . . ."

Jani strangled a sigh. "I got a mercenary hacker and a missing kid here! Corporate can go take a flying—"

"Jani! Hard aport!"

Before Jani had time to react, a star swallowed her whole. White light blinded her. Jani signed sharply for signal clearance but didn't get it. The light persisted, forcing her to close her eyes.

"My apologies, Madame Guide," said a man's voice.

Jani opened her eyes. She stood in a book-lined office that had neither doors nor windows. Behind a heavy mahogany desk sat a big-boned man with a gray suit, gray eyes, and gray hair. "You would like an explanation, I'm sure." He extended his hand toward one of the deep leather armchairs in front of the desk.

Jani didn't move. She searched the room with her gaze instead, looking for a crack, a blur in the details or a blank spot in the paneling. Anything that might indicate a signal leak or a way out.

"I'm Leverette Rhodes," the man went on. "I am the attorney for Simona Dale's former husband Derek Guinsburg."

The only secrets in net-space are the ones you keep in your head. Jani sighed and folded her arms as if trying to hold her anger back by physical force. "Deliberately interfering with an established channel is illegal."

"If you want to take me to a court-space and prove I deliberately tapped and obstructed your channel, you're welcome to do so," Rhodes said. He made a gesture with two fingers, and a polished wooden door appeared between the bookcases.

"Jani?" said Control. "You still with us?"

"It's okay," she told them, even though she wasn't sure that was the truth. Something nagged at her. Something was not right, and it wasn't just Rhodes's abrupt way of getting through to her. The detail of the room reminded her sharply of Simona's rose trees for no reason she could define.

"On the assumption you want to talk about Ninon Dale, I'm listening." Jani's restless eyes scanned the environment, willing it to reveal the source of her discomfort. Aside from the desk and its owner, there was nothing but books. Copies of the *Harvard Law Review*. Volume upon volume of state, city, and UN legal codes. Funny. The last time she'd been in a lawyer's office outside, there had been no books. There had been filing cabinets full of papers and a networked terminal. She'd dealt with lawyers inside both for personal business and as clients for Lockmaster. The offices had been variations on that theme.

"Actually, it's Simona Dale I wanted to talk to you about." Rhodes leaned back in his chair, watching her examine his walls. "I thought I'd save both you and security some time." He pushed an optical disk the size of Jani's palm across the desk. "This is the public synopsis of the proceedings my client has initiated against Simona Dale."

Jani picked the disk up and ran her fingers over its surface, scanning the information. There was a summary of the divorce agreement, which gave Derek Guinsburg the right to "his daughter's unaccompanied physical presence for a period of forty-eight hours every three hundred and thirty-six hours." This was followed by a series of complaints that Simona Dale was obstructing the "physical presence" clause by neglecting to schedule the med-service to come and let Ninon out to visit her father. Then came the lengthy petition from Guinsburg to regain custody of Ninon on the basis that Dale had not only violated the divorce agreement but was subjecting Ninon to physical abuse and mental cruelty by keeping her inside net-space against her will.

Jani remembered Simona Dale's voice as she said, "I want my daughter back."

Jani's thoughts clicked over all at once and she knew what was wrong, because Simona had also said, "can't keep up with the way the world is changing."

Books were anachronisms. Either Derek Guinsburg had hired himself a lawyer who was old-fashioned to the point of eccentricity or Jani was dealing with somebody who had no idea what a lawyer's environment really looked like.

"I can also supply recordings of conversations in which Ninon is on a public channel apologizing to her father for her mother's behavior and insisting she will try to get out soon," Rhodes went on. Something dark crept into his voice. "Unfortunately, as a minor, she does not have authority to contact the med-service on her own behalf."

"So where is Ninon Dale?" Jani asked, looking around the shelves again. This time she knew what she was looking for.

Rhodes sighed theatrically. "You're not the only one who wants to know that. We think her mother's hired a hacker to deliberately obstruct her signal so that Ninon is unable to contact her father or anyone else for assistance. Which is the reason, we think, that she is trying to reach a guide."

"Jani," said Control's voice suddenly. "We got a problem here."

We got one here, too. Jani's heart began to thump painfully. Down in the corner of a shelf, half-hidden by the desk, stood three fat, familiar books. The urge to grab Rhodes by his virtual neck and demand to know what was going on washed over her but she held it back. He controlled this environment and she couldn't risk getting trapped inside it.

"Be with you in a minute, Control." She turned back to Rhodes, or whoever this was. "You don't mind if I take this to security with me?" Jani held up the disk. "To do a match with what's in their databases?" *Of course you won't. This is a distraction. You're doing something somewhere else, and you've had plenty of time to finish it, too, whatever it is.*

"Certainly not. You'll find everything in order, stamped and sealed." Jani tucked the disk into her pocket and "Rhodes" continued. "As I said, I simply thought I'd save us some time."

"Well, I appreciate your consideration." Jani mustered a courteous tone. "And I'll take it into account while I'm checking all this out. Good-bye, Mr. Rhodes."

The door opened onto her veranda and Jani stepped through.

"Control!" she called as soon as her feet touched the porch boards and Rhodes's door vanished.

"We've taken Control off your channels, Ms. Renard." Esdras Delgado appeared in front of her.

All the fury Jani held back in the hacker's environment burst out at once. "You've got no right to cut me off, Delgado!"

"I don't, but Lockmaster's assistant vice-president for this region does. You're forgetting, Madame Guide—" he managed to make the title sound like an insult "—you and your Control work for Lockmaster, not the other way around. Your behavior today lost us a five-year, nine-million-dollar account!"

I haven't got time for this. I've got to tell the net-secs what's going on. I've got to find out what that hacker has done to me and to Ninon. "My behavior today was in accordance with—"

"The law says that you have to notify net-security of the channel the lost party is transmitting through, not that you have to run after them!"

Jani felt real fatigue settling in. "Look, Esdras. The 'lost party' is a fifteen-year-old kid who has either been kidnapped by her father or is being held prisoner by her mother!"

Esdras pulled back as what she was saying sank in. "You should have told net-security, Jani."

"Control already has. I was on my way with the latest information when I got cut out by the hacker who's been hired by one or the other of the parents to keep the kid from helping herself. Every second I waste here is one more he's going to have to screw up my chances of getting to her."

Esdras had suddenly lost his ability to look her in the eye.

Jani folded her arms. "If there's something else coming, get on with it."

"You're suspended."

Jani ground her teeth together. "Why am I not surprised? Okay. I know you were looking forward to telling me that yourself since I screwed up your commission. You've done it. I'll file my appeal and see Lockmaster in court. Now get out of here." She made a slicing motion across her throat and Esdras vanished as her private secruity system cut his signal out of her space.

She clamped down her frustration and opened herself a door onto net-security.

Jani didn't make it back to her home environment for five hours. The security agent she had dealt with had insisted on going over every nanosecond of the conversation with "Rhodes." The net-sec put out a warrant on the hacker and began organizing a search mission while Jani waited. But when Jani asked what was being done about Ninon Dale, she was rewarded with a bland smile and a speech about domestic affairs and lawyers' petitions. This was an argument for the outside courts and social services, he said. They were handling it. The job of net-security was to track down the hacker. Madame Guide had done everything she could, now if she'd just pull back to her home-space and wait, that would be best, thank you.

Alone, Jani sat glumly on her grass and stared at the flowing river. Her sun sank below the tops of the willows, tinting the silver waters rose and gold. She stared at the clearing on the far bank where the archive data-environment should have appeared. It wasn't there. Her link to the library archives had been cut. That was no surprise. It was the obvious thing to do.

Jani ran both hands through her hair. Without Control to help her think, her mind felt hollow. The hacker could easily have found a new place to shuffle Ninon's signal through. He probably had already. That was probably what he was doing while she was standing in the office environment pretending she didn't know what was going on. That was the way wars were fought inside. You created a diversion to keep your target busy while you finished your attack.

Tired. Jani hung her head. *Too tired to even think straight. Maybe I should just let the net-secs handle it*, she thought. *Never should have left*

the Comm office. How much currency, how much space do I really need?
Then she shook her head. *No good, none of this. Can't let this go.
Inside or outside, Ninon needs somebody's help.* Jani stared out across
the water made up of a hundred million shifting, drifting signals.
*Okay, let's see. If the hacker's working for Simona, he should be shuffling
Ninon's home-space around so nobody can trace her to her origin point.
Which means my best bet is to try to trace the hacker, which could take
years and might just get the net-secs to yank my license for interfering
with an investigation. I could hunt up the data-spaces again and try to
follow the trail that way . . .*

*But if he's working for Guinsburg and Ninon is outside, then he
might be buying time until Guinsburg can win his case against the senior Ms. Dale, In that case, Guinsburg might move Ninon, or confine her
altogether if he knows she's gotten inside. I could go digging for the links
and try to find her last point of entry. But the hacker'll have thought of
that.*

*If he's any good at all, he'd have used his time to bury every single
path and erase all the links, because he knows where they're coming from
and I don't.*

A chime sounded through the evening air. Jani's head jerked
up. A space cleared on the river and a new message printed itself
across the surface.

JANI. ARGUING OUR CASE WITH CORPORATE NOW. GETTING NASTY.
WILL KEEP YOU POSTED. WANTED TO LET YOU KNOW THAT THE NUMBERS
NINON GAVE AFTER HER NAME WERE HER COORDINATES ON THE CITY
MAP AND EIGHT-FOUR-ONE-NINE IS A STREET ADDRESS. TWELVE-FORTY-
SIX IS AN APARTMENT NUMBER DEREK GUINSBURG IS NAME ON LEASE.
CONTROL.

Jani's breath caught in her throat. Damn it! Control didn't
know what Jani'd been through in the "law office." If the hacker
was watching her lines he now knew Jani had Ninon's physical
location. He'd tell his employer. He'd be doing it at this second.
She raised her head as if she expected to see the signal flash by.
And she couldn't cut it off, because she had no idea what channel his signal used, or where Guinsburg was.

*By the time I find a way to bring this home to the hacker, Ninon could
be in an unwired building in San Salvador, if she's not stark raving mad*

from being adrift inside for so long. The hacker knows too much. Jani knotted her fists.

I've been laying trails for twenty years, I've got more links to more spaces out there than even Control can keep track of. There's got to be something I can do that the hacker couldn't trace. Got to be. The problem is, he's had enough time to establish a way to trace just about anything I do in the whole of net-space. Jani straightened her spine up one joint at a time. *So what if I did something outside net-space?*

No. Ridiculous. I haven't been outside in twenty years.

"System," she said slowly. "Confine information parameters to my secured environment. Identify my physical location relative to Ninon Dale's physical location."

The river sank and dwindled until it became a chattering creek, running past the tops of her shoes. In front of her sprouted a tourist information map of Manhattan adorned with two red dots. The first was labeled YOU ARE HERE. The second, at grid coordinates 27H, was labeled NINON DALE.

Jani felt her jaw drop. Ninon Dale was maybe the length of a football field away from her.

Which explains why she was signaling me. Jani closed her mouth. *I'm the closest guide to her.* She got to her feet, breathing slow and heavy as the implications of what she was about to do sank in.

No. No. Jani, this is stupid. Call somebody else. Anybody else.

And who do I know who's less than an hour away? How can I be sure that my signal will get through? How do I know what's being done to Ninon right now? I can be there in fifteen minutes. Get her back where she wants to be. It'll take me fifteen minutes once I'm unhooked. Fifteen minutes.

Jani glanced around at the world. Her willows swayed in the evening breeze. The twilight turned the air a pale blue. Soon the moon would be rising and the evening stars would come out to shine on the night birds and will-o'-the-wisps.

Jani grit her teeth and raised her right hand. This was not how it was supposed to go. After an extended period inside, she was supposed to contact her med-service and get out under supervision.

One letter at a time, Jani spelled L-O-G-O-U-T.

Her home faded to black.

The weight of the outside world pressed against her. Smooth fabric muffled every inch of her. Metal struts hugged her body, supporting all her weight and keeping her standing.

With clumsy motions, Jani reached behind her head and tore the Velcro seam that held the mask over her face and let it dangle under her chin. Without the mask, she could look down at her body encased in cottony fabric, steel rods, and fiber-optic threads.

The release key was a big red button at eye level on one of the cage supports. Jani pressed it. The bars and their fibrous tethers drew back and left her standing on her own. Jani took two steps and fell over. The floor slammed against her knees and shoulder. The bags of nutrients and waste hanging on her suit squished and sloshed. Jani lay where she fell, blinking stupidly at the floor until the chill from the tiles began to soak through her.

Well, gravity still works, she thought ludicrously. She pushed herself into a sitting position with a groan. She hurt. She sagged. Something was wrong. Jani stripped the gloves off and looked at the backs of her hands. Mottled skin bunched around a web of bulging blue veins.

Oh, God. She traced a hollow where her cheek should have been and fingered the pouch of flesh dangling from her throat.

Should have known. Should have known. I was thirty when I went in. What's that make me now? Fifty? Fifty-three? I've lost track. She squeezed her eyes shut a couple of times, trying to clear her blurry vision. *And I've gone nearsighted. Oh, Christ, what've I done?*

"Jani! Jani!" A familiar voice burst out from someplace past her right shoulder.

"Control?" God! Was that raspy noise her voice? She swallowed, cleared her throat and tried again. "Control?"

"Back here!"

Jani shoved herself onto her knees and looked behind her. Aside from the empty exoskeleton, the only thing in the room was a long, metal-topped table. The boxes and bottles stacked there belonged to the med-service that looked after her. Above it hung a flatscreen terminal that Jani had forgotten she owned.

One of the members of Control looked down on her. Jani stared at the slender, Chinese woman in a scarlet blouse with VR gloves on her hands and audio-link headphones covering her ears.

Hsing-Yi. Jani tried to reconcile what she saw with the tenor voice she heard. *This one is Hsing-Yi.*

"I'm okay." Jani took a deep breath and got to her feet. She made it to the table in three lurching steps and caught herself against the edge before she could fall again. "Why'd Lockmaster let you back online to me?"

"They didn't," Control said. "Get back in here, you idiot!"

"Not unless you know an outsider who's closer to Ninon Dale than I am." Jani explained what she had worked out about the hacker and the real extent of the problem. Her voice still sounded too high and too reedy to her own ears, but at least it had cleared up.

Control was silent.

"Okay then." Jani straightened her back experimentally and found she could hold the position. "I could really use your help. I'm not sure what it's like outside anymore."

Control shook her head. "Okay, Jani. But get out of the net-suit first, all right?"

"Just tell me what to do."

Getting out of the suit was a tricky business. Control prompted her so she didn't tear any of the tubing, or injure herself removing the feeds that dealt with the necessary body functions. Underneath the net-suit, she wore a second, thinner jumpsuit that was assembled of Velcroed sections that could be removed in pieces. Control pronounced it funny-looking but adequate.

"Now," said Control briskly. "The door to the outside's locked. Twist the latch above the knob clockwise to open it. Go ahead."

Jani took one step toward the blank, beige door and then another. Her stomach churned, but this time, she did not fall. The latch turned smoothly and Jani pulled the door open.

Daylight exploded in front of her. Jani buried her face in the crook of her arm.

"Jani?" called Control.

"I'm okay, I'm okay. " Blinking hard, Jani raised her head. Her eyes adjusted themselves in painful stages until the blurs of light and shadow separated into recognizable shapes.

Most of those shapes were people. A river of people from every climate and culture flowed by her ancient stone porch. Beyond them, a broad stretch of burgundy had replaced the street. Closed vehicles whirred by on it at insane speeds. On the far side, more people moved. The summer wind was full to bursting with noise.

A lump formed in Jani's throat that might have been wonder or fear. In front of her porch, a tidy row of children in uniform paraded past. A quartet of police officers shouldered their way through the crowds. A host of caterers with hot boxes stepped around them. Between the people's ankles scurried things that looked like a cross between a cat and a hamster, except they were the size of collie dogs and had bright purple fur. One of the things scuttled up to a pile of dead leaves and old paper and began eating its way through the debris. A street vendor hawked flowers and sun visors. Across the street, a woman in brown overalls spatulaed what looked like tarry putty onto a lumpy wall of wood. The wall was constructed at a skewed angle to run into another wall that rose behind the woman until it cast a shadow over the whole street.

Wait a minute. Jani looked up and realized her gaze was traveling up the trunk of a tree. A huge tree. Jani had seen redwoods. This thing would have dwarfed them. It wasn't the only one either. She could see eight others without even turning her head. Jani felt her eyeballs try to pop out of their sockets. Glass-and-stone buildings sprouted like squared-off mushrooms from between the gigantic trees. Bridges and catwalks had been slung from building to building and from building to tree. Transparent elevators glided up and down the mammoth trunks, past windows set into the living wood and the market stalls and shops that rested on the spreading branches.

"Control? Where'd . . . Trees?" Jani was suddenly unable to construct a full sentence.

"Trees?" Control sounded puzzled. "Oh, the ironwoods.

They're the Republic's answer to the O_2 crisis. The project kicked into production phase maybe ten years ago. You're living in one of the fully foliated districts."

"Oh," said Jani faintly.

"Ninon is in one of the handmades . . . the buildings across the street, " Control told her. "You can't walk on the road. That's for the autoports . . . automated transports. Private cars got outlawed inside city limits about the time they phased the trees in. You're going to have to take the walkway. Look to your right."

Jani did. A gleaming network of tubes supported by living trees arched over the street. The structure connected the sidewalks to half a dozen of the buildings and three of the closest ironwoods.

She eyed the walkway skeptically. "Must confuse the hell out of the chickens."

"What?" asked Control.

No time. No time, Jani, she reminded herself fiercely. "Never mind. What do I do once I get in there?"

"Hang on . . . Okay, we've got the map. When you're inside the walkway, the tunnel will split into three branches. Take the one to the left. Then, take the first set of stairs you come to, those'll also be on your left. They'll lead you straight out to the roof of the building. You'll need to—"

"Control?" Jani jerked her head around. Darkness filled the screen.

Oh no.

Corporate had cut them off. Or the hacker had. It didn't matter. The last bridge to the world she knew had just gone up in flames. Jani faced the outside and fear tightened in her sunken chest.

Move, Jani! she ordered herself.

Leaning heavily on the rusty porch railing, Jani hobbled down the steps to join the flow of people along the sidewalk. A few faces glanced at her curiously and then pointed their eyes straight ahead. City indifference. Some things had not changed. One woman in an elegant suit of lime green silk quickened her pace to get out of Jani's way. Jani thought about what she must be seeing. A shambling, aging woman in ridiculous clothes gawking at her surroundings as if she'd just dropped down from another planet.

"Hey, lady, you got the skej?'

Jani teetered around. A skinny, brown man in a gray jumpsuit squinted down at her.

"Wha—?" she stammered.

"Name a'th'Proph't, Lady, just wanted the skej." He scowled and stalked off into the crowd. Jani stared after him. Somebody bumped into her at full force and she staggered.

"Move it, will you?" sneered a woman's voice as it passed.

Think about Ninon. Jani stumbled forward. *Keep your mind on what you're doing, Jani. You know how to do that. You do it all the time inside.*

But inside, distractions weren't coming from her own body. She didn't ache. Her eyes didn't blur when she tried to focus them. Her chest didn't heave as she tried to catch her breath. Inside, she wasn't old and lost.

Finally, Jani made it to the mouth of the walkway. The flow of pedestrians divided itself up to pass through a series of turnstiles. Each stile had an attendant sitting on a stool beside it. Jani saw a man in what looked like a rumpled kimono flash a pass at an attendant, who punched a button on the gate as the man walked through.

While Jani watched all this, the attendant at the stile closest to her looked up. "Coming through or checking in?" Both his face and his voice registered extreme boredom.

"Uh, coming through," said Jani. The man grunted and jerked a thumb over his shoulder.

Jani swallowed and pushed herself through the turnstile. The white glow of lighting panels replaced the gold daylight. The curving metal walls forced the pedestrians to crowd together as they all headed up a steep set of cement stairs. Somebody bumped Jani's shoulder and she winced. Cloth swished against the back of her hand and she jerked away. Voices bounced off the walls and circled round her head. There was no wind in here, just stale air being inhaled and exhaled by a thousand other lungs.

"Control," Jani murmured, "I think I'm claustrophobic."

There was no answer.

Jani reached the top of the stairs and froze in her tracks. This wasn't just a walkway. People lived in here. Stacks of metal boxes about the size of coffins protruded from the walls. A panel in one of the boxes slid open and a pale, wrinkled woman in shapeless clothing climbed out, stretched, and ambled over to a nearby spigot, shooing a gaggle of kids out of the way with grumbled curses. Other women hung laundry from cords stretched between the modules. A crowd of men surrounded a hot plate and helped themselves to what smelled like beef stew out of a battered aluminum pot. One of them had a vest made of purple fur. Jani's throat tightened around her bile. She looked away, trying to find something else to think about.

She found it. People were watching the crowd flow by from the tops of the metal boxes. Old people, teenagers, women with babies in their arms hunkered down on the stacks of bunks. Their eyes picked out Jani and tracked her like searchlights.

Jani's hands moved reflexively, signing for room, for a cut off. Instinctively, she tried to shape herself a world with air and space and silence.

Nothing happened. Of course nothing happened.

"Stay with us, Jani." She tried to imagine it was Control's voice she heard instead of her own. "Do you see the branch?"

Jani forced her eyes to move, to search past the shifting mass of people. Up ahead, the echoing tunnel split into three separate tunnels.

"I see it. I'm on my way."

The tunnel sloped upward. Jani managed to angle her path so she joined the current of people moving through the left-hand opening.

"Now where?" she asked herself, stretching her neck, trying to see some break in the flow of people. The walkway's residents who perched on the bunk-boxes looked down on her. All of them looked down on her at once. Jani shrank back, trying to hide between the bodies that bumped and prodded her as they passed.

"The first set of stairs. On the left. Stay with us, Jani. You're almost there."

Jani shuffled along. Her hands twitched, signing useless commands. She dropped her gaze onto the gritty floor, but she couldn't see where she was going like that. Jani bit her lip until she tasted blood and aimed her eyes straight ahead. But her peripheral vision would not go away. The eyes watched her. The world was full of eyes. Eyes dissected her. Bodies pressed and bumped and bustled, making the world too warm, too loud, too small. Too many people shoved too close together, using up all the air. Her foot hit something soft that squealed and she stumbled over a trash-eater. She fell against a broad, white-haired man who snarled something about drunks and shoved her away. More eyes. More hands. Her hand lashed out, signing for cutoff. On the downstroke it smacked against a railing. She gawped at the opening on her left without understanding. Her fingers signed the word *stairs*, and her brain managed to identify the objects in front of her.

Reflex forced her feet to start climbing. More voices. Perfume. Hairspray.

Sign for air.

White light, white skin, white silk, white leather. Steel.

Sign for room.

Cooking meat. Eyes. Screams building up in her throat, choking off her breath and squeezing her heart.

Sign for help.

Concrete and dirt and turnstiles and eyes and eyes and eyes.

Daylight and the summer wind engulfed her. Jani collapsed onto a bare stone ledge. She curled in on herself, shaking uncontrollably.

"Hey," said a voice. Not her own voice, or Control's voice. "Hey, lady, you okay?"

A warm hand touched her arm and reflexively Jani looked up. A young man with deep ebony skin and eyes like the midnight sky bent over her. His face was full of quiet concern.

"You need help? Want me to get a cop or something?"

For a minute, Jani just stared wildly at him. Then she drew a long, shuddering breath. "No," she managed to say. "I . . . I'll be okay. Could you . . . help me up, please?"

"Sure thing." He grasped her wrists and pulled her easily to her feet. "Maybe you should just get yourself home, huh?" He nodded toward a metal booth. "Net-screen'll let you call a cab." He walked off into the tunnel.

Net-screen? Jani stared at the booth. *Net-screen!*

Jam staggered to her feet, and as fast as her ankles would let her, she ran to the booth. The metal booth surrounded a flatscreen terminal in front of a battered metal stool. A pair of VR gloves dangled from the bottom of the terminal. Jani shoved both hands into the gloves before her backside even touched the stool. The screen lit up with a series of squares and commands glowing in friendly green letters and a voice said, "Hello, I am the net-space default system."

"And am I glad to see you!" Jani's hands began to move, but not across the touch-sensitive screen. They signed her name and license number, signed SOS, and screamed for Control.

"I'm sorry," said the system. "This link cannot handle your request."

Jani swore at it and tried again, slower this time, with simpler grammar and fewer shortcuts.

This is a link for outsiders, after all. The smug thought wormed through the cotton wool smothering her brain and Jani felt it begin to clear. The world she knew was at her fingertips.

The world she knew. The battleground she knew. The tactics she knew. Jani felt her thoughts drop into place, one by one.

"Jani!" Control appeared, grinning from ear to ear. "How'd you—?"

"Never mind! I'm on the roof of Ninon's building. I need a diversion," she said. "Can you leak this signal?"

"What?" Control's forehead wrinkled.

"Can you make it look like I'm on the line to my home-space environment from this terminal? I want Guinsburg and his hacker to know I couldn't handle it out here and that I'm screaming for somebody to come and get me. If the hacker hears, he'll call Guinsburg to say that the immediate panic's over. If the net-secs got a trace on Guinsburg's comm lines . . ."

Control's smile became absolutely devilish. "Done and done, Jani. What else?"

"Get me down to where a taxi would pick Guinsburg up if he was leaving the building."

Control turned away and said something Jani couldn't hear to someone she couldn't see.

"We can route a hardcopy map to the terminal you're at, Jani. Go get 'em!"

In one motion Jani pulled her hands out of the gloves and got up. A sheet of paper extruded from a slot below the screen. She tore it free and studied the map. A red line showed her the route across the catwalk and down the tree-elevator to the sidewalk in front of the building. Next to the map glowered a picture of a man's heavy, square face. Guinsburg.

"Thanks again, Control." Clutching her map, Jani started forward.

Guinsburg's hacker would have warned him Jani was coming. If Jani had been in Guinsburg's place, she would have stayed locked up tight at home until the danger had passed. Then, when the danger was said to be gibbering helplessly on the rooftop, she would have moved her daughter to a safer location, somewhere she had no chance of getting into net-space from.

If there's anybody still listening to me, please, let me be right!

The trip across the roof and down the elevator was a piece of cake. Jani emerged onto the crowded sidewalk. People bumped and brushed past her. She ignored them. She knew what she was doing now.

The building provided its tenants with a covered and carpeted area outside the foyer to wait for their cabs. Ferns and vines hung from the awning, reminding Jani of the willow trees in her office.

Guinsburg waited under the awning, tapping one foot and scanning the street for his cab. What Control's picture did not show was that Guinsburg topped Jani by a foot and a half and at least a hundred pounds. He was also at least fifteen years younger. One heavy hand clamped onto the shoulder of a gangly, white-faced girl.

You're on, Jani. She straightened an imaginary tie. *I am wearing a business suit, I am combed and washed and rested. I am. I am.*

Jani strode up to the waiting pair as lightly and easily as if she were still inside.

"Ninon Dale?" Jani said to the girl. "I'm Jani Renard. I'm here to escort you home."

Ninon mouthed her name without making a sound and something between hope and terror shone in her eyes. Derek Guinsburg turned ponderously and looked all the way down his blunt nose at her.

"I don't believe I know you," he said.

Jani flicked him a brief glance. "No, I don't believe you do. As soon as you're ready, Ninon, we'll go." She gave Ninon her best professional, reassuring smile. At least, she hoped she did.

Ninon glanced at her father and shivered. "I . . ." She licked her lips. "There's a problem."

"Oh?" Jani arched her eyebrows. She could feel Guinsburg's anger radiating from his glaring eyes.

"You can tell my wife this won't work." Guinsburg's hand tightened on Ninon's shoulder until she winced. "I will not permit my daughter to become a skeleton freak incapable of dealing with reality."

Jani held her ground. *If I'm a skeleton freak, you're an arrogant outsider. You don't care about the law and you don't care what your daughter wants. You can't see beyond your world and your way of life. Which is something you have in common with Simona Dale.*

"Mr. Guinsburg, your permission is not required. I am here to escort Ninon home." Jani deliberately laid her frail hand on top of his where it clutched Ninon. "Or are you the problem to which Ninon is referring?"

Guinsburg's thick lips twitched into a smile. "Ninon's home is with me and this," he nodded toward Jani's hand, "is grounds for assault. Leave now and I won't call the police."

Jani let her face sag into a puzzled expression. "Mr. Guinsburg, the police are already on their way. And net-security is recording this entire conversation." She tapped her ear, as if indicating a communications link. "We're trying to handle this as quietly as possible, but it's getting difficult. Someone has leaked a story to the news services that loving father and prominent respected businessman Derek Guinsburg, a man who 'lives on his reputation,' I believe the Lockmaster files say, has kidnapped and imprisoned his daughter."

Guinsburg towered over her. She could see his pulse throb in a purple vein in his forehead. His breath smelled of mouthwash and martinis. His beefy fist knotted so tightly his knuckles turned stark white.

"Is there a problem, Mr. Guinsburg?"

Jani jerked around in time with Guinsburg. A uniformed woman with a shoulder badge that read SECURITY leaned out of the apartment-building door.

"No problem." Ninon shook herself free from her father's loosened grip. "My mom's stuck at work and she sent a guide to take me back inside." Ninon slid sideways until she was on the far side of the door from Guinsburg. "Dad just wanted to check her credentials."

Everybody builds worlds, you see, Mr. Guinsburg, thought Jani. *Insiders just have practice doing it on the fly.*

Jani couldn't see Ninon's face to tell if she felt triumph or anguish for her expert lie, but Guinsburg's breath grew fast and shallow and his face twisted itself up in pain. Against all expectation, Jani felt a twinge of sympathy for the man. He wanted his world to continue through his daughter and this shriveled old woman was taking her away.

"Mr. Guinsburg? " said Jani quietly. "May we go now, or do you want to press that assault charge and have this all over the gossip lines in fifteen minutes?"

"My attorney will contact you," he croaked.

"Of course." Jani nodded and turned around. "Let's go, Ninon."

"Good-bye, Dad." A little too fast, Ninon turned on her heel and shoved her way into the crowd. Jani caught up with her with difficulty.

"He's not really . . . I mean, it's . . ." stammered Ninon. "I know Mom didn't send you. She wouldn't let me out to see him. I used her code to get the med-service to cut me loose. Then Dad wouldn't let me back in, so I made a patch to try to call for help, but he'd hired a hacker and—"

"I know," Jani squeezed Ninon's hand. "You're going to have some decisions to make, Ninon. But first, you're going to have to help this old lady across the street."

Inescapable Justice

Aaron Rosenberg

During the day he could fool himself, convince himself that he was just like everybody else. But late at night, after he had finally tossed off to sleep, the dreams came again, the memories, haunting him, taunting him. . . .

"What did you say?"

"You heard me." He glanced around at all of them, seated there at their fancy table with the insignia etched into the top—Lady Arcane, Captain Power, Flare, Umbra, Galladia, the White-Out Kid. His allies. His teammates. His friends.

"I said I quit."

It was Galladia who spoke up first, as usual—short on tact and long on common sense, she had always been the foundation of the Patrol.

"But, Justice, you can't just quit—we need you! The people need you!"

"No they don't." He didn't raise his voice, but the edge carried across the room anyway, and it was hard to tell who he was arguing with more, Galladia or himself. "They don't need me. They have you."

"But you're Justice," Flare blurted out. "You're the leader of the team—you're the strongest of us all!" Flare was still a kid under his brightly colored costume, and he still acted like it at times. Justice was his hero, his role model, and he knew the betrayal the kid must be feeling now, to see his hero cutting out like this. The betrayal all of them were feeling.

"I just can't do this anymore," he told them desperately, but if it was understanding he was looking for, it never came. "I need to get away from all this, to get back to my life, to be myself again. I've been Justice for so long, I've almost forgotten what Michael Shirken feels like." He glanced from face to face, hoping that one of them would nod or smile, to say that it was okay, that they understood, that he could go and they would cover for him. But no one met his eyes, and he finally bowed his head and turned away.

"I'm sorry."

He walked out of the meeting room and down the marble hall, his heavy boots ringing sharply on the polished floor. At the doors he stopped to glance behind him, but no one was there— no one to see him off, to wish him good-bye. Then his ears picked up the faint whine, the ring of the alarm, and he knew that within seconds the rest of the team—now all of the team—would be mobilizing, flying or leaping or running to the Patroller and then shooting up into the night sky, off to save some poor woman or stop some bank robbers or prevent yet another maniacal fiend from taking over the world. For a moment he considered joining them—he could easily catch up to the Patroller jet, even pass it if he chose to, and when they landed at the trouble site it would be the same as it had always been, the Patrol to the rescue, with Justice right in front. But the moment passed, the roar of the jet faded off into the distance, and he turned sadly back toward the doors and heaved them apart as if he were prying the lid off his own grave. The heavy thud when they closed again sounded like a death knell, and a part of his heart shut down in sympathy. Then, with the echo from the door still ringing in his head, he turned and trudged away.

It woke him up—that one always woke him up, and there was no getting back to sleep afterward, either. So he clambered out of bed, stalked over to the kitchen table, and dropped down into a chair, lighting a cigarette and watching the smoke fade away into the shadowy room. The spark of his cigarette caught his eye, reflected in the windowpane, and he turned to study his reflection, hunting for signs of the hero he used to be. Same features, under the thick beard—strong jaw, harsh nose, heavy brow, dark eyes set back over pronounced cheekbones. Hair dyed from black to reddish brown, but still glossy and thick. Same powerful frame, with as little fat as when he'd started out, and just as much muscle. Just for the hell of it he floated up from his chair, until his feet were brushing the tabletop, fluttering the sports section in the breeze, then settled back down with a gentle swoop. The powers were still there, untouched for all these years. But something else—something was gone. Something crucial.

He remembered when he had first started out. There had been that explosion down on the docks, and he had been caught full-force, knocked straight into the water. His body had felt as if it were burning up, and the cool water did nothing to quench the flames that he was sure were consuming his flesh. He floated there for two days, unable to move, barely conscious, before a tugboat spotted him and hauled him ashore.

They took Mike—that was him then, just plain Mike Shirken—to the hospital, and there he stayed for a week, fading in and out of consciousness, as his eyesight gradually cleared again and his strength slowly returned. The doctors couldn't figure him out, and there was frequently a small huddle of them in front of his bed, pointing to spots in the charts and whispering among themselves.

"It's a miracle he's still alive," they said, and "Why can't we find a pulse on him?" and "Did you see what happened to the needle when Nurse Jenko tried to get the blood sample? It's unbelievable!" At first he found it insulting that they would talk about such things right in front of him, as if he weren't there. After a while he started to find it funny, though, just to sit and listen to them. Then one day it occurred to him that he could still hear them talking, even when they were in the office down the hall, and it stopped being quite so funny.

When they finally released him, all of the doctors begged him to stay and let them run tests, claiming everything from the chance at a Nobel Prize to the cure for cancer to the possibility of some future risk to his own health. He ignored all of it, and walked out into the sunlight, swearing then and there that he would never step inside a hospital again.

The next day he had gone back to the docks, back to work—the foreman eyed him carefully before putting him back on the schedule, and some of the boys seemed a bit leery of him at first, but he just went back to driving the forklift and unloading crates, and within a few days everything went back to normal.

Until Greggie fell down.

The fall itself wasn't a problem—a stray bit of wrapping tape left lying on the dusty floor, and Greggie's shoe catching in it, tangling it around his leg until he couldn't help but topple over, cursing more out of habit and surprise than any real pain. A few of the others saw it and laughed, including Mike. That would have been the end of it, just a slightly embarrassing moment, no harm done. Except that Greggie fell in the path of the retreating forklift, and Davis wasn't watching behind him.

It was never really clear what made him move—after all, he'd worked the docks for years, and he knew as well as anyone that there was no stopping a forklift once it decided to go in a certain direction. But Greggie had taken him in when he'd started, after his dad had died, had taught him the ropes and defended him against the bullies, had made working there bearable, even enjoyable at times. Which was why Mike found himself diving in front of Greggie and scooping him out of the way, fending the forklift off with one arm like a crossing guard stopping some way-ward kid from running in front of a car. It wasn't until the smell of burning rubber and the sound of grinding metal reached him that he realized what he was doing—the forklift was whining petulantly, like a small child, and when he lowered his arm it went shooting across the floor as if the speed had been building up inside it for hours.

Greggie was fine, but he turned white when Mike approached him and started backing up, even while his mouth was muttering thank-yous. The other workers did the same when he turned to them, and in frustration he ran outside, past the foreman, past the still-smoking machine, away from the dock and into the cool afternoon air. It was two days before he stopped running, and he found himself halfway across the country—his shoes were burned to tatters, but he felt no pain, no hunger, nothing but an aching loss that opened up in the pit of his stomach.

When he finally calmed down, he started testing himself, to see what he could do. There were still cliffs in the center of the country with man-sized tunnels driven through them, and mountains with his finger-and toe-prints dug into their sides. By the time he reached New York he knew that he could never go back again, and at the tender age of twenty-three he didn't want to. Suddenly he had the power, the might, to change the world, to make people sit up and take notice of him! And that was exactly what he set out to do.

The cigarette had burnt out long ago, smoldering to ash between his uncaring fingers. He pinched it out and lit another one, taking several long drags to fill his lungs and clear his brains—but the memories persisted, swirling around him in a fog of their own, as cloying as the smoke and twice as durable. The first time he had stopped a mugger flashed through his mind, with the priceless look on the man's face when the bullets bounced off of him, and the effusive gratitude of the older couple he had rescued; it was the woman who looked down on the still form at his feet—he hadn't yet learned to control his strength, and the mugger never woke up—and muttered something about "justice." Two weeks later his costume was finished, that first one with the tacky-looking scales on the front, and Justice stepped out into the light.

Those first two years had been insane, looking back. He had been so eager to fight crime and right wrongs that he never gave a thought to his own life, to making a home for himself. The dockworkers had accepted him easily enough, and that daytime routine was comforting, but he never made time for the social side, never went out for drinks after work, never met anyone new. By the time Galladia and Captain Power found him, he was so desperate for someone to talk to that he jumped at their offer of a partnership, and never looked back.

It had been Captain Power who dubbed them the Patrol, saying in his old-fashioned way that they needed to "clean up the streets and make things safe for decent folk again." Justice and Galladia had accepted the name because it wasn't really important to them. Only their deeds mattered, and those were making the headlines more and more, as New York slowly began to realize and then even appreciate the trio of costumed strangers who fought to protect them from all manner of harm. When the city finally chose to honor them with the Hall and its equipment, and to set up a stipend for the members to support them, Justice was convinced that he was home—he had finally found his calling in life.

Even now, after all these years, it still called to him.

The next day passed in a haze, as so many of them had for so long—but he was used to the fog, used to working around it, and his motions were as smooth and as even as ever. The disadvantage to dockwork was that it was steady, uniform, monotonous— as a youth this had given him time to daydream about how he was going to become a success someday and change the world. Now all it did was allow the memories to creep back in again, dancing before his eyes in a wash of color and emotions until they became more real than the crates and barrels that he gripped between his hands. For years he had tried to fight them off, but they kept coming back, crowding into his head until he couldn't breathe, just like those fateful two days when he had lain in the river—not quite dead, but not fully alive.

It was two years before he saw his old comrades again. He had taken the money he had saved from his time with the Patrol and made a few investments, and he was running a packing-supply store when Galladia and Captain Power found him. At first he didn't even recognize them—despite all of their time together, he had never really gotten used to her without her protective skin or him without his armor, and at first all he saw was a towering woman with long red hair and a slim man with white hair and the overly tanned skin of a retiree. Then they got close enough for him to notice the boneless grace in his stride and the way her skin shone slightly in the sunlight, like iridescent metal—by the time they entered his shop, he was ready for them.

"Hello, Michael." He didn't turn around, didn't look up, but he could feel Captain Power's voice rolling over him in waves of firm authority, and for an instant he considered letting himself drift into them again, floating once more into the world of capes and superpowers. But the moment passed, as it always did.

"Hello, Jonathan. Mariel." The package he had been sealing was finished, and he had no choice but to face them again. "It's good to see you both again. What can I do for you?"

"We need your help, Mike." Galladia/Mariel still didn't waste any time, but he had always liked that about her. "Agamemnon has been causing trouble again."

"Yes, I saw that in the papers. You'd think that he'd learn after all these years, but he's certainly a persistent little runt. You almost have to admire him for it, if it weren't for those homicidal tendencies."

"This is no time for games, Michael." The Captain's eyes were every bit as piercing as when they had first met, and Mike found himself trapped in a wall of jade fire. "He's planning something big, and we need to put a stop to it."

"So why don't you, then? Why tell me about it?" Mike waved his hand around the place. "Were you looking for some tape to trip him up? Or maybe a good wooden crate for his remains?" The banter faded away, and his mouth twisted. "You've been beating him for years now without my help. What makes this any different?"

"Because something's happened to him, Mike." Galladia was leaning over the counter in her urgency, and he could see the tiny stress fractures forming in the wood as her full weight came down on it, echoing the tension in her voice. "We don't know how, but he's gotten stronger, more powerful. We can't take him alone. We need you." She glanced around quickly, checking for eavesdroppers. "We need Justice."

Her eyes were warm and strong and maybe a little frightened, something he'd only seen in her a few times over all those years, and for a moment he thought about it, but then he realized that to give in would be to start it all over again, and he heard his voice rasp while he was still trying to decide what to say.

It decided for him. It said, "Justice is dead."

And he turned his back on his two oldest friends and waited until their footsteps had receded beyond his range before he shattered the counter with a blow from his fist.

That was the problem with being the strongest, he'd discovered—everyone started to depend on you. Captain Power was a far better fighter than he would ever be, and his ability to sense people from a distance was invaluable to rescue missions, but without his suit he was just an old man with a lot of training and a talent for finding things. Galladia could direct the power of the earth, controlling earthquakes and shaping rock and dirt to her bidding, and she could absorb more damage than a granite block without flinching, but her weight made her slow for pursuit, and she was limited when not dealing with large-scale problems on dry land. Flare had turned out to be a powerhouse, with his flight and his endurance and his plasma generation, but he was too young to have much control, and too volatile to trust with delicate missions. Lady Arcane . . . ah, she was amazing, but her powers exhausted her with every use. And the White-Out Kid had just enough power to convince himself that he could deal with anything, and more than enough delusions and bad luck to prevent that from being the case.

And then there was him—Justice. His power just seemed to keep growing, until he wondered if it would ever stop. At thirty he was twice as strong as when he'd started, and able to fly beyond the speed of sound. Two months before his thirty-first birthday he'd discovered the ability to blur his body between molecules, so that he could pass through buildings and even people without harming them, and could grab a small child through a falling wall and pull her to safety. He was the vanguard of the team, the star center, the pillar. And for a while it was great, always being in demand, always having the others look to him for aid and support.

But pillars never got to take vacations, were never supposed to call in sick. When Flare's mother had died, he went home for a month to comfort his father and help set affairs in order, and the Patrol survived without him. Every year Captain Power disappeared for a week in August, to mourn the anniversary of his wife's death. Galladia occasionally took trips to volcanic regions, to study their effects. Lady Arcane had a torrid love affair with a young movie star, and although it tore at him personally, the team managed while she was gone. And the White-Out Kid stormed off to pout so often it was a running bet whether he'd show up on any given mission.

And yet, the one time Justice had taken a break—after news had reached him that Greggie had died—the entire city cried out for his return. Papers asked why he had deserted them in their time of need, talk shows discussed whether this were an omen that he was going to leave them for good, and people on the streets demanded to know what made him think that he could up and leave like that, any time he chose to. One particularly angry state representative had even demanded that Justice's stipend be cut, "to reflect his flagrant dereliction of duty."

He was gone for one week—and it took two months afterward for people to stop demanding answers from him. After that, he never took a vacation again, and every time one of his teammates did, it galled him deep inside, until the resentment built up to the point where he could no longer ignore it.

So he had quit. And to go back meant that he would have to face all of the questions again, the accusations, the guilt, the overdependence on his always being there. It meant that he would have to give up his life again, to sacrifice himself once more for all those people who demanded his help but never showed any gratitude for it, any kind of understanding of what it was like for him. And that was something he wasn't willing to do.

The fight wound up being broadcast on television, a few days later. A news crew had heard the commotion and rushed to the scene, and so he was able to watch it all in glorious color on the little set placed behind his counter.

He saw it all. He stared with unblinking eyes as the Patrol

launched itself at Agamemnon in perfect unity: Galladia erecting a bulwark of earth and concrete to shield bystanders from the conflict and limit escape routes; Captain Power coordinating events from beside her, using his limited mental powers to link everyone in telepathic communication; the White-Out Kid firing a patch of ice under the diminutive villain to distract him and take away his footing; Flare launching himself from the air and unleashing a stream of supercharged plasma directly at the evil mastermind's head; and Lady Arcane weaving a mystic web that drifted toward him over the heads of her teammates, to bind him tightly and render him harmless.

He saw Agamemnon retaliate as well, with the ease and grace and speed of a true adversary; somehow he reflected Flare's attack back out, cutting through Lady Arcane's spell before it had fully solidified and striking the Kid full in the chest, which immediately took him out of the combat. Then the villain was airborne, negating the effects of the Kid's ice patch and allowing him to evade the closing earthen wall falling from behind—an energy blast of some sort struck Flare and enveloped him, and Mike watched from his store as the young man who had idolized him went rigid with shock and fell from the sky like a wounded bird. Captain Power dove into the fray then, igniting his rocket and taking to the sky himself, but Agamemnon evaded his charge easily, and a casual eyebeam struck the Captain's rocket pack from behind, shorting out the controls and sending him careening into the side of a nearby office building. That left only the ladies, and a sudden cascade of force ended their threat, lifting the hefty Galladia off the ground and hurtling her back several feet, to land in a crumpled heap—on top of Lady Arcane, who was too stunned to react. The news crew captured every detail as the villain gazed around him at the defeated superheroes, then grinned at the camera, laughed, and nonchalantly flew away into the clouds. Mike didn't move as the news anchor came back on and began to recap what had just happened in hushed tones, but when the inevitable "Where is Justice?" picture flashed up on the screen he picked up the set and flung it through the front window, into the path of a passing truck. The satisfying crunch of glass and plastic under hardened rubber eased the throbbing behind his eyes, and after another moment or two he was able to pick up the phone and call the Hall to find out where his injured friends were going to be taken.

As it turned out, for some of them there was never a choice—both Galladia and Flare were killed outright, and their funerals were held two days later. Mike didn't attend. The White-Out Kid survived with only a concussion, second-degree burns, and some cracked ribs, but refused to stay hospitalized, and disappeared—he was never seen again. Captain Power was in a coma, and they were uncertain if he would ever recover, or if he would be able to walk again even if he did. And Lady Arcane . . . the beautiful, elegant, charming Elaine McGinnis who had captured his heart the first time they met was now a paraplegic, most of her spinal column crushed by the weight of Galladia's massive form. Her magicks might have been able to help her . . . if her hands and arms weren't completely paralyzed, and her vocal cords damaged beyond repair. He went to see her, despite his oath, and sat by her bedside for hours, never saying a word. She never moved, never realized he was there—her eyesight had also been taken from her, and he was too afraid to speak up, afraid that she would curse him for what had happened, blame him the way he blamed himself. After what seemed an eternity, he crept silently out of her room and down the hall.

Jonathan Walden, also known as Captain Power, was in Intensive Care; his once-glittering armor had been carefully removed and replaced with the IVs that stabbed through his too-tan skin and kept him alive, and with the bewildering array of sensor lines that let the nurses down the hall monitor his condition. Without the green fire of his eyes he looked much older, and in unconsciousness the firm lines of his face sagged slightly, more like the features of a tired old man.

Ah, Captain, how did it ever come to this, Michael wondered. *We were supposed to save the world, to lead people to a new and brighter age. We were never supposed to grow old, to get injured, to die.* Then he bowed his head, as if in confession—and even with his former mentor in a coma, unable to respond to him or even recognize him, that was exactly what it felt like.

I know, I should have been there. We probably could have taken him then, and everyone else would still be alive. You and Elaine would still be all right. We would still be heroes. But I ran out on you, turned my back, and look at what happened because of it. Because of me.

Well, I know I was wrong—regardless of my personal feelings or misgivings, you're my friends, and I should have helped you. I know it's too late to fix it, but I'd like to make up for it, if that's possible. What can I do?

He paused then and lifted his head, as if listening. There was nothing to actually hear, beyond the steady beat of his own pulse and the quaver of the man beside him, but that didn't mean there wasn't an answer to his question. He had known the Captain for more than seven years, and during that time he had come to understand the man, so that now he heard in his own mind those things that would have been said aloud under other circumstances.

The Captain forgave him, of course—he always had, in that gruff but gentle manner of his. Everyone made mistakes, including the illustrious Captain Power, and so he knew better than anyone that people shouldn't be held to their past errors indefinitely. But there were three conditions. The first was the obvious one, and Michael had already accepted it—stop Agamemnon. The second was more personal—every August, make sure to place fresh flowers on the grave of Nancy Walden, the Captain's former wife. But the third . . .

At first he refused to accept that as real, tried to discount it as some outside hint of morbidity, but the Captain finally convinced him—every tremulous beat of his heart, every wheezing breath, every sudden spasm, reassured him that it was the truth. And, because this was the man who had taken him in and trained him and taught him how to help others, Michael complied. With one large, roughened hand he reached out and tapped the Captain once, quickly, on the temple—the resulting burst of blood vessels killed him instantly, without pain, without a sound. A blue light flashed on the console at the side of the bed, and he could hear nurses shouting down the hall, already running for his location, but he rose and turned away casually, almost dazedly, and walked on down to the end of the hall and out of sight as countless medical workers rushed to the old man's bedside. The Captain had never approved much of grief, which was why he had tried to keep his own so carefully hidden—the best way to show respect was to keep his promises, and accomplish the tasks he had agreed upon. One of those was already taken care of, and it would be several months before another.

That only left the third.

People still talk about that fight occasionally—the day Justice returned and sought out Agamemnon for a knock-down, drag-out, no-holds-barred fight to the death. He found him easily enough—actually, it was news of the villain's whereabouts and actions that drew him out at that particular time. The little madman had stormed the United Nations building, and was in the process of announcing his new supremacy over the world to the gathered delegates when Justice came hurtling in through the roof.

The man was fast, he had to give him that. Before he could close the distance Agamemnon had turned and obliterated the French and Italian delegates with a vicious energy burst, and then faced front again. His shout reached Justice in time to slow him down, and he came to ground with the central seal still spanning the gulf between them.

"Stay where you are, Justice!" The cry rebounded through the room, but despite its shrillness it didn't sound frightened, only passionate. "Come any closer and I'll destroy more of them—it makes no difference to me, but your little moral code will never forgive you."

That might have been true once—he could clearly remember a time when he had vowed not to take a life, or cause one to be taken. But the memory of his fallen comrades and the promise made to a dying old man who never opened his eyes sustained him, and those strictures vanished in a haze.

A step forward, and the Israeli delegate died. Another, and the British delegate was only a charred memory. He paused and looked around the room then, either to see how many were left or to judge their reaction . . . and met the gaze of the American vice-president.

"Finish this, Justice," the man said calmly, as if his own life were not hanging by a thread. "We are expendable, but this madman must be stopped."

"Silence, you fool!" the "madman" screamed. "Do you think it is only your own pathetic little existences at stake here? You're not even worthy of notice—no, I have far greater scope than a few self-important little politicians!" Even across the distance Justice could feel the glare burning into him, trying to cut away his heart through sheer hatred. "My minions are watching around the globe, and they already have their instructions—for every delegate, there is a bomb somewhere in their country, and their death is the signal to detonate. France, Italy, and Israel have already been devastated . . . shall we make the United States next?"

Justice still remembered the vice-president's calm—he had admired it then, amazed at how this unpowered, unprepossessing man with the receding hairline and the watery eyes could retain his demeanor in the face of such grave danger. But his voice never wavered, and he ignored the villain ranting a few yards away to fix his gaze on Justice instead.

"It doesn't matter how much damage he does here" were the words that etched themselves into his brain. "More harm would result if he were allowed to achieve his true goals. 'Give me liberty or give me death' has always been our motto, and that still holds true." It was unbelievable that those watery blue eyes should hold such power, such magnetism—they rivaled the green fire in the Captain's eyes, in their own way. "No matter what the cost, you have to stop him."

"Enough!" The air sizzled from the force of the bolt, and before his eyes the vice-president was reduced to a blackened husk, his eyes and his voice vaporized in an instant. For a moment silence reigned in the vast room, broken only by harsh breathing and the hushed crackle as the remains of the man slid to the polished floor. Then, around the room, people began to nod their heads, to clap, to shout.

"He was right!" "Finish him!" "Save the world!" Soon the chamber was ringing with noise, and Justice had no choice but to accept the mandate of the world once again. He squared his shoulders, set his jaw, and stepped forward across the floor.

One step—Germany perished in flames. Another—China ceased to exist. A third—Saudi Arabia disappeared, and almost took Turkey with him. Then Justice was across the gap, and the force of his blow sent Agamemnon hurtling backward into the wall. But an instant later the little man was back, only the dents in his breastplate showing where he had been hit, and the battle was truly joined.

The blows struck were titanic, on all levels. Agamemnon's bolts would have leveled mountains, and the seepage demolished walls, tables, stray people; Justice's punches caused shock waves to ripple throughout the room, and most of those who hadn't yet escaped felt their eardrums burst from the pressure. The two men took to the air to avoid the rubble, and traded attacks while diving and wheeling like giant birds, taking and giving wounds between snarls and glares that would have cowed a hunger-mad tiger.

The fight was not without penalty, on both sides: Justice took a beam that blackened his skin and turned the muscles in his legs to jelly, and if he hadn't been flying he would have crumpled to the ground in pain; in return, he vibrated his hand through his opponent's chest and then resolidified, taking organs and tissue with him when he pulled back. Their sweeps and wheels slowly retreated back to the ground as they exhausted themselves, until their feet hung mere inches from the floor, and they locked in one final embrace.

It was Justice's ability to evolve that saved him, in the end—with a strength that he had never shown, Agamemnon matched his powerful limbs and held off the punch that would have crushed his head, and then locked gazes with him. Too late Justice remembered the eyebeam that had ended Captain Power, and saw the embers glowing deep within the crazed circles of his adversary's eyes—the beam lanced out at him, directly for his eyes, and burned its way through his retinas, arcing toward his brain. Then he felt a strange new sensation, an electrical tingling, jumping up through his head and into his eyes, and they began to burn, almost the way the tongue burned after a peppermint, cool and calm and strangely refreshing.

And the beam that should have blinded him, killed him, was absorbed into the tingling, channeled through it, strengthened, and redirected back out again, reversing the flow back into Agamemnon's startled gaze, and searing through his optic nerves straight into the channels of his brain. There was a wet popping sound, and the air behind them was sprayed with blood and organic matter as the beam exited the villain's head; the body pitted against Justice tightened once, then froze in place, its power gone, and he was able to drift back to the floor and drop to his knees as the corpse fell from his grasp and collapsed in a heap on the ground. It was several minutes before he could move again, and then he dragged himself up and went to check on the damage the would-be ruler had caused before he died.

The devastation was frightening—one thing that Agamemnon had never done was bluff, and the bombs had gone off just as he had claimed, some in major cities, some in oil fields or military bases or food basins, but all almost crippling in their effect. And after he had died some of his henchmen had fled for safety, but others had set off their remaining targets out of retaliation.

Justice spent the next week without sleep, shoring up broken dams, clearing away collapsed buildings, defusing activated nuclear weapons, sealing ruptured gas lines and oil wells, and doing his best to minimize the damage around the globe. At times he wished the Patrol were there to help, but the reminder only served to sadden him further, and he worked twice as hard to make up for their absence. When it was over, when he had done everything he could to fix the problems, he returned to the Hall to rest and try to recover, and it was there that the remaining world leaders came to him and requested an audience. Expecting the usual recriminations, mixed with perhaps a little gratitude, he wearily complied, and had them led into the meeting room, where he sat at the head of the empty table with its defunct emblem, and waited for the gathered powers to speak.

They surprised him. First, because the accusations he had anticipated never arose—no one so much as asked him where he had been. Second, there was a distinct absence of thanks, as if it were assumed that he would do all of the prodigious work he had just performed, not as a favor but as an obligation—that he had almost expected, because it was so in keeping with all of the reasons he had left in the first place. But third was what they did say.

They asked him to take over.

The world structure had been severely damaged, they pointed out—several of the presidents and premiers and emperors had actually been present during the battle, and had died in that once-proud room. Others had perished from the bombs that had gone off across the world, and a small handful had taken their own lives out of shame and misery. Without a unified leader, the nations would devolve into a chaotic jumble of minor squabbles and skirmishes, and the current civilizations would be lost in the wave of anarchy, possibly forever. And there was only one man that everyone would listen to, the man who had saved them from an even worse fate, who had pitted his life and his strength against the very essence of evil and had won. Justice.

And despite his misgivings, despite the fact that this was everything he had feared for so long, everything he had tried to avoid, an image of green fire came into his head, and he found himself agreeing.

"But not for good," he added, startled and worried by the looks of relief that had crossed these men and women's faces. "Only until you get your countries back on track, and we can restore some semblance of normality. Then I'll step back down, and you'll have to take over again."

Oh, of course, they all agreed. That's fine—we just need time to straighten things out, and someone to guide us through this. And, when he asked for an estimate, they all agreed that two years would probably do it. Two years to rule the planet.

It was ironic that, after battling Agamemnon, who had desperately wanted to rule the world, Justice got handed that very position—particularly since he had never wanted it. But they always said that anyone who wanted to rule was obviously unfit, and if that was true, then he was perhaps the most fit of all. So he took the job, and, with the assembled leaders at his side, left the table and went out to begin the business of leading the world back to a semblance of order and stability.

By the time two years had passed, Justice thought they had done a pretty fair job of it—granted, there had been some problems, some countries who refused to follow his lead, and others who tried to play on his apparent inexperience to their own benefit. But the ones who tried staying independent eventually realized that it was far safer and more profitable to be working with everyone else than to be avoided, and those who tried manipulating him learned to their dismay that Justice was not as naïve as they had thought, that he did not tolerate such ploys, and that he never made the same mistake twice. Some of the national boundaries collapsed under his rule, and new conglomerates were formed, but that was simply a result of evolution and changing times—most of the damage was healed, the wounds smoothed over, and people in general were still healthy and reasonably happy. Even crime went down, which was a definite advantage to having a superhero as a ruler. "Justice prevails" became a common phrase, and the letter of the law went from a trifling annoyance to a serious guideline.

But when he tried to step down the former leaders, who had since become his advisors and delegates and regional directors, reacted in horror and fear. You can't leave yet, they squeaked, and the tremor in their voices convinced him that their concerns were genuine. We've only begun to recover, they complained— true, it may look good on the surface, but there's still a lot of work to be done, jobs to create, famines to cure, wars to prevent, cities to rebuild. We still need you here. And because he honestly believed them, he agreed to stay on another year.

And another year after that.

And the year after that.

By the fifth year, he had become fed up with their excuses, their constant complaints and claims and gripes and hedges. In a scene that seemed strangely reminiscent, he called them all into the Hall, which had once again become his headquarters and capital, and announced his intentions.

"I quit. And no, don't try to give me any more of that 'but there's still so much to be done' crap," he demanded, warding off the panicked looks and the anguished cries. "This world is in far better shape than it was before Agamemnon's attack, and you know it. You just don't want to have to deal with the responsibility again—most of the innovations over the last few years have been yours, but this way you could always hide behind me if something went wrong, so you were willing to take a few risks. Well, no more." He stood up and faced them all down, waited until they were all silent. "I've done more than my part—now it's your turn again. I've got my own life to lead, and you've got a world to run."

He turned his back on them, and for the second time he swung the heavy doors shut behind him, praying silently that the results would be better than the first time. And he walked away, leaving Justice far behind, to find Michael Shirken again.

But it wasn't that easy, of course, he thought as he moved another crate, swung himself into the forklift's chamber, and deftly geared the machine up. No, it hadn't been that easy at all. He had hoped that he could just go back and pick up his investments again, perhaps reopen his store or get a new one, meet some new people, maybe have an honest-to-God relationship. Build a life.

Instead he had discovered that his former assistants and advisors had figured out at some point that Michael Shirken and Justice were the same person, and they had attempted to insure that he wouldn't leave them; all of his assets had been coopted by the government, and all government files around the world listed his real name and his photo, with instructions to keep constant tabs on him. Every attempt to get a loan had been denied, and the phone rang so often that he had finally pulled it out of the wall, only to have them switch to letters and spontaneous visits instead. So he had fled to the only place he could, the safest place he knew—the docks. A little hair coloring and a full beard had changed his appearance enough, and he knew enough about the machines and the procedures that the foreman didn't hesitate to hire him on the spot—with free education now available, there were fewer people willing to take this work, and even someone without references or ID was better than no one. And so he settled back into the familiar routine, saved his money, and bided his time.

After a few months, he had heard from a coworker about a guy who did fake IDs, and had gotten a driver's license under the name Joseph McKiernan, so that at least he could own a car and buy beer without any problem. But the lack of references or background material, or even a high-school diploma or a birth certificate, made it difficult for him to find any other job, and increased the chance that they would discover where he was and start hounding him again. So he stayed where he was, and waited.

Then, a year or two ago, the revelation came, the final piece of bad news: he wasn't aging. It was the only possible explanation. It had occurred to him when he had been reminiscing one night that over thirty years had gone by since he had first started out as Justice. He had been twenty-five at the time, so that would make him fifty-five now. But he didn't look fifty-five. In fact, he could easily pass for mid-thirties, and his driver's license claimed that he was almost thirty-six, which seemed to fit. It could just be that his active life and his powers were keeping him fit, but no, it was more than that. He could feel it. Just like with his eyebeams—he had tested them, in those five years, and learned that he could now produce them upon command—he could sense somehow that his body was slowing down, not in its activity and its vitality, but in its aging. He wasn't getting any older. He had no way of knowing how long this would last, or if it would be indefinite, which would mean . . . the true enormity hit him, and he had to take a quick swig of beer to keep from crying.

He could be immortal.

Wouldn't that just be the kicker—he had been harboring a secret hope that his powers would start to fade as he got older, until he was no longer strong enough to be useful, and could honestly decline to help on the grounds that he wouldn't be able to do anything. But no such luck. Instead, he would be this healthy and this strong for a long time, and probably continue getting more and more powerful, to boot. His dreams of a family and a real life seemed to be fading by the minute.

He couldn't even stay here on the docks, he realized. Eventually people would start to wonder why Joe McKiernan didn't seem to be getting any older, didn't seem to be slowing down at all, and then someone would check his records and discover the curious lack of background material. A few discreet calls and the government would know where he was again, and the hounding would start all over again. The only way to avoid that was to keep moving, to never stay in one place long enough for anyone to get suspicious—and his dreams went up in smoke, vanished with only a bitter aftertaste.

Ever since then he had lived in a daze, only counting the time and wondering how long he had before he would be forced to run to the next hiding place. He never went out with the other workers, for fear they would notice something odd and shorten his time even more. He never tried to meet anyone, because he knew that he would only have to disappear eventually, and he couldn't stand the thought of losing them, whoever they might be. He even gave up on saving his money—what was the point, when he'd never be able to stand still long enough to spend it? All he did was go to work, go home, drink, and try to stop the nightmares from haunting him.

It was August when the change came. He had made his annual pilgrimage back to New York, and laid the flowers on the grave of a woman he had never met—she had died years before he had ever seen that city, and it was her loss that had prompted Captain Power to resume his fight against crime. Now Michael kept his vow and paid his respects every year, in honor of the man he had once known, and the things that man had done for him.

It occurred to him then, standing over the grave there in the soft rain, that the Captain had been as alone then as he was now—no family, no friends, no place to go. Galladia had mentioned once that the Captain had been back on the streets for almost three years before she had met him and convinced him to team up with her, and that he had refused at first, saying that he preferred to work alone. So for three years he had been alone in the world, just as Michael was now. How had he endured?

The answer came on a wet breeze, mingled with the crisp tones of a born leader and the reassuring flash of green fire. Michael had once asked, after that debacle with his first and only vacation, why they bothered, why they cared; and the Captain had answered, "We do this because we can, and because we must. These people rely on us, look up to us, count on us to help them to the best of our ability. We cannot let them down."

"Why not?" he had asked. "Who are they to us, that we have to take such responsibility for them?"

And the answer had come then, the one he had been avoiding for so long, the one he knew was right: "They are our family, our blood, our kin. They are our children, and we are their parents. It is not always a pleasant task, and it is often a thankless one, but we do it nonetheless, because we love them, and because we want them to be happy."

The words still lingered on the breeze, and it was only the echo that revealed that he had been saying them out loud, uttering each syllable as it rolled from the back of his head and lit his eyes like fire. Nancy Walden's tombstone bore the legend SHE WILL BE LOVED FOREVER, and her husband had requested that his own read, HE LOVED WISELY.

But it was not only his wife he was referring to. It was the world.

The next day, at precisely noon, a bolt of light shot across the sky, bisected the clouds, and landed with a flash at the steps of the Hall of Heroes. Bystanders gasped and stepped back, then began to cheer as the brilliant light resolved itself into the form of a man, a man they all knew, the man who had guided them and shielded them and protected them. The form of Justice.

He waited until they had quieted down, then strode calmly toward the doors and flung them open. This was where he belonged, what he had been born to do—there was a lot of work involved, and no end of hardship, and he might never be appreciated, but that didn't matter anymore. At least he knew now that he would never need to be alone. The whole world was with him.

"Tell the world," he announced in ringing tones to the people who gathered behind him, "that I have returned. Tell them that Justice prevails once more, and that I will never leave them again."

They need me, he admitted to himself as he faced the long corridor again. *But just as important, I need them. They give me purpose.* And he stepped over the threshold and headed down the hall, to the place where his destiny lay patiently waiting.

Walking Contradiction

Nancy Jane Moore

I stared into the bathroom mirror, trying to tell if I needed to shave. Once a week usually does it for me—I'm naturally blond, though my beard comes in pretty gray now. So does my hair, but I do something about that.

I got my hair cut yesterday. I go to Kevin's place, and I always use Kevin, not a bot. Vanity, I know, and I pay for it. But I like the way the waves fall after he cuts it.

Kevin's always telling me to get a laser zap for my face. "Once a year," he says, "and you won't have to shave again." But I resist, even though I never let the beard grow full: It takes too long, and comes in too light. Sometimes I just want to look like I need a shave.

But not today. I could feel a bit of fuzz. And besides, I was about halfway through my period. My beard always grows faster then: testosterone kicks in when estrogen drops. So I shaved.

And then washed out the sink thoroughly. I'd hired a cleaning service the day before, and didn't want to undo their work. Not before Jace saw it.

I looked back at my reflection, and laughed at myself. I was acting as if Jace were my lover, instead of my child. Likely Jace won't care, I thought. I didn't care at Jace's age.

Though Carroll did. I remembered Carroll and me—both of us six months pregnant—scrubbing floors on our hands and knees because our parents were coming to visit. Carroll never trusted the bot to get things clean enough.

Carroll raised Jace, so things might be different. But I doubted it. Still, I shoved all the dirty towels into the hamper and put out fresh ones.

I heard the beep of the phone as I opened the bathroom door—I don't keep a receiver in the bath; some places should be private—and managed to punch in ahead of the bot. I was still naked from the shower, so I didn't hit visual. "Morgan Doyle."

"Oh," the caller said. "You're Morgan Doyle?" Deep voice. If the caller was a norm—or something close to one—probably male.

"That's right."

"Uh," said the caller. "Mr. uh, Ms. uh."

That made it a hundred to one the caller was a norm. Somebody had given him my name, with no honorifics, and he'd probably assumed I was male. But my voice didn't sound male to him. Back when I sang in college choir, I was a mezzo.

"Just Doyle. Or Morgan. I'm not very formal. What can I do for you?"

"My name's Vincent. Paul Vincent. A guy I know gave me your name. Said you're the, uh, the one to call in a situation like this."

"Like what?"

"Could I meet you somewhere? It's not a conversation for the phone."

"Sure. Should I come by?"

"No, no. Better that I come to you. My friend said you have an office on Nineteenth. In about an hour?"

"I'll see you there."

A client. It would give me something to do besides clean the fucking apartment while waiting for Jace.

My apartment's not big—a one-bedroom with den—but it's got a balcony on the south and gets a lot of morning sun. Location and extras cost in Washington, but I like nice surroundings.

My office lacks those amenities. I rent seventy-five square meters of interior space in an anonymous office building. No windows, no special effects. I've put some pictures on the wall, arranged some comfortable chairs around a table so I can meet with clients, even stuck an old comp on a desk in the corner to make the place look like someone works there. But I mostly work at home. I use the office to meet people.

Actually, I don't meet with clients a lot. Most of my work consists of corporate investigation, and is both hired, and done, over the net. But from time to time, people want to talk in person. And people in trouble usually tend to be folks you wouldn't want in your home. So I keep the office.

Paul Vincent was a beefy, red-faced man pushing sixty. About my age. He wore one of those black choke-collar jackets that are considered de rigueur in business these days. It looked like it was strangling him.

He stared at me as I invited him in. I don't go in for formal business dress, but my attire would pass: dark green slacks, with a matching open jacket. But he wasn't looking at my clothes.

"Well, what are you?" he said. "A man or a woman?"

Not good manners but lots of people assume they don't need good manners to talk to a detective. And, anyway, I get variations on that question a lot—it's the price I pay for living in mixed society. I've gotten reasonably good at not taking offense.

"Both."

"Oh, shit. That bastard Bergman. What a sick joke. He knows how freaked I am, so he sends me to you."

Actually, I did take some offense at that point. But I allowed for the man's stress. "If you mean Aaron Bergman, I doubt he sent you here for a joke. I handled something for him a while back, and he was pretty satisfied."

"Yeah, well, he still should have told me you were ambi what you call it."

"Ambigendered. And why the hell does it matter?"

For a moment I thought he was going to walk out, but I guess he had committed himself before he got there. "It's my son. He's joined this group, and now he wants to have a sex operation. See, somebody like you who's done it, you won't want to help stop it."

"Mr. Vincent, calm down and give me a few facts. I don't know whether I'll want to try to stop him or not unless I know what's actually going on. And just for the record, I was born ambi."

He looked startled.

"So tell me about it. Is your son an adult? Is he in his right mind? What does he want do: become a woman; become ambi?"

"Neither. He wants to be neutered."

I have to say, it freaked me out as well. Easy to be very high-minded and say people have a right to their own lives, but neutering. How could anybody healthy want that? I mean, you don't want to have sex, don't have sex. Sex drive too much? Take some hormones. But why cut up your body?

"And, no, he's not in his right mind. He's under the influence of that goddamned cult."

"The True Virgins?"

"That's the one. Sick."

I agreed.

"It's bad enough what they do to themselves, but why do they have to go try to convert people?"

"Well, they can't very well have children, so how else are they going to keep their sect going?"

He didn't think I was funny. "So, are you willing to work for me?"

I hesitated. I'd heard enough about the True Virgins to consider it probable that they had brainwashed Vincent's kid, but dealing with cults can be tricky business. "I don't know. Is your son of age?"

"Yeah. He just turned twenty-six."

"That makes it stickier. Do you have any evidence of undue influence on him?"

"No evidence, exactly, but he hasn't been the same since he started going to those meetings."

"Did he have a normal sex life before?"

Vincent actually blushed. His red face got even redder. "Sure. I guess so. We didn't talk about it."

I sighed. But then, parents are rarely the best source of information about their children.

"Look, I think it's likely that the True Virgins do qualify as a cult. But if your son is of age, getting him away from them is very iffy legally. I can't just snatch him. That's considered kidnapping."

Vincent said, "Oh, I don't want you to grab him. I want you to get something on the cult, something I can use."

He must have already grabbed the kid and found a deprogrammer. Good. Snatching people isn't my line, anyway.

"Something you can use to convince your son they've brainwashed him."

"That, or something I can use to convince them they don't want to bother with him."

I got the idea. "I'll see what I can do, Mr. Vincent." We spent a few minutes on the paperwork and other niceties. Messing around with groups like the True Virgins can get sticky, and I wanted to get paid for it.

He stood up to go, then asked, "Were you really born that way?"

"Yeah. I'm third generation."

He said, "Really," like he didn't think it could possibly be true.

"Yeah, really. Some biologists who'd altered themselves surgically started out with the idea of changing the chromosomes on a fetus, but once they'd figured out how to alter the DNA enough to give a child both sets of working sexual equipment, it was easy to make it heritable."

"I thought that kind of experimentation was illegal."

"It was, here in the States. But not in Denmark a hundred years ago. I grew up there, in an ambi community."

"You ever regret it, being what you are?"

"No. Do you regret being male?"

"Of course not."

"I'm happy with the way I was born. Most people are." But not all.

I thought about what Vincent had said about regrets as I drove out to meet Jace's plane. Like most of the middle-aged, I have plenty of regrets. Choices made, roads not taken.

But it's never occurred to me to regret being ambi. Frankly, I've always felt sorry for the norms.

Virtually all business operates internationally these days. And with growing colonies on Luna and Mars, plus some habitats out in the Asteroid Belt and plans for a science station on Titan, we're not even planet-bound anymore. So you'd think national borders would have started to fall by the wayside.

You'd be wrong. The nation states of Earth, small and large, are still clinging tightly to their borders, regardless of the fact that they control a smaller and smaller amount of what goes on within them. They get their revenge at customs.

Jace's plane came in as scheduled, but it took an hour before we actually saw each other. Not that they searched Jace; they just hadn't bothered to put enough people on duty to cope with the number of people on the flight.

We'd waved at each other from opposite sides of the partition—customs is very picky about keeping visitors from actually meeting anyone until they've been checked through. It was a long enough look to remind me how much Jace looked like me.

The younger me, of course. Jace's hair was the pale blond mine had once been, longish, and pulled back with a clip. The eyes, though, green with flecks of amber, those belonged to Carroll. Mine are bluish gray.

People often assume I gave birth to Jace, when in fact it was Carroll. Our other child, Arden, was my birth child. And Arden looks more like Carroll than me. When it comes to genetics, the father is equal to the mother, and the mix is seldom predictable. Though if you've both given birth and sired a child, you know the mother puts more into the actual process.

They're virtually twins, Jace and Arden, born a day apart. Not uncommon among ambis. Partners tend to get pregnant together. I last saw them both at Arden's wedding, two years ago.

Jace finally came through the customs door, wearing a large pack and pulling an even bigger wheeled bag. The visit to me was just a brief stop on a move to Mars.

We hugged clumsily, both because of the backpack and because Jace held something back. Not exactly surprising, but a little painful nonetheless.

I'd left when the children were five. I'd been on the verge of leaving ever since I'd weaned Arden, but it took me several years to get up the courage to go. Oh, I'd been responsible, sending regular money, visiting when I could, bringing them over from time to time. But I had moved halfway around the world.

Arden was the one who cried, the one who schemed to get Carroll and me back together. Jace never said anything. But there's always been a bit of a wall.

Carroll had remarried, of course. They had other children. In truth, the divorce probably didn't hurt Carroll or the children as much as it hurt me. And it was my idea. I guess that's fair.

"Nice of you to meet me," Jace said. "I could have just shuttled in. And you wouldn't have had to wait around for customs."

I shrugged. "Gives us more time together. And what's the use of a car, if you don't drive it occasionally?" Maybe I was showing off a bit.

I took the rolling bag from Jace, and we made our way through the crowds.

"So, Mars, huh," I said, after we had settled into my two-seater and hooked into the system so we could get back to the city. There are a few places out west where you can actually drive a car, but here on the East Coast you just program it and link up.

"Yeah. It's a good place for an exobio postdoc."

"Long way from home, though."

Jace shrugged. I recognized the move. It was mine.

"E-mail works between here and Mars about as well as between here and Denmark."

I heard the undercurrent, and didn't answer it. "I was thinking more of a long way from the rest of the family."

"Arden cried, of course. And Carroll really doesn't understand why anyone wants to leave." Jace gave me a look.

No, Carroll was very happy there, and wanted everyone else to stay.

"Well, exobiology sort of requires that you go a long way," I said. "By definition."

"I'm going to try for one of the out-of-system missions." Jace kind of blurted out that sentence.

Even I blinked at that one. I went halfway around the world, but Jace was talking about leaving the system. If that happened, we wouldn't ever see each other again.

"Uh," I said. "Have you told Carroll?"

"No. I'll wait and see if it happens. Carroll's upset enough at Mars."

We drove along in silence for a while.

"Might not be any other ambis on an out-of-system mission," I said.

That shrug again. "I'll get by. There aren't too many on Mars, either."

Jace hadn't seen my apartment before. "Nice digs. I thought private detectives were scroungy characters who didn't make much money, if they were honest."

"You've been reading too much fiction." My tone was a little sharp. "A detective who does good work, and works hard, can make a good living without being a crook." Actually, I kind of crossed my fingers at that last part. Not that I'm a crook. But anyone who makes a living ferreting out secrets that others don't want to give up breaks the law now and again.

"Sorry. Didn't mean to tread on the sore toe. And it is a nice place." Jace took a deep breath. "I didn't think you could get roses to grow indoors. Smells wonderful."

"It's a hybrid." Like Jace and me. "I thought we might go out to dinner. A nice Asian or African place maybe."

Jace's eyes brightened for the first time. Denmark is no longer a monoculture; they took in lots of immigrants during the troubled years and have been home to other unusual folks besides the ambigendered. But they still don't have the variety of cultures we have in the States. Just walking in the neighborhood around my apartment I can find fifty different kinds of restaurants, including some of the new experimental cuisines.

"Yeah. I want to get my fill of good Earth eating. Food's pretty bland on Mars, from what I hear."

"Maybe you can smuggle along some peppers and such. Let me check into this program I have running, and then we'll go."

I'd set my comp to dig into the True Virgins while I was gone. Just the superficial stuff: news clips, public documents, nonprofit status. An investigation starts with sifting through the on-the-record stuff. You look for the holes, the things that don't match.

And then you start digging deeper into those. It's not exactly lurking in doorways, tailing a suspect.

I started out as a reporter, got into the investigative stuff, and finally figured out that doing it privately paid a whole lot better than coming up with the scandal of the week. Let me work for myself, too: Most companies don't want investigators directly on the payroll. Independent contractors give them greater deniability.

I scanned quickly through the True Virgin data. Interesting that they had tax-exempt status from the U.S. federal government. Religions get that as a matter of course, but the U.S. Supreme Court has tap-danced around the definition of religion in recent years, and it's hard for some of the groups perceived as cults to get it.

When I looked closer, I realized that they got the status as an education group, supporting sexual morality. Pretty foxy. I wondered if they'd just snuck it by a bored bureaucrat, or if there was something more sinister involved. That would bear more investigation.

Their finances looked a bit interesting, too. Large donations from members. Probably typical cult stuff: getting members to turn over assets. Might be some messy stuff in that, too.

I set a search bot to compare their tax returns with those of their donors, just to see what it turned up. And I also started a search in motion to find out the history of their tax-exempt status. All this stuff is public record.

Two more things caught my eye: a bunch of ugly publicity around a member's suicide (post-operation) and about half a dozen feature-type articles on the children of prominent corporate execs who'd joined the cult. I set the bot to look for other data that matched those.

Then, letting my comp do my work for me (state-of-the-art equipment pays off), I took Jace to dinner. We'd decided on Ethiopian, and headed off to a place two blocks up from my apartment.

Jace put on a short tight skirt and a billowy sleeved top for dinner. Hot, I found myself thinking. I gave myself a mental slap. One doesn't use words like "hot" about one's children.

But the skirt showed off Jace's gently curved hips and muscled legs. And the shirt hinted at more breast than was actually there. Most norms who saw us were going to peg Jace as a woman, unless they got close enough to notice the mustache forming. Jace hadn't shaved for me.

I've got too much middle age in my middle to dress that way anymore. And anyway, I prefer to dress in ways that can be taken either way. Jace is still young enough to want to startle people; I'd rather leave 'em guessing.

The Ethiopian place is traditional—low tables, and food served commonly on huge platters. You eat with spongy bread instead of forks. The place was crowded, and smelled of spices and peppers. And the hostess welcomed us warmly. Funny how even in a big city, in a fast-paced modern world, little islands of old-fashioned hospitality still exist. It felt like we were sitting in someone's living room, waiting for the dinner we could smell cooking.

I went to Ethiopia once, and found that few people eat the old way. They use knives and forks and mostly eat packaged food just like we do. That may have a lot to do with the famines and wars and diseases that racked Africa for so many years. There's probably more old Ethiopian culture in the U.S. than in Ethiopia.

Over local ale, I asked Jace questions about exobio and the Mars project. I cared, somewhat abstractly, but mostly I wanted to figure out how the child's mind worked. Not really a child, I reminded myself: almost thirty and with a Ph.D. But still so young.

"Of course," Jace was saying, "most of the stuff we're going to work with on Mars is fossilized. But it's a training ground, a way to refine our methodology."

"For the out-of-system projects?"

"And the ones on Titan. Out-of-system is probably a ways off. If at all. I shouldn't have mentioned it."

"No, it's okay. Gives me some time to get used to the idea."

"I'd rather you didn't tell Carroll."

"Don't worry." Carroll wouldn't get used to it.

"It's highly competitive. I might not get selected."

"You'll find a way, if you want it bad enough."

"I want it." Jace shifted in the chair, looking uncomfortable.

"It's not that I don't love them, you know. Carroll, Arden, the whole family . . ."

I noticed my absence from the list during the pause.

"It's just that I want things I can't find there. It's too homey, too comfortable. I need to be surprised once in a while. And we don't have much wilderness left on Earth."

"Well, you're an exobiologist. Off-Earth makes sense."

"It's not just my work. It's something else, a drive to go somewhere, see things that I've never seen before, things maybe no one has seen before."

"Be someone no one has ever known before?"

Jace laughed. "Something like that. Just go places where my role's not already set out for me. You understand?"

"All too well."

Jace looked at me, then, one adult to another. "I guess maybe you would."

Definitely my child. The biologists and sociologists can debate if it was because of my genes, or because I left and set that example. Of course, Arden got the same genes and the same example. The same factors can produce such different results.

"How is Arden doing?" I asked.

"The research is going well. Going to be some new ways to cure disease in the future with Arden's name on them. And the marriage is a good one, I think. I guess Arden told you they're both pregnant."

It was probably obvious from my face that I hadn't heard.

"Oh, shit. I guess they were waiting for the lab results before telling you. Don't let on that you know. I'm sure Arden wants to be the one to tell you."

"No problem," I lied. "It's always hard letting folks know long-distance." Funny thing about being a birth parent: You think you ought to be the first to know about a pregnancy—well, after the spouse—even if you live halfway around the world.

It wasn't until we were drinking a little brandy after our meal that I asked a delicate question. "You thought about having kids?"

"And leaving them behind?"

I didn't flinch visibly. "It might make it easier for Carroll."

"I'd never leave any kids of mine behind," Jace said.

I couldn't stop the flinch that time.

We strolled down the street, a few inches and a great gulf between us.

"The night is young," Jace said. "Let's hit some bars."

"What kind of bars did you have in mind."

I got a withering look back. "What kind do you think? I haven't been in a big city in months, and you know how dull the scene is back home."

I'm sure the dullness hadn't kept Jace from trading favors with others. Unmarried ambi life tends toward the promiscuous.

"I don't think I'm up to it," I said.

"You're not going to tell me you gave it up." Jace's voice held a note of incredulity.

Once they're past the insanities of adolescence, you shouldn't lie to your children. "No."

"So why not?"

Truth, damn it. "Because watching you flirting, or knowing you're watching me, will freak me out."

"Oh, come off it, Morgan. You know I have sex; I know you do. What's the big deal?"

"Damned if I know. I didn't say it was logical. But I'm not going to the bars with you. If you want to go, though, I recommend Waugh's on Lamont if you're looking for adventurous norms, or the Fair-Haired Child on Oregon Place if you want just the ambi scene."

"You won't go with me, but you'll tell me where to go?"

"I may be a coward, but I'm not a hypocrite."

Jace laughed. The distance between us shrank down again. "I don't want to abandon you, but life on Mars ain't likely to be all that spectacular. I figure I should play while I can."

"Go, go. I've got work to do anyway. We can talk more tomorrow."

"Do we have more to say?" The wall back in place.

Jace took a cab to the Fair-Haired Child. I found myself thinking of how the regulars would react, and felt a combination of lust and parental anger. I wanted them to admire Jace, and I wanted them to keep their goddamned hands off my baby. Definitely nothing logical about it.

When I got back to my apartment, the programs had finished running. Lots of people just use pocket comps for their research these days, but I like a big screen that lets me see everything I've got. I had data galore to analyze. I downloaded everything into my personal sorting program—my own reworking of an off-the-shelf job—read just enough to come up with some data parameters, and started the sifting process once more.

And then I noticed the e-mail light on my public port. One message: "Stay out of matters that don't concern you, freak."

Fuck. My initial searches weren't carried out in my name—I'm not an idiot—but I hadn't put any extra security on them since I was just going after public record. The True Virgins must have put some fancy bots in place, to find someone getting public info from systems they didn't even control. And to be able to track me down and figure out exactly who and what I was. Unless they called everybody who hadn't had their operation "freak." I'd had the word thrown at me enough to take it personally, but cults have their own definitions.

Good thing I'd charged Vincent a high fee. This one could get ugly. I felt a little scared. And energized. We all pick our lines of work for a reason.

I needed a new approach. People were probably searching True Virgin info regularly, but now I'd be on the list of people they'd check out anytime they spotted something. So standard encryption wouldn't help. I made a pot of coffee to counteract the effect of beer, and settled in at my desk.

What I needed was something to distract them from the likes of me. Something big enough to take all their attention. Maybe multiple somethings. An investigation by one of the big net magazines or holovision talk shows. The U.S. feds. Interpol.

And maybe something corporate. Multinationals scare folks more than governments.

I sifted through my data. The bot had come up with a lots of bits and pieces about the kids of corp execs: enough to hint at a pattern. Could they actually be targeting these people? What did they hope to get? Respectability? Or maybe clout?

I reset the parameters on my sorting program. And started mapping out a general strategy. Disguise my ID. Use public terminals. Drop hints to some reporters I know; directly to some, anonymous e-mails to others. Same thing with the various cops. Drop a line to the legal department of some of the corps involved.

Or—how about pretending to be a major corp's legal department? Not legit; the corp would jump on me with all fours if they traced it. But if they ended up in a big fight with the True Virgins, it might not occur to them for some time to figure out how the fight started. I ought to be able to conceal my tracks well enough to be long gone by the time they started looking.

I got so deep into figuring out how to do this (definitely from a public terminal) that I jumped when I heard a key in the door. I'd forgotten all about Jace.

I checked the clock. Three A.M.

"Waiting up for me?" Jace sounded like a resentful teenager.

"Working."

The signature shrug. I knew it meant Jace didn't believe me.

"The current investigation got a little sticky, so I got caught up figuring out ways of getting what I want without attracting attention. Got carried away." But my brain had clicked into parent mode. Had Jace met anybody? Maybe not, I figured. It was late, but not that late: even casual sexual encounters between ambis tend to go on for several hours. With a double set of erogenous zones, we're not much into quickies.

I wasn't going to ask. "You have fun?" I said instead.

Jace unbent a little. "Good music. And the people were pretty diverse. Made a change from home. I'm beat, though."

"Take the bedroom. I'm still kind of wired. Think I'll play with this a while longer."

In the end, I didn't sleep all that well: too much coffee and perhaps a little worry. I got up before Jace, and mixed up pancake batter while sipping coffee.

The smell of breakfast drew Jace out of bed around ten. "Pancakes. I haven't had those in years."

"Easy enough to make," I said, putting another batch on the griddle.

"I guess. I'm just lazy. Left to my own devices I do whatever's simple." Jace poured some coffee. "You look tired."

Ah, youth. I hadn't been up that much later than Jace, but fatigue shows more when you hit my age. I shrugged. "Worked too late."

Jace gave me a funny look; maybe the shrug looked familiar. "You were really working?" A skeptical tone.

"Yep. I'm trying to find some dirt on the True Virgins."

"That weirdo cult?"

I nodded.

"Who'd pay you for something like that?"

"A man who doesn't want his son to join them."

"Oh. God, why would anybody want to do that to themselves? Gives me the creeps."

"Me, too. Hey, how do you feel about doing some exploring? I need to go out to a couple of places out of the city, and we could make an afternoon out of it. We could have dinner out at this barbecue place out in the sticks. They brew their own beer out there, too. Old-fashioned beer."

"Sounds good. Sounds wonderful. But only if you cook for me tomorrow, and not just breakfast. I miss your cooking."

An overture. I am a good cook; it's one of those things I take pleasure in. But Jace couldn't have eaten my cooking all that often.

As we started out the door, Jace said, "You really weren't waiting up for me last night, were you?"

I shook my head.

"Probably forgot I was here."

Truth hurts.

Traffic in downtown Washington wasn't too bad, for a weekday. I pulled into a lot about a dozen blocks from the FBI building, and we walked the rest of the way.

The feds keep a tight rein on the official part of the city, so the sidewalks were clean and the trees were trimmed. The temperature wasn't particularly hot, either, even though it was only the end of October. Been some talk about putting a dome over the city, to counteract the heat we get nine months out of the year, but nothing's been decided yet.

Janelle Dawson was a prosecutor back in the days when I was a reporter, but she got hooked on the investigative side of law enforcement and moved on to the FBI. She actually specialized in cults, which made her a good person to talk to. We weren't exactly friends, but we didn't hate each other either.

She squeezed me in between a couple of meetings, probably because she'd found me useful in the past.

"This a client, Morgan?" Janelle was giving Jace a definite look. Jace looked good, too, though definitely different from the night before, dressed in classic academic clothes—jeans and a T-shirt—and now unshaven enough to show just the beginning of a five-o'clock shadow. Almost male.

"My child. Jace Livingston."

Janelle cooled a bit. She's not into ambis. "What's up, Morgan?"

"Looks like the True Virgins are targeting the children of big corp execs." That was stretching things a bit, but if you want info out of feds, you have to make them think you know something that they don't.

Something flickered across Janelle's face that made me think I had guessed right. But she said, "Sure you're not just seeing some coincidences? After all, the kids of corp execs tend to go to extremes. The high-powered don't make the best parents."

"My digging shows that it's happening often enough to pass the statistical margin for coincidence." Actually, I didn't have that much info. "Plus the Virgins are paranoid. They've got lots of security out there. They must be doing something more extreme; that stuff costs."

Janelle grinned. "They caught you looking into them."

"Well, kind of."

"So, actually, you're looking for help."

"More like protective coloration. I don't want to be the only person looking into them."

"Using the government to do your work."

"Hey, you're supposed to protect citizens. I'm a citizen. Anyway, you're obviously looking into this too."

She didn't waste any more time pretending she wasn't. I gave her the correlations I'd noted, and tried to sound like I was holding something back. Something I said must have triggered something the feds hadn't noticed, because she actually promised to do more digging.

As we left Janelle's tiny office—the feds put all their money into big impressive buildings, and don't do much in the way of interior decoration—I noticed that no one was in the next couple of rooms. Out to lunch, probably.

"Let me know if anyone's coming," I told Jace. I doubted a phone call from the FBI building would be traced to me.

I called a reporter to let him know the feds were looking into the True Virgins. Calls to Janelle from the press would trigger more work on her part. I was going to call a couple of others, but Jace was looking highly uncomfortable, so I passed on the opportunity. Just as well, because the owner of the office came back just as we walked up the hall.

"You do stuff like that a lot?" Jace asked.

I shrugged.

"Not exactly straightforward, is it?"

"Got to take advantage of circumstances." But I got the impression that exobiologists didn't work that way.

Our next stop was a coffee shop out past Tysons, Virginia. Although the entire region looks like one huge city, it's actually a blending together of a number of separate ones. This part of Virginia used to be a Washington suburb, but it's long since developed a separate culture. Office buildings are much smaller than the massive government structures—and fancier on the inside as well. Enclosed walkways connect them to each other, and to parking garages.

The coffee shop sat in a strip mall providing the usual range of consumer services: groceries, drugs, hardware, cleaning. Most of the parking-lot traffic consisted of delivery vehicles, from electric bikes to vans. Anyone who can afford it gets the routine stuff delivered these days. However, the coffee shop was about half full of local workers on break.

I like this particular place because they'll rent you a public comp terminal for cash. And they don't care how you log on. I sent out a flurry of anonymous e-mails.

Jace watched me. "You sure you're honest?"

I sighed. "Look. The people I'm investigating are obsessed and paranoid. And they've figured out that I'm investigating them. I don't want everything I'm doing to be traced back to me."

"Sounds kind of dangerous."

I could hear Carroll's voice. Carroll, who would work in a lab with any number of toxic chemicals, was always worried by my work with human beings. Though I suppose human beings are a lot less predictable than chemicals.

"Probably more annoying than dangerous," I said, and hoped I wasn't lying.

The last working stop we made was at Interpol's tiny office out past Dulles Airport on the way toward the new spaceport. The one Jace would leave from in a few days. Here I was on friendly ground; the chief U.S. Interpol agent is ambi.

I'd called Adrian to say I was coming by. If the Virgins were tapping my phones, all the better. Interpol should make them nervous.

Adrian welcomed us warmly, offered tea (a welcome respite from all the coffee), and was interested to hear about Jace's plans for research on Mars. A very civilized way of doing business. I sat back and watched Jace get animated, explaining the proposed work.

Adrian has black hair with streaks of red (and a bit of gray) and café au lait skin. I've always wanted to get much closer, but Adrian is very happily married, with half a dozen kids. Some married ambis do play around—we're human—but I don't seem to meet them.

Adrian's primary job is watching what the U.S. is doing— Interpol's presence is mostly a formality here. So I used Janelle's work to pique Adrian's interest.

"Hmm. So the FBI thinks the True Virgins are actually target-ing kids of corp execs?"

"They're looking into it, at least."

"Seems to me I've seen some similar reports from Europe. Let me dig around and see what our people have to say."

All in all, a successful day of work. An hour's drive beyond the spaceport brought us into actual countryside. Leaves were just beginning to turn; we get some winter and the trees do shed leaves. The barbecue and beer lived up to my advance billing, and Jace seemed to relax and have a good time. Our conversation steered clear of touchy subjects. It wasn't all that late when we got home, so we sat up awhile drinking a bit of good brandy and listening to music. I found myself thinking that we'd managed to make some peace between us without discussing all the possible touchy subjects. It felt good.

Jace started to fade out around eleven, but despite the brandy and my sleep-deprived state, I felt a little antsy. So I went out for a walk.

It's a city neighborhood, my part of town: restaurants and shops and theaters. People on the street until all hours. All kinds of people. Washington is an international town.

A few blocks away from my place, the businesses get less tony. But they're still open late, the African groceries, South American restaurants, little shops where those so inclined can shoot craps in the back. Funny. All the fancy, high-tech forms of gambling these days, and some people still want to bet their futures on little plastic cubes (no ivory these days). It's the history of those cubes that makes people call this neighborhood "dicey."

It's just a long-standing Washington tradition: bad neighborhoods bumping up against good ones. I knew where the change lines were, and I turned up my instinctive radar when I crossed them.

I'd changed before I left the apartment, put on loose jeans and an oversized sweatshirt. If you're going to walk alone in a less-than-stellar area, it's best to look male. Boringly male. Females of any age short of decrepit attract attention. So do obvious ambis and well-turned-out men. But a middle-aged man in shapeless clothes is virtually anonymous.

I stopped in at a bar I frequent. Just a neighborhood bar, for a neighborhood that never quite gentrified. A reasonable selection of beer and whiskey, but none of your twenty-year-old Scotches or fancy brews made from that new strain of hops they developed in the Asteroid Belt. The clientele's budget doesn't run to that stuff.

A couple of guys seated at the bar were staring at a wrestling match on the viewscreen up in the corner. They didn't get excited when one of the wrestlers pinned the other. Just something to look at, I guess. No one else was paying attention. I got a beer from the bartender, and took it to a quiet corner.

I thought I was puzzling over the case, but I found myself thinking more about Jace and me. I wondered if maybe we'd come out of this visit better friends. I wanted to be friends with my children now that they were grown.

I registered a person walking across the room, but I didn't pay close attention, so I was a little surprised when someone said, "Mind if I join you?"

I glanced up, annoyed. "I'd rather be alone," I said, and then actually looked at the person.

Tall, slender, but with wiry muscles. Short curly dark brown hair. A skin tone somewhere between olive and brown.

Ambi radar kicked in: not male, not female. And then: not ambi.

"I won't stay long, Doyle."

It—that's the pronoun the True Virgins prefer, so I'm told— had to know it had caught me off guard. But I was damned if I was going to show it. "Sure. What's on your mind?"

"Snatching adults to brainwash them is a crime, Doyle. I'm sure you know that."

"I haven't kidnapped anybody."

"The law covers accessories."

"I deal in information. No law against researching anybody. Even the True Virgins." I didn't see any point in pretending I didn't know what it was talking about.

"Sometimes it's not what you actually do, but what it looks like you did, that gets you in trouble."

"The brainwashing law cuts both ways. Certainly applies to cults."

It didn't like that word. "No need to be insulting, cuntdick. We're not all that different."

I laughed. Being called names by a neutered freak doesn't sting like it might from a norm. "Yeah, we are. I haven't mutilated my body."

"No, someone else did that. You're just the end result. But ambis aren't the only people who can use biology to their own ends. A little DNA, an artificial womb . . ." It shrugged and smiled.

I got the picture: a child born neuter. I didn't succeed in keeping the fear off my face.

"Why so freaked out? It's what your people did, isn't it?"

"That's different," I said. Not exactly witty repartee.

"Why? Because you can fuck anything that moves?" The expression on its face was one of disgust. "We're creating a higher form of human being, leaving the animal functions behind." Not just muscle for the Virgins. A zealot as well.

"Going to figure out how to live without eating and shitting next?" I'd regained some of my composure.

"Just stay out of our business. You don't need the kind of trouble we can bring down on you. Or your kids." It stalked away.

I sat there, taking deep breaths. Okay, so not only had the Virgins caught me looking into them, but they knew some things about me. Like where I hang out. And the fact that I have kids. Did they know Jace was in town?

The personal threats bothered me some, with Jace around. But I've been threatened before. What freaked me out was the idea that the cult was creating neutered babies. I'd heard the rumors, but like most people listening to things I didn't want to hear, I'd ignored them.

And the accusation that it wasn't really any different from what my great-grandparents had done made it creepier. Of course it was different, I told myself. But most norms wouldn't think so. My client Vincent wouldn't think so.

Maybe if the only ambis in the world had been surgically constructed even I wouldn't think so.

I'd known my great-grandparents. They hadn't seemed like

creepy zealots to me. But as a child, you take what you know as normal.

Was there really a difference between creating ambis and creating neuters? My heart cried out yes, and argued its point: We might have been constructed originally, but we could reproduce normally. The neuters could never do that. What they were creating was not human.

But my reason, honed in a world in which more options for making babies are created every year, my reason wasn't so sure.

I felt pretty edgy when I left the bar, so I spotted the two men pretty easily. Big guys, one mostly black, the other maybe white. Not out of place, except that I'd seen them earlier, near my building.

I deliberately left the main drag for a more residential street, to see what they'd do. They didn't follow me. But I saw them again when I came back out onto U Street. Clearly they knew enough about both me and the area to be able to predict where I'd end up.

Not really a tail then, since they didn't care where I went. More likely they wanted to cause some kind of trouble, and were looking for the right opportunity. I decided to give them one. Since they hadn't followed me into the neighborhood— maybe assuming that people would call cops if they heard a scuffle—I picked an alley that ran behind the Fourteenth Street theater district.

The front of the theaters is clean and slick, but no one bothers to clean alleys. I ducked behind a pile of broken furniture, and waited. The white guy passed right in front of me a few minutes later. He didn't see me, and I wouldn't have seen him if his skin hadn't been pale enough to reflect a little light. The black guy had probably run around to the other end of the alley.

Maybe I could have hidden out for a while, waiting for them to give up. But they might start looking through the junk for me, and anyway, I wanted to know what was going on. While my work doesn't usually call for fights, it's not like I can't get physical. Service in the Danish Army is mandatory, and includes a lot of self-defense skills. Danes serve in most of the international peacekeeping operations.

So I jumped white guy from behind. He hadn't expected me,

but he was quick enough to keep me from getting a chokehold. As he slipped under my left arm, he tried to grab my right wrist. I let him think he was getting it, and then took hold of his wrist. I cranked it back toward him while moving under his arm. He was dancing backward, trying to get loose.

I heard running footsteps. Using white guy's arm like a fishing rod, I threw him in the direction of the noise. A thud that sounded like head hitting pavement was followed by an "Oh, shit." I caught just the flash of a white T-shirt bouncing around, and guessed that black guy had nearly tripped over white guy. Keeping my eye on the shirt, I jumped for black guy, and this time I moved fast enough to actually get the chokehold.

"What the hell is going on?" I asked, releasing my pressure on his neck just enough to allow an answer.

"A good question, Doyle," said a voice I hadn't heard before. Light from a handheld spotlight struck me in the eyes. I found myself temporarily blind, so I tightened my grip on black guy and ducked my head behind his.

"Sorry," the voice said in a tone that didn't sound sorry at all. The light moved away from my eyes, and as I recovered from the glare I could make out a woman standing there. Tall, broad-shouldered. She looked like trouble, especially since she was holding a gun in her hand. A projectile weapon of some sort.

"You going to tell me what the fuck is going on?" I asked.

"Actually, I was thinking about shooting you," she said.

"You're going to have to shoot your friend here first."

She shrugged, like it didn't much matter to her. Then she said, "Leave the Virgins alone, Doyle. We can always find you again. We know where you live, where you go."

"What's the deal here? You figure the threat from the freak in the bar wasn't enough?"

Something about the way she moved suggested she didn't know what I was talking about. I wished I could see her face, see if it showed something. But there wasn't that much light.

"Whatever it takes," she said. And then added, almost as an afterthought. "We know how to find your kid, too. Made a quite splash at the ambi bar the other night."

Black guy gurgled as my grip tightened.

The light went out, and I couldn't see the woman anymore. Hoping they hadn't put any people behind me, I dragged black guy back to the opening of the alley, and dropped him just before any of the pedestrians on U Street saw us. He collapsed in a heap, and I walked as steadily as I could out of the alley. My heart was still racing, but I made the effort to walk like everyone else.

When I got back home, though, I raced up the stairs instead of waiting for the elevator. The apartment didn't look as if anyone had broken in, but I tiptoed into the bedroom to make sure Jace was okay. I heard regular breathing, and the light from the living room showed me Jace's face, relaxed and childlike in sleep. I remembered checking on the children when they were babies. I resisted the urge to go adjust the covers or stroke Jace's forehead. Babies sleep through things like that, but adults don't.

The next morning dawned sunny, but not hot. I got up ahead of Jace, and called Janelle to tell her what happened.

"You sure these folks were really men and women?" she asked. "Not neuters who just dressed that way?"

"Well, I didn't get a chance to inspect their genitals," I said. "But, yeah, I think they were norms. They were different from the one in the bar. Didn't have that prepuberty look to their bodies."

"They don't have to do that, though," Janelle said. We had the vid on and I could see dissatisfaction in her face.

"What they looked like—and sounded like, and acted like— was muscle," I said. "Pro muscle."

"Yeah," she said. She still looked dissatisfied. I watched her punching commands in on the computer. "Well, the guy who hit the pavement didn't show up in either the morgue or the hospital. But you should have called the cops."

"And then I still wouldn't be home yet. They threatened my kid, Janelle. I'm not going to let Jace out of my sight until the ship takes off for Mars."

She grinned. Janelle didn't really care if I called the cops or not. "Pro muscle," she said. "Doesn't sound much like cult stuff to me. The guy in the bar sounds more like the real thing. Though I guess the Virgins can hire muscle, too. Muscle isn't usually picky about who it works for." She still looked dissatisfied when she punched off.

I logged on and discovered that my work had borne fruit: a couple of newslines had hints of a major investigation under way on the True Virgin cult. Adrian had sent me an update—encrypted—with European data confirming the targeting of kids of the powerful.

Jace woke up in the same mellow mood from the night before. I didn't mention the Virgin in the bar or the fight.

We decided to take advantage of the nice weather, and go out to museums and parks—those things you do in your own city only when you have out-of-town company.

We admired the French Impressionists in the decaying east building of the National Gallery, though more because we thought we ought to than because we really liked them. Then we argued amicably over the latest modern art in the gallery's new south building, a sharp-angled hexagonal monstrosity that has eaten up the last of the open space between the White House and the Capitol. Jace and I disagreed on the worth of almost every piece. The ones I liked, Jace pronounced old-fashioned; if Jace admired one, I found it form without content.

We were leaving the mall, headed for Eastern Market on the other side of the Capitol to buy fresh vegetables and meat for a nice dinner, when my phone buzzed. It was Vincent.

"Glad you called," I said. "I should have some results for you by tomorrow or the next day."

"No," he said. He almost shouted. "No. Call it off. Quit the whole thing."

"Mr. Vincent, I'm afraid it's not that simple. I've already done a lot of work."

"I'll pay for your time, Doyle. I'll pay the whole damn fee. Just stop it. Now."

He hung up before I could explain that it was going to be pretty damn hard to stop it, given what I'd set in motion. I tried calling back, but he wouldn't take my call.

It ruined the mood. Jace and I continued on to the market and bought the makings of curry, but I was distracted.

Instead of going home, we reversed steps back to downtown and went by Vincent's office. He worked in one of the new office buildings that replaced similar—but out-of-date—office buildings along K Street. Office buildings are like clothes: Designs come in and out of fashion, and are mostly notable for not being what they were last year.

Vincent headed up the lobbying office of a consortium of biotech multinationals. The support staff didn't want to let me through, but I persisted. When Vincent saw me, he sighed, but he motioned to the staff to let me be. "Let's take a walk," he said. I left Jace in the company's reception room, though not without worrying a little.

Walking on K Street isn't exactly pleasant. Pedestrian traffic is wall-to-wall and cars creep along. The computerized system solved actual gridlock, but it can't make an overabundance of cars move fast. But there's privacy in chaos.

Vincent looked hollow-eyed, completely worn out. "Look, Doyle," he said. "They're threatening my kid. And they proved they can get at him. Can you understand that?"

"Sure. I've got kids." And I was worried about mine, too.

He blinked. I guess he hadn't thought of ambi kids. "Anyway, as long as I get you to lay off, they'll leave him alone."

"And?"

"What do you mean, 'and'?"

"And what else do you have to do?"

"What makes you think there's something else?"

"Come on, Vincent. They targeted your son for a reason. They want people in important positions under their thumbs. They're getting something from you."

I think he actually wanted to tell me about it. But he was the kind of man who takes the ugly stuff of life and deals with it on his own. He probably hadn't even told the boy's mother what was really going on. That's the kind of stress that kills people young, even if they've had all the gene intervention and take the right drugs. The human body isn't meant to handle that much stress.

"Just get out of it Doyle. Call off whoever you've brought in.

Leave it be. Just leave it be." He pushed an envelope into my hand and went back to his job.

I didn't look in the envelope until Jace and I got back home. It contained about double the contract price. I couldn't decide if it was extra payment for getting out, or a sign that he really wanted me to continue.

Not that it mattered, really. No way in hell I could call off the FBI and Interpol. Or reporters. But unless they came on something quick, or some thorn in their side like me kept pressing on them, they'd all move on to the next crisis soon.

I could just stop, and let it ride. Jace would be off to Mars in two days, safe from the Virgins. Things would die down, and the creeps probably wouldn't bother with me anymore. No real reason to keep digging, without a client.

It bugged me. I don't like being threatened, and I wanted to fight back. But I didn't want my kid in the middle. So I compromised with myself. I'd leave things alone until Jace took off for Mars.

I sent Vincent an e-mail—with just enough encryption to make it look like I didn't want anyone else to know about it— telling him I was following his instructions. And then I made a few plans for Jace and me that would ensure we'd stick together like glue.

But as I may have said, human beings can be unpredictable. Or maybe it's more that we ignore signs we don't want to see.

Jace sat on a stool in the kitchen, watching me chop vegetables by hand. Yeah, I know: You can toss all the ingredients into the combiner and push the right buttons and end up with something that tastes pretty much like what you had in mind. But as far as I'm concerned, that's not cooking.

My mind wasn't on the job, though. I was constantly rummaging through a cabinet, looking for the ingredient I'd forgotten, a spice here, a vegetable there. If it hadn't been for Jace, I'd have just called for take-out.

"What do you think about the Virgins using their DNA and artificial wombs to create neuter kids?" I asked Jace.

"Yuck."

"That the professional biologist's response?"

"No. That's the human being trying not to throw up. I hope you're kidding."

"I don't think I am."

Jace shivered.

"As a biologist," I prompted.

"Okay, so as a biologist I know that life can reproduce any number of ways. And that over the past century or so humans have figured out how take complete control of it. Plus as an ambi it's hard to argue that it's wrong to alter genes. But it still gives me the creeps."

"Me, too."

"Why do you think your client wants you to get out?" Jace asked.

"He's scared. And the Virgins told him they'd lay off his kid if he'd pull me off, and give them some data on his company. That's the real scheme here: blackmail corp execs by going after their kids."

"What kind of data are they looking for?"

"I don't know."

"You don't know? That sounds like the most important part of the whole puzzle."

Jace was right. Why the hell was a cult going after corp execs? What use was it to them? I hadn't really given it much thought. I'd been defining the job pretty narrowly: Get the Virgins off Vincent's kid.

"It's a good question, all right. Vincent lobbies for a consortium of biotech companies. I think they mostly manufacture generics, after the patents run out on the initial drugs. I can't quite see what the Virgins might want with them, though. Doesn't really matter. I don't have a client anymore."

"So what? Those people are dangerous. They need to be stopped."

"The FBI and Interpol are looking into it. It's their job, not mine."

"Ducking responsibility. That's your specialty, isn't it." Jace's voice was bitter.

"Look, I can't—" Jace didn't let me finish.

"You just do what they pay you to do, right? Do your duty according the fucking rules. But whenever it gets tough, you cut out. Like with Arden and me."

I got a little pissed myself. "What I do for work and what went on with our family are two separate things, Jace. They've got nothing to do with each other."

"Like hell. You're walking out on something that needs doing, just like you walked out on the family."

"Jace." But I didn't really know what to say.

"Why the hell did you have kids, if you weren't going to stick around? No, wait. I know the answer to this: It's an ambi's duty to have kids, right? There are too few of us. Got to build up the population. So be sure and reproduce, even if you're not going to be a real parent. That's why you want me to have kids, even if I have to leave them behind. That's your definition of duty."

"It's more complicated than that," I said. My answer sounded pretty feeble to me, and probably worse to Jace.

"Sure it is." Jace's voice dripped contempt.

"Look, damn it. I loved Carroll, love you and Arden. But I couldn't live that comfortable, isolated life. You ought to understand that. I needed something else I couldn't get in there."

"Lack of commitment, maybe?"

I tried again. "Jace, I was committed to you. You're my kid. Nothing changes that."

"Then why didn't you take me with you when you left?"

"What?"

"I wanted to live with you. I always did. I've never been happy in that comfortable domesticity either. I wanted out."

"Carroll would never have allowed it. You know that. The birth parent has greater rights; the law might have let me take Arden, but not you. And Arden wouldn't have wanted to leave."

"You never asked. You never tried. Maybe you couldn't have done it when I was five, but when I was a teenager you could have. The courts would have listened to me then. Carroll would have considered it then."

I avoided Jace's eyes.

"You didn't want me, did you?"

I couldn't answer. I tried to look at Jace, and failed miserably.

"You selfish bastard." Jace stood up, shoved the stool violently under the counter, and stalked out of the kitchen.

I just stood there, trying to come up with something, anything to say in my defense. I couldn't think of a thing. Jace was right. I never wanted to raise kids. I wanted to be exactly what I was: the absentee parent, sending expensive presents for birthdays, visiting occasionally, bragging about their accomplishments.

It hurt, though, having it thrown in my face like that. I couldn't lie to myself anymore, say that my leaving didn't really hurt my kids. Oh, they hadn't starved, or been mistreated. They'd been loved. But they'd known that something besides them mattered more to me, and that leaves scars.

The wall between Jace and me was my fault. And it wasn't going to come down. My kid—whom I loved greatly in my selfish way—was probably going to go hundreds of light-years away sometime in the next few years, and the wall between us would be cemented in place.

And I didn't have any right to beg Jace to make peace with me, because it had been my choice in the first place.

I stood in the kitchen feeling sorry for myself. It was about three minutes after I heard the hall door slam that I realized Jace had left the apartment.

Time alone would cool Jace down, I told myself. Not that we'd make peace, not really. Just get back to not talking about it.

And then my errant brain kicked in: Jace was out on the street, alone. And the True Virgins and their muscle likely still believed they needed to do something about me.

I did remember to turn off the stove as I dashed out the door.

They hadn't seen Jace in the Fair-Haired Child. "No, hasn't been in tonight," the bartender said, looking at the picture of Jace I carry with me.

"You sure?"

"Oh, yeah. I'd have noticed. That one broke a few hearts the other night, dancing till almost dawn and then going home alone. This business, Morgan?"

"Personal," I said grimly.

I stood in front of the club and tried to think. The Child had been my best guess. Now I couldn't think of where to look. An ugly voice in the back of my head was saying, "Maybe the Virgins grabbed Jace already." If so, they'd probably call. It was me they wanted. I reached in my pocket to be sure the phone was there.

But what if they decided to hurt Jace in the meantime? I kept my hand on the phone. Maybe I should call Janelle, see if I could get some locations for the Virgins. Though that sounded like looking for the proverbial needle in the haystack. Bound to be more than one place.

And maybe they hadn't pulled off the snatch yet. Think, I told myself. Jace is a lot like you. Where would you go if you were pissed off?

Waugh's. Of course. I'd go to Waugh's. And Jace knew about that place; I'd mentioned it. Waugh's, where the adventurous norms hang out to meet ambis.

The norms at Waugh's are looking for a kinky sexual experience, not a relationship. It's not something I go in for much, except when I'm in a spectacularly bad mood. Quickie sex with someone I probably wouldn't even want to know seems to work about as well as getting drunk. Not that it cures the mood, exactly; it's more like wallowing in the mud.

I went to Waugh's because it was less painful to think of Jace having casual sex with norms than it was to think of what the Virgins might have done.

It was only when I got there that I realized I wasn't exactly dressed for the place. The person running the door looked at my rumpled shirt and slacks with the kind of disdain that such gatekeepers develop to a high art. But I got in. They rarely turn an ambi away, even an underdressed one. We're the draw.

The place was packed, and underlit. Not the best crowd for looking for someone. And I had the feeling that the management might decide to toss me out if I was too obvious about looking.

I finally spotted a waiter I knew slightly, and showed Jace's picture. "Oh, yeah." A definite look of appreciation. "Try the back bar."

The music was quieter in the back bar, but the lights were even dimmer. Still, I spotted Jace sitting on a barstool, next to a woman. They were deep in conversation, and the woman had a hand on Jace's thigh.

I didn't like it, not at all. And I didn't think it was just the parental blood pressure skyrocketing. Something about the woman bothered me. I knew my judgment was skewed by the situation, though, so I wanted a better look. Preferably without Jace seeing me.

I moved close to bar, staying on Jace's blind side. Now I could see the woman a little better. Tall. Broad-shouldered. Dressed conservatively—that was one of the things that bothered me. Most norms dress outlandishly for Waugh's.

I wouldn't have thought of her as Jace's type, and, indeed, as I watched, Jace pushed her hand away. She laughed, and turned her head enough so that I could see more of her. It was the woman who'd pointed the gun at me the night before.

She leaned close to Jace, and whispered something. Jace reacted to the whisper. The two of them got up and started out.

The stairs in the back bar at Waugh's lead to some private rooms. But they walked past that, headed toward the main exit. I watched them start across the big room—with its wall-to-wall dancers—and decided the odds were they were leaving.

There's an exit from the back bar, though like most exits in public places, it's alarmed. That might be a problem, except that I carry a small device that will override it. I've had the urge to go out the back way before at Waugh's. And a few other places.

So I went out through the alley and got around to the front door just as Jace and the woman came through it. A car was parked in front, and the woman was herding Jace toward it. She didn't seem to be holding a gun on Jace, though she might have one on her. What she'd said in the bar had apparently been enough to convince Jace to go with her.

As they got close, I shouted, "Don't get in the car." Jace froze suddenly. The woman looked briefly confused, as if she couldn't figure out what was slowing them down. She hadn't understood what I'd said; I'd yelled it in Danish.

She gripped Jace's left wrist with her left hand, and reached behind Jace's back to grab the other one. Jace didn't wait for her to grab. Spinning to the right, Jace sent an elbow into the woman's throat. And then grabbed around the back of her neck and threw her forward.

Jace was in the Danish Army, too.

The driver of the car was getting out. It was the black guy from the previous night. He hadn't spotted me, though. Too many people on the sidewalk. So he was surprised when I took hold of the hand in which he was holding a gun and forced it back toward him. He went down, and I bent his wrist enough to get him to let go of the weapon.

Jace had seen me by that point. "Morgan. The bastard said you'd been hurt, and that she was taking me to see you."

"I figured it was something like that." I could hear sirens. I kept the gun trained on the guy I'd taken it from, and pulled out the pocket phone to call Janelle. The local cops would probably buy my snatch story, but FBI backup wouldn't hurt anything.

We all ended up down at the police station. Jace and I just sat around, eating junk out of the candy machines and waiting. Janelle got to sit in on the interviews, though—local cops don't like feds, but they don't have much choice—and after a couple of hours she came out and filled us in.

"Pro muscle, just like we thought. The woman's the brains of this little crew, or what brains they've got, anyway. And she's got a long enough record that she's willing to cooperate a bit."

"So the Virgins are hiring muscle?"

"No. The guy who hired her tried to pretend he worked for the Virgins, but she didn't buy it and did some digging of her own. To protect herself in a situation like this one. He worked for one of the biotech multinationals." She named a company. It wasn't part of the group Vincent worked for.

"Some kind of legislation pending that affects drug companies?" I asked.

Jace looked at me like I was an idiot. "Haven't you been paying attention? Those people have a patent on the tailored drugs that knock out about half of the immune-system disorders.

They're trying to extend it. And the lobbying group Vincent heads represents the generic manufacturers. They want a piece of the action."

"How do you know so damn much about it?"

"Arden was following it pretty closely, just before I left, and told me about it. What the U.S. decides about these things usually affects what goes on in the rest of the world, so Arden keeps up with all these companies. Who's doing what and where matters if you're in biomedical research. I'm surprised you didn't e-mail Arden and ask about them, once you found out what kind of work Vincent did."

I should have thought of that. But I still think of Arden as a child, I guess. Jace, too. Pretty stupid. "So the Virgins aren't even involved?"

Janelle shook her head. "Apparently not. Or not directly. I think the guy who did the hiring had checked out Vincent and found his kid was playing around with the cult, and chose that strategy."

On the way home, Jace and I decided junk food from the machines didn't constitute dinner. We called for delivery on the way, and met the guy on the front steps of my building just as we got there. Back upstairs we spread the food around on the dining-room table, and opened a bottle of wine.

"God," Jace said. "I don't guess I've fought anybody since the Army."

"How'd it feel?"

"I kind of liked it." A big grin. "I definitely liked it. Stupid bastard figured I was just a punk kid." Jace gave me a look. "Underestimated you, too."

"Yeah." But not by much. The fight had released some of my tension, too, but I was still displeased with myself. It shouldn't have happened.

We ate in silence, polished off the wine, and opened a new bottle.

"Morgan, what I said earlier. Look, I'm sorry. I didn't really mean it."

"Yes, you did. And you've got nothing to be sorry about. You just told the truth."

"Well, sort of. My take on it, anyway."

"I'm the one who should be apologizing. I'm sorry I wasn't much of a parent, Jace. It wasn't that I didn't love you; it was just . . ." I let my voice trail off.

"You wanted other things more."

"Yeah." Bald truth. Cruel to say it, but worse to keep lying.

"You know, Morgan. I understand it now. I know why. I even sympathize. But as a kid . . ." Now it was Jace's voice that trailed off.

"It wasn't fair to you or Arden."

"And you wouldn't do anything different, if you had it to do over."

Now was the place for a comforting lie. But there was too much between Jace and me for that. "No. I wouldn't."

Jace nodded. And changed the subject. "How'd you find me tonight, anyway? Did you tail me?"

I shook my head. "Lucky guess. It's where I'd have gone."

"Oh, fuck. People are always telling me how much I remind them of you. And here I did it again."

"Afraid so."

Jace said "Oh, fuck" again, then took the rest of the wine without offering to share any with me, and sat there staring off into space, sipping it.

I don't think being like me was a pleasing thought. I kind of like seeing bits of myself in my children, but I can get very angry when I see my parents in myself. So I understood how Jace felt. But it still hurt.

I went out to Vincent's house early the next morning, and caught him before he left for work. He looked like shit.

"Whatever you agreed to do, you're off the hook," I said, and told him about the pro muscle and the corp that had hired them. "They found your son's flirtation with the Virgins, and used that."

"My God. I knew they could fight dirty, but it never occurred to me they'd do something like that. So my son is safe."

"Well, the Virgins might still want him. But what they do won't have anything to do with how you lobby on Capitol Hill. I brought you some material that might help." I handed him a folder full of printouts.

I'd sat up late the night before, going over my data. After I'd sorted and resorted the data enough times, I'd found a pattern that showed substantial fraud in the way the Virgins got new members to sign over their assets. Plus some data on how they'd managed that tax-exempt status.

"If the Virgins bring down some heat on you for grabbing your son back, you ought to be able to convince them to let it be. Convincing him he's not interested is up to you."

"Thanks." His face looked even redder than usual. "And thanks for not quitting. I was just scared. It was my kid."

"I know. Act on that stuff quick. I'm going to pass it on to the feds pretty soon. But I thought I'd give you time to use it first. You paid for it."

I did manage to cook a good meal before Jace left, and we did some more of the tourist routine. I even overcame my parental issues. The night before the Mars shuttle took off we went to the Child and both danced until the wee hours.

At the spaceport, when I gave Jace a final hug, I could tell that the wall between us had come down completely. Nothing was held back. All the anger and resentment were mixed in with the love. It hurt like hell, and I didn't want to let go.

But I kissed Jace good-bye, and then turned away as the passengers began to board. I didn't want anyone to see me cry. Some things should be done in private.

It actually got a little cold the day after Jace left. A front blew in from the northwest, and brought heavy rain with it. I curled up in my most comfortable chair, and sat in the dark in my apartment, staring out at the rain, trying to make up my mind. The afternoon before, I'd had a long talk with Janelle at her request—debriefing, she called it—and I'd picked up a few bits of interesting information.

I came to a decision about the time the rain slacked off. Choosing about ten of the e-mail addresses for the True Virgins in the public records, I sent off a message—"Tell the same guy to meet me at the bar tonight"—and signed it.

It showed up about ten o'clock, while I was nursing my third beer.

"I hear you figured out it wasn't us blackmailing that lobbyist. Thanks for the help."

I meet the slightly sarcastic tone with one of my own. "Anytime."

"That why you wanted to see me, get your thanks in person?"

I pushed an envelope across the table. "The corp that was using you had a line into your organization. The FBI knows where it is. I figured you ought to know, too."

Surprise ran across its face. "Why are you doing this? You hate us."

"I'm not even sure. I hate the way you target vulnerable people. I hate the way you use the folks who join you. The idea that you might be creating neuter babies creeps me out. And zealotry gets on my nerves. But . . ." I paused.

"But?"

"But I hate to see the big corps get away with using anybody, just to promote some financial gain. I figure everybody needs ammunition against them. And . . ." I took a very deep breath. "And maybe a little of what you said about humans controlling our own evolution rang true. I don't like your methods, and I don't think humans should put their animal selves behind them, but maybe we find that out by trying it."

It gave me a look. "I don't like all our methods, either. But we're at war."

Zealots. "So you owe me something," I said. "How'd you figure out I was looking into you so quick?"

"So that's why." It looked relieved, as if believing I had ulterior motives was easier than believing I might have meant what I said. "We keep a database of everyone we think might cause us trouble. Reporters, private cops, folks like that. Anybody hits on certain net sites, we run them through it. It's geared to cut through basic encryptions."

"Paranoid."

"Even paranoids have enemies. And we have lots of them. You come at us again, be prepared for a fight."

"Don't worry."

"I hear you got grandchildren on the way. I guess congratulations are in order." The way it said "grandchildren" made it sound like a four-letter word.

I responded to the chill I felt. "The Virgins touch any member of my family, ever, and I'll kill you. You, personally."

It grinned. "I know you will. You ambis are very predictable that way. So are the norms. Easy to control you through your families. We don't have that problem. You're forced to threaten me, personally."

"You start this cloning program, you'll have those same kind of ties."

"No, we won't. No birth parents. No ties between the DNA donors and the kids. We won't have all that crap." A look of disgust passed over its face.

Just for a moment, I wondered what kind of childhood this person had suffered, to lead him or her—I couldn't tell which and I refused to believe it had been ambi—to take the drastic step of surgically removing everything connected with sex. And to hate the basic concept of parent and child.

But I couldn't do anything about that. I said, again, "You, personally."

And this time I walked out.

Of a Sweet Slow Dance in the Wake of Temporary Dogs

Adam-Troy Castro

Before

1

On the last night before the end of everything, the stars shine like a fortune in jewels, enriching all who walk the quaint cobble-stoned streets of Enysbourg. It is a celebration night, like most nights in the capital city. The courtyard below my balcony is alive with light and music. Young people drink and laugh and dance. Gypsies in silk finery play bouncy tunes on harmonicas and mandolins. Many wave at me, shouting invitations to join them. One muscular young man with impossibly long legs and a face equipped with a permanent grin takes it upon himself to sprint the length of the courtyard only to somersault over the glittering fountain at its center. For a heartbeat out of time he seems to float, enchanted, over the water. Then I join his friends in applause as he belly-flops, drenching himself and the long-haired girls wading at the fountain's other rim. The girls are not upset but delighted. Their giggles tinkle like wind chimes as they splash across the fountain themselves, flinging curtains of silver water as their shiny black hair bobs back and forth in the night.

2

Intoxicated from a mixture of the excellent local wine and the even better local weed, I consider joining them, perhaps the boring way via the stairs and perhaps via a great daredevil leap from the balcony. I am, after all, stripped to the waist. The ridiculous boxers I brought on the ship here could double as a bathing suit, and the way I feel right now I could not only make the fountain but also sail to the moon. But after a moment's consideration I decide not. That's the kind of grand theatrical gesture visitors to Enysbourg make on their first night, when they're still overwhelmed by its magic. I have been here nine nights. I have known the festivals that make every night in the capital city a fresh adventure. I have explored the hanging gardens, with all their deceptive challenges. I have climbed the towers of pearl, just down the coast. I have ridden stallions across Enysbourg's downs, and plunged at midnight into the warm waters of the eastern sea. I have tasted a hundred pleasures, and wallowed in a hundred more, and though far from sick of them, feel ready to take them at a more relaxed pace, partaking not as a starving man but as a connoisseur. I want to be less a stranger driven by lust, more a lover driven by passion.

So I just take a deep breath and bask in the air that wafts over the slanting tiled roofs: a perfume composed of equal parts sex and spice and the tang of the nearby ocean, all the more precious for being part of the last night before the end of everything. It occurs to me, not for the first time, that this might be the best moment of my life: a life that, back home, with its fast pace and its anonymous workplaces and climate-controlled, gleaming plastic everything, was so impoverished that it's amazing I have any remaining ability to recognize joy and transcendence at all.

In Enysbourg such epiphanies seem to come several times a minute. The place seems determined to make me a poet, and if I don't watch out I might hunt down paper and pen and scrawl a few lines, struggling to capture the inexpressible in a cage of fool amateurish June-moon-and-spoon.

3

The curtains behind me rustle, and a familiar presence leaves my darkened hotel room to join me on the balcony. I don't turn to greet her, but instead close my eyes as she wraps me in two soft arms redolent of wine and perfume and sex. Her hands meet at the center of my chest. She rests a chin on my shoulder and murmurs my name in the musical accent that marks every word spoken by every citizen of Enysbourg.

"Robert," she says, and there's something a little petulant about the way she stresses the first syllable, something adorable and mocking in the way she chides me for not paying enough attention to her.

By the time I register the feel of her bare breasts against my bare back, and realize in my besotted way that she's mad, she's insane, she's come out on the balcony in full view of everybody without first throwing on something to cover herself, the youths frolicking in the fountain have already spotted her and begun to serenade us with a chorus of delighted cheers. "Kiss her!" shouts a boy. "Come on!" begs a girl. "Let us see!" yells a third. "Don't go inside! Make love out here!" When I turn to kiss the woman behind me, I am cheered like a conqueror leading a triumphant army into Rome.

Her name is Caralys, and she is of course one of the flowers of Enysbourg: a rare beauty indeed, even in a country where beauty is everywhere. She is tall and lush, with dark eyes, skin the color of caramel, and a smile that seems to hint at secrets propriety won't let her mention. Her shiny black hair cascades down her back in waves, reflecting light even when everything around her seems to be dark.

I met her the day after my arrival, when I was just a dazed and exhausted tourist sitting alone in a café redolent of rich ground coffee. I wasn't just off the boat then, not really. I'd already enjoyed a long awkward night being swept up by one celebration after another, accepting embraces from strangers determined to become friends, and hearing my name, once given, become a chant of hearty congratulation from those applauding my successful escape from the land of everyday life. I had danced the whole night, cheered at the fires of dawn, wept for reasons that puzzled me still, and stumbled to bed, where I enjoyed the dreamless bliss that comes from exhaustion. It was the best night I'd known in a long time. But I was a visitor still, reluctant to surrender even the invisible chains that shackled me; and even as I'd jerked myself awake with caffeine, I'd felt tired, surfeited, at odds.

I was so adrift that when Caralys sauntered in, her hair still tousled and cheeks still shining from the celebrations of the night before, her dress of many patches rustling about her ankles in a riot of multiple colors, I almost failed to notice her. But then she'd sat down opposite me and declared in the sternest of all possible tones that even foreigners, with all their worries, weren't allowed to wear grimaces like mine in Enysbourg. I blinked, almost believing her, because I'd heard words just like those the previous night, from a pair of fellow visitors who had caught me lost in a moment of similar repose. Then she tittered, first beneath her breath and then with unguarded amusement, not understanding my resistance to Enysbourg's charms, but still intrigued, she explained much later, by the great passion she saw imprisoned behind my gray, civilized mien. "You are my project," she said, in one expansive moment. "I am going to take a tamed man and make him a native of Enysbourg."

She may well succeed, for we have been in love since that first day, both with each other and with the land whose wonders she has been showing me ever since.

4

We have fought only once, just yesterday, when in a thought-less lapse I suggested that she return with me on the ship home. Her eyes flashed the exasperation she always showed at my moments of thoughtless naïveté: an irritation so grand that it bordered on contempt. She told me it was an arrogant idea, the kind only a foreigner could have. Why would she leave this place that has given her life? And why would I think so much of her to believe that she would? Was that all she was to me? A prize to be taken home, like a souvenir to impress my friends with my trip abroad? Didn't I see how diminished she would be, if I ever did that to her? "Would you blind me?" she demanded. "Would you amputate my limbs? Would you peel strips off my skin, slicing off piece after piece until there was nothing left of me but the parts that remained convenient to you? This is my country, Robert. My blood." And she was right, for she embodies Enysbourg, as much as the buildings themselves, and for her to abandon it would be a crime against both person and place. Both would be diminished, as much as I'll be diminished if I have to leave her behind.

5

We leave the balcony and go back inside, where, for a moment in the warm and sweet-smelling room, we come close to collaps-ing on the bed again, for what seems the thousandth time since we woke sore but passionate this morning. But this is the last night before the end of everything, when Enysbourg's wonders emerge in their sharpest relief. They are not to be missed just so we can keep to ourselves. And so she touches a finger to the tip of my nose and commands that it's time to go back into the world. I obey.

We dress. I wear an open vest over baggy trousers, with a great swooping slouch hat glorious in its vivid testimony to Enysbourg's power to make me play the willing fool. She wears a fringed blouse and another ankle-length skirt of many patches, slit to midthigh to expose a magnificent expanse of leg. Dozens of carved wooden bracelets, all loose enough to shift when she moves, clack like maracas along her forearms. Her lips are red, her flowered hair aglow with reflected light. Two curling locks meet in the center of her forehead, right above her eyes, like mischievous parentheses. Somewhere she wears bells.

Laughing, she leads me from the room, and down the narrow stairs, chattering away at our fellow guests as they march in twos and threes toward their own celebrations of this last night. We pass a man festooned with parrots, a woman with a face painted like an Italian landscape, a fire-eater, a juggler in a suit of carnival color, a cavorting clown-faced monkey who hands me a grape and accepts a small coin in payment. Lovers of all possible, and some impossible, gender combinations flash inebriated grins as they surrender their passions in darkened alcoves. Almost everybody we pass is singing or dancing or sharing dizzy, disbelieving embraces. Every time I pause in sheer amazement at something I see, Caralys chuckles at my saucer-eyed disbelief, and pulls me along, whispering that none of this would be half as marvelous without me there to witness it.

Even the two fellow tourists we jostle, as we pass through the arched entranceway and into the raucous excitement of the street, become part of the excitement, because I know them. They are the ones I met on that first lost day before Caralys, before I learned that Enysbourg was not just a vacation destination offered as brief reward for earning enough to redeem a year of dullness and conformity, but the repository of everything I'd ever missed in my flavorless excuse for a life. Jerry and Dee Martel are gray retirees from some awful industrial place where Dee had done something or other with decorating and Jerry had managed a firm that molded the plastic shells other companies used to enclose the guts of useful kitchen appliances. When they talk about their jobs now, as they did when they found me that first night, they shudder with the realization that such things swallowed so many years of finite lives. They were delivered when they vacationed in Enysbourg, choosing it at random among all the other oases of tamed exoticism the modern world maintains to make people forget how sterile and homogenous things have become. On arriving they'd discovered that it was not a tourist trap, not an overdeveloped sham, not a fraud, and not an excuse to sell plastic souvenirs that testify to nothing but the inane gullibility of the people who buy them, but the real thing, the special place, the haven that made them the people they had always been meant to be. They'd emigrated, in what Jerry said with a wink was their "alternative to senility."

"Was it a sacrifice for us?" Jerry asked, when we met. "Did it mean abandoning our security? Did it even mean embracing some hardships? Of course it did. It meant all those things and more. You may not think so, but then you're a baby; you haven't even been in Enysbourg long enough to know. But our lives back home were empty. They were nothing. At least here, life has a flavor. At least here, life is something to be treasured."

Living seven years later as natives, spending half their time in the capital and half their time out in the country exploring caves and fording rivers and performing songs they make up on the spot, they look thirty years younger than their mere calendar ages: with Jerry lean and robust and tanned, Dee shorter and brighter and interested in everything. They remember me from nine days ago and embrace me like a son, exclaiming how marvelous I look, how relaxed I seem in comparison with the timid creature they met then. They want to know if this means I'm going to stay. I blush and admit I don't know. I introduce them to Caralys and they say it seems an easy choice to them. The women hit it off. Jerry suggests a local inn where we can hear a guitarist he knows, and before long we're there, claiming a corner table between dances, listening to his friend: another old man, an ancient man really, with twinkling eyes and spotted scalp and a wispy comic-opera mustache that, dangling to his collarbone, looks like a boomerang covered with lint.

6

"It's not that I hate my country," Jerry says, when the women have left together, in the way that women have. His eyes shine and his voice slurs from the effects of too much drink. "I can't. I know my history. I know the things she's accomplished, the principles she's stood for, the challenges she's faced. I've even been around for more of it than I care to remember. But coming here was not abandoning her. It was abandoning what she'd become. It was abandoning the drive-throughs and the ATMs and the talking heads who pretend they have the answers but would be lucky to remember how to tie their shoes. It was remembering what life was supposed to be all about, and seizing it with both hands while we still had a few good years still left in us. It was victory, Robert; an act of sheer moral victory. Do you see, Robert? Do you see?"

I tell him I see.

"You think you do. But you still have a ticket out, day after tomorrow. Sundown, right? Ach. You're still a tourist. You're still too scared to take the leap. But stay here a few more weeks and then tell me that you see."

I might just do that, I say. I might stay here the rest of my life.

He dismisses me with a wave of his hand. "Sure you say that. You say that now. You say that because you think it's so easy to say that. You haven't even begun to imagine the commitment it takes."

But I love Caralys.

"Of course you do. But will you be fair to her, in the end? Will you? You're not her first tourist, you know."

7

Jerry has become too intense for me, in a way utterly at odds with the usual flavor of life in Enysbourg. If he presses on, I might have to tell him to stop.

But I am rescued. The man with the wispy mustache returns

from the bar with a fresh mug of beer, sets it beside him on a three-legged stool, picks up a stringed instrument a lot like a misshapen guitar, and begins to sing a ballad in a language I don't understand. It's one of Enysbourg's many dialects, a tongue distinguished by deep rolling consonants and rich sensual tones, so expressive in the way it cavorts the length of an average sentence that I don't need a translation to know that he's singing a hymn to lost love long remembered. When he closes his eyes I can almost imagine him as the fresh-faced young boy staring with earnest panic at the eyes of the fresh-faced young woman whose beauty first made him want to sing such songs. He sings of pain, a sense of loss, a longing for something denied to him. But there is also wonder, a sense of amazement at all the dreams he's ever managed to fulfill.

Or maybe that's just my head, making the song mean what I want it to mean. In either event, the music is slow and heartfelt until some kind of midverse epiphany sends its tempo flying. And all of a sudden the drum beats and the hands clap and the darkened room bursts with men and women rising from the shadows to meet on the dance floor in an explosion of flailing hair and whirling bodies. There are children on shoulders and babies on backs and a hundred voices united in the chorus of the mustached man's song, which seems to fill our veins with fire. Jerry has already slid away, his rant of a few moments before forgotten in the urgency of the moment. I recognize nobody around me but nevertheless see no strangers. As I decide to stay in Enysbourg, to spend the rest of my life with Caralys, to raise a family with her, to keep turning pages in this book I've just begun to write, the natives seem to recognize the difference in me. I am handed a baby, which I kiss to the sound of cheers. I hand it back and am handed another. Then another. The music grows louder, more insistent. A wisp of smoke drifts by. Clove, tobacco, hashish, or something else; it is there and then it is gone.

I blink and catch a glimpse of Caralys, cut off by the crowd. She is trying to get to me, her eyes wide, her face shining, her need urgent. She knows I have decided. She can tell. She is as radiant as I have ever seen her, and though jostled by the mob she is determined to make her way to my side. She too has something to say, something that needs to be spoken, through shattered teeth and a mouth filled with blood.

During

8

There is no sunlight. The skies are too sullied by the smoke of burning buildings to admit the existence of dawn. What arrives instead are gray and sickly shadows, over a moonscape so marked with craters and shattered rubble that in most places it's hard to tell where the buildings stood in the first place. Every few seconds, the soot above us brightens, becomes as blinding as a parody of the light it's usurped, and rocks the city with flame and thunder. Debris pelts everything below. A starving dog cowering in a hollow formed by two shattered walls bolts, seeking better haven in a honeycomb of fallen masonry fifty meters of sheer hell away. But even before it can round the first twisted corpse, a solid wall of shrapnel reduces the animal to a scarlet mist falling on torn flesh.

I witness its death from the site of my own. I am already dead. I still happen to be breathing, but that's a pure accident. Location is all. The little girl who'd been racing along two paces ahead of me, mad with fear, forced to rip off her flaming clothes to reveal the bubbling black scar the chemical burns have made of her back, is now a corpse. She's a pair of legs protruding from a mound of fallen brick. Her left foot still bears a shoe. Her right is pale, naked, moon-white perfect, unbloodied. I, who had been racing along right behind her, am not so fortunate. The same concussion wave that put her out of her misery sent me flying. Runaway stones have torn deep furrows in my legs, my belly, my face, my chest. I have one seeping gash across my abdomen and another across one cheek; both painful, but nothing next to the greater damage done by the cornice that landed on my right knee, splintering the bone and crushing my leg as close to flat as a leg can get without bursting free of its cradling flesh. The stone tumbled on as soon as it did its work, settling in a pile of similar rocks; it looks like any other, but I still think I can identify it from over here, using the marks it left along the filthy ground.

I have landed in a carpet of broken glass a meter or so from what, for a standing person, would be a ragged waist-high remnant of wall. It is good fortune, I suppose; judging from the steady tattoo of shrapnel and rifle fire impacting against the other side, it's that wall which for the moment spares me the fate of the little girl and the dog. Chance has also favored me by letting me land within sight of a irregular gap in that wall, affording me a view of what used to be the street but which right now is just a narrow negotiable path between craters and mounds of smoking debris. My field of vision is not large, but it was enough to show me what happened to the dog. If I'm to survive this, it must also allow me to see rescue workers, refugees, even soldiers capable of dragging me to wherever the wounded are brought.

But so far there has been no help to be seen. Most of the time even my fragmentary view is obscured by smoke of varying colors: white, which though steaming hot is also thin and endurable, passing over me without permanent damage; black, which sickens me with its mingled flavors of burning rubber and bubbling flesh; and the caustic yellow, which burns my eyes and leaves me gagging with the need to void a stomach already long empty. I lick my lips, which are dry and cracked and pitted, and recognize both hunger and thirst in the way the world pales before me. It is the last detail. Everything I consumed yesterday, when Enysbourg was paradise, is gone; it, and everything I had for several days before. Suddenly, I'm starving to death.

9

There is another great burst of sound and light, so close parts of me shake apart. I try to scream, but my throat is dry, my voice a mere wisp, my mouth a sewer sickening from the mingled tastes of blood and ash and things turned rotten inside me. I see a dark shape, a man, Jerry Martel in fact, move fast past the gap in the wall. I hear automatic fire and I hear his brief cry as he hits the dirt in a crunch of flesh and gravel. He is not quite dead at first, and though he does not know I am here, just out of sight, a collaborator in his helplessness, he cries out to me anyway: a bubbling, childish cry, aware that it's about to be cut off but hoping in this instant that it reaches a listener willing to care. I can't offer the compassion Jerry craves, because I hate him too much for bringing fresh dangers so close to the place where I already lie broken. I want him gone.

A second later fate obliges me with another burst of automatic weapons fire. Brick chips fill the air like angry bees, digging more miniature craters; one big one strikes my ravaged knee and I spasm, grimacing as my bowels let loose, knowing it won't matter because I released everything I had inside me long ago. I feel relief. He was my friend, but I'm safer with him gone.

10

I smell more smoke. I taste mud. I hear taunts in languages I don't recognize, cries and curses in the tongues spoken in Enysbourg. A wave of heat somewhere near me alerts me that a fire has broken out. I drag myself across ragged stones and broken glass closer to the gap in the wall, entertaining vainglorious ambitions of perhaps crawling through and making it untouched through the carnage to someplace where people can fix me. But the pain is too much, and I collapse, bleeding now from a dozen fresher wounds, having accomplished nothing but to provide myself a better view.

I see the elderly musician with the huge mustache stumble on by, his eyes closed, his face a sheen of blood, his arms dangling blistered and lifeless at his sides, each blackened and swollen to four times its natural size. I see a woman, half-mad, her mouth ajar in an unending silent scream, clutching a tightly wrapped but still ragged bundle in a flannel blanket, unwilling to notice that whatever it held is now just a glistening smear across her chest. I see a tall and robust and athletic man stumble on by, his eyes vacant, his expression insane, his jaw ripped free and dangling from his face by a braided ribbon of flesh. I see all that and I hear more explosions and I watch as some of the fleeing people fall either whole or in pieces and I listen as some are released by death and, more important, as others are not.

Something moving at insane speed whistles through the sky above, passing so near that its slipstream tugs at my skin. I almost imagine it pulling me off the ground, lifting me into the air, allowing me a brief moment of flight behind it before it strikes and obliterates its target. For a moment I wish it would; even that end would be better than a deathbed of shattered rock and slivered glass. Then comes the brightest burst of light and most deafening wave of thunder yet, and for a time I become blind and deaf, with everything around me reduced to a field of pure white.

11

When the world comes back, not at all improved, it is easy to see the four young men in identical uniforms who huddle in a little alcove some twenty meters away. There is not much to them, these young men: they all carry rifles, they all wear heavy packs, they're all little more than boys, and their baggy uniforms testify to a long time gone without decent food. When one turns my way, facing me and perhaps even seeing me, but not registering me as a living inhabitant of the corpse-strewn landscape, his eyes look sunken, haunted, unimaginably ancient. He is, I realize, as mad as the most pitiful among the wounded—a reasonable response to his environment, and one I would share if I could divest the damnable sanity that forces me to keep reacting to the horror. He turns back to his comrades and says something; then he looks over them, at something beyond my own limited field of vision, and his smile is enough to make me crave death all over again. His comrades look where he's looking and smile the same way: all four of them showing their teeth.

The three additional soldiers picking their way through the

rubble bear a woman between them. It is Caralys. Two stand to either side of her, holding her arms. A third stands behind her, holding a serrated knife to her throat with one hand and holding a tight grip on her hair with the other. That soldier keeps jabbing his knee into the small of her back to keep her going. He has to; she's struggling with every ounce of strength available to her, pulling from side to side, digging her feet into the ground, cursing them to a thousand hells every time they jerk her off her feet and force her onward.

She is magnificent, my Caralys. She is stronger, more vibrant, than any one of them. In any fair fight she would be the only one left standing. But she is held by three, and while she could find an opportunity to escape three, the soldiers from the alcove, who now rush to help their comrades, bring the total all the way up to seven. There is no hope with seven. I know this even as I drag myself toward her from the place where I lie broken. I know this even as she struggles to drive her tormentors away with furious kicks. But these boys are too experienced with such things. They take her by the ankles, lift her off the ground, and bear her squirming and struggling form across the ravaged pavement to a clear place in the rubble, where they pin her to the ground, each one taking a limb. They must struggle to keep her motionless. The soldier with the darkest eyes unslings his rifle, weighs it in his arms, and smashes its butt across her jaw. The bottom half of her face crumples like shattered pottery.

There is nothing I can do but continue to crawl toward her, toward them.

Caralys coughs out a bubble of fresh blood. Fragments of teeth, driven from her mouth, cling to what's left of her chin. She shrieks and convulses and tries to kick. Her legs remain held. The same soldier who just smashed her face now sees that his job is not yet done. He raises his rifle above his head and drives the stock, hard, into her belly. She wheezes and chokes. She tries to curl into a ball of helpless misery, seeking escape within herself. But the soldiers won't even permit that. Another blow, this one to her forehead, takes what little fight is left. Her eyes turn to blackened smears. Her nose blows pink bubbles which burst and dribble down her cheeks in rivulets. She murmurs an animal noise. The soldier responsible for making her manageable makes a joke in a language I don't know, which can't possibly be funny, but still makes the others laugh. They rip off her filthy dress and spread her legs farther apart. The leader steps away, props his rifle against a fragment of wall, and returns, dropping his pants. As he gives his swollen penis a lascivious little waggle, I observe something wrong with it, something I can see from a distance; it looks green, diseased, half-rotted. But he descends, forcing himself into her, cursing her with every thrust, his cruel animal grunts matched by her own bubbling exhalations, less gasps of pain or protests at her violation than the involuntary noises made as her diaphragm is compressed again and again and again. It doesn't last long, but by the time he pulls out, shakes himself off, and pulls his pants back up, the glimpse I catch of her face is enough to confirm that she's no longer here.

Caralys is alive, all right. I can see her labored breath. I can feel the outrage almost as much as she does. But she's not in this place and time. Her mind has abandoned this particular battlefield for another, inside her head, which might not provide any comfort but nevertheless belongs only to her. What's left in this killing ground doesn't even seem to notice as one of the other soldiers releases his grip on her right arm, takes his position, and commences a fresh rape.

12

There are no words sufficient for the hate I feel. I am a human being with a human being's dimensions, but the hate is bigger than my capacity to contain it. It doesn't just fill me. It replaces me. It becomes everything I am. I want to claw at them and snap at them and spew hatred at them and rip out their throats with my teeth. I want to leave them blackened corpses and I want to go back to wherever they came from and make rotting flesh of their own wives and mothers. I want to bathe in their blood. I want to die killing them. I want to scar the earth where they were born. I want to salt the farmland so nothing ever grows there again. If hatred alone lent strength, I would rend the world itself. But I cry out without a voice, and I crawl forward without quite managing to move, and I make some pathetic little sound or another, and it carries across the smoky distance between me and them and it accomplishes nothing but advise the enemy that I'm here.

In a single spasm of readiness, they all release Caralys, grab their weapons, scan the rubble-field for the source of the fresh sound. The one using her at the moment needs only an extra second to disengage, but he pulls free in such a panicked spasm that he tumbles backward, slamming his pantless buttocks into a puddle of something too colored by rainbows to qualify as water. The leader sees me. He rolls his eyes, pulls a serrated blade from its sheath at his hip, and covers the distance between us in three seconds.

The determined hatred I felt a heartbeat ago disappears. I know that he's the end of me and that I can't fight him and I pray that I can bargain with him instead, that I can barter Caralys for mercy or medical attention or even an easier death. I think all this, betraying her, and it makes me hate myself. That's the worst, this moment of seeing myself plain, this illustration of the foul bargains I'd be willing to make in exchange for a few added seconds of life. It doesn't matter that there aren't any bargains. I shouldn't have wanted any.

I grope for his knife as it descends but it just opens the palms of my hands and christens my face and chest with blood soon matched by that which flows when he guts me from crotch to rib cage. My colon spills out in thick ropes, steaming in the morning air. I feel cold. The agony tears at me. I can't even hope for death. I want more than death. I want more than oblivion. I want erasure. I want a retroactive ending. I want to wipe out my whole life, starting from my conception. Nothing, not even the happy moments, is worth even a few seconds of this. It would be better if I'd never lived.

But I don't die yet.

13

I don't die when he walks away, or when he and his fellow soldiers return to their fun with Caralys. I don't die when they abandon her and leave in her place a broken thing that spends the next hours choking on its own blood. I don't even die when the explosions start again, and the dust salts my wounds with little burning embers. I don't die when the ground against my back shakes like a prehistoric beast about to tear itself apart with rage. I don't even die when the rats come to me, to enjoy a fresh meal. I want to die, but maybe that release is more than I deserve. So I lie on my back beneath a cloudscape of smoke and ash, and I listen to Caralys choke, and I listen to the gunfire and I curse that sociopathic monster God and I do nothing, nothing, when the flies come to lay their eggs.

After

14

I wake on a bed of freshly mowed grass. The air is cool and refreshing, the sky as blue as a dream, the breeze a delicious mixture of scents ranging from sea salt to the sweatier perfume of passing horses. From the light, I know it can't be too long after dawn, but I can tell I'm not the first one up. I can hear songbirds, the sounds of laughing children, barking dogs, music played at low volumes from little radios.

Unwilling to trust the sensations of peace, I resist getting up long enough to first grab a fistful of grass, luxuriating in the feel of the long thin blades as they bunch up between my fingers. They're miraculous. They're alive. I'm alive.

I turn my head and see where I am: one of the city's many small parks, a place lined with trees and decorated with orchid gardens. The buildings visible past the treeline are uncratered and intact. I'm intact. The other bodies I see, scattered here and there across the lawn, are not corpses, but sleepers, still snoring away after a long lazy evening beneath the stars. There are many couples, even a few families with children, all peaceful, all unworried about predators either animal or human. Even the terror, the trauma, the soul-withering hate, the easy savagery that subsumes all powerless victims, all the emotional scars that had ripped me apart, have faded. And the only nearby smoke comes from a sandpit not far upwind, where a jolly bearded man in colorful suspenders has begun to cook himself an outdoor breakfast.

15

I rise, unscarred and unbroken, clad in comfortable native clothing: baggy shorts, a vest, a jaunty feathered hat. I even have a wine bottle, three-quarters empty, and a pleasant taste in my mouth to go with it. I drink the rest and smile at the pleasant buzz. The thirst remains, but for something nonalcoholic. I need water. I itch from the stray blades of grass peppering my exposed calves and forearms. I contort my back, feeling the vertebrae pop. It feels good. I stretch to get my circulation going. I luxuriate in the tingle of the morning air. Across the meadow, a little girl points at me and smiles. She is the same little girl I saw crushed by masonry yesterday. It takes me a second to smile back and wave, a second spent wondering if she recognizes me, if she finds me an unpleasant reminder. If so, there is no way to tell from the way she bears herself. She betrays no trauma at all. Rather, she looks as blessed as any other creature of Enysbourg.

The inevitable comparison to Caralys assigns me my first mission for the day. I have to find her, hold her, confirm that she too has emerged unscathed from the madness of the day before. She must have, given the rules here, but the protective instincts of the human male still need to be respected. So I wander from the park, into the streets of a capital city just starting to bustle with life; past the gondolas taking lovers down the canals; past the merchants hawking vegetables swollen with flavor; past a juggler in a coat of carnival color who has put down his flaming batons and begun to toss delighted children instead. I see a hundred faces I know, all of whom nod with the greatest possible warmth upon seeing me, perhaps recognizing in my distracted expression the look of a foreigner who has just experienced his first taste of Enysbourg's greatest miracle.

Nobody looks haunted. Nobody looks terrorized. Nobody looks like the survivors of madness. They have shaken off the firebombings that reduced them to screaming torches, the bayonets that jabbed through their hearts, the tiny rooms where they were tortured at inhuman length for information they did not have. They have shrugged away the hopelessness and the rampant disease and the mass graves where they were tossed beside their bullet-riddled neighbors while still breathing themselves. They remember it all, as I remember it all, but that was yesterday, not today, and this is Enysbourg, a land where it never happened, a land which will know nothing but joy until the end of everything comes again, ten days from now.

16

On my way back to the hotel I pass the inn where Caralys and I went dancing the night before the end of everything. The scents that waft through the open door are enough to make me swoon. I almost pass by, determined to find Caralys before worrying about my base animal needs, but then I hear deep braying laughter from inside, laughter I recognize as Jerry Martel's. I should go inside. He has been in Enysbourg for years and may know the best ways to find loved ones after the end of everything. The hunger is a consideration, too. Stopping to eat now, before finding Caralys, might seem like a selfish act, but I won't do either one of us any good unless I do something to keep up my strength. Guilt wars with the needs of an empty stomach. My mouth waters. Caralys will understand. I go inside.

The place is dim and nearly empty. The old man with the enormous mustache is onstage, playing something inconsequential. Jerry, who seems to be the only patron, is in a corner table waiting for me. He waves me over, asks me if I'm all right, urges me to sit down, and waits for me to tell him how it was.

My words halting, I tell him it doesn't feel real anymore.

He claps me on the back. He says he's proud of me. He says he wasn't sure about me in the beginning. He says he had me figured for the kind of person who wouldn't be able to handle it, but look at me now, refreshed, invigorated, ready to handle everything. He says I remind him of himself. He beams and expects me to take that as a compliment. I give him a weak nod. He punches me in the shoulder and says that it's going to be fun having me around from now on: a new person, he says, to guide around the best of Enysbourg, who doesn't yet know all the sights, the sounds, the tastes, the joys and adventures. There are parts of Enysbourg, both in and outside the capital, that even most of those who live here don't know. He says it's enough to fill lifetimes. He says that the other stuff, the nasty stuff, the stuff we endure as the price of admission, is just a reason to cherish everything else. He says that the whole country is a treasure trove of experience for people willing to take the leap, and he says I look like one of those people.

And of course, he says, punching my arm again, there's Caralys: sweet, wanton Caralys, whom he has already seen taking her morning swim by the sea. Caralys, who will be so happy to see me again. He says I should remember what Caralys is like when she's delighted. He says that now that I know I can handle it I would have to be a fool to let her go. He chuckles, then says, tell you what, stay right here, I'll go find her, I'm sure the two of you have a lot to talk about. And then he disappears, all before I have said anything at all.

Onstage, the man with the enormous mustache starts another song, playing this time not the misshapen guitar-thing from two nights ago, but something else, a U-shaped device with two rows of strings forming a crisscross between ends and base. Its music is clear and resonant, with a wobbly quality that only adds to its emotional impact. The song is a slow one: a relief to me, since the raucous energy of Enysbourg's nights might be a bit much for me right now. I nod at the old man. He recognizes me. His grin broadens and his eyes slit with amusement. There's no telling whether he has some special affection for me as a person, or just appreciates the arrival of any audience at all. Either way, his warmth is genuine. He is grateful to me for being here. But he does not stop playing just to greet me. The song continues. The lyrics, once again in a language unknown to me, are once again still easy to comprehend. Whatever the particulars, this song is impossible to mistake as anything but a tribute to being alive. When the song ends, I toss him a coin, and he tosses it back, not insulted, just not interested. He is interested in the music for music's sake alone, in celebration, because celebration is the whole point.

17

I think hard on the strange cycle of life in Enysbourg, dictated by law, respected as a philosophical principle, and rendered possible by all the technological genius the modern world can provide: this endless cycle which always follows nine days of sheer exuberance with one day of sheer Hell on Earth.

It would be so much easier if exposure to that Tenth Day were not the price of admission.

It would be so much better if we could be permitted to sail in on the Day After and sail out on the Night Before, enjoying those nine days of sweet abandon without any obligation to endure the unmitigated savagery of the tenth. The weekly exodus wouldn't be a tide of refugees; it would be a simple fact of life. If such a choice were possible, I would make it. Of course, I would also have to make Caralys come with me each time, for even if she was determined to remain behind and support her nation's principles, I could never feel at peace standing on the deck of some distant ship, watching Enysbourg's beautiful shoreline erupt in smoke and fire, aware that I was safe but knowing that she was somewhere in that no-man's-land being brutalized and killed. And there is no way she would ever come with me to such a weekly safe haven, when her land was a smoking ruin behind her. She would know the destruction temporary the same way I know it temporary, but she would regard her escape from the regular interval of terror an act of unforgivable treason against her home. It is as she said that time I almost lost her by proposing that she come back home with me, a suggestion I made not because home is such a great place, but because home would be easier. She said that leaving would be cowardice. She said that leaving would be betrayal. She said that leaving would be the end of her. And she said that the same went for any other attempt to circumvent the way things were here, including my own, which is why she'd despise me forever if I tried. The Tenth Day, she said, is the whole point of Enysbourg. It's the main reason the ships come and go only on the Day After. Nobody, not the natives like Caralys, and not the visitors like myself, is allowed their time in paradise unless they also pay the price. The question that faces everybody, on that Day After, is the same question that faces me now: whether life in Enysbourg is worth it.

I think of all the countries, my own included, that never know the magic Enysbourg enjoys nine days out of ten, that have become not societies but efficient machines, where life is all about keeping that machine in motion. Those nations know peace, and they know prosperity, but do they know life the way Enysbourg knows life, nine days out of every ten? I come from such a place and I suffocated in such a place—maybe because I was too much a part of the machine to recognize the consolations available to me, maybe because they weren't available to be found. Either way I know that I've never been happy, not before I came here. Here I found my love of being alive—but only nine days out of ten.

And is that Tenth Day really too much to endure, anyway? I think about all the countries that know that Tenth Day, not at safe predictable intervals, but for long stretches lasting months or years or centuries. I think about all the countries that have never known anything else. I think about all the terrorized generations who have lived and died and turned to bones with nothing but that Tenth Day to color their days and nights. For all those people, millions of them, Enysbourg, with that Tenth Day always lurking in recent memory and always building in the near future, is still a paradise beyond comprehension. Bring all those people here and they'd find this choice easy, almost laughable. They'd leap at the chance, knowing that their lives would only be better, most of the time.

It's only the comfortable, the complacent, the spoiled, who would even find the question an issue for internal debate. The rest would despise me for showing such reluctance to stay, and they'd be right. I've seen enough, and experienced enough, to know that they'd be right. But I don't know if I have what it takes to be right with them. I might prefer to be wrong and afraid and suffering their disdain at a safe distance, in a place untouched by times like Enysbourg's Tenth Day.

18

I remember a certain moment, when we had been together for three days. Caralys had led me to a gorge, a few hours from the capital, a place she called a secret, and which actually seemed to be, as there were no legions of camera-toting tourists climbing up and down the few safe routes to the sparkling river below. The way down was not a well-worn path, carved by the weight of human feet. It was a series of compromises with what otherwise would have been a straight vertical drop—places where it became possible to slide down dirt grades, or descend from one rock ledge to another. Much of the way down was overgrown, with plants so thick that only her unerring sense of direction kept us descending on the correct route, and not via a sudden, fatal, bone-shattering plunge from a height. She moved through it all with a grace unlike any I had ever seen, and also with an urgency I could not understand, but which was nevertheless intense enough to keep me from complaining through my hoarse breath and aching bones. Every once in a while she turned, to smile and call me her adventurer. And every time she did, the special flavor she gave the word was enough to keep me going, determined to rush anyplace she wanted me to follow.

The grade grew gentler the closer we came to the river at the gorge bottom. It became a mild slope, dim beneath thick forest canopy, surrounded on all sides by the rustling of a thousand leaves and the chittering of a thousand birds. Once the water itself grew audible, there was nothing but a wall of sound all around us. She picked up speed and began to run, tearing off her clothes as she went. I ran after her, gasping, almost breaking my neck a dozen times as I tripped over this root, that half-buried rock. By the time I emerged in daylight at a waterfront of multi-colored polished stones, she was well ahead of me. I was hopping on one leg to remove my boots and pants and she was already naked and up to her waist in midriver, her perfect skin shiny from wet and glowing from the sun.

She had led us directly to a spot just below one of the grandest waterfalls I had ever seen with my own eyes. It was an unbroken wall of rushing silver, descending from a flat rock ledge some fifty meters above us. The grotto at its base was bowl-shaped and just wide enough to collect the upriver rapids in a pool of relative calm. The water was so cold that I emitted an involuntary yelp, but Caralys just laughed at me, enjoying my reaction. I dove in, feeling the temperature shock in every pore, then stood up, dripping, exuberant, wanting nothing in this moment but to be with her.

She caught my wrist before I could touch her. "No."

I stopped, confused. No? Why no? Wasn't this what she wanted, in this perfect place she'd found for us?

She released my arm and headed toward the wall of water, splashing through the river as it grew deeper around her, swallowing first her hips and then her breasts and then her shoulders, finally requiring her to swim. Her urgency was almost frightening now. I thought of how easy it might be to drown here, for someone who allowed herself to get caught beneath that raging wall of water, and I said, "Hey," rushing after her, not enjoying the cold quite as much anymore. I don't know what fed that river, but it was numbing enough to be glacial runoff. Thoughts of hypothermia struck for the first time, and I felt the first stab of actual fear just as she disappeared beneath the wall.

The moment I passed through, with sheets of freezing water assaulting my head and shoulders, was one of the loudest I'd ever known. It was a roaring, rumbling, bubbling cacophony, so intense that it drowned out all the other sounds that filled this place. The birds, the wind, the softer bubbling of the water downstream, they were wiped out, eliminated by this one all-encompassing noise. I almost turned around. But I kept going, right through the wall.

On the other side I found air and a dark dank place. Caralys had pulled herself onto a mossy ledge just above the waterline, set against a great stone wall. There she sat with her back to the stone, hugging her legs, her knees tucked tight beneath her chin. Her eyes were white circles reflecting the light passing through the water now behind me. I waded toward her, found an empty spot on the ledge beside her, and pulled myself up too. The stone, I found without much surprise, was like ice, not a place I wanted to stay for long. But I joined her in contemplating the daylight as it prismed through a portal of plummeting water. It seemed brilliant out there: a lot like another world, seen through an enchanted gateway.

"It's beautiful," I said.

She said nothing, so I turned to see if she was all right. She was still staring at the water. She was in shadow, and a trick of the light had shrouded most of her profile in darkness, reducing her outline to a dimly lit crescent. The droplets balancing on the tip of her nose were like little glistening pearls. I saw, too, that she was trembling, though at the time I attributed that to the cold alone. She said, "Listen."

I listened. And heard only the sound of the waterfall, less deafening now that we'd passed some distance beyond it. And something else: her teeth, chattering.

She said, "The silence."

It took me a second to realize that this was the miracle she'd brought me here to witness: the way the waterfall, in all its harmless fury, now insulated us from all the sounds we had been hearing all morning. It was as if none of what we'd heard out there, all the time it had taken us to hike to this place she knew so well, now existed at all. None of it was there. None of it could touch us.

It seemed important to her.

At that moment, I could not understand why.

19

I am in the little restaurant, thinking all this, when a soft voice calls my name. I look up, and of course it's Caralys: sweet, beautiful Caralys, who has found me in the place where we prefer to think we saw each other last. She is, of course, unmarked and unwounded, all the insults inflicted by the soldiers either healed or wiped away like bad rumors. She looks exactly like she did the night before last, complete with fringed blouse and patchy dress and two curling strands of hair that meet in the center of her forehead. If there is any difference in her, it lies in what I now recognize was there all along: the storm clouds of memory roiling behind her piercing black eyes. She's not insane, or hard, the way she should be after enduring what she's endured; Enysbourg always wipes away all scars, physical and psychological both. But it does not wipe away the knowledge. And her smile, always so guileless in its radiance, now seems to hold a dark challenge. I can see that she has always held me and my naïveté in the deepest possible contempt. She couldn't have felt any other way, in the presence of any man who had never known the Tenth Day. I had been an infant by Enysbourg's standards, a man who could not understand her or the forces that shaped her. I must have seemed bland, dull, and in my own comfortable way, even retarded.

I find to my surprise that I feel contempt as well. Part of me is indignant at her effrontery at looking down at me. After all, she has had other tourists. She has undertaken other Projects with other men, from other places, trying time and time again to make outsiders into natives of her perverse little theme park to savagery. What does she expect from me, in the end? Who am I to her? If I leave, won't she just find another tourist to play with for ten days? And why should I stay, when I should just see her as the easy vacation tramp, always eager to go with the first man who comes off the boat?

It's hard not to be repulsed by her.

But that hate pales beside the awareness that in all my days only she has made me feel alive.

And her own contempt, great as it is, seems drowned by her

love, shining at me with such intensity that for a moment I almost forget the fresh secrets now filling the space between us. I stand and fall into her arms. We close our eyes and taste each other's tears. She whispers, "It is all right, Robert. I understand. It is all right. I want you to stay, but won't hate you if you go."

She is lying, of course. She will despise me even more if I go. She will know for certain that Enysbourg has taught me nothing. But her love will be just as sincere if I stay.

It's the entire reason she seeks out tourists. She loathes our naïveté. But it's also the one thing she can't provide for herself.

20

Jerry Martel stands nearby, beaming and self-congratulatory. Dee has joined him, approving, cooing, maternal. Maybe they hope we'll pay attention to them again. Or maybe we're just a new flavor for them, a novelty for the expatriates living in Enysbourg.

Either way, I ignore them and pull Caralys close, taking in the scent of her, the sheer absolute ideal of her, laughing and weeping and unable to figure out which is which. She makes sounds that could be either, murmuring words that could be balms for my pain or laments for her own. She tells me again that it's going to be all right, and I don't know whether she's telling the truth. I don't even know whether she's all that sure herself. I just know that, if I take that trip home, I will lose everything she gave me, and be left with nothing but the gray dullness of my everyday life. And if I stay, deciding to pay the price of that Tenth Day in exchange for the illusion of Eden, we'll never be able to acknowledge the Tenth Day on the other days, when everything seems to be all right. We won't mention the times spent suffocating beneath rubble, or spurting blood from severed limbs, or choking out our lungs from poison gas. I will never know how many hells she's known, and how many times she's cried out for merciful death. I'll never be able to ask if what I witnessed yesterday was typical, worse than average, or even an unusually good day, considering. She'll never ask about any of the horrors that happen to me. These are not things discussed during peacetime in Enysbourg. We won't even talk about them if I stay, and if we remain in love, and if we marry and have children, and if they grow up bright and beautiful and filled with wonder; and if every ten days we find ourselves obliged to watch them ground beneath tank treads, or worse. In Enysbourg such things are not the stuff of words. In Enysbourg a certain silence is just the price of being alive.

And a small price it is, in light of how blessed those who live here have always been.

Just about all Caralys can do, as the two of us begin to sway together in a sweet slow dance, is continue to murmur reassurances. Just about all I can do is rest my head against her chest, and close my eyes to the sound of her beating heart. Just about all we can do together is stay in this moment, putting off the next one as long as possible, and try not to remember the dogs, the hateful snarling dogs, caged for now but always thirsty for a fresh taste of blood.

"The mere absence of war is not peace."
—PRESIDENT JOHN F. KENNEDY

For J.H.

BIOGRAPHIES

Award-winning author and editor **Janet Berliner** continually breaks the mold of the average novelist. Her most recent novel, *Artifact* (Forge), is an action-adventure thriller coauthored with her friends Kevin J. Anderson, Matthew J. Costello, and F. Paul Wilson. "Totem" is taken from her work on a new novel, *Birthrite*, a sequel to her first novel, *Rite of the Dragon* (twentieth anniversary edition available from Wildside Press). With George Guthridge, she wrote *The Madagascar Manifesto* (Meisha Merlin Publishing), which includes the Bram Stoker Award-winning novel *Children of the Dusk*. Janet's editorial work includes the anthologies *David Copperfield's Tales of the Impossible*, coedited with David Copperfield, and *Snapshots: 20th-Century Mother-Daughter Fiction* (David R. Godine Publishers), coedited with Joyce Carol Oates. The latter was chosen by the New York Public Library for its 2001 list of Recommended Reads for Teens. More information about Janet and her work can be found on the BerlinerPhiles Web site at http://members.aol.com/berlphil.

Adam-Troy Castro made his first professional sale to *Spy* magazine in 1987. Since then, he's published more than seventy short stories, including the Stoker nominee "Baby Girl Diamond" and the Hugo/Nebula nominees "The Funeral March of the Marionettes" and (with Jerry Oltion) "The Astronaut from Wyoming." Adam is the author of four Spider-Man novels, including the trilogy that culminated in 2002's *The Secret of the Sinister Six*. Adam's short stories are reprinted in his collections *Lost in Booth Nine*, *An Alien Darkness*, *A Desperate Decaying Darkness*, *Vossoff and Nimmitz*, and *Tangled Strings*. The owner of four cats, including Jones, Maggie, Lipless Louie, and the acronymic P.I.T.A., Adam credits his wife, the lovely and long-suffering Judi Castro, with refusing to accept a damn fine first draft and instead insisting on the critical changes that moved "Of a Sweet Slow Dance in the Wake of Temporary Dogs" past the finish line and into the kindly editor's mailbox.

Keith R.A. DeCandido has been an author, critic, editor, anthologist, interviewer, musician, and TV personality in over a decade in the SF and comics fields. He has edited or coedited over a dozen anthologies, some from behind the scenes. The more public ones include *OtherWere: Stories of Transformation* (with Laura Anne Gilman), *Urban Nightmares* (with Josepha Sherman), *The Ultimate Alien* and *The Ultimate Dragon* (with Byron Preiss & John Betancourt), the collection *Virtual Unrealities: The Short Fiction of Alfred Bester* (with Robert Silverberg & Byron Preiss), and the forthcoming *Star Trek: Tales of the Dominion War* (to be published in the summer of 2004). He is also the best-selling author of a variety of novels, short stories, eBooks, comics, and nonfiction books told in assorted media universes, including *Star Trek, Farscape, Gene Roddenberry's Andromeda,* Marvel Comics, *Buffy the Vampire Slayer, Doctor Who, Xena,* and more. His first original novel, *Dragon Precinct,* is due in 2004. Through Albé-Shiloh Inc., he is producing several projects besides *Imaginings,* including the science-fiction trilogy *The Inconstant Moon* by Pierce Askegren, to be published by Ace Books. Find out more at www.albeshiloh.com.

In the twenty-five years of **Craig Shaw Gardner**'s professional career, he's published around thirty novels, forty short stories, and three dozen reviews and articles. The day he went to see *Viva Las Vegas,* his very first Elvis film, he stayed to watch it twice.

Charles L. Harness was born in a little town in West Texas in 1915. He has degrees in chemistry and law. He worked as a patent lawyer in Connecticut and Maryland for forty years. His first SF story was published in 1948. Many of his subsequent stories and novels dealt with the patent profession, and several were nominated for Hugo and Nebula Awards. In recent years, NESFA Press has published two collections of his short fiction—*An Ornament to His Profession* and *Cybele, with Bluebonnets*—as well as *Rings,* an omnibus of his novels *The Paradox Men, The Ring of Ritornel, Firebird,* and *Drunkard's Endgame.*

H. Courreges LeBlanc is a native of New Orleans. He expatriated to Minnesota in 1980, and attended Clarion in 1996. Since then, he's sold several stories to *Strange Horizons*, *Terra Incognita*, *Tales of the Unanticipated*, and *Darkling Plain*. He has written a novel, *Tainted Cotillion*, which his agent is dutifully flogging. In addition to his literary pursuits, LeBlanc is also a musician. He is in the improvisational jazz ensemble the Moon, and an electronic music ensemble Eight Minutes to Wapner (www.mp3.com/eightminutesto). His other interests include recumbent bicycles, vintage cars, permaculture, and free software.

Nancy Jane Moore's fiction has appeared in several anthologies, on the Web site Fantastic Metropolis, and in magazines ranging from *Lady Churchill's Rosebud Wristlet* to the *National Law Journal*. She has trained in martial arts for more than twenty years and holds a black belt in Aikido. Her Web site is http://home.earthlink.net/~nancyjane.

Daniel Pearlman got his Ph.D. in Comparative Literature at Columbia University and teaches creative writing at the University of Rhode Island. His ironical/fantastical stories and novellas began appearing in 1988 in magazines and anthologies such as *Amazing Stories*, *The Silver Web*, *New England Review*, *Quarterly West*, *Semiotext(e) SF*, *Synergy*, and *Simulations*. His books of fiction to date are *The Final Dream & Other Fictions* (Permeable Press, 1995); a mainstream novel, *Black Flames* (White Pine Press, 1997), a twisted excursion into the Spanish Civil War; a second fiction collection, *The Best-Known Man in the World & Other Misfits* (Aardwolf Press, 2002); and a science-fiction novel, *Memini* (Prime Books, 2003). His new novel, *Weeds in Franco's Garden*, is based on his prolonged residence in Spain (1971-74) and is currently seeking a publisher. His work has received outstanding reviews in periodicals such as *Publishers Weekly*, *Booklist*, and the *Washington Post*. If you'd like to get in touch, his e-mail is dpearl@uri.edu.

Aaron Rosenberg was born in New Jersey, grew up in New Orleans, graduated high school and college in Kansas, and now lives in New York. He has published short stories, poems, essays, articles, reviews, and nonfiction books, but for the last ten years the majority of his writing has been in role-playing. Aaron has written for more than ten game systems (including *Lord of the Rings*, *Vampire*, DC Universe, *EverQuest*, and *Star Trek*) and is the president of his own game company, Clockworks (www.clockworksgames.com). He has two degrees in English, and misses teaching college English, which he did for several years. In 2001, Aaron's *Star Trek: S.C.E.: The Riddled Post* was published as an eBook; it was recently reprinted in book form in the *S.C.E.* omnibus *Some Assembly Required*. A second *S.C.E.* eBook, the two-part *Collective Hindsight*, was just released.

Harry Turtledove, an escaped historian, writes science fiction, fantasy, and historical fiction. He is perhaps best known for his alternate history, including such titles as *The Guns of the South*, Nebula finalist *How Few Remain*, *Ruled Britannia*, and the Hugo-winning novella "Down in the Bottomlands." He lives in Los Angeles with his wife—the writer Laura Frankos—and their three daughters.

Sarah Zettel was born in California, and since then has lived in four states, ten cities, and two countries. She has been practicing the art of writing fantasy and science fiction since the sixth grade, and hopes to get it right one day. Her most recent novels are *The Usurper's Crown*, *Kingdom of Cages*, and *A Sorceror's Treason*. She currently lives in Michigan with her husband, Tim, her son, Alex, and her cat, Buffy the Vermin Slayer.

Printed in the United States
By Bookmasters